SPELLS IN THERAPY

Michaela L Cane

A HellBound Books Publishing LLC Book
Houston TX

**A HellBound Books LLC
Publication**
Copyright © 2019 by HellBound Books Publishing LLC
All Rights Reserved

Cover and art design by
HellBound Books Publishing LLC

www.hellboundbookspublishing.com

Printed in the United States of America

Spells in Therapy is dedicated to all those readers who fell in love with Lauren and David from the start, as well as all of you readers and writers who've supported me in spilling out their crazy journey.

Micheala L. Cane

SPELLS IN THERAPY

Chapter 1

Crouched by her bed, Lauren ran her fingers along the edges of a hand mirror she'd appropriated from the bathroom. She'd been doing this each morning for a week, trying to force some of the magic she felt to trickle into the mirror, to give her some active use of it, but nothing had yet worked. The most she'd accomplished was pushing some newly potted plants in the living room to flourish more quickly than was strictly natural, and getting an herb garden going outside of the garage. Already taking impressive form, the little plot she'd arranged and begun cultivating was lending itself to aid in cooking (and allowing her to build up a better stock of frozen poultices and treatments than the men had before kept on hand). It all added up to something, but not enough, and Lauren sensed that the little magic she had to feed her instincts was only diminishing.

And it had been that way ever since she and David had separated at the warehouse, too. The space between them had been eating away at what reserves she'd built up in that cage, and she knew it.

But part of her wondered if it was her own fault—if she was mentally sabotaging herself, somehow. Perhaps it was just waiting on her to…what? Desire it enough? Maybe, she thought, she just wasn't there yet. Because what would happen if it did come back, and David and Josh found out? She could be honest enough with herself to know that she'd rather not get it back than get it back and lose it once again.

The problem came down to Nell and Johanna, who were still out there somewhere. No matter what David and Josh might think, she knew those women well enough to understand that they'd be feeling all the more determined to locate Lauren, and also exact their revenge on the agents who'd brought their coven down. They wouldn't have disappeared or fled the country, let alone given up. And that wasn't fear speaking—that was experience. When Lauren went to bed at night, she saw their faces leering at her in her dreams, as if she were back in that cage with David or locked in that closet of a space they'd kept her in. They were out there, and it was just a question of who found who first. And who would be more prepared when that happened.

Finally tired of the effort involved in getting no return, Lauren let the little magic she felt in her fingers draw back into her blood and slid the mirror under her bed. At moments like this, when she'd just been trying to use her magic, she could almost feel it sinking back into her core, as if to say that it wasn't ready, or that she wasn't offering what it needed. And, of course, she knew what it required to have a chance at flourishing…it wanted David's touch—to re-enliven that spell still soaked into her bones so that it had something to feed from. But she wasn't ready for that, and she couldn't take the chance, anyway.

Taking a look at the clock, she realized David and Josh would be working by now; she'd spent longer than usual staring into the blasted mirror, and it was time to get the morning started. She thought for a moment of whether she ought to duck into the common room to say hello, if they were here instead of gone off on a case, but decided she'd rather let it go.

She'd go straight down to Josh's room instead. There'd be comfort there, as always.

Slipping down the stairs, Lauren let her hand trail along the banister, thinking about how surprising it was, the way she'd grown into being a part of the place. This stairwell was one of the spaces of the house she liked most; she only passed through it, of course, but it was like a little passage between the realm of the men and the realm of the operatives, on some level. Down here, they seemed more like people who she just happened to be living with, and less dangerous. They seemed real, and her world felt more natural, though she couldn't quite say why. Maybe it was the hidden memories of being with David, or maybe it was the extra warding, subtly offering a bit of added safety that she didn't have upstairs. Or maybe it was just the way she'd grown into trusting Josh.

Lauren had never had a brother, or even such a close friendship with a male as to say she'd felt like she had, but she imagined that this was the ideal brother-sister dynamic. Whenever she needed Josh—even when she didn't realize it, in some cases—he was there. There to keep David at a distance, and to trade small-talk with, and to simply be a presence. Somehow, they'd become easy with one another. Piece by piece, she'd even told him some of what had happened while she and David had been held by the coven, though she wouldn't have thought she'd be brave enough. It had actually helped her leave it behind somewhat, so that the horrors experienced there weren't flashing into her mind at every moment. At least, it wasn't so much when David wasn't around. And for

Josh's part, he'd made it clear—even with his few words—that she was family now, so far as he was concerned. Her giving herself up to the coven for David had apparently sealed that for him, though Lauren hadn't quite realized it to be the case at the time. And now he was what she had to rely on…even if he did get frustrated with the distance she and David kept from each other.

The rhythm of the house had been uneasy at first, but lately she'd been finding that there was almost a comfort in the quiet awkwardness of things, hard-pressed as Lauren would have been to explain it.

The first few days she'd been back, David had been in the hospital—with no way to explain the aggression he'd felt driving him to pound his fist into the wall, short of magic, the doctors had labeled it self-destructive and kept him for observation. Meanwhile, Josh had all but fawned over Lauren, worrying about the retreat she'd made into herself and the renewed weight loss even as he and Barry had reinforced the wards a hundred-fold, making sure it was safe for her to remain in the guestroom they'd essentially gifted her. He'd also kept David at a distance, per her request, when he'd first returned, and then after a few days they'd started going off to work again. And with that, strangely, things had settled. The main reminder of things had actually been her tattoo, which she was slowly growing to like the look of more and more as each day passed.

She'd once feared it would forever remind her of what had happened with David in the coven's warehouse, but as the weeks passed, those memories felt more like nightmares, and the tattoo itself more a symbol of the fact that they'd be able to find her again if they had to. If Nell and Johanna came after her, and found her.

Now, Lauren spent her mornings in Josh's suite, using his tablet to scour the internet for signs of Nell and

Johanna's presence. Then she made coffee and a sandwich—for herself if the men were out, or for the three of them. She took her own meals in her room, or downstairs with Josh's tablet if she'd stopped in the middle of something and wanted to continue, leaving the kitchen to Josh and David. She tried, diligently, to not be in the same room as David.

In the afternoons, she'd taken to spending her time outside, working in the little garden spaces she'd set up near the house for various herbs and vegetables. The medicinal herbs that wouldn't be used in cooking were outside the garage, tucked back within a little wire fence that Josh had built up upon her request, given that some of them might be poisonous if ingested. Around back, near the patio, she'd begun building a solid garden full of vegetables and herbs. She'd yet to leave the property, or even the grounds immediately surrounding the house, but Claudia and Josh had brought her any seeds she'd requested, even ordering some, and the work was relaxing, as well as being a little drawing up of what magic remained in her blood. She told herself that exercising it made a difference, fearing all the while that she was only milking herself dry of it.

Most days, she spent hours outside, and her pale skin had grown tanner for near on the first time in her life. On rainy days, she simply read or studied herbal remedies, planning the gardens' expansions.

Josh calling her to get dinner had become her sign that it was time to quit for the night, and though she ate in her room, she'd then do what she could to help around the house before retreating to a bath and a book, if her eyes were up for more reading. Despite protests from both of the men, she'd also taken to insisting on doing the dishes, foregoing the dishwasher, and doing their laundry, as well. This was the only reason she went into the men's suites, beyond her morning internet use—when they were out, she retrieved their clothes from their hampers. After she'd twice delivered washed and ironed clothing to the common area upstairs after dinner, Josh had stopped protesting, reluctantly admitting that her ironing left better and more comfortable results than what he got from the nearest dry cleaner. And, she didn't mind. It was something she could accomplish without any trouble, and it made her feel like she was helping out since she'd essentially moved in, and wasn't contributing any money (whether they needed it or not, as they never forgot to remind her).

But she spoke very little, and tried not to think beyond the present moment. When she'd look up, she'd catch David watching her, looking like he was about to say something, and she'd flee. More than once, she'd heard Josh demanding David give her more time, and wait till she was less skittish. It was embarrassing, but she couldn't deny that she appreciated it. Josh had only been remotely harsh with her once, when she'd suggested that it might make sense for her to just use his tablet in her room. He'd put his foot down then, saying she only wanted to hide away further and never leave the space they'd given her, which they thought was cramped and she thought was cozy.

He'd been right.

And, always in the back of her mind when she thought of hiding away or when she thought of spending more time with them, either one, there was her magic in the back of her mind and in her blood, just there enough for her to know what it wanted as it pushed along the base of her blood, wanting *him*. Wanting her to give in and be near him—to touch him, however she could, whenever she could. Each time she saw him, it was asking, bribing her with thoughts of what she could have again if she'd only…

But she wouldn't. Or, at least, she hadn't yet. How could she, given what he'd done to her, and that there was no guarantee that her magic could or would be anything more than a tingle, no matter the time they spent together or the contact they had? There was just no way to know, and she wasn't even sure, anymore, that she could handle knowing one way or another.

Plus, the witches would be found. They had to be. David and Josh wouldn't give up any more than Nell and Johanna would, and for the sake of Lauren's nightmares, that had to happen soon. After that, then maybe she could think about what to do about her magic, assuming there was anything to be done. For now, the remaining coven members came first.

***

Three weeks. He'd given her three weeks of space, and hiding, since he'd come back from the hospital. And he'd even planned on giving her four. Part of his patience had come from Josh's prodding him to leave her alone it was true, but he also knew she was in a hard spot. All he'd put her through, and she still didn't have anywhere else to turn—not with the danger of Nell and Johanna still out there, and any plans she'd once had for the near future demolished. Hell, even the far future plans she'd harbored had been demolished.

And he'd hurt her. He'd done more to her than he could make up for, and regardless of the fact that he'd been driven to hurt her because of the damned coven's actions, it had been his face and his body pushing her to her limits, taking advantage of her weakness.

So, yeah, he'd given her time, but now his hand was being forced.

He stopped at the entrance to the kitchen, leaning into the edge of the island and watching as she washed the dishes, careful of every detail and soapsud before she placed the pieces one by one in the dish rack to dry. They'd long past given up on extolling the merits of the dishwasher, and she was right that her hands were more dependable than its mechanics anyway. Truth be told, he liked to stand here and watch her doing them—he'd stopped here to observe her more than once over the last few weeks, slipping away before she noticed. It drove him nuts that she was doing her best to turn herself into a maid for them, but he guessed he would have been doing much the same if he'd been in her position, stuck as she was. And if it made her feel better about being here…well, he didn't want her to think about leaving, so anything to that end was welcome.

Like this, busy and occupied with daily chores, she was easy to watch. Tonight she wore a sleeveless blouse, cotton and black. The tone in her muscles had come back, and all the time outside had given her skin a glow—he thought she might even be healthier now than she'd been when he'd first met her. From where he was, he could see her shoulders moving, flexing, her head tilting as she thought, and he could enjoy the way she brushed strands of hair from her face with her knuckles so that she didn't have to dry her hands or get soap in her hair. Most of her hair was pulled up, black and smooth, showing off the curve of her neck and the blue teardrop earrings she so often wore. Working, she was easy and graceful, and he knew this was why he'd given her so much time. He liked her being here, and he didn't want to scare her away. He wanted her a lot closer, in fact.

"You know that wasn't me in the cage," he said, seeing her take up the last mug in her hands. He'd wanted to speak before she finished, and before she could stumble over an excuse and leave him alone here without saying anything at all. She froze at the sound of his voice, though, tension rippling through her as she stilled for seconds upon seconds, and then she finally went back to what she'd been doing. "And we need to talk about it, kid. Tonight, Lauren."

She stilled again, the sound of her name on his lips enough to bring a flush to her face that he could see from where he stood. Arousal spiked through his blood, telling him to move straight to her, but he held himself back. He couldn't afford to scare her away right now.

Lauren pressed her hands into the coffee mug she held, grounding herself in her task. God help her, but that voice alone warmed her. "I get it, yeah…it wasn't you," she made herself answer, "but, I mean, it also was," she added quietly, almost to herself. She hadn't yet even glanced his way. "I don't know how to…leave that part of it behind, you know? Or…if I should." Finished rinsing the dish she held, she took a heavy breath before turning to face the man behind her. As always, his presence was magnetic. It was too easy to see him and flash to the feel of his stubble against her skin, his hands pressing her legs apart again and again. "Can we not do this now?" she asked, letting her gaze move sideways to the window. It was too hard to look at him, and then not either move toward him or run away.

He looked like he had when she'd met him. All muscle and hard edges held back by t-shirt and jeans, his hands hanging by his sides like they were ready for anything…for her. And with his brown eyes focused on her…

"When then?" he asked.

Lauren nodded at the question, as if that was any kind of an answer. He'd asked a fair question, and they both knew it.

Standing straight, he took a small step forward, and then another and another, until her gaze out the window was awkward, he was so close by. *Close enough to touch,* she thought to herself, and then he was.

David had reached for her without warning, one of his fingers curling into a belt loop on her jeans as his other hand came up to her shoulder, just trailing along lightly so that she could barely feel the pressure of his touch, and then pressing in ever so slightly. She could feel herself shivering in response, and knew he could probably feel the tremor running through her just as well as she could, but she didn't flee. Her skin had already begun warming to him, and she knew desire would soon begin distracting her more and more, the longer she let this go on.

I should pull away. This close, she could smell his aftershave, and feel the heat of him pushing against her presence. The skin of her arm was already heating beneath his touch. Even the skin at her hip, feeling the light press of his hand there against the fabric of her jeans, was raising heat, drawing reaction.

Lauren closed her eyes instinctively, letting herself melt forward to forget how awkward things had been over the previous weeks. What did it matter now? Breathing him in, she felt her hands raise of their own will and land on David's chest.

"Your heart's pounding," she said. It was thumping against her palms, almost violent. She'd known her own was, but to find out that David's was somehow mirroring her own…it was something else. Comforting, almost. For the first time since he'd approached, she tried to meet his eyes, pushing back enough to where his gaze could meet hers. "You did…. I mean…"

"I missed you," he finished for her. "I've been trying to give you space, Lauren, I swear to God, but Jesus, I've missed being close to you."

She didn't want to understand the feeling, but she did. Her bottom lip caught between her teeth, she let herself enjoy his touch, breathing him in as her hands rested against his chest, hard and pounding.

"We need to talk about the spell, kid. About how you react to me and where we are, and everything between us. I don't know what it means for you, but the spell doesn't affect me, and I still want to be with you, close—like this," he added, and when she looked away, he leaned in and kissed her temple, his lips lingering on her skin before he drew her in closer against his body. "I don't know what it means for you, or how to deal with it, unless you talk to me. We can't just hide from it," he added, and she nodded after only a second passed, figuring they'd both done enough of that.

"But we shouldn't," she began, more to herself than to him. "Not when I'm…stuck in this limbo here with you guys, with the coven out there, and not when you…" Stopping herself, Lauren leaned into him again, telling herself she'd just stay with him here for another few moments more, and then she'd cut herself off. Because that was what he was, she realized—he was an addiction. Being around him was addictive, driving magic up from her very bone marrow into her veins so that it wanted release, and wanted more of him. And she couldn't give it that, not without endangering it altogether.

"When I what?" he asked after a moment.

"David…you, I mean…"

He leaned back from her, his eyes finding hers again. "Spit it out."

"You're the one who, I mean…hell, David. You and Josh gave me that potion to begin with!" she finally said, blinking her eyes hard to fight back the emotion that was bubbling up. She hated herself for allowing this to come up—for not just taking the moment and hoping he wouldn't think of or notice her magic if it came. And yet, this close to him, she didn't know how to keep from telling him everything in her head, whatever he ended up doing with the knowledge. It was like her body wouldn't let her even keep secrets from him anymore, not while he was this close, and it wouldn't let her pull away, either—she was just stuck, whatever he did with what he told her, and whatever he thought; more than anything, this made her want to run, and she had to blink hard to keep tears from dribbling out as she began speaking again, almost without being aware of them.

"I feel the magic that the spell left in me when I'm with you, and I don't know…I don't know whether it will get stronger or not—maybe it won't—but you don't want me to be a witch, and I don't want you to take it away from me again if it does come back. I don't know…I don't know where that puts us, or if I could handle losing it all over again," Lauren surrendered, making a move to step away for the first time, but David held tighter to her belt loop and his other hand also moved down to her waist so that his hands rested on her hips, holding her close to him with his fingers tangled in her jeans.

"That's what's keeping you away from me? Fuck, Lauren, I wouldn't do that. *We* wouldn't."

"Why not, though?" she sputtered, raising a hand to swipe at the tears she could feel on her cheeks now, both embarrassed and mad at herself. This was her life, right? Her magic, her blood, her life—he'd been the one to step in and fuck it all up. Why was she the one left crying?

"Jesus, Lauren, I don't know," he breathed out, looking up from her to stare at the wall. He should have seen this conversation coming, he realized now, but he hadn't. "I've been wondering whether we had any business doing it to begin with," he said finally. "I thought—back then, I mean—I thought it was the right thing to do, but now that I know you, and know what happened as a result, with the coven coming after you? And who you are?" David shook his head, taking a moment to run a hand through Lauren's hair, brushing it back and wishing she'd look at him straight. "We thought you could turn bad; I don't know how else to say it. And that taking away your magic wouldn't keep you from mostly going on with your life as it was. Hell, we didn't even know that magic had had a hand in you choosing a grad program or career—to us, you were a witch and a grad student, and those things weren't related. We didn't see how they could be. We don't think that anymore, that you could turn bad or give us reason to go after you. That's not even possible."

"So, if it came back…"

"You won't have to hide it, or worry about us trying again. You've got my word on that, if you'll take it," he promised. "I felt it…in the cage, with you; I couldn't *not* feel it. I knew it was running through your blood, making you…pushing you toward me. Once Nell told me, I…fuck," he said, stopping. Each time he thought of the spell, the guilt came back, stabbing him in the guts. What he'd taken from her without even knowing it.

Forcing himself away from thoughts of the coven, he leaned his head against hers, playing his hand along her arm and feeling the shivers running through her in reaction. The guilt running through him suggested he ought to be running away, going back to his basement suite and calling Josh, telling him to talk to her about what would happen the next day—anything to get her out of his presence.

But he could smell the garden on her, the mint she'd been planting that day upon Josh's request, and the lemongrass she'd picked and brought in for Josh to cook with. Above those scents, he could smell the honey of her shampoo. "You're not backing up," he said softly, blocking out what he'd been trying to explain, but couldn't, and inhaling the scent of her instead as he let his hand run more confidently up and down her arm. He'd missed this—the heat and the quiver of her skin beneath his touch. "I didn't mean to touch you, but we need to talk," he added after a moment, when she still hadn't spoken, "and I've missed being around you, Lauren. I've fucking missed it so much," he breathed out as she trembled again, but her hip was pressing back into his hand, like she wanted him there.

"Yeah?"

"Yeah," he answered. The breath of the syllable still lingering in the air, he leaned in, veering away from her lips at the last moment so that his breath was landing on her cheek instead, and then on her neck before he let his lips come down to feel her soft skin, his hands still stationed carefully at her waist and on her arm. "This okay?" he muttered, and he felt her nod against him, her body wafting toward his—almost imperceptibly, and certainly without intention.

For a moment, he let himself go with it, and just enjoyed the trembling of her heated skin beneath his hands and his lips. The dreams he'd been having of her hadn't done the memories justice, and now that he was this close, he didn't want to back off.

He let his lips close around her earlobe, his tongue playing at her flesh, but the sudden mewl of desire that slipped from her lips was so helpless, so honest, that it jarred him back to the reason he'd been staying away from her to begin with.

Fuck fuck fuck fuck fuck me, he thought, jarring himself upward with a gasp. He didn't step away, but he looked up at the ceiling, trying to re-center himself, reminding himself what they'd just been talking about.

The spell. We have to talk about the fucking spell, and then everything else.

"Fuck, I'm sorry. I didn't mean to do that. I know you didn't have any choice when it came to me. I know you don't…have enough choice now. I'm sorry. I didn't know that the spell was why you were staying away from me here, though. Maybe I should have, I guess. But I don't know what it means—whether it means I should stay away or shouldn't. I don't even… you're not pulling away now, but maybe you want to. Maybe I'm forcing you to be near me again," he added, "hurting you just as much as before."

There was a gruffness in his voice that Lauren hadn't heard in weeks, since he'd been holding himself back from her in the cage, and it was enough to run a tremor through her blood that warmed places she'd been trying to ignore ever since.

"No, you're not hurting me," she whispered, letting her hands find his wrists in front of her, and running them along his forearms. Her blood had warmed to him already—she felt safer, standing here in his light grip, than she had since that one night she'd spent in his bed. "I want to be close to you, and that's what scares me. I liked you the moment we met. There was no spell then, David. And before we slept together, before that first time, I…" she trailed off, shrugging and seeking out the window so that she wouldn't have to meet his gaze. "I hate admitting it," she told him, "but I couldn't not want you. It was…I don't know what it was."

"Automatic. Chemistry," he commented.

"Yeah, I guess so," Lauren breathed out. "And I didn't think the spell would be so strong, the attraction…but it didn't start with the sex, so it's me, too, still. You should know that," she added, nodding to herself. "And then, that night after I fell in the pool, when I saw the way you were looking at me—that was the first time I realized maybe you were, uh…"

"Thinking about you also," he finished for her, again somehow understanding what she'd been about to say, though she wouldn't let herself dwell on how he could read her so easily.

She nodded and gulped down air. "It's why I didn't, couldn't, tell you. I realized maybe I should at that point, that maybe there could be something between us, I thought, maybe," she stumbled, hearing the embarrassment in her own voice. "But with the spell, I just couldn't."

"You didn't want me to feel guilty," he said quietly. Her hand stilled on his arm for a moment, but then she nodded, and suddenly she noticed the flush in his neck, his speeding pulse matching her own. "Because you can't say no to me."

She froze, and then seemed torn between agreeing and disagreeing. "I think I could, but sometimes…I don't know, David. I don't know. I guess the point is that I don't *want* to say no to you, and on one hand I know that's not right, but on the other…I liked you before the spell."

David's fingers ran along her skin, and the magic all but warmed the air, twisting beneath the contact between them. He could feel the way it wanted them together, touching, and didn't know whether he ought to feel excitement or guilt at the thought. No—he *should* be feeling a deeper guilt than ever. He just couldn't quite bring himself to.

"I want you to have a choice about me, Lauren. I don't want you…forced to like me. To not have choice. If you were staying away from me to give yourself a choice, because that's the only way…okay, I get it. I'll back off," he added, though he couldn't bring himself to let go of her. Not yet.

"I like you, David, spell or no spell. I haven't been staying away from you because of this…compulsion, this chemistry, whatever it is. That's not the problem…it's the magic. You can feel it now. I know you can. There's a part of me that's been trying to push it down, I think," she whispered. "I mean, at times, I've really been trying to draw the magic out, but mentally, I'm not sure I haven't been pushing it down also. Like having it back and losing it again would be worse than not getting it back at all. And with the magic being tied to the spell, which is tied to you…it's hard for me to know what I should be doing, thinking. I was just starting to get used to not having it to rely on when it…started humming again, around you. I didn't expect it, after everything, and I even…even thought maybe you guys were right," she admitted. "That I could turn into my mom if I wasn't careful, and might be better off without it."

Instead of answering right away, he tightened his grip on her and drew her fully in this time against his body until she leaned reluctantly into his chest, practically thrumming with nerves. His hands had tightened on her now, grounding her against him, and his voice had gone deeper when he responded. "You're not her."

His words rang in the air, and Lauren tried to believe them, but it was hard to think, being so close to him, and harder still to know what to believe. His hand moved along her arm and another wave of desire rushed through her, catching her breath in her lungs so that she had to force herself to take a heavy step away, and then another.

"You made it sound like there wasn't time anymore for you to give me more space, like we needed to talk tonight," Lauren said after a beat. Threading her fingers through her ponytail and backing away to lean against the island, she caught her breath from the heat of his closeness and tried to regain some control over her own thoughts. He'd said everything she'd needed to hear, and yet, it was hard to believe he could mean all of it. And then, there was the memory of when they'd last been together, fighting for attention and telling her he was just as dangerous as he'd ever been; that voice was hard to ignore.

"Yeah." David coughed—awkwardly, she thought, as if he'd forgotten his own purpose in bringing it up. "Adrias, the guy Josh and I report to, who generally sends cases our way, or at least options for what comes next…he called earlier. He wants to meet tomorrow. With you, too."

The air hung between them, and finally David shrugged before he went on. "There's another case on the radar that he hasn't briefed us on yet, though Josh has been on it for a few days, doing some legwork for him; Adrias says he thinks you could be an asset. I don't know any more than that and haven't had a chance to mention it to Josh, but I didn't want Adrias coming in here tomorrow before we'd even really talked again. I thought we better clear the air for whatever's coming. It's not often that he brings a single case to our attention and pretty much demands we take it, though it's happened before, but I think this is going to be one of those times, where he wants us on it."

"And it's not the coven?"

"No—a lead like that, he would have passed it on right away. We're at the front of that search anyhow, so it'd be us giving him information. I figured I ought to tell you in advance that something's coming, though."

"Yeah, I guess so," Lauren acknowledged, her mind running with what it could be. "Does he know…?"

"No," he cut her off. "We haven't said anything about traces of your magic re-emerging. Don't plan to, either,"

David added. "And I won't try to order you to keep it a secret, but…"

"But you think I should," Lauren finished for him, seeing the discomfort on his face.

"Yeah, kid, I think you should."

Chapter 2

Lauren generally stayed to herself after the evening's meal and clean-up ended, but once she'd left David in the kitchen and retreated to her room, she didn't know what to do with herself. After he'd told her about meeting with Adrias tomorrow, he'd seemed to back off from the tension between them, and she'd done the same. These weeks of avoiding each other had made the sudden re-immersion into his presence overwhelming—enough to stop her ability to think—and she'd welcomed the chance to flee as soon as it came.

Everything about his presence had warmed her blood and made her want more, despite the memories, and the desire in his eyes and his voice had been just as clear. All of it terrified her.

But now, the book she was reading suddenly seemed unappealing, and she'd spent enough time on the internet for one day. Plus, Josh's tablet was downstairs, and she wasn't sure she felt brave enough to go down those stairs and chance running into David on his private turf. If Josh had been there, maybe she could have suggested they all watch a movie together, just to keep the ice breaking, but he was out on a date with Claudia, having left as soon as the three of them had had dinner together. He'd been spending so little time with her lately, there was no way Lauren would allow herself to intrude on their time together tonight via text. No matter how much she wanted something to distract herself.

Because, of course, her focus kept drifting back to David. To how worried he'd looked, to the fact that he didn't seem to care any longer whether she had magic running through her or not. To the way his hands had felt on her, on her arm and even through her clothes, and the way his breath had felt on her neck…

Her body still hummed with the warmth of it, and the energy. He'd stopped short of kissing her on the lips, yes, but the way her heated blood felt now, she wasn't sure whether she ought to be relieved or frustrated by that. *But I couldn't even think*, she reminded herself. No way should she be making out with him in their kitchen if his presence had such an effect on her. If anything, she had to get used to him again slowly—to his very presence, let alone his touch.

But as she thought about it, and *him*, it was the tiredness in his voice that struck her more than anything…as if he was resigned to her not wanting to be around him, or able to trust him, but was still working toward it anyway. It had been kind, and somehow felt to her like a weakness, as if she'd been the one in control. Which was absurd.

Finally lying on her bed, Lauren thought back to the way it had been when she'd been downstairs in his apartment, pressed against him for the whole of a night. It had felt like love then, if she was being honest with herself. But that was just as absurd as thinking that she might be more in control of things than him—it was just her blood responding to him, and the bits of magic still residing there in her mother's spell, that had her feeling like the word 'love' could be even remotely appropriate. How could she possibly know what love felt like anyway? Real love? With her background, everything about that train of thought was nonsense.

The knock brought her back to herself, and told her in an instant that, wherever David had been since she'd left him in the kitchen, he'd also found it impossible not to linger on that night.

"David?" she answered.

The door nudged open, and only his hand came in, holding two wine glasses. "Interested?" he asked, and Lauren—for a moment, with the sound of the surrender in his voice—forgot everything that had made her hesitate earlier.

"Yeah, come in," she answered as she pulled herself upright, leaning back against the headboard. Had this been her plan all along, she wondered—to wait till he came to her, dignity at least partially in hand, to see if she'd let him in and forgive him? Still, just the sight of him made it not matter.

He'd pulled on a hoodie to cover his muscled arms, and with the wine and glasses in hand, the effect was that of a handsome college guy who'd just happened onto some wine and didn't quite know what to do with it, the image was so incongruous. Paired with the worry in his face and the heady brown of his eyes, it made him irresistible.

"I didn't want us to end the night on that note when we just started talking again," he said too lightly, setting the glasses down and fishing a corkscrew from his pocket. "Thought we could cap it off with a drink—maybe talk about something that doesn't matter? Save the spell conversation for later?"

Lauren nodded, slipping her feet up so that he'd have more room to sit at the foot of the bed and still not be tangled so near to her feet, should he want to.

"I was thinking that, too," she said as he handed her a wine glass. "I thought about coming back to find you, but…" she stopped, watching him focus on the bottle. She didn't know what she'd been about to say. She hadn't even realized she'd been thinking about going after him until she'd said it aloud, though now she realized that she only hadn't wanted to admit the desire to herself.

Struggling against the desire to move closer to him, she forced herself to do the opposite, pulling her legs up and wrapping her free hand tightly around one ankle. He'd felt so good, against her in the kitchen before she'd managed to pull away—it was hard to remember, now, why she'd left his arms at all, or why she was holding back after everything he'd said. As David began talking about the movies in the theater—rambling, really, as he fiddled with the corkscrew—she could pretend they could be this casual, wandering over thoughts of entertainment and thinking about going to a theater that weekend, and she responded when he prodded her about what she liked or didn't as he sat at the edge of the bed, though the conversation nearly flowed around her, in one ear and out the other, so that she could only focus on his presence and couldn't have said what movie they spoke of at any given moment.

David kept his eyes down, focused on his fast emptying glass, and wondered at the fact that, after everything, they were having to get accustomed to being alone together all over again. That seemed like either a good sign or a bad one, but he wasn't sure which. He turned and filled Lauren's glass two thirds full when she held it out to him for a refill, then topped off his own. Only then did he consider whether he actually ought to be sitting on her bed, but when she'd tucked her feet up tighter beneath her, he'd taken the cue from her and sat sideways at the foot of it, facing her. It felt natural, if dangerous.

Maybe he should have invited her out to the living room for a drink rather than intruding on the one private space she had to call her own. He felt sure that's what he should have done, in fact, now that he thought of it.

She was practically vibrating with nerves as he watched her, coiled and tight as if she was ready to flee, and he wished not for the first time that he could have met her earlier, before there'd ever been a case pitting him against her mother, or suggesting in any way that she and his work could potentially collide, let alone put her at odds with his beliefs or duties. That could have made things easier, he guessed—or made it so that they might never have spent more than five minutes together, and never touched and found themselves skin to skin.

Trying to put her at ease, he moved from talking about movies to trying to get her to talk about the herbs she'd been planting, and then he found that he was talking about movies again, though he wasn't even sure half of them were still out, it had been so long since he'd bothered to pay any attention. Could he see himself taking her on an old-fashioned movie date, if they even decided it was safe? Right now, it was somehow both impossible and easy to imagine.

The wine tasted good, and Lauren was drinking quickly, matching his own nervous drinking; he could see her struggling, and guessed she was fighting back the instinct to tell him to leave. Giving her the space she seemed to need, David picked up the wine bottle from the floor and poured himself another glass. He'd drunk the first down fast, even with the top-off, doubting his motives for interrupting her in her room; now the drinking was just something to do—action to keep the stillness from becoming awkward. And though he'd put on the sweatshirt on her behalf, so that there'd be *some* barrier between her skin and his own if they got that close, now it was stifling, and he hesitated for only a moment before rolling up the sleeves so far as they would go. God, what had he just been talking about? He didn't even know, but now there was silence again. He didn't think she'd been paying much attention anyway, but still…

"Back in the kitchen, you said Adrian…" she began, stumbling at the name.

"Adrias," he corrected her. He wished she'd meet his eyes. Waiting for her to continue, he took another sip of the wine and watched her tuck her hair behind her ears, seeming to gather herself. So much for not talking about anything serious.

"Right. Adrias. You said he'll be here in the morning. Is this regular? I mean… does he often come over to give you guys assignments, or do you guys usually work with people like me, who aren't, uh, trained?"

David glanced sideways and away, shrugging and trying to hide how disconcerted he'd been by the request when it had come through that afternoon. "Nothing about this situation is normal—not even you being here; you being involved? Forget it. Last time or this time," he added.

Leaning back on one hand, he turned sideways so that he could see her more easily, facing her straight-on. "I never asked you why you did it—giving yourself up and coming in after me." *If she's getting serious, I might as well ask what I've been wanting to*, he thought.

"Yeah," she answered simply, taking another small sip of the wine. "Ya know, I didn't think I'd be here after. I thought that was something I could do to…to do good, to help. Saving you, if nothing else, or at least trying. Like, make up some for my mom's actions, you know?" she asked.

Her head was down, and David wasn't sure he wanted to see what was in her eyes after that comment anyway, but her words were echoing in the air, and suddenly he realized that Josh must have meant to hide him from this additional guilt, if he even knew how she felt. David licked his lips, taking a deep breath. "So, you mean you thought it was a suicide mission, coming in after me. You thought I was already dead?" he asked.

Lauren jerked, her elbow knocking into the headboard and nearly spilling the wine. "No...no, I didn't think they'd kill you 'til they had me, but I wasn't sure if Josh would get there before—" she stopped, breaking off and taking a gulp of her wine before she sat staring into her nearly empty glass, leaving him to finish the thought, should he want to.

"Before we ran out of time," he said.

"That's right," she agreed, still apparently unable to meet his eyes.

"More wine?" he asked after a minute or so had passed.

"Why not?"

David retrieved the wine bottle and poured them each another half-glass, telling himself to go slow. They'd gone through most of the bottle now, and he hadn't been in the room long. This time, though, when he put it back down on the floor, he walked around the foot of the bed so that he came to the side across from Lauren, and nodded down his request as he handed her her glass.

Acquiescing, Lauren scooted closer to the edge and smiled up what felt like a welcome. Taking it for what it was, David lowered himself onto the bed and leaned back against the headboard beside her with a sigh.

He didn't know what to say to what had just been

revealed, so he sat silently beside her, sipping at the wine in his hand and maintaining the bit of space between them. It was enough, for now, to be able to smell her shampoo and feel her warmth this close. Maybe he shouldn't have let himself touch her earlier, in the kitchen, but it had seemed like the only way to get her to face him. At least that was what he'd told himself in the moment.

"I'm glad you came by," she said quietly. "I knew we needed to talk."

David took another sip from his glass, letting the silence fill the little bit of space between them. This was part of what he'd missed—the nature of the air when she was with him, warm and electric as if they were near a fireplace. And, too, it was her. The way she looked at him and the way she spoke…and the way she cared. He couldn't, and wouldn't now try, to wrap his mind around the fact that she'd gone into a proverbial den of wolves to save him, not expecting to make it back out. He couldn't think about that now.

"I thought I was just coming by to talk, I swear. But it's hard not to touch you, Lauren, I have to tell you. I didn't realize it would be so hard to just…not," he finished. "It was the same thing in the kitchen—I just meant to speak to you, kid, I swear."

Lauren was nodding beside him, and he hoped she could feel the truth in what he said, and that her thoughts echoed his.

"David, about the spell…it's got its effects, we both feel them, but you don't have to worry about me being forced into caring about you. It just means I can't ignore the connection, you know? And that I'll always have a weakness for you. But me not wanting to say no to you isn't the same thing as me not being able to. You have to know that. It's just…I'm having a hard time knowing how to navigate all this, and with all that happened with the coven, I've just been struggling to figure out what makes sense."

"That's what I'd been worried about," he answered quietly. "That you'd never had any choice when it came to me, even that night downstairs. When Nell told me about the spell, I couldn't believe I'd been so fucking dense. But by the time you got to me…I was barely me, Lauren. You have to know that. Their spells in that cage—I couldn't think straight. Couldn't breathe for what they were doing to me."

"I know," she whispered, thinking back to the days in the warehouse. He hadn't been himself, and she just had to forget who he'd been there.

Reading his doubt, her hand edged sideways between them, so that her fingertips brushed the roughness of his jeans, indenting the fabric until he could feel her touch against his thigh with the slightest of pressures. He took a deep breath when she hesitated at the resistance, holding himself back. He didn't touch her, letting her make her own foray, just as he'd taken his own liberties in the kitchen.

He could feel it, though—the magic. Energy running through her veins, desire bubbling in her even from touching him this much. He hadn't realized how strong the spell was until tonight, how it must be distracting her even when they weren't touching. She'd brushed against him the day before in giving him coffee and then jerked back from the brief contact, but he hadn't chalked it up to the spell or to desire so much as to discomfort. Now, feeling her quivering beside him, he realized he'd been wrong.

Her hand pressed into his thigh, not hiding the contact anymore, and paused there before it kept running back and forth along his leg as if remembering the feel of him.

Swallowing down lust and doubt combined, he realized he'd been wrong—he couldn't control himself with her, not when they were alone, and when it had been so long…and she couldn't control herself, either, he now saw. Coming to her room like this, wine in hand, had been a mistake, tonight of all nights, and he geared himself up to leave even as he felt his dick thickening in reaction to the chemistry between them.

And then, he heard her bite back the slightest of moans.

For a moment, David thought he'd imagined the sound. That little moan of pleasure that he'd first heard when she'd been handcuffed in the room right next door to this one and his lips had first found her skin. But he hadn't imagined it, no matter how it echoed in his memory—that sound had come up in the here and now, with her fingertips fussing against the leg of his jeans and her eyes twisted downwards away from his.

His glass suddenly emptied again, he set it to the side on the nightstand and then shifted toward her, not letting himself think about what he was doing. When she didn't jar away from him after his hand rested on her thigh, he let it remain there before allowing his fingers to play up and down a bit, until his fingers were naturally reaching in so that he could better simply hold her leg, and she was leaning toward him in return, almost humming with warmth as he felt her nerves begin acknowledging his touch, her hand gripping his jeans now.

He looked up, from his hand to her half-closed eyes, and let the look on her face draw him forward into a kiss. She opened her lips to his, slowly, and he moved in only then, one of his hands coming up to cup the nape of her neck and bring her in closer. There wasn't anything to be said—this was what he'd wanted, what he'd come in here for even if he wouldn't have admitted it to himself.

He began unbuttoning her blouse as he told himself he wouldn't go any further, but she angled towards him so that he could better reach her, his fingers brushing her skin and causing her to shiver as they moved. She let him take her mostly empty wine glass from her fingers and murmured assent into his neck, laying her hands against him and holding on.

A mewl of pleasure escaping her lips, Lauren slid down from the headboard so that she lay prone beneath him, his body half covering hers as her hands moved beneath his sweatshirt and even the fabric beneath it, finding his skin.

"You wore this for me," she whispered, her eyes closed.

"So our skin wouldn't meet accidentally," he agreed huskily. "I didn't plan this."

But already he'd finished opening her shirt and dipped his lips to her breasts, teasing her skin and her nipples above the cups of her bra as his hands explored, pulling more tremors from her and relishing each of them as she gasped beneath him. Her nipples hardened into nubs at the tugging of his fingers, and he let himself remain distracted by them, teasing them with his tongue and his teeth until she gasped and he noticed she had one hand wrapped into his sweatshirt, holding onto him. When he slid his knee between her legs, she opened to him and pushed back against him when she felt the hard length of his cock against her thigh, pressing through his jeans.

"You want this?" he whispered into her ear, rubbing against her, and he felt her heart pounding back at him, her body instinctively lifting upward against his. Sliding down, he trailed his lips down her belly and lower, following the retreating fabric his hands were drawing down as Lauren gripped the comforter and shivered beneath him, her body humming with that intoxicating energy he'd missed over these past weeks.

Lauren's body shifted and turned instinctively beneath his hands, relaxing into the connection and his breath as he trailed along her body, until she was naked beneath him, and he was left tugging away his own clothing to leave it in a pile with hers beside the bed. When his lips came back to where they'd left off, trailing along her belly until he could lap lightly at her center as his hands pressed her legs far apart, she called out his name for the first time in what felt like ages, and then he felt her reaching for him, pressing her hands into his shoulders.

"David—you, I want you, in me," she gasped out, her breath lost to what he was doing and the pleasure of being against him again, this close, skin to skin. He could feel her magic rising up to meet his breath and his lips, her veins running hot with it now that his attention was focused on her once again.

"Wait," he demanded, his lips at her clit, before he pushed two fingers into her and laid his mouth against her so that she bucked beneath him, gasping with the sudden pressure and the pleasure it brought. Pumping his fingers into her, he lapped at her juices and felt himself growing even harder at the sounds of her breath and her soaking pussy taking his quick movements and demanding more. She was whimpering, wanting him, and it was irresistible.

His lips on her body, he looked up to see her eyes on his, her lips parted and gasping, her hands clenched in the comforter beside her sweat-slicked body. Holding her gaze, he put his lips against her clit and put his free palm against her belly, pressing into her and heightening that pressure he knew had been building as his other hand pumped into her, and then she went rigid beneath his attentions, screaming his name as a tremor rocked through her body. Her scream bled into a whimper of pleasure, and he found himself grinning against her, massaging her skin with his hands.

He felt her go limp with sudden relief from the tension of sensations when he rose up and took away his hands and his lips, and then he hesitated in reaching for the nightstand, where he thought there might be some condoms. He hadn't even thought of it until now, but they hadn't used anything at all while they'd been in that energy cage. And with that memory fresh, and the taste of her juices on his lips even now, he didn't want to use anything tonight if he didn't have to.

Leaning up beside her, he pulled strands of hair away from her face and brushed at her cheek until she looked straight at him, her blue eyes dilated and heavy with pleasure. "God, David, what are you waiting for?" she asked. He knew Lauren could feel his hard cock against her thigh, and even more than that, now he knew she was aching for him, wanting this just as much as he did.

Instead of answering, David palmed one of her breasts and played his fingers around her nipple until she gasped, one of her hands clenching at the bed while her other reached for his cock. She stroked teasingly until he jerked heavily beneath her grip and had to bring his hand to cover hers, stopping her movement. "We didn't use protection, the last few times," he bit out. "Are you on anything…?" he trailed off, loosening his hold on her to allow her to keep exploring, teasing both of their bodies. Her head was still, though, easing away from the contact. "Lauren?" he asked.

She paused, then whispered, "I can't get pregnant."

The air went still—that had been the last thing he'd expected to hear, but then she dipped her tongue out against his lips, her eyes closed, and moved her mouth closer to his ear. "Just take me," she added when he hadn't said anything after another moment, and then she breathed again only when he began moving over top of her, his lips insistent on her neck again and his hand gripping her breast as he tasted her. She shifted beneath him so that they both felt his cock sliding against her slit, demanding more.

This was what he'd been craving, pressing her down into a bed with his body above hers, slick with sweat, the hard plains of his body pulling the breath from hers. When David's hands moved to her wrists and pulled her hands above her head, she surrendered, helpless beneath him and giving in to the pleasure. With her wrists held over her head by just one of his hands, he let his other trail down her ribs as his cock prodded her folds, drawing little gasps from her. His nails tickled her skin and wrung tremors from her body as he moved against her wet heat, teasing her with every breath.

When he finally lifted and then thrust down into her, she screamed into his chest with the release of it, bucking beneath him. Her center had already been soaked with want, but she was hot and tight, the pressure of her channel around him now re-adjusting to him, getting used to him all over again as she clenched around him, panting with the pressure.

David held still, buried within her and panting against her neck already as her pussy worked to accept him again. "God, you're tight," he murmured before he began to move slowly, keeping her still beneath him as her body practically vibrated with the warmth of their coupling. She was wet and heated, and holding onto him with everything she had, clenching around him and gasping each time he pushed into her. Steadily, he thrust into her again, going deeper each time and breathing her gasps in, holding her wrists down with one hand and gripping her hip with his other. With nothing between them, he could feel the warming of her body responding to his, pulsing around him.

This wasn't like the frantic sex they'd had in the cage, on a hard floor and with a spell driving them. That had been violent, dangerous, and he hadn't had more than an ounce of control. Now, he took his time and focused on each sensation—each pulse of her body and quiver of energy, each moment of warmth and wetness as she engulfed him and moaned encouragement. He bent his lips to one of her nipples and angled her breast to his mouth, sucking in until she whimpered and he moved to the other, and then to her neck, until he had to catch his own breath and just let himself breathe against her shoulder, allowing himself to enjoy the rhythm he'd built and the fact that she was matching each of his movements with her own, even quivering as she was. Her hands were still above her head, her wrists held still, and she wasn't fighting him; she'd given in to the pleasure and to his control, and he wanted it to last. He wanted this desperation he felt in her to last—it was built from pleasure instead of pain, and what he should have been giving her every moment they'd been together. Forcing himself to slow down even more, he breathed in her skin and pressed in as deeply as her body would allow.

Lauren moaned suddenly when he bottomed out within her and then pulled back, just barely. The pleasure of being this close to her again was almost torturous when he moved this slowly, this carefully, and then she pushed up, clutching at his hand with her fingers. She was aching for him to just take her—to make her scream against him again with his cock filling her, with both her body and her breath muffled by his skin, his presence.

David pushed into her again, gripping her wrists tighter as he whispered into her ear. "Ready?"

"Yeah—God, yes, David, please," she breathed out.

Pressing into her hard then, David began slamming into her, going deep and holding her down, knocking her breath from her with each thrust of his cock. When she screamed out another release, he held himself pressed into her, licking at a nipple and caressing her hip, and then he began moving more slowly again when she'd caught her breath, her body all but limp beneath him.

He pulled out, leaned into her ear, and whispered to her to turn over.

This time, when he entered her, he went more slowly and kept the same pace. She was slick and hot, and he enjoyed each thrust forward as he watched the muscles of her back bent down beneath him with her ass in the air, round and gorgeous beneath his hands. He reached out to trace her spine, and then the lines of the vined tattoo leading down from her shoulder that glistened with sweat, and then he held onto her hips. "Hold on," he told her quietly, and then he sped up, taking her and moving her body to meet the rhythm he set for them.

Thrusting faster, he grunted and then called out her name when he finally jerked with the sensation of coming within her, exploding with the release he'd been holding off as their bodies slid against each other. She moaned beneath him, accepting him and pressing herself backward into him, her face sideways against the mattress.

When he slid from her to lay beside her, she rolled into him, her eyes already closed as her hands landed on his skin, on his chest and his shoulder. Her body thrumming with warmth, and with energy. He pulled her closer in, shutting his own eyes.

Chapter 3

David was gone when Lauren woke, and she could almost have pretended the evening had been a dream—from meeting him in the kitchen right on through to the wine and then falling asleep in his arms. Almost. But there was the soreness in her body, along her wrists and her core, and the stickiness she could feel along her thighs, and finally, of course, the fact that she was bare of any clothing.

She didn't know what time Adrias was supposed to arrive, but anything like that would have to wait; she needed a shower. Turning on the bathroom light, she touched her fingers along her swollen lips and then slicked them through her hair—she looked a mess, but she felt alive. Awake. She could practically feel how her body had warmed since being with David, coming more alive with energy and with the heat of magic. It was circling in her blood. Maybe she wasn't yet back to herself, but for the first time, she could believe that might be the outcome she was headed for. That she'd not just be able to feel the magic in her blood again, but work with it and from it in the way she'd dreamed might return. Now it seemed possible, finally.

In the shower, she took her time washing off, wanting to savor the time alone, and the time before whatever would come next that had seemed to have David on edge. Only when there was no more time to be wasted—when she'd shampooed and conditioned her hair, and washed and shaved and moisturized the daylights out of her skin, did she reluctantly shut off the water and reach out for her towel.

***

David didn't know what he'd expected, but it hadn't been this.

Telling them to move her out already, so she'd tempt the still-at-large witches into the field of play? *Maybe.* Getting her input on something to do with covens or spell-casting, or even asking her to talk to the witches they'd already found to see if they'd missed something? *Possibly, yeah.* Telling them to get a move-on with the hunt or report on their progress? *Sure.* But asking them to pull her into a brand new investigation where she'd be put at risk—a girl who'd been through hell already, had her life rolled out from beneath her, and who didn't have a lick of training when it came to investigative anything, let alone self-defense or military tactics?

"The two of you must have something more than chemistry," Adrias continued. "She went in after you and survived it when Josh didn't think she would. And, what's more, she's still here. You're telling me that doesn't mean anything?"

David met his boss' eyes, glaring. Hell if he was going to give him the view into his private life that would come close to explaining their relationship. "Fuck off, Adrias. You know that's not what I meant."

"Let's let her decide then, shall we?"

David looked up to find that Lauren had just slipped into the room to lean nervously against the wall. Dressed in a long, white A-line skirt that came to her ankles, and with a long-sleeved button-up shirt open, its ends tied over a tank at her waist, she looked so young. Fresh. Her hair was still wet from a shower, and he could tell even from where he sat that her lips were swollen from the night they'd spent together. Wondering for a moment whether his lips had left a mark on her neck, he felt himself thickening and looked away from her, back to the moment.

Adrias was leaning forward intently, his hand gesturing for her to take a seat. "Lauren, it's nice to meet you. I've heard a lot about you, so it's good to put a face to the name."

Forcing a nod, she returned his smile with a thin one of her own. She wouldn't call his bluff, but knew perfectly well that, all things considered, he'd certainly known what she looked like before now, and probably even before David and Josh, what with him having been the one to give them her mother's case to begin with. "Same," she answered simply, sitting a foot away from David on the couch. With no way to avoid being distracted by his proximity, she figured she might as well stay close enough for comfort.

Adrias himself stayed quiet for a moment, and then continued. "We've found ourselves in a minor bind here, and given the lack of progress in finding what's left of the coven your mother was involved in, along with your...*connection*, we'll say...to David, I thought you might be willing to help us out. If you'd be open to listening?" he invited, a false friendliness slipping from him with every word.

Glancing to David, Lauren nodded once again. She didn't trust this man in front of her, with his slicked back hair and perfectly pruned eyebrows, but she trusted David and Josh absolutely. If they trusted him enough to take the jobs he handed them and report to him, which she knew they did, he couldn't be all bad. But why wasn't Josh there also?

"Good," he said. "There's something going on in upstate New York, and the truth is that it might just be one of these new-agey, off-the-grid cults that's sucking people in, and that people are just dim-witted enough to go for it. It may be nothing we need to be concerned with, in other words. But it might be more malicious—murder, human trafficking, or something else entirely. We don't know. But eight couples have gone missing in three months that we know of, and these are just the ones who've been reported. There could be more."

"What he means," David interrupted, "is that those are the couples whose families have thought something was wrong. All of the individuals involved reached out and said they were going into therapy, and then into a couple's retreat for more intensive therapy. Next thing their families knew, they were getting calls to tell them goodbye—that they were going off the grid indefinitely to focus on each other and simpler living. The couples we know of are the ones whose families didn't buy it."

"Right," Adrias picked back up. "The ones who felt the couples were on the brink of divorce, or who are sure the folks involved loved their work or other aspects of their lives more than each other. And there's evidence enough to support it."

Lauren looked between the men, trying to catch up. David was scowling, gauging her reaction, and Adrias seemed to be examining the two of them. "And you think we can find them?" she asked belatedly. "When others haven't?"

"No. Maybe," Adrias corrected himself an instant later. "But we think you can go in, as a troubled couple, and figure out what the hell's going on."

***

The first three shots went down easy—he was pissed off and antsy, anxious for any change to come and settle things. It was the fourth that stopped in his throat. *It's one o'clock in the fucking afternoon. What am I doing?*

He'd left soon after Adrias, giving in to stalking out in what had been the equivalent of a tantrum. He hadn't known what else to do. Lauren had wanted to talk about the case, to talk about logistics and find out what he was thinking, and that wasn't something he could go into. How could he tell her what a mission like this would actually mean? What Adrias had told him their ruse would have to look like, before she'd entered the conversation, and what more he'd gleaned from reading between the lines? She'd just begun trusting him again— she'd just in the past night looked into his eyes and opened herself up to being vulnerable to him, trusting he wouldn't hurt her any more than he already had. But telling her that that was why this case wasn't an option…it was the same as admitting that he'd be capable of hurting her again, and without a spell to compel him. Hell, it was the same as admitting that he *would* hurt her again.

And even aside from what lay between them, and whatever relationship they might have a chance at, he didn't want Adrias dragging Lauren into another case and potentially putting her in more danger. The problem was, he also didn't know how he could really object. Rules had been bent all over the place since Josh had brought Lauren back from the hospital—and at their request, too.

It was true that they were in a sort of indefinite stasis, and that Lauren couldn't help but be aware of their schedules and investigations in a way that no one beyond their colleagues should be. It had been a spot of contention at the agency even when she'd been recovering, that two active operatives were also letting their home serve as a safehouse for someone who'd been a suspected accomplice to murder not that long ago. And Adrias had gone to bat for them, making sure the exceptions got approved because he trusted them to take care of their business, and because of how good they were at their jobs. That had been huge—and appreciated.

But this… this felt too close to taking advantage of her, at best. And whatever there was between them, he didn't know what came next, but pretending to be in a non-working relationship where he'd have to play a dirtbag of a husband…well, that sure as hell didn't seem like the best option.

Looking at the re-emptied shot glass in front of him, he pulled a menu closer, and then ordered a burger and a beer when the bartender came back by. Grease was better than having nothing but liquor in his stomach.

Waiting for the food, he texted Josh again. His partner hadn't answered his phone earlier, or responded to the quick text he'd sent to try to get his input.

Answer? Thoughts? he wrote now.

Adrias had told him that Josh had been on the case for a few days, trying to find other options. The man had expected Devlin to be at their meeting that morning, too, but he hadn't shown.

A moment later, the response came: *Home soon.*

Fucking great, he thought, *that's helpful.*

He texted back: *I'm not there, I'm drinking.*

As expected, no response came.

By the time his burger came, he'd broken down and taken another shot, shrugging off the bartender's invitation to share his troubles. He'd give the guy a good tip for leaving it at that and doing his job without fanfare.

When a body slid in next to David, he ignored it at first, but curiosity got the better of him. The woman was likely his age or just short of it, but older than anyone he'd normally have taken the time for, whatever that said about him. More than anything, though, this habit of acknowledging only younger women came down to him being practical. Women his age were looking for relationships—something more than casual laughs and the equivalent of a one-night stand, which he hadn't had the time or the patience to endure. Not till Lauren had entered the picture, at least.

Glancing sideways, he caught her looking his way and nodded, turning quickly back to his beer. He didn't need the distraction, but he knew before she spoke that she was going to.

"Wanna talk about it?" she asked, and he nearly snorted into his beer—it was exactly what he would have expected her to open with, word for word.

"No, sorry," he answered, and then he held up a finger to the bartender and gestured for another shot. Fuck it, but if there'd ever been a time where he wanted to day-drink and could actually afford the loss of focus it brought along in the bargain, it was today.

"I'll have one, too," she told the man when he set down the whiskey in front of David. "Rough day all around, I guess," she added when he glanced her way again.

"Must be," he said noncommittally. He sensed more than saw her downing her own shot and gesturing for another.

Don't engage, he told himself. *Not now.*

He stared blankly at the television above the bar until his burger came, and then he focused on the food, ordering another beer to accompany it. When the woman beside him asked if the fries were any good, he shrugged and then nodded, and gestured after a moment that she could take one. It surprised him when she did, but he stayed focused on his food. He needed to get home he suddenly felt, before he did something he'd regret.

After paying his tab and giving the bartender a hefty tip, he nodded to the woman whose name he'd never gotten, and wouldn't, and headed toward the bathroom to run some cold water over his face. In the mirror, it was hard to reconcile what he saw with what he felt. He felt exhausted, as if the morning's conversation had aged him a decade, but the man in the mirror actually looked like he had it together—maybe a little bleary-eyed if he tried being critical, but nothing worse. And he'd dressed in a button-down for the meeting, so that now he looked like a businessman, just calling the day quits early. No wonder the woman had been coming onto him, brushing his arm every chance she got. He looked as responsible as could be expected, given the place and the time. He ran his hands under the faucet again and then swiped them over his face before pulling down a paper towel to dry himself off.

The woman was in the corridor outside waiting for him.

"I'm not pretty enough or young enough?" she asked abruptly, blocking his path out. "Is that it? It's what my boyfriend—my ex-boyfriend," she corrected herself, "—clearly thinks. Is that it?"

"No, it's not," he said quietly, moving to go around her. "I have…someone at home," he finished.

"A girlfriend?"

"Or something like it," he said. In the next breath, he planned on asking her to move aside, but then she stepped closer and he breathed in her perfume and the desperate look on her face. Whatever he'd been about to say faded into something that would be easier on her, and he paused. "You're pretty, but I'm not…"

She cut him off with a kiss, and with the liquor's push, he caught her naturally and stepped backward as she pressed into him. His hands were on her and, before he knew it, his back was swinging open the restroom door behind him and they were inside, and he was backing her up against the sink, his hands scrabbling at the buttons on her blouse as hers found their way beneath his undershirt and ran over his abdomen.

It felt good suddenly to be back in the arms of someone where there was no emotion, no background, and not even any knowledge of name or where this woman might have been an hour before they'd met. There was just her desperation, and her crotch grinding against his hard cock pressing at his jeans. When he bit her lip, she moaned and gave into the pressure of his body, and then one of her hands was at his belt.

In a flash of awareness, with his hands on her cool, desperate skin, he realized what he was doing, and what he was missing in the warmth that his hands were seeking out instinctively, waiting for and not finding. There was no shiver here. No blood rising to his touch, no sweet tremble of energy responding to every one of his breaths and moves.

"Fuck," he gasped, jerking away so that he stood across the small room from her, his eyes on her bared breasts and then the needy look on her face. "Fuck," he repeated, running one hand through his hair. "I can't do this."

Re-buckling his belt as he fled, he moved before she

could say another word, and before either of them could let the liquor they'd consumed take hold all over again. *I shouldn't have come here at all*, he thought to himself as he hit the door to the parking lot.

Out in his truck, he sat for a few minutes leaned back heavily against the driver's seat, closing his eyes before he took a look at himself in the visor mirror. "Fuck," he muttered yet again, seeing the woman's lipstick smeared around his own lips. He used the edge of his sleeve, probably wiping at his face about ten times more than necessary. "Of all the stupid shit…"

Slamming shut the visor, he jammed his key into the ignition and pulled the truck out with a kick at the accelerator, swerving out of the parking lot to get back to the house. His mind veered between the woman at the bar and Lauren, spurring his dick to stay hard and his hands to remain clenched on the wheel white-knuckled.

***

When the landline rang, Lauren skidded away from the laundry room and reached the phone just before their answering machine cut in, breathing out a fast 'Hello?' before she even had the phone all the way to her ear.

"Lauren? You okay?"

"Josh. Yeah," she breathed out, leaning back on the little hall table where the phone lived. "Where have you been?"

"Researching. You guys talked to Adrias this morning?"

Lauren caught herself nodding instead of answering, and gave him a quick affirmative that, she hoped, begged for information more than more questions. He took the hint.

"Yeah, sorry I couldn't give you a heads-up. I should

have, but I just heard about what he was planning a few days ago and, well, I kept putting off bringing it up. I've just been trying to dig into the case to get you guys out of having to consider it at all. Haven't had any luck…"

Lauren listened as Josh kept talking, repeating a lot of what Adrias had said and voicing his own frustration until he suddenly cut himself off. "Is David back yet?"

Lauren scoffed. "I thought he'd gone off to find you. He left almost as soon as Adrias did…he was pissed."

"Yeah," the other man answered, and Lauren heard him sighing before he continued. "I am, too, honestly, but we can talk about that later. David texted me and wanted to know if I was there with you, though, and I got to wondering. I think he didn't like you being alone right now, but fuck if I know why he left if that's the case. Listen, before I go—you and David are, uh, talking again? I, uh, I mean…look, I looked for David when I got back last night, and the truck was there, but…"

"He was with me." *Was he ever.* Lauren bit her lip to keep from saying more. She was flushed from thinking of the night before, and Josh's stumbling had made it clear he didn't exactly want details. She'd let David tell him what he wanted to later on and leave it at that.

"Good. I'm glad, really. You doing okay?"

Lauren grinned into the phone, wondering how often people saw into this side of Josh Devlin. Sure enough, he sounded like a concerned parent. *My big brother*, she couldn't stop herself from thinking. "I'm good, Josh, thanks. Just a little worried about this thing with Adrias. David cut me off before I could remind him I can't lie, and he clammed up after Adrias left, so I…I mean, I don't know how it could work, you know?"

She listened to the silence on the other side of the line, and was just about to ask if Josh was still there when his voice came through with some assurances that sounded empty even to her ears. It was hard to tell whether he'd forgotten about that detail, or whether he had other reasons to be stressed, but maybe now wasn't the time to chime in an opinion, on the phone like they were and when David wasn't even there.

"Don't worry about details now," he said. "We'll talk later, and I'll be there after a while. I just want to finish up some research I'm in the middle of, but figured I should check in. You're okay on your own right now?"

"Yes, *father*, I'm okay alone right now," Lauren tried to joke. God, but she hoped her voice didn't sound as flat as she felt. "I'll see you when you get here, yeah?"

"Ha, yeah, you got it. Talk soon."

Lauren stared at the phone for a moment after Josh hung up, trying not to give much thought to how stressed he'd sounded about not being able to make it back right away. Where did David get off anyhow, demanding Josh get home when he himself couldn't be bothered to stick around and talk things out? He'd jetted out as if what his boss had requested had only stood to affect him, and not her, as well. Lauren had been left alone to puzzle through it, with one of the men she'd met with seeming to assume she had to say yes and the other acting like she ought to be mortally offended for even fucking considering it.

And it wasn't as if she could, anyway, given that she couldn't lie. Right? Not that David had allowed her to tell Adrias that. No, he'd cut her off before she'd barely gotten a fucking word out, alpha male down to his bone marrow.

With the laundry folded and all of the morning's dishes done, Lauren turned her attention to unnecessary clean-up, just to keep focused. Her mind still fuming over David's behavior—first overprotective and then dismissive—she leaned over the island and scrubbed at it before turning to the counters.

Fucking ass, she thought, slamming her fist into the sponge she held with her other hand, ringing it out over the sink. *And he leaves me here alone after all that, when I don't have a fucking clue what happens next. Tells Josh to check up on me because he doesn't feel like it, putting him in the middle of it, and won't just talk to me himself. Right when I...*Lauren cut off the thought, grimacing.

But she didn't know how he could just stalk off when so much seemed to be up in the air. What was about to happen? Anything? Were they going in even though she couldn't lie, or had he simply split with no thought of what came next or what they'd done last night? That's what it felt like, that he'd just left—and it was what was bothering her, too, far more than she was bothered by the prospect of what Adrias had proposed or the stress in Josh's voice. It felt like David had deserted her. And since the time she'd spent alone in her apartment before meeting up with Josh, this was the most alone she'd felt. The most vulnerable.

And it shouldn't have been. Not after everything she'd been through.

Lauren caught herself staring out the kitchen window once again, and this time she found that it was an effort to pull herself away. She wasn't even sure whether she expected, or wanted, Josh or David to return first at this point, but being alone was beginning to get to her. What was she supposed to do—sit here and stew until the two of them decided what came next? She deserved to be a part of the decision here, whether David wanted to acknowledge the fact or not. And yet, she figured that that was playing right into Adrias' hands—she'd been able to see it in his expression, that he expected her to want to make up for all they'd given her by helping out in this way.

Fucking hell. He knew it before he came in here, that

bastard. He knew I'd be ready to put myself in danger again because I feel like I owe them.

Because, yeah, there was no question that David and Josh considered this to be dangerous—she'd figured that much out for herself just from the way they were skirting around decisions and details.

The thought spurred her away from the window, and she headed to her bedroom to change clothes. She refused to sit and sulk in her own worries—she could at least try to be productive. At one time, she'd planned to use today to organize the shelves in the garage, which were crammed full of everything from paint cans to boardgames, rags and boxes of junk on to cases of water and discarded magazines. Even at a glance, anyone could see the men had used the shelves for anything that didn't have a place elsewhere, leading to the mess they had now. She guessed that half of the paints and cleaners were out of date, and judging by their age, she wouldn't be surprised if half of the games had missing pieces—it seemed like that sort of an area, which might have collected things they'd brought in from previous dwellings without giving them much thought, and then just dropped there to be forgotten.

As she stripped out of the nice clothes she'd donned for the morning's meeting, her mind went back to Josh's call. He'd expected David to be there because apparently David had been demanding to know where *he* was. She'd set him right, of course, but that wasn't the point distracting her now.

Sure, Adrias had given him a heads-up of what he wanted tackled next to give Josh a day's start in seeing if an extra set of eyes on the case would make a difference before they got a 'civilian' involved. But though Lauren hadn't said anything in return, she knew the ulterior motive of their boss also, in giving him the heads-up—

Adrias had been dismayed to see that Josh wasn't there that morning, to serve as a mediator. She'd seen it in his face. No, that man had *wanted* Josh on his side ahead of time, another person David would trust to communicate the seriousness of the case and convince him that their involvement was the next logical step. But no…he'd still been reading up on things, and he'd been unwilling to say what he thought, too, which told Lauren clearly enough that he was indeed on Adrias' side of things. He just wasn't ready to admit it yet.

Why wouldn't David let me tell him? I couldn't do it if I wanted to, could I…? The question had been haunting her, and Josh had shrugged it off. It was true, though—how could she pretend to be married to David when she couldn't lie? How could she present a believable front for whatever story they came up with if she could only tell the truth? And yet, David hadn't been willing to halt the discussion by saying just that. She'd gotten the words out once—'I can't lie'—and David had cut her off, facilitating Adrias' belief that she'd simply meant she was a bad liar. She'd tried to say it again and he'd given her a look that could have cut glass, which had stunned her, much as she would hate to admit it to him. All they'd been through, that look had only told her how hard he could be, when he needed to be or felt the need to show it, whereas she once would've said that he wouldn't be able to look at her like that. At least, she would have after the night they'd shared, assuming he wasn't under some spell to push it from him.

Now, knowing that weak spot on his part had been an illusion…it was just one more thing clouding her brain.

The look remained in her mind as she pieced through items on the shelves in the garage. Everything was mixed up, but she began by plucking out the various boardgames and stacking them to the side; later on, she could take these inside and go through them piece by piece to see which were worth keeping. Next came the paints. These went to a pile on the floor if they were still good, and to a spot by the trash cans if they were near-enough on empty or past their expiration dates. Based on some of the colors she saw, Lauren felt positive that a number of the paint cans had been left behind by previous owners—wondering about which was which was enough to keep her preoccupied, so that she didn't hear the front door.

With the garage door to the house open, Lauren had thought she'd hear anyone come in the front, but at some point she must have stopped listening. She was stretching up to reach another paint can when David's hands landed on her hips and pulled her around to face him.

The shriek had barely died on her lips when his mouth landed on hers and he pressed her back against the shelving, his fingers suddenly gripping her back and her ass, holding her to him like they hadn't seen each other in months instead of hours. Breathing in his kiss, Lauren couldn't think about anything but his presence—as always, her blood was humming to his, warming her and begging for the man whose arms were around her. She couldn't resist him.

"I don't understand," she murmured as his lips found her neck, sucking at her skin, and then his hands were beneath her blouse and his lips were back on hers, his tongue tangling with hers.

The whiskey on his breath and lips sank into her, and she wanted to pull back to just have a conversation, but he pressed harder into her when she made a move to squirm away. Feeling his desire against her, she gave herself up to the hum running through her skin, the magic pooling in her blood as he kissed her. He felt desperate for her, and her blood wanted to respond. All of the hesitation she'd felt earlier, thinking of that look he'd given her, was gone;

she could only give in to him. Without thinking about what she was doing or where they were, she let her fingers find the waistline of his jeans and she began tugging his shirt from them, anxious to touch skin and to have more of his skin against hers. Sucking his lower lip between hers, she swallowed up the lingering taste of whiskey and arched into him, moaning against his lips when one of his hands reached further up beneath her shirt and groped a breast.

"What the hell are you doing in here?" he growled out as his lips went to her neck, nibbling gently so that she gasped, her fingers suddenly frozen on his belt; the magic was more alive than she'd felt it in months, suddenly, responding to the gruffness in him and the tug of his rough fingers around her nipple.

She'd barely heard the question, and in fact could barely think with the pressure of him there, the feel of him against her. His cock was hard, pushing against her belly through their jeans, and she could feel her own body reacting more with each second. "Orga…organizing… stuff," she gasped finally, feeling herself be pulled upward so that he was holding her, her legs locking around his waist instinctively, and then he was carrying her over to the edge of the workbench where she'd once tended to his injuries and setting her ass on the edge of it.

"God, your body's warm, baby," he mumbled, the words nearly lost as his lips explored her skin.

Lauren leaned forward into him, cooperating as he pulled her shirt up over her head; she was untangling it from her arms when his lips found one of her nipples, and she wrapped her legs around him again, anchoring herself to him, against him, as she arched backward and one of his hands cupped her, angling her nipple so that he could suckle and tease at her more easily as his hand massaged her skin.

Taking advantage of the arch in her back when he sensed it, David used one hand to press her back over the bench so that her upper body lay prone before him and he could look at her, clad in only her jeans. She appeared stunned, flushed and confused, and he grinned as he saw one of her hands wander to her own breasts, toying with her nipples in turn now that he'd let her go—the unselfconscious move told him she wasn't thinking of anything but desire, and satisfaction. Keeping his eyes on hers, he pulled her legs from around his waist and nudged them down against the edge of the workbench, shaking his head slightly to stop her when she began to close them. Obediently, she froze under his gaze with her lips parted, watching for his next move as his power over her sung through him.

He undid his own jeans first, letting them drop to the floor around his ankles before he undid hers and then shifted her body, manhandling her until he could slip hers down with her panties to land on top of his, and then he spread her legs again. Now she was naked before him, spread for him. This was what he'd been wanting, what he'd needed to center himself, and he could see she was soaked for him already, trembling with want and with the cool air.

Pressing her legs further open, he held her gaze as he nudged his cock forward to prod her slit, and then let it rub up and down over her clit so that her eyes widened, her mouth gasping open for more air. When she reached to pull him forward, he caught her hands and held them at her sides helpless, and only licked his lips at the mewling sound she let out in response.

He watched her close her eyes, already breathless, and felt the magic running along her skin, thrilled at his touch. This was what he'd been missing. He moved into her and let his dick tease her pussy, his legs holding her open to him as he kept her helpless. She arched upward again, and then he took her without warning, thrusting forward all the way as he pounded into her, not giving her time to get used to his size—she'd taken him the night before, and her body remembered, opening up to him more easily now, soaked as she was with want. Once again, she'd reacted to his taking control, and where he'd been gentle the night before, this was all he wanted from her right now.

This submission, this desperate want, this magical soul of hers bending to his.

Wanting to keep her like this, helpless, he slowed down and began teasing her. He rotated his hips, brushing his hand against her nipples and then her clit, and then back again, and then he pulled back so that only the head of his dick was parting her folds, burning into her as she squirmed against him, wanting more now that he'd slowed down.

"Look at me, baby," David told her, nudging forward again just barely, and smiling down at her when she let out a moan and opened her eyes in response. "You're about to come, yeah?" he asked, half out of breath himself with the way he'd been teasing her. When she nodded, swallowing heavily, he held himself still inside of her and pressed down each of her hands so that she lay immobile in front of him, and he held them still against the table. "Keep your eyes open, kid—I want to see them when you come," he told her, nudging forward again into her slickness. Fuck, but she was so tight and hot, he wasn't sure how he'd held off this long.

"Yeah," she breathed out again, her dazed eyes still on his.

"Yeah," David echoed, and then he pushed into her again, his eyes on hers, and he felt her orgasm shaking through her, pulsing, as he did, until he fell onto her as he pressed all the way in, bottoming out as he leaned over her. He held her blue eyes with his as he exploded, gripping her hands as he spasmed within the heat of her and she milked him for more, helpless to the power of it and bucking beneath him as his orgasm rocked her backward against the table.

When he stepped back, his dick still hard, her legs fell limply away from him and he noticed her eyes following his, still obediently on him in a way that made him suddenly realize he wasn't done with her by a long shot. Pulling her toward him, he was swinging her around even as her feet touched the floor, pressing her to lean forward over the bench. Later, there was a lot for them to talk about, but none of it mattered right now. He leaned in, pushing his dick down so that it rested against the crack of her ass, nudging forward. He was slick with her juices, and she slid her legs apart, welcoming him.

Reaching down, David caught one of her knees and lifted, stretching her thigh up and sideways so that she was spread apart, one of her legs resting on the bench where her chest was, her body now diagonal to him as he pushed three of his fingers hard into her and pumped back and forth once, scissoring his fingers against the pressure of her channel so that she groaned in response, her pussy pulsing around his hand and begging for more. He could feel the heat of her, and feel her being beyond words and still wanting more.

He pressed the head of his cock in, going just beyond her entrance, and stopped her with one hand when she began to press backward against him. "You ready for all of me?" he asked instead, and in response he could have sworn that he felt magic run through her, along her body in a shiver that went from her shoulders to her toes in one long, nodding tremble that nearly made him gasp with the tension it took for him to stay still inside of her rather than lunging right then. He heard her take a deep breath, and saw her nod against the table, her cheek on its surface and her eyes closed.

Without letting another moment pass, he shoved into her canal, welcoming the heated pressure that came with the thrust of his hips and then pulling back immediately, pumping into her over and over again. He held her hips for leverage, his eyes on her lips as they gasped for breath and on her hands as they clawed at the bench for purchase as she pressed back into him, her body welcoming his with each desperate breath. He leaned back, arching into her and shutting his eyes to try to hold out longer, but when he felt her body begin spasming around him, he couldn't wait.

"Fuck, fuck, fuck," he grunted out, pumping into her violently with three last jerks of his cock bucking into her with cum and with need, unable to get enough of her.

When he slid out, he took a step back, and then sideways, until he could lean on the table beside where she still lay spread out, a slight smile on her parted lips.

Chapter 4

David knew what he wanted to talk to her about—he wanted to sit and talk to her about what she meant to him, and how he couldn't get enough of her. He wanted to focus on who they were together, and how they fit into each other's lives, the coven be damned. He wanted to know why she couldn't have kids, and why it had taken her so long to tell him, and whether she'd wanted kids. He wanted to know what more she'd thought about her future, if anything, and whether she could forgive him for being the monster he'd been to her in that cage, and for dropping himself back into her life—and, let's be honest, her body—so suddenly and completely, without any time for her to acclimate. Like today, when he'd come back from a bar and all but landed on top of her with a caveman grunt and a hard dick.

But there wasn't time, and he knew it. All of that, all of those conversations, would have to be put on a back-burner until they figured out what to do about this case, and how he and Devlin could tackle it without her being involved. Because that wasn't happening.

He dripped some Irish Cream creamer into her coffee with a packet of Splenda and poured a heavy dose of straight sugar into his own cup before stirring both drinks. She reached up for her mug from the living room couch where she'd curled up after changing clothes, and he took a seat in the armchair diagonal to where she sat, crossing his leg so that his foot brushed against her knee. He watched her drink down some of her coffee, and let her. He wanted another few minutes to sober up, and then they'd get this over with.

"Josh called before you came in," she started a moment later, her eyes landing on his. "He thought you'd be here."

Man, she jumps straight in. David swallowed, and fought down the impulse to put aside his coffee and silence her with his touch—again. That wouldn't solve anything. "Sorry about that. I needed air. Adrias caught me off-guard."

"Me, too," Lauren said pointedly. "But, look, you wouldn't let me say it before, but it's not like there's anything to talk about here, right? I mean, if I can't lie..." she trailed off, watching him. "You've got a way around that, don't you?" she breathed out a few seconds later. With that, she reached out and gripped his ankle, hard, the point of emphasis bringing his eyes straight to hers. She pressed her fingers into his joint and her lips set in determination when he winced in reaction. "Truth, David—I deserve it."

He gulped down some more of his coffee and then rested the cup on his knee, meeting her eyes again. "Yeah, Lauren, we can figure a way around that. It's not hard— I've done enough undercover work that I could talk our way around it. And you're good at sidestepping when you want to, just not answering what you can't. You wouldn't have to lie—we could finagle things, the way things started between us, all that's happened…I'm not gonna lie to you. Some coaching would take care of it. But that's not the point. You'd be in danger, and maybe get hurt, and we're not doing that. What you need to understand…"

"What I need to understand? Seriously?" Lauren yanked her hand away from his ankle and slid away, landing herself in the middle of the couch. "Stop treating me like I'm a fucking child, alright? Okay? Because I'm not. I can see reasons you wouldn't want me to help you guys on this, and that's fine, but don't make it about protecting me," she hissed. "I'm tired of you—both of you—treating me like I'm helpless and don't know what's in my own best interest or what I'm capable of. Me needing your help with the coven does not translate into me being incapable of making a single fucking decision of my own. If you can't get over that, maybe I do need to leave," she bit out, unable to stop herself. It was true, though. Josh turning into her big brother was one thing— the two of them treating her like an invalid or a child was something else entirely.

David stared at her, hard, and then leaned forward, placing his empty coffee cup on the table between them. "Okay, Lauren, fine. So, let's say it like this. You're a civilian. Devlin and I are trained operatives with a military background—we're trained for this shit, and we've done it a thousand times. We signed up for this, just like we signed on to protect you, whether you like it or not. Adrias has no business asking you to get involved here and—"

"So, there's another way?" Lauren cut him off, holding his gaze.

"What?"

"Another way to fix this. Another way to figure out whether couples are being killed or kidnapped or whatever Adrias thinks is going on. You've got another way."

David looked out toward the window. "You can't tell Adrias you can't lie," he said instead of answering.

"David…"

"No, Lauren, I'm serious." David turned back to her and leaned forward. He reached out to catch her hand, but she shuffled herself further backward on the couch, out of his reach. Sighing, he accepted the distance and sat back, taking a deep breath into his lungs. "If Adrias knew you were being affected by magic that strongly, or that you had any magic left in your blood, it would be asking for trouble. And you not being able to lie outright? Fuck, kid. He'd consider you a liability, for us, just being here."

Lauren had been ready to push for answers to how else they might address the case, but that word—*liability*—stopped her. The man in front of her looked dead serious. Not afraid…but not comfortable. "Are you saying he'd…David, are you saying he'd kill me?"

"What? Jesus, no—fuck, no!"

She watched as David reached for his coffee cup, saw it was empty, and sat back in his seat again. "That's not…no, that wouldn't happen. But he wouldn't ignore it. And on some level, he'd be right—you're exposed to our lives here, Lauren, whether we like it or not. Somebody comes after us, they're gonna find you here. You not being able to lie, and being around our work? It's just not safe, you wanna hear it like it is. Adrias finds out, he'll want you in some other safehouse, somewhere else. I don't want to trust strangers to take care of you. Neither does Josh," he finished belatedly.

The flatness of the comment caught in her gut, but Lauren held back any reaction. "Because I'm your responsibility," she answered quietly after another moment went by.

"Yes…no." David stood abruptly and sat down on the couch beside her, before she could move away. He caught her hands in his, and finally she looked at him, feeling her skin all but begin humming beneath his hands once again, the chemistry between them pulling magic to the surface of her blood in a way that she knew even he could feel, now he was aware of it. "I *want* you to be my responsibility, that's what I'm telling you. Professional, personal, all of it. I want you here, with me. I don't know what we are, and I guess we have to talk about that, soon, but the point is that I don't want to give Adrias reason to try to yank you out of *this* safehouse, with *me*. You got me?" he finished.

She didn't meet his gaze, but he felt her fingers curl around his after another few seconds passed, and then she leaned against his shoulder. "Okay," she said quietly. "But I don't want to be in the dark, David. It's my fault I've been so apart from things, I get it," she said in a rush, before he could point it out, "but now that we're talking, now that we're together again…I need you to not treat me like a child."

David smirked. "Children don't do what we've been doing, kid."

She knocked her head against his shoulder in a joke of a reprimand, fighting back a laugh. "You know what I mean."

It took a moment before he agreed, but when he did, she let herself relax against him.

"Okay," she said, snuggling closer as he draped an arm around her shoulder and pulled her in. "So, we don't tell Adrias that we're connected by my mom's spell, and we don't admit that I can't lie. Where does that leave us? What are you and Josh gonna do about this cult Adrias is worried about?"

After a few seconds of silence passed, she realized he didn't have an answer, and the part of her that had counted on one paled with the realization. "David," she began carefully, "Adrias said the only way to do this is for a couple to go in. And he said the only other agents who were qualified and tried got called on it and dismissed. But he wouldn't have brought the case up if… if he didn't think people were being hurt, right?"

She felt him shrug against her, but his silence spoke volumes.

"We'll talk when Josh gets home. Maybe he'll have figured something out."

Lauren swallowed down her nerves and protests as David fished out his phone and texted his partner, then relaxed back into the couch and turned on the television, switching it to a baseball game. Her mind was elsewhere, wrapped up in what options there were. If Josh didn't have another solution…what did that mean? And how did she even feel about it?

She watched the game blankly, allowing herself to curl in against David and go limp against him. This was what he and Josh did. So, if he said they'd figure it out…they'd figure it out. When David took her hand after a few minutes, she let herself just focus on the warmth there, and on the smell of his cologne seeping into her senses.

"What you said last night," he began, "I didn't get a chance to ask you about it. About you not being able to have kids," he clarified after a moment.

She put her head back down against his chest, the hand that wasn't already encased in his slipping behind his back and resting near his belt so that she was near hugging him, however loosely. "Is that…a problem?" she asked quietly.

He coughed back a laugh and answered a moment

later. "No, it's not a problem. But you can't be surprised I'm wondering what happened, or why."

"I never wanted kids," she answered, knowing it wasn't actually an answer.

He waited for her to keep going, but her eyes were on the game again, her pulse racing against his hand, hoping he'd just leave it be. "See what I mean about you getting around lying?" he prodded.

"David, come on. If it's not a problem for you, and I never wanted kids…why does it matter?"

For a minute, he didn't speak, but she couldn't help the tension that had crept back into her body, or the bitterness she'd heard in her own voice that she knew he wouldn't ignore.

Disengaging his hand from hers, he rubbed his hand along her arm, up to her shoulder, and began a gentle massage there until she felt herself relaxing into him again, despite wanting to run away. By the time she felt her heartbeat slowing, her magic reacting to his touch and warming her skin, wanting him, she'd almost been able to forget what had brought the tension back into the room, but then he reached sideways for the remote and flicked the television off.

Lauren closed her eyes when she felt his hand reach up to her face as if to tilt her head to meet his eyes, but his hand froze when his fingertips met her cheek and found the moisture there, so that she twisted her head away and attempted to dry the tears against his t-shirt, avoiding his gaze.

"I guess it matters because you're crying," he said, his lips close against her ear.

"I really didn't want kids," she reiterated, wondering how many times she'd said it before. Hundreds, probably. The way her mom had treated her, and the way things had ended up between them. She couldn't chance passing on powers to a child—they came with more bad than good. "After what Mom did to me," she told him, "how could I, right?"

"Okay," he answered. "I get that. But Josh said you're terrified of hospitals. He said the nurses had to give you a sedative when he took you to Bartlett General, just to make sure you wouldn't injure yourself worse from panicking, so you can't tell me you sought out a doctor to keep you from having kids. So, what," he asked after a moment, "did you cast a spell on yourself, too?"

Lauren huffed out a laugh against his chest, letting her fingers clench into his t-shirt as more tears came. "I guess I could have. I never thought about it."

David leaned his head back against the couch, and she could see the effort it took for him to be this patient. "If you weren't so upset, Lauren, I'd let it go, I swear to God I would, but you can't seem to stop crying, and so you can't tell me not to worry about it or that it doesn't need to be discussed. I'm gonna keep wondering till you tell me, and I'd just as soon it not be taking up space between us—especially if it doesn't bother either of us, right?" he emphasized, pulling her closer so that he was hugging her back now, and one of her legs uncurled and found its way over his, tangling beneath his knee as if she was aching to get as close as she could.

Lauren swallowed again, and took a swipe at her eyes. She'd pushed herself not to think about that night or what had come after it. And not saying it aloud, that this had happened…it hadn't felt so real till now. But David was right. He'd wonder now, if she didn't just tell him.

"The doctor told me when Josh was out of the room," she said. "One day when he came by the house and I was more…aware. They didn't do a rape kit at the hospital, but they gave me a full exam when I was unconscious, because he was worried about internal bleeding or other damage."

Other damage. The phrase echoed in the room, and then David pulled her in tighter against his body, holding on like he could go back in time and protect her. "The guy who attacked you," he said tightly. "Before you called Josh."

She nodded against him. "He was too rough, and the bruising went so deep, and I guess there was…internal damage. Not the type of thing I'll feel or that will affect me, now that I'm past it, but…yeah. I don't…I don't even remember what the doctor said. I was still hopped up on pain medicine. But that's what it comes out to."

David hugged her in closer and let his chin sit against the top of her head as she cried into his t-shirt. Maybe it was true that she'd never wanted kids, but that didn't change the fact that the bastard who'd attacked her had taken yet another choice out of her hands.

"I've got you now," he said simply, rubbing his hands along her shaking form. "I've got you."

***

Josh hung up just as he pulled his Mustang into the drive, having been on the phone for the last half hour with Adrias. The man didn't have any more of an idea of what they were facing than he did, but both of them felt, in their guts, that something about this couples' retreat was not just suspicious, but downright malicious. They weren't talking about money disappearing—they were talking about people. People who'd had troubled, abusive marriages, in some cases to the point of talking about divorce, but who'd never given any indication that they might be the types to disappear into a commune. And, just as much to the point, there hadn't been giant shake-ups in the world or in any of their lives that might suggest a sudden catalyst for a move like what these folks had supposedly embraced.

The more Josh looked into it, the less he liked what he saw and the more questions he had. And while none of it made him feel better about putting Lauren into a situation where she might be in danger all over again, he also hadn't seen any new options arise. And what Adrias said was true—he either trusted his partner and his instincts or not, and he did. He trusted David Fredericks with his life, and on any normal day, he would have trusted anyone's life to his hands. He'd just never had to holster his own gun and send someone else into the proverbial line of fire with him. The closest he'd come had been letting Lauren give herself up to the coven, but at least that case had directly involved her, and *there*, there'd truly been no choice. This was different.

And then there was the fact that this involved David and a girl he seemed to be falling for, for real…and to make Adrias' plan work, he'd have to put Lauren through hell. Even if he kept her safe, this wouldn't be a walk in the park they were moving into. Instinctively, Josh figured that was why his partner had disappeared that morning—he'd seen the writing on the wall and wanted no part of it.

Inside the house, the sight in the living room stopped him for a moment, and despite the day he'd had, it garnered a smile. David had a beer in his hand and was wrapped up in a baseball game on the television, Lauren curled into his side with her hand resting lightly on his chest. His free hand was tangled in her hair, as if he'd been running his hand through it without thinking, and her feet were tucked beneath her into the overstuffed couch. They looked like they belonged together.

"Took long enough," David said without looking up, and Lauren glanced upward blearily with a look in her eyes that suggested she might have been falling asleep. From the caution in her eyes, though, Josh guessed she'd come to the same conclusion he had, even without the benefit of the research.

"Sorry," Josh answered. "Looks like you guys did okay without me."

Offering fast apologies, he moved to the kitchen to get himself a beer, and then he paused at the island, watching David and Lauren from there. Nervous as she was, he'd been able to see her practically glowing with the effect David had on her—feeding off of his energy, reflecting it. When she was within a few feet of him, she was flushed with his presence. More herself, and confident in the way she'd been before David had ever slept with her. Apart from him, she was Lauren still, but somehow less present, less grounded. As if she needed David there to really complete her.

And his emotions affected her constantly, though it was more obvious now than ever before. Josh had seen it between them in the past weeks, though David seemed mostly unaware of it so far. Each of his moods affected her, and the closer they were, the more drastic the effect. He'd thought to himself earlier that anyone in the world would believe the two of them were connected, married and taken with each other but struggling. Whether they realized it or not, it broadcast from them when they were together. Maybe it was no wonder, given the rollercoaster of a relationship they'd had so far.

But the why of it didn't matter.

What mattered was that they could literally put the two of them into counseling as they were, painting them as a domineering man with a smitten wife who was going through an identity struggle because of her chosen mate…and although that was taking it out of context, and painting both of them in a light that wasn't entirely fair, it was also a hundred percent believable. And it would work, if they did it. Maybe that was understating things, and David would have to play more of a controlling, hurtful jerk to her than either of them would want, but it would work.

And, Josh told himself again, they could prepare Lauren for that. They could make her understand why it was necessary if it meant saving lives.

But the fact that the two of them were together again…he didn't know if that made things better or worse. What Adrias was asking would be hard on both of them, whether they said no or yes. They could say otherwise, and Adrias could say the same, but there was no way around it. The two of them were wired that way— wanting to help other people, caring about other people even when they didn't need to, and despite the shit that David had put Lauren through and how hard he could be, he was a good guy. If they said no to this case, they'd be taking on the guilt of knowing they might have been able to help and had turned their backs. And if they said yes, there was no telling what they were walking into.

But that didn't make anything easier. Not when it felt like they didn't have any choice in the matter. Again. And whether Adrias realized it or not, Josh had begun to fear that getting involved in what he proposed would tear all of them apart. Lauren was family now, whether Adrias liked it or not—Josh didn't want that to change.

Running through his options, few as they were, Josh downed a beer in the kitchen as he stood there contemplating what came next, and then he pulled out fresh ones for himself and David, pulling a third out for Lauren after another moment's thought. Then, bottles in hand, he finally headed for the living room.

David had stayed where he was, knowing his partner would be back in shortly. For the last hour, the case had been pushed to the back of his mind, Lauren's admission grounding him beside her. Whether she'd wanted kids or not didn't matter—the knowledge that it wasn't an option because of the monster who'd attacked her would haunt her, and be one more tangible reminder of what had happened. If David could have gone back in time and killed the man before he ever touched her, he wouldn't have hesitated, and it killed him that all he could do was sit here now, dealing with the aftermath instead of the action. What made it worse was understanding that he himself couldn't even promise not to hurt her again—not with what Adrias was proposing lurking in the very air they breathed, waiting for a decision.

When Devlin returned with beers in hand, David picked up the remote control and muted the television, turning his attention to his partner. He'd left early that morning, before David had made it to the kitchen, and it looked like he hadn't bothered with anything more formal than a t-shirt and jeans, which meant that he'd been stuck at a computer all day and had planned it that way. It also meant he was stressed, and the circles under his eyes highlighted that fact in broad relief. David nodded thanks as he took the beers for himself and Lauren, and then commented as he opened them, "Adrias said you've been on this since the day before yesterday, looking into the case."

"Trying to find a way around you guys going in," Josh acknowledged, his eyes darting to Lauren's. She was awake now, wary.

"Well, I hope you managed it, cuz we're not putting Lauren into that place."

"It'd be you *and* Lauren," Josh answered. "She wouldn't be on her own."

David froze, his muscles tensing even against Lauren's warmth.

"It's not happening," David bit out, letting his fingers press into Lauren's skin to lever her head back against his shoulder. He wanted her with him on this. "We don't know what we'd be walking into, but we know enough to know it's not safe. To know it wouldn't be good. You can't tell me you want to put her in that situation, Devlin. Hell, I wouldn't want to put you and Claudia in, and it's the same thing, yeah?"

Josh shrugged, clearly uncomfortable, his eyes on Lauren instead of his partner. David looked down to see that she'd closed her eyes, and had a flush spreading along her neck and into her cheeks, practically a beacon of energy feeding from his proximity.

Josh caught David's eyes and held his gaze, pushing down the bile in his throat that questioned what he was about to say. "She's strong, and I trust you to take care of her. I think we ought to leave it up to her."

Her fingernails dug into David's palm and Lauren took a shallow breath, her eyes still closed. Beside her, David tried to let her be, and to let her answer. This had been what he'd expected, but not what he'd hoped for; he hadn't wanted to put the decision on her. He could feel her running warm beside him, her blood still pulsing with magic from being with him all night and most of the day, and after the emotional afternoon they'd had, the last thing he wanted was to raise his voice against hers or call what they had into question. This case was a minefield of uncertainty, and that would have been the case even if their relationship had been rock solid.

Eventually, David's hand pressed into her knee, asking for an answer, and she opened her eyes to see his jaw moving, suggesting he was grinding his teeth to keep himself silent. She glanced over to Josh next, who looked like he was in physical pain just from suggesting what he had. She wanted to say no—so, so badly—but if Josh felt they were the best option for helping…

"I don't want to put you on the spot," Josh said quietly. His eyes met hers, and she saw the truth of the apology in them and nodded slightly, trying to swallow down her nerves. "It's not like you have to decide tonight, let alone now, but all of the research I've been doing has only brought up more questions. It is what it is," he finished, shrugging. "It wouldn't be easy for you, or David," he added belatedly, meeting his partner's eyes, "but Adrias has already run through a lot of options, and this seems like it could work, if you're both willing."

She glanced sideways to David, who wasn't meeting her eyes, and reached her hand from his chest to land over his on her knee and grip it. "And couples are disappearing… regularly?"

Josh nodded. "Yeah. That's why we're talking about this and why I didn't tell Adrias to get lost. You're not qualified for something like this, but David is, and right now, with the connection you guys have and the fact that your connection is real, visible…you guys are the best bet we've got of figuring out what's actually happening in there. They've been on this for a while without us, and this seems like the first workable plan anyone's hit on, tell the truth. The other operatives who've gone in posing as couples—and FBI agents before them, before it got handed to our agency—have all been turned away, the doc in charge telling them they weren't suitable for the program. Somehow, she's seen through them; even turned away a couple of cops who were actually a couple for some reason."

Lauren nodded, a sigh pressing from between her lips. "And what about the coven? I haven't even left the grounds…" she began, picturing the faces of Nell and Johana as they appeared in her memory and dreams. She'd been hiding out, waiting on the point when they'd be caught.

Josh and David traded looks, and she felt David shrug against her before he spoke. "As long as you don't use your magic, and as long as we make it quick…we should be okay. There's been no sign of Nell or Johana. I'm starting to agree with Adrias, that they're laying low or maybe have left the country. We're going to find them, Lauren, but…"

"But not immediately," she answered for him, a pinch in her chest. She didn't add that their just being together was, in some way, waking up her magic. He already knew that. And if this was a quick trip, she could certainly avoid using it—they wouldn't be able to sense it from wherever they were without her actively using it, surely.

"Lauren," Josh cut in, "we're not talking about letting our guard down when it comes to the coven. That's not happening. We're talking a few days away from the house, in the middle of nowhere, with agents on hand. It'll be a week away from the house at most, and with no sign of Johanna or Nell on the radar, I think we'll be okay as long as you don't try using whatever… whatever juice you've got left," he finished awkwardly, trading looks with his partner.

She felt David tensing all over again before she even spoke, but knew it was because he could predict what she was about to say. "So, if there's a way around me not being able to lie, and David says there is, and we're not worried about the coven for now…then we figure it out. We go in."

Josh nodded, and David's hands gripped her more tightly, on her shoulder and her knee, but she knew that the two partners couldn't disagree with what she'd just said. She'd felt it in David all day, and seen it in Josh from the moment he'd walked in. Once again, they seemed to be pressed into a situation where there were no good options, no assurances, and once again she and David would be venturing into a lion's den, together and without any other choice.

But at least they'd be going in together this time.

The weight of the decision settled her against David's frame on the couch, and she nodded blankly when Josh announced a moment later that he was going to get up and make dinner, and that they'd take the night to think about it.

She knew he was right. They would take the night to think about it, and she and David would talk about it, but the decision had been made.

Chapter 5

So, they have nothing in common is what you're saying," Lauren cut Josh off, putting her hand up to stop him turning another page in the file he'd printed out. "Just say it, and stop acting like I can memorize all this in one sitting—I can't," she added, looking pointedly at the two men who sat with her at the kitchen island. They'd been sitting there for hours, ever since dinner, going over files and information and statistics that showed that none of this was normal, and if anything, she only felt less prepared for what she was being pulled into.

"We just need you to remember them well enough that you'll recognize their faces if you run into them," Josh answered quietly. "If you know something about them, all the better. Plus… the more you guys know about them, the more you might be able to mirror the commonalities in their relationships."

Lauren sighed and ran her fingers back through her hair, leaning away from the table. Beside her, David sat bent over his notes, his eyes running up and down the chicken-scratch he called handwriting. She looked back to Josh and caught his eye, feeling herself bristle through her tiredness. "David will be there, and he'll have all of this memorized the way he's going. And it's not like we have their clinical files—you said those were hardcopy in the offices and we can't get copies. What are we going to learn about these people from the bare facts, Josh?" She caught him looking toward David, and reached out and grabbed his wrist, stopping him from evading her, again. "I mean it—what are we getting at here? And what are you not telling me?"

Finally, he met her eyes and nodded. "I wanted to lay it out for you first, so you guys could talk about how to present yourselves and all this would be here for you to draw on," he began, and then he paused, weeding out the pictures of the various disappeared individuals and grouping them into clusters as he spoke, regrouping them to prove his points as he went along. "Eight couples," he reminded her. "Six of them straight; two gay. No children among them. And," he said pointedly, "that's not normal. More couples might be deciding not to have kids, but eight couples out of eight…even if two are gay, that's long odds, especially considering these are couples who could afford the expense. All of them with at least a middle-class tax bracket, though that's not all that surprising—"

"Why not?" Lauren broke in, thinking that it finally felt like they might be getting to the meat of things here, talking about these people in groups instead of one by one.

"You'd need at least that to afford the type of retreat they're offering—room and board, long weekends away as a couple. I don't know of any run-of-the-mill insurance that would cover marriage counseling, let alone on that scale. Plus, you're talking time away from work—that's lost income on top of flat cost. This place is for couples that are willing to make a real investment in therapy."

Beside them, David scoffed, but Lauren ignored him. "Okay, so, what else?"

Josh regrouped the couples in front of her. "These six couples have an uneven dynamic—one primary breadwinner between them, and it's the male in all of the straight couples here; the spouse in each case has an income, but a lower one. Teacher married to a lawyer, freelance writer married to an engineer, you get the picture. One spouse brings in more than twice the income of their partner. That makes for a certain power dynamic, especially when there aren't kids to suggest that one person being more of a home-maker makes sense."

Lauren glanced to David uncomfortably, wondering if the comments about children would have drawn a reaction, but she didn't see any. She looked back to Josh as he reached out to rearrange the couples' pictures again.

"These four have had suspicious injuries suggesting some violence at home," he said quietly, pulling aside two of the pictures of gay men and two of the women. "Nothing extreme, not like what happened to you," he added, "but serious enough to raise eyebrows about their spouses. Doctors' reports and records. Especially when you look at the fact that *none* of those who got injured are the primary breadwinners, so they'd be on the underside of the dynamic I mentioned."

Once again, Josh separated out the pictures. "These three men have multiple DUIs and hold high-stress jobs— two lawyers, one surgeon—and this guy, the engineer, he's moved six times in eight years and his wife has had to move with him, which is bound to create some stress at home. Might even be why she freelances instead of having a regular career."

Lauren felt her throat tightening, and nodded as Josh

kept going. She was finally starting to get the picture of the kind of 'troubled marriage' he and Adrias needed them to represent. And beside her, David had gone tense, as if he was primed to move now, and the stress of it had sucked the air out of her lungs so that her body hummed with the aggression pulsing in his; she nearly had to bite back a gasp in response to the force of it. Any emotion that ran through him, when she was connected like this to him, even just with his hand brushing her neck through her hair as it was now, as if in comfort—it was like a live wire of magic and energy, thrumming into her blood and beckoning her closer. She closed her eyes, trying to hide the reaction as the men kept speaking.

"We've got records showing that these three women have all left their husbands at some point, and gone to stay at hotels or with friends, and then come back. At least five of the individuals here have consulted divorce attorneys, and it could be more. It's worth saying that we know for a fact one of the men in each of the gay marriages did so, and divorce isn't as common among the LGBT community as it is in straight marriages, so that's saying something."

Josh glanced up to David, as if to see if he wanted to chime in, but he remained still, studying the various profiles.

"That's it?" Lauren prodded.

"Mostly," Josh answered. "But there are a lot of texts, and one assault charge. The assault charge was filed by a friend of one of the women—he was having dinner with her and, allegedly, the woman's husband walked in and decked the guy. Charges were dropped a few days later, but he put him in the hospital."

"So, she was cheating on her husband?" Lauren asked.

Josh shrugged. "The texts, in all but two marriages, suggest that one partner is over-protective to the extreme.

Checking in constantly, asking questions…you get the picture. It's uneven. A normal relationship, texts show up as conversations, and the number's about even—each spouse texts the other about the same amount; more often than not, it's an exchange. *'Please pick up carrots at the grocery store.' 'Okay, will do.'* … That sort of thing."

"Okay, and…"

"And, this isn't that. This is one person sending five or six times as many texts as the other person. Asking where they are, what they're doing—even giving commands, in a few cases." Josh pulled up a document on his laptop, which had been sitting nearby, and showed her a screen-capture Adrias had sent. "This is from one of the couples, the texts for one day—the Saturday before they ended up making an appointment at the in-take center to talk about a weekend therapy session. And it's not one of the more extreme examples from this group."

10:15   Evan: Where are you?

10:17   Evan: Why aren't you   home?

10:25   Evan: Would you fucking answer me?

10:33   Evan: Why the fuck aren't you answering the house phone? Where are you?

10:38   Jillian: Sorry I'm at the store. Didn't hear my phone. Get you something?

10:50   Jillian: Sorry Evan. Love you.

12:15   Evan: I'll be home at 5:30.

12:20   Evan: Told Bill he can come by for the game tonight. Make sure the case

   of beer in the garage gets put in the fridge.

1:35 Evan: Did you put the beer in the fridge? Buy some more if you go out, too.

1:50 Evan: Why is it so hard for you to answer your fucking messages?

1:52 Evan: Bet you'd be answering if this were that jerk from your office. Or your goddamned sister.

2:30Evan: Place was a mess last time Bill was over. Don't embarrass us and

remember to clean up okay?

Lauren pushed the laptop back towards Josh, shaking her head. "I don't need to read more than that. I get it. I wouldn't blame her for cheating on him." From the corner of her eye, she caught David exchanging a look with Josh. "What?" she asked as the laptop got closed.

David answered first. "Lauren, a guy like that doesn't have a cheating wife; he just thinks he does. He'd probably put her in the hospital for real if she cheated on him."

"He's a possessive jerk, and he's probably a shitty husband, but I'd be willing to bet she wasn't cheating on him," Josh agreed. "Not with trains of texts like that. Closest she came to going behind the guy's back was talking to a divorce attorney, but based on the timing, I think that's what sent them to the in-take center—this guy realizing she was serious about leaving him."

For a moment, Lauren thought about how sad that was—that this guy had tortured his wife with possessiveness, and then gone into a panic only when he'd realized he might lose her. Thinking back over the train of texts she'd just read, she couldn't imagine sticking in a relationship that got to that point, and the lack of power that woman had to have experienced on a daily basis.

And then her breath caught in her throat.

She looked between the men at her side, and saw from the way that they weren't meeting her eyes that this was what they'd been avoiding telling her.

"This is how you guys want me to act. Scared of David, like this, like…like I'm some helpless victim he's taken advantage of. Like he tells me what to do at every minute of the day, and beats me if I…if I…if I fucking *disobey* him. That's what you guys aren't saying. That's why…" she looked sideways, and saw David grimacing. He'd seen it the day before, right away. "That's why Adrias thinks this is so perfect," she breathed out. "Because he sees me as some victim David's taking advantage of, without any power, and thinks it'll be a perfect fit because that's all I fucking am in any of this. To him, right? That's all this is. And if this is going to work, that's what we need to look like, isn't it? Like I'm scared of David, and he's just, just… and I'm just…" she choked back whatever was coming next, and the words died in her throat.

Before either of the men could say anything, Lauren slid from the stool and rushed from the kitchen. Reaching her room, she slammed the door behind her and leaned against it, breathing hard. All this time, she'd done everything she could to chip in, to feel like she was contributing and helping and not just serving as the never-ending houseguest who'd slipped into David's life as a victim and remained one. And here was their boss, assuming that was all she was. A victim. Asking to capitalize on the one thing that had made her feel insecure over the past weeks, the one thing she'd been terrified of her identity being reduced to as she waited for them to find the last of her mother's coven. And what did that say about David, or what Adrias thought about David? Because if the men David worked with thought she was a victim, and nothing more, then that meant…

She cut off the thought before she could finish it.

"Lauren?"

Josh. Fuck, just give me one minute, please.

"Lauren? Let me in."

She took one deep breath and then another, and took a

fast swipe at her eyes to get rid of the moisture that had built up suddenly. Then she turned and opened the door, but she didn't back up to let Josh enter. He could talk to her from the hallway. "What, Josh?"

The agent in front of her had the grace to look ashamed, at least. What looked like a blush had even risen to his face. "Can I come in? Or will you come out?"

"It's your house," she answered, and with that she moved sideways to let him do as he would. She wasn't going to feel guilty for shaming him over this.

"And it's your room," he answered, still standing in the hall.

Lauren swallowed, hard, and then moved to her bed and took a seat. "Whatever. Come on in, Josh."

Josh glanced around the room before he entered, at the blue walls Lauren had re-painted since moving in and the ocean landscape by the door. A spread of ferns and cacti covered the dresser, where another girl might have kept makeup or hair products, and a stack of books and journals lay sprawled across the desk. With the quilt covering the bed and the cream-colored area rug spread over the wood flooring, it looked homier than it had ever looked before she'd moved in. It looked like her, and it felt right being there in their house, too.

He took a seat at the desk and played his fingers over the surface in the silence, trying to think what to say. He'd hoped that the night would go better. That she wouldn't see through to what had drawn Adrias to come up with this scheme. He should have known better.

"I'm sorry I didn't tell you up-front that these aren't just troubled marriages in general, and that there might have been more than convenience to Adrias thinking you and David could pull this off," he acknowledged, speaking slowly. "But he doesn't know you. This has nothing to do with who you actually are, to me or to

David," he said. "It's a shitty coincidence, that what Adrias knows of you makes you look like a victim, and David…"

"Look like an abuser," she finished for him.

There it is. "It is what it is," Josh allowed, nodding.

"And he's not," Lauren hissed, glaring up to meet Josh's eyes finally. "But with where we are, and everything, it's not fair to put us in this…in this…"

"Situation," Josh finished. "I know."

Lauren met his eyes. "I was going to say 'set-up'—but I could think of ruder things to call it."

Josh remained silent, knowing there wasn't much he could say to any of this. Lauren was right, and he was honest enough to recognize it. He wouldn't disrespect her by pretending otherwise. She'd been fighting against the role of victim ever since he'd met her, tooth and nail. Ever since they'd met her. They'd already managed to take her life from her, and with the spells her mother had cast on her, she had little enough agency left right now. And here they were asking her to take a flying leap into the role she'd feared falling into, and that wasn't even the half of it.

Truth be told, Josh had been as worried about David's mindset as Lauren's when he'd first heard about what Adrias wanted them to do. His partner hadn't been serious about a girl, not like this, since he'd met him…what, more than a decade ago? And he'd already been pressed into putting Lauren through a lifetime's worth of shit that had him feeling guiltier than hell—Josh could see it, even if nobody else could. He hadn't had time to make restitution for what he'd already done, or get back on track with this girl who he'd clearly fallen in love with, for better or worse, and yet his boss was demanding he welcome in a situation that would all but demand he turn himself into a possessive prick while she got forced into playing a victim, the same role she'd been trying desperately to escape ever since they'd met her. Hell, since before that if you brought her mother into the equation.

"I'm sorry," he finally said. "It's another shit situation you've landed in the middle of because of us, and you've got every right to pass it up."

"So does David," she pointed out. And, after a moment, as he'd known she would, she added, "But he won't, because it's his job and there are people who need help."

"You wanted to do this, Lauren—you said as much today," David commented, suddenly appearing in the hallway and leaning against the doorframe.

Lauren looked back and forth between the operatives, and Josh could see what she was thinking. She and David had just begun talking again, and the three of them could finally be in the same room without the tension of that discomfort as a distraction, and suddenly it was all going to hell again. He wished they could all have had a few more days of simply coexisting before this had been thrown into their laps, too. All this time, he'd felt like he was living in the middle of them, mediating a middle ground and trying to hold them in the same orbit until something changed and they came together. If only they'd had a few more days, maybe she and David would have spent it talking.

"The roles you guys would play, and what Adrias thinks of you…none of that changes anything," Josh said gently. "It's why I couldn't protest. These couples are disappearing, and something's happening. Somebody has to look into it if we want it to stop, and all things considered, you guys might be in the best position to do so."

Josh set his eyes on hers, waiting. The arguments for

and against were swirling around them, but this was her decision to make as far as he was concerned. They'd be putting her and David into danger and putting their relationship on the line. And, as much as she didn't want to be cast as a victim, it was what it was. Embracing the role wouldn't change how they saw her, even if they couldn't convince her of that.

"Okay, but you tell your boss that I'm not a fucking cowering victim who's being pushed around by you cavemen. And, David," she added, turning to face him, "you make him understand that whatever it is that's between us isn't some Stockholm shit, either, because we both know it's not."

Sitting at the desk, Josh was the first to let loose the laughter he'd attempted to choke back. When David joined him, Lauren let a giggle slip a moment later, and then sat on the bed laughing along with them.

With the release valve pressed on the tension, Josh grinned at her, finally catching his breath. His little sister had teeth, and he was glad to see them coming back out.

Chapter 6

Not much less than seventy-two hours later, Lauren found herself sitting in the passenger seat of David's pickup, waiting for him in the loading area in front of a hotel that lay a few miles from the therapy center's in-take office. They only did entrance interviews with couples on Thursdays and Fridays, given that they wanted to bring couples in for long weekends—at least—and it had been a tight thing for them to feel prepared enough and get an interview scheduled for the next day, before having to wait another full week. Now, Lauren rather wished they hadn't managed it.

When she and David had first begun talking again, and then fallen into bed together, she'd thought that would be the state of things, but since that last hot-and-heavy reconciliation that had followed David's coming home from the bar, and the admission that had followed once they'd sat down to talk, they'd barely managed to be alone together, and she'd felt her blood and her magic screaming for more time, more attention. Instead, he'd been wrapped up in preparing for the case and making sure she was as prepared as could be. They hadn't even shared a bed the past few nights, as he'd pulled an all-nighter two nights before and then they'd both passed out separately last night, exhausted from a day of talking over what to expect and going over strategies that would avoid her having to give them away because of her inability to lie. More than once, the process of that had made her wonder whether the whole thing should be called off, but David had been adamant that she'd be fine. And she had to trust him, particularly since Josh was in agreement.

The only time they'd really talked one-on-one had been when Josh had awkwardly told David to tell her what to expect from him, before disappearing off to prepare dinner the night before. She'd tried to fill in the silence, saying she knew he had to act the domineering jerk, and he'd mostly let it go at that. But she'd seen more in his face. She just hadn't been willing to push, afraid of what would come. Josh had asked at dinner if they were on the same page, ready, and she'd said yes…but she wondered.

And then, in the men's house that morning, Josh had presented the two of them with fresh papers—everything from driver's licenses to insurance cards and phones registered in their names. Her legal one, and David's reading David Merriweather since him taking her last name made for one less lie she'd have to slip through upholding. She'd been amused to see it at first, but recognized the utility. The awkwardness had come only when Josh had brought forth a baggie—literally, a whole Ziploc baggie—of gold wedding bands and told them to find ones that fit. Lauren felt sure that her face hadn't looked so shocked ever before in her life; it had been a step she'd been nowhere near prepared for, and neither of the two operatives had thought to warn her.

"It's just for show," David had told her, passing her the Ziploc baggie after fishing out a few men's rings to try on. She'd been so dumbfounded that she'd managed to drop the whole bag, and then the three of them had spent a few minutes down on their hands and knees hunting down stray wedding rings that had scattered across the wooden floor of their living room. In the end, she'd found one that was thin and slid easily along her finger—its only ornamentation a light engraving of vinework that circled it, barely discernible unless you looked for it. It seemed to her that it offered a pleasing symmetry to the vinework tattoo she'd gotten when she'd given herself up to the coven, though David had seemed less than amused over the connection. She'd tried to balk at wearing an engagement ring, as well, but he'd insisted and Josh had backed him up, telling her that a marriage like the one they were representing would look traditional from the outside, and that meant a diamond engagement ring to go with the wedding band. He'd had another baggie of those, and the smallest of bands had been a perfect fit. It was a large diamond, especially considering the ring normally lived in a plastic bag.

Examining it again now, she could only be thankful that she'd at least slipped it onto her own finger, rather than either of the men play-acting a suitor and slipping it on for her.

"We're set," David announced, pulling open the door and sliding in beside her. "Any thoughts on dinner?"

Lauren looked up from her ring and watched the hotel's windows pass by as he drove around to the side. "We really need to go out? Ordering in sounds awful good about now."

Reaching over as he pulled his truck into a spot by the side entrance, David gripped her hand and squeezed.

When she met his eyes, he leaned over and kissed her, holding the nape of her neck and letting his forehead rest against hers.

"They'll have people watching us soon, if they don't already. We'll be quick, but we need to do this. I'm gonna take our bags upstairs and then we'll get food. I'll order for you, we'll eat fast, and then we'll come back here and have the night to ourselves. Just us," he promised. "But this is where it starts, okay? You know that?" David asked.

She nodded against him, gripping his wrists with her hands and wondering what she'd gotten herself into as he kissed her again, pressing her back into the seat in a way that promised she'd have his full attention later on.

***

They found a nondescript bar and grill nearby, and David swallowed down guilt over what he was about to do as he rolled down his sleeves, buttoned the cuffs at his wrists, and went around to open her door for her. What he was about to put her through hadn't been part of the plan, but he'd realized it had to be as they'd made the drive that day. Telling her to treat him coldly, like he was an abusive asshole, wasn't enough. The way she looked at him, anyone could see she was head over heels for him, attracted to him in a way that couldn't be ignored. The way they were now, together, nobody would believe he made a habit of causing her pain.

But, that was the point. That was what they needed to get this done.

He'd seen what she looked like when she was afraid, and he didn't want to see it again, but that was the only way this was going to work. If he reminded her how cruel he'd been to her before, and gave her reason to look at him like that again. He simply had to remain in control, and remember who she was to him, and what they had at stake once all of this was over. He just couldn't let things get out of hand.

Before she could get out of the truck, he reached out to stop her and pulled her closer, willing her to understand where he was coming from as he felt the energy bubbling from her blood, warming and rising to his skin as he breathed in her honeyed scent. "You sure you're ready for this?" he asked.

She nodded, and he brushed his lips against her forehead, feeling the magic rise to meet his lips as he did. He knew he was misleading her even now. He also knew he didn't have a choice.

Inside, the place was like a million other restaurants all over America, with kitsch decorating the walls and overly excited servers wearing suspenders over black uniforms, the men's clothes a little too tight and the women's just a tad too revealing to be classy. He demanded the hostess give them a booth and send a server over right away, and Lauren's eyes got bigger than hers at the rudeness in his voice.

As soon as they sat down, she leaned forward and caught his eye. "You didn't have to be mean to *her*," she hissed quietly.

"I'll leave a big tip," he sneered, trying to ignore the shock in Lauren's face upon seeing his reaction. The way he'd just spoken to her. He picked up the menus the woman had left and pushed one into Lauren's hand. "Tell me what you want to eat—I'm ordering for both of us."

He held her eye for a second more as her lips pursed doubtfully, and then he looked down to his own menu. When the waiter came, he ordered waters, along with whiskey for himself and a house red for Lauren. And when she began to speak up to tell him she'd wanted white, David let her get only far enough in for the waiter to realize what she'd been about to say before he cut her off, corrected her, and reaffirmed to the waiter that she wanted the house red. He didn't miss the apologetic look the waiter sent her, and he caught Lauren's eye as the man walked away. David had thought she might be trying not to smile—they'd scripted that whole exchange down to every syllable before walking in the door—but, if anything, she looked like she might cry.

He leaned forward, nudging her ankle with the toe of his loafer to get her to look at him. "Last chance, kid. Are you okay?" he whispered.

She jerked her head back and forth in some approximation of a confused nod, her black hair falling in gorgeous waves around her face. "It's just…embarrassing," she breathed out. "And uncomfortable for the waiter."

She's worried about the fucking waiter's feelings? Jesus. David stared at her for a moment more, at the way she tucked her dark hair behind her ears, her skin flushed as her eyes darted up to his and then back to her menu. He'd had a lot of reasons for not wanting to get into this situation with her, all of them big ones. What hadn't occurred to him was how hard it was for her to think about hurting anyone. He'd seen her spend fifteen minutes catching a snake in their garage so it wouldn't starve a few weeks before, and witnessed the struggle she'd faced when they'd talked about going after her mother's coven, no matter what they had done and would do to her. Even hurting a stranger's feelings was something that got to this girl in front of him. It made him wonder all over again if they were doing the right thing. If she was faced with putting her own safety over someone else's, or defending herself at their expense, would she do it? Could she?

And what would happen when he took things further in the next few minutes?

Pressing guilt down once again, he looked back to his menu. He ordered salads and entrees for them when the waiter came back with their drinks. As planned, Lauren kept her eyes down and didn't speak a word, and David answered every question about her meal, from what salad dressing she wanted down to the temperature of her steak. When the waiter left, he cut into the bread the man had left, buttered a piece lightly, and reached across the table to press it into her hand. She ate it mechanically and sipped her water.

She didn't look up at him, and he told himself that was better. He'd surprise her, and maybe she'd be upset and flustered, but what he did would remind her that he was supposed to be the one in control here, from start to finish. That that's what they had to project.

Time to go off-script. He knew someone in this restaurant was watching them, carefully, and he needed them to see a man who didn't particularly care for his wife's feelings. A man focused on sex and property more than love and commitment. Telling Lauren what he'd been thinking hadn't made sense earlier; knowing she couldn't lie, and knowing her, he'd thought maybe she'd have trouble keeping a straight face, not flirting back with him.

From the discomfort bleeding out of her features now, he realized that he'd been incredibly wrong, but that didn't change the image he needed to send out.

He slipped out of one loafer and then pressed his foot forward between Lauren's, nudging at her ankles. Her eyes shot upward to his, her hand jumping against her silverware and jangling it with the surprise of the contact. Keeping his eyes flat, he sipped his drink and held her gaze, kicking at her ankles slightly. Insistently.

She took the hint and opened her legs. He let his foot trail up and down her naked calf, and then farther up, pushing beneath her skirt. Across from him, her breath hitched, and he watched her hands tense along the table, one on her wine glass and one gripping the table edge as if to hold herself back from pushing his foot away. A flush was rising along her chest, neck, and cheeks, and when he paused his socked foot along the top of her thigh, he thought he detected a tremor in her skin. Nerves, or did the magic really work even with fabric in the way? More importantly, would it work even when she didn't want it to, when she was this uncomfortable? It had worked in the cage, but she'd been exhausted then, in no shape to fight it or even think about it. Sipping his drink, he saved the question for later and pressed his toes against her slit, and he felt her warmth even through the fabric of her panties and his sock, as well as the jerk of a reaction that ran through her body.

Her eyes met his, pleading for him to back off, and he barely caught himself from smiling, wrong as that might be. She was uncomfortable, but there was arousal there in her blue eyes staring back at his. That girl who'd trembled when he'd handcuffed her to a bed and driven her crazy was there in front of him all over again, but this time she'd signed up to be here with him. And, just now, she'd opened her legs when he'd pressed. She'd let him in, and there was no denying that that thrilled him.

He shouldn't have been having fun and he knew it, but knowing her body reacted to him like this…it was hard not to enjoy it, and every muscle in his body wanted to drag her out of this restaurant and back to their hotel.

Instead, he kept toying with her as he sipped his whiskey, running his foot along her panties and up and down her leg. Pressing into her skin, into that wet warmth at the core of her, to feel and watch her react. He kept going until the waiter came with their food, and then he let her be, only kicking lightly against her heels and leaving his foot outstretched between hers, a present reminder of what he'd just been doing.

Across from him, she kept her eyes down and nibbled at her food. She'd drunk her wine down in dealing with his antics, and he ordered her another glass. He couldn't apologize; he'd do that later. Whether he'd enjoyed it more than he should have or not, there'd been a purpose. He'd seen other diners noticing his movements, noticing what he was doing to her, from the corner of his eye. A man dining alone at the window, who he thought might be the one sent to watch them and seemed to be doing an awful lot of looking their way. A man dining with his own girlfriend or wife. Two drunk girlfriends having a night out.

He'd gotten them a booth to make sure they were visible without being too public, but he'd also gotten them attention, and the dynamic between them had caused whispers already—that was easy enough to see from the side-eye waitresses were sending him as they passed by.

Mission accomplished.

With the food gone, he ordered another whiskey and another glass of red over Lauren's quiet protests. She'd pressed her back into the seat across from him, and it occurred to him that she now looked even younger than she was, especially up against his persona.

She also looked like she might be about ready to cry.

"Drink your wine," he told her too loudly when the waiter dropped it off. "I'll take the check," he added before the waiter could say whatever he'd been about to say, based on the angered look on his face. With one glance to Lauren, the man nodded and disappeared.

One more thing. Then we'll go. He brought his foot up Lauren's calf again, and wasn't surprised when she clamped her legs shut against him, her wine jarring in her hand so that drops splashed out onto her hand.

"Stop it!" she hissed, anger popping in her eyes as she struggled to hold his foot still with her legs.

He reached across the table and gripped her free hand in return, squeezing it until she looked away, down to her clenched hand and her shivering drink. He hoped she didn't break the glass. When he gripped her hand tighter, her eyes got wide and he forced himself to squeeze still harder, knowing he was hurting her, pressing their hands into the table until her eyes watered. Finally, she let her legs fall open with a small groan and he moved his foot up, perching it on the seat in front of her pussy. A moment later, he squeezed her hand a last time for emphasis, so that she let out the barest of whimpers, and then he let go. His foot stayed where it was, unmoving, emphasizing the intimacy of the space and what he could do if he wished.

He knew he hadn't injured her, but disgust with himself moved through his blood in a wave as he watched her take her other hand to cover the redness his grip had left behind, massaging feeling back into it.

"Use the ice against it," he muttered, and then he moved his toes against her slit again purposefully, feeling her warmth and her wetness through her panties as she closed her eyes and breathed in, and he let himself toy with her some more until his whiskey was gone, telling himself that this was who he had to be, and how she had to look at him, if this was going to work.

Ushering her from the restaurant, he didn't miss the disgust he saw on the faces of their waiter and any number of diners, including the man who'd sat by the window and watched them through most of the night. In that face, though, he thought he saw more interest than disgust.

Outside, rain dappled their clothes and skin as David held his hand in the small of Lauren's back and rushed her forward to the truck. At the passenger door, he held it open for her and then slammed it shut as soon as she was inside, hurrying back around to his side as the rain began coming down faster. Pulling himself up into the driver's seat, he glanced over to see that she'd curled into herself, her arms around her knees and her face hidden.

He pulled out of the restaurant with barely an eye to the windows, pushing down the guilt that was trying to insist he take her straight back to the ranch house and spend the rest of the night—hell, the rest of the fucking month—apologizing. "I had to be a dick, Lauren. I had to hurt you like that if you were going to know how to look at me and show that guy what he needed to see, and I had to make sure we got noticed by the guy sent to watch us, and start us off on the right foot. There's no point in us being here if they don't bring us into the treatment center and—"

A cry erupted from her, cutting him off. "Stop, okay? Just stop. David, you *humiliated* me in there," she sobbed out suddenly, jerking in her seat so that she better faced him, her back half against the door. "I get that we're supposed to be in a bad marriage, but what you did in there…"

"What I did in there was get us started," he said flatly, forcing himself to keep his eyes on the road. "And now you know how it would feel…to be married to a guy like the one I'm pretending to be for them. You can channel this. You have to, Lauren. Use this when they want you to talk about me. You were worried about not knowing what to say, how to lie about the way we've been recently. Now you've got material, on top of…on top of the way I acted when I first brought you to the house, and when we were with the coven," he finished.

He glanced sideways at her with that, but she'd buried her head in her arms again, and he could see from the way she was breathing that she was sobbing.

"Lauren, you've gotta understand that you can't look at me like…like you were before we went to dinner. They'll see right through us if you do." His hands gripped the steering wheel harder as he turned his truck into the hotel, thinking over the night and how hard he'd been on her. He'd had to be, but that didn't make it easier. "I'm sorry it had to be like that. I'm sorry I didn't warn you."

When he came around and opened the truck door for her, she slid down to the asphalt beside him and hurried by, speed-walking to the side door of the hotel and waiting there for him until he reached her and inserted the key card.

"Upstairs. 318."

Without looking at him, she turned into the stairwell beside them and moved up the stairs, leading the way to their room until she again had to pause and wait for him to insert the key card. Inside, she rushed into the bathroom and shut herself inside.

Outside the bathroom door, David leaned into the frame and thought about how the night had gone. He listened to hear her crying, but no sound came from inside. They weren't even into the interview yet, and he felt as if he'd been torn apart, pulled away from her in a fashion that wouldn't be repaired.

"Why don't you get a bath?" he called out, thinking maybe that would calm her down even if he didn't dare say it.

A minute passed, and then he heard her faint reply. "Yeah."

That was it then. He'd let her re-set, and then he'd come back and they'd try for the night he'd hoped they could have. It was only seven. There was plenty of time.

"Listen, I'm gonna go down to the bar while you get a bath and relax. I'll bring you back a glass of wine?" he offered.

Inside the bathroom, Lauren sank down onto the floor and let her head fall into her hands. He sounded like himself again. Like the guy she knew. *How am I going to get through this?* she suddenly wondered. And then she heard the door outside click shut, and realized he'd left.

Lauren had kept her eyes clenched shut as he'd parked and avoided looking at him as they'd come upstairs, trying to get past the anger and humiliation burning through her. All day, she'd looked forward to tonight. To having David to herself in a hotel room, without case files or Josh trying to help them prepare or any talk of what to wear and how to talk. Just her and David, in a nice hotel room alone, with one more night to relax before getting this mission started. Now, she felt like it had been stolen from her, yanked out of her grasp and stomped into shards of a pretty picture that was disintegrating in front of her eyes. And like she didn't know David at all, if he could flip between personas so easily, going from gentle to cruel without so much as a warning.

It was only as she reached out to turn on the bathwater that she realized she'd actually begun to shake.

***

At the hotel bar, the distance from Lauren gave him enough perspective to know that he'd pushed her a lot further than expected, and to know that this was what Josh had warned him about.

His roommate had caught him before they'd gone upstairs that morning, and told him in no uncertain words to be careful, to not get so carried away with the role he was playing that he hurt her or did something he couldn't come back from. At the time, David had brushed off the warning. Lauren was a submissive, even if she didn't know it. She leaned into his advances and ran with them, and gave in to him at every turn. She practically melted beneath his hands when he held her down. And it wasn't just the spell, either. The way she reacted to him when he pushed her, when he controlled her…none of that was spellwork or learned behavior. That was her natural instinct, and it fed into everything he craved. The fact that she didn't think of herself as submissive, or wouldn't have used the word, didn't matter.

That morning, he'd told Josh as much, and told him he knew what he was doing. That he was in control, and as long as he stayed in control, she'd feel safe and be okay with what they had to do to get through this. And he'd promised he wouldn't get lost in the role, too.

But he'd already done that, hadn't he?

And now Josh's words kept echoing in his head, despite the liquor he'd used up in trying to drown them out. *"I know how far into undercover work you go. She's not another agent, man, and she needs you to be you if she's gonna get through this in one piece. You have to be you as much as you can. For her."*

In one piece. What did that even mean? Lauren knew who he was and what he did for a living, and she knew what he'd been like when they'd first met, that first week when they'd kept her at their house and all the cards had been on the table. She knew who he was and that he'd do whatever it took to solve a case.

His eyes on a baseball game on the television above the bar, David kept half an eye on his watch. Whatever Lauren was thinking upstairs, he needed to give her the time to get over the night. So they could go forward. Tomorrow wouldn't be so drastic, and once they got in, once they were inside and playing their parts, they'd be in this together, and the lengths he'd gone to in the restaurant would be done with. But they had to get in the door, and tonight had gone a long way to making sure that happened. Now, he just had to convince her that his intention hadn't been to embarrass her or hurt her.

When he'd been downstairs for near on two hours, he decided she'd had enough space and headed back upstairs with drinks in hand—red wine for her, whiskey for himself. Shuffling the glasses into one hand so that he could unlock the door, he paused in surprise and double-checked the room number above the door when he opened it up to perfect darkness. But, no, it was the right door.

He slipped inside in the dark and nudged the light switch with his elbow so that the overhead light came on. From where he stood, he could see a tenting up of the bed's comforter, far to one side of the king-sized bed, and he realized she'd turned in without him. For the first time since they'd gotten back to the hotel and he'd headed downstairs, he felt real doubt. All day, she'd been looking forward to them having a night together, alone, where they didn't have to focus on preparing or going over files. And he'd known that. Knowing it would be too dangerous to have signs of the case on them, even electronically, they'd made sure that the electronics they had with them were virgin-clean, right out of their packages. Tonight would have been reserved for them, David and Lauren, without any worry of role-play or impression.

Without asking her, he'd taken that away from her—forgotten about it entirely, in fact, he'd been so focused on the case.

Lauren shifted slightly in the bed as he approached, proving she was awake, but she was cuddled so deep under the comforter that David couldn't barely see any of her. Silently, he leaned in between the wall and the bed, and placed the wine he'd brought her on the nightstand beside a bottled water he guessed she'd gotten from the mini-fridge. When she didn't move, he stepped back and to the foot of the bed, trying to decide what to do. She was obviously determined to pretend sleep, and the idea that he might say something only to be ignored was enough to hold his tongue.

Instead of fighting her on the ruse, he picked up his shaving kit and retreated to the bathroom, where he took his time shaving and showering off the day. When he came back to the bed, he noted that her wine had gone untouched, and she hadn't bothered to get up and turn off the light he'd left on.

He dropped his dirty clothes on the floor by his suitcase and moved around to take the other side of the bed, watching her to see if she'd flinch or move in reaction. *Nothing.* "Mind if I turn on the television?"

No reaction.

David forced aside the annoyance he felt and picked up the remote control from the bedside table, and then he began flipping channels. The baseball game he'd been watching had long since gone off, but he found another and let the channel remain there as he sipped his way through what was left of the whiskey he'd brought upstairs, shooting occasional glances to Lauren's still form.

Chapter 7

She'd wanted to be asleep when he came back to the room, but the nerves running through her body had made that impossible. Instead, she'd gotten a fast bath and then lain awake in the dark, wishing she could chance calling Josh—though she didn't know what she'd have said—or had sleeping pills, or even more wine, just to try to help her get some rest. The bath had done almost nothing to relax her, though, and with only one bed in the room, it wasn't as if she could somehow suggest that he take another.

So, she'd feigned sleep, even knowing he likely saw through it, and remained quiet through everything. Trying and failing to sleep as he shaved and showered, and then laying frozen as he watched television, reclined on the other side of the bed. When he finally turned the television off, she bit back a sigh of relief.

And then, before she even had time to be surprised, his hand landed on her shoulder and he pulled her backward so that she lay on her back beside him, staring up into his face. He'd shaved so cleanly, she wasn't sure when she'd last seen him look like this. And that hard set to his jaw… he was angry with her, and maybe hurt, judging by the look in those deep brown eyes of his and the fact that he seemed to be waiting for her to speak.

"You wanted us to do this," he said after a moment. "I tried to convince you not to, and gave you every out, and you said we had to do it."

Instead of answering, she jerked her shoulder from beneath his hand and went to turn over again, but before she'd managed it, he'd moved sideways and above her, hovering over her on his hands and knees, trapping the comforter around her as surely as if he'd tucked her in. This, of course, was something else. His eyes were on hers, waiting, and she wasn't in a position to escape his gaze.

She meant to curse at him, or demand he move, but when he kept staring at her, the words that finally came out of her mouth only reflected the thought that had been circling her mind all night. "I don't know how to deal with you going back and forth; two people. I wasn't expecting it to be like this. Like you're Jekyll and Hyde."

For half a second, she thought he wouldn't answer, but then his jaw softened, ever so slightly. "It's the job, Lauren. I tried to warn you and so did Josh. We're going undercover, and I've gotta sell it. Especially since you can't lie, it's on me. And…" he trailed off, his eyes glancing away from hers.

"And?"

David met her eyes, and his voice was harder when it came out, gruff in the way she remembered it being on those first days at the ranch house when he'd worked to intimidate her. "And," he began, "maybe I thought it would be good, tonight, for you to…see me as a bad guy again. Controlling. *Mean*. Considering what we're going into. What you're going to have to focus on and who you need to be if they're gonna believe we are what we say we are."

You can't fucking be serious.

Lauren groaned aloud and pushed outward against his arms, but he wasn't budging. "Christ, David. Seriously? You think the way to get me to be believable as an abused wife is to fucking abuse me? And you didn't think it was worth having that discussion yesterday? Or the day before?"

"That's not…" David cut himself off. "I wasn't going to hurt you," he corrected himself, apparently having decided against whatever he'd been about to say. "It was a show, the best way to get to you and get to the guy watching us *without* hurting you."

Lauren jerked her arms against his for emphasis, holding his gaze. He hadn't sounded nearly so sure of what he'd just said as she might have hoped. "You sure of that? 'Cuz it kind of looked like you were having fun until we got into the car and you saw how upset I was. And at that point, the phrase 'too little, too late' comes to mind, don't you think?" She jerked her arms again, and this time he let her up, sitting back so that she could squirm upward and sit away from him against the headboard.

"Look," Lauren offered, "I get that you like undercover work. I get that that's part of what makes you good at what you do. And it's not like I've forgotten who you were when we first met," she added more quietly. "But you could have warned me if you had all that planned, like you said. I was expecting you to order for me, and maybe insist I have a particular thing or drink, but…David, I can't…" She shook her head, and suddenly took up the glass of wine he'd brought for her, draining half of it before she turned to him again. "It's not fair for you to…to count on me reacting to you, to push me like that physically when you turn into… when you turn into the other guy."

"*The other guy?* Lauren, I'm not the fucking hulk."

She met his eyes, knowing the darkness there was showing again because she was hitting close to home. "Yeah? Well, you could have fooled me. Maybe I wasn't tied down, but in that booth, knowing what all this depends on, it sure as hell felt like I might as well have been back in that chair in your interrogation room, with you calling all the shots and me just waiting to see what I'd have to deal with next. And to have my magic pulling me into you at the same time…" Lauren took another sip of the wine, and then she muttered, "It's just not fair. And you know that."

The air had seemed to thicken around them, and it took him a minute to answer, but she could hear that gruff desire from earlier in his voice when he did, and knew her body was reacting to it even as she fought her attraction to him.

"You like me being in control," he finally answered, "so I don't know how you can complain if I take control and don't broadcast everything I'm about to do."

Lauren glared back at him and swallowed the last of the wine he'd brought her. "So, that means you don't respect me enough to tell me what's happening? What you're planning when so much is at stake and we're not alone? Yeah, we both know it, that I like when you…when you're in control," she said, her voice tight, hating even to hear herself admit it, "but that's between *us*. It's not you hurting me, David, or humiliating me in public. You can have control and still fucking respect me," she finished. And although she hadn't consciously thought it before, or recognized it, she knew in her gut that it was true. Maybe she did love it when he held her down and pushed her, and took all of the control he

110

wanted even. But until tonight, she'd always, however oddly, felt respected. Even that first week, when he'd taken advantage of her attraction and she'd allowed herself to totally lose control, and he'd just kept pushing and pushing until there was no going back…even then, she'd never felt like he didn't respect her, odd as that might have sounded to someone looking in from the outside. But now…he'd sunken into the role of an abusive, condescending jerk and embraced it, and left her to deal with the consequences.

She put the wine glass down and sank back down in the bed even as he watched her, curling to the side again and tugging at the comforter until it was gathered around her shoulders, hiding the bare skin that had shown around the tank she wore. "I want to go to sleep, David. You either get it or you don't." And she did, she told herself. She wasn't going to forgive him for the way he'd acted—not so easily, at least.

David watched her for a moment, letting his mind catch up to his feelings. What she'd said, about him being willing to abuse her in order to put her into character, had pushed a ball of lead into his stomach that hadn't yet lifted. Had that been what he'd been thinking? Put like that, it sounded absurd that he could have felt that way or had that plan in mind, but…was she seeing more clearly than he was? If she hadn't reacted so strongly, like what little he'd done had hurt her, what would he have done when he'd gotten her back to this hotel room, wrapped up in the role as he'd been? If she'd taken what he'd been doing as flirtation, and run with it, and never looked at him like she had?

This was what Josh had warned him about, that he'd let the persona take over and end up pushing her too far, and no matter how close they'd been a few days before, the look she'd just given him had said it all. Maybe she'd been scared of him in the past, but right now she was only disgusted.

For a moment, he thought about just letting her sleep and hoping the emotion could wear off. But then they'd be walking into that interview tomorrow with this between them… and while that might make the tension between them all the more believable, the distance wouldn't be safe. She had to feel like he had her back, like he was in there with her even when they weren't in the same space. She had to be willing to come to him if she needed him.

Knowing he was about to make yet another unforgivable move against her and take advantage of her, he dropped silently into bed behind her without turning off the light, and slipped his hand between her bare thighs as he moved up behind her, resting his hand there as her body tensed. Half of the bed was behind him, and she didn't have anywhere to go.

"I want to go to sleep, David," she repeated, digging her hands into the pillow beneath her head.

Using his other hand to pull her hair away from her neck, David bent over her, knowing how sensitive she was there. With his hand still on her thigh, feeling the trembling warmth of her skin and her magic beneath his palm, he began kissing along the side of her neck, biting down lightly to hear her gasp. Her skin was soft, pliant and ready for him. And he needed to leave marks tonight, whether she liked it or not.

Lauren tried to clench her legs together when she felt his hand begin massaging her skin, but he knew the magic was already racing in her blood, begging for more and helping him along as he pushed. He stretched around her, moving so he could see her face, and then he began nuzzling her neck, sucking her skin between his teeth as he kissed her roughly, feeling the magic rising beneath her skin. Her eyes had closed and she was fighting to ignore him, to hold herself still, but he could feel her skin warming to him, and see her face flushing with the contact.

"You belong to me, kid," he whispered into her ear then.

She flipped back to face him, a hurt sneer on her lips. "You don't have any right—"

His kiss cut her off, sucking up her words and forcing her back and into the pillow as he moved over top of her, letting his hands wander. She'd only worn panties with the tank top, and he nudged them down until his hand could find her center and prove to himself that she was turned on. She was, and he ignored the part of his brain that told him he'd gone from being practical to being cruel, even brutal, with what he was doing.

Lauren whimpered beneath him, her hands pressing into his chest, but his fingers found her slit and pressed into her just as he took his lips away and let her breathe, and she gasped in air as two of his fingers entered her and his teeth came down at the base of her neck, driving shivers through her. He could feel her letting go now, giving in to him again. Giving up. Her whole body was thrumming beneath his, warming to the press of his lips and the way he worked her body. Pleasure was already sliding through her, radiating from her soaked pussy and the playing of his fingers—he could practically feel her arousal pulling her over to his way of seeing things.

David listened to her moan as his fingers found one of her nipples, and the sound was enough. He'd moved her panties near to her knees already to get access to her, and now he used one of his feet to rip them down the rest of the way and off her feet. Shifting, he replaced his fingers with his cock and pushed into her so that she gasped as her nails dug into his side for purchase—not trying to hold him back, he noticed.

He caught the hair at the nape of her neck in one of his hands and held her head still, forcing her to face him as he pressed further into her, all the way in. Her face was wet with sweat, and…

He froze. The moisture he'd felt wasn't sweat, but tears that had begun leaking from her eyes silently. And when she met his gaze, it was as if she was daring him to deny them and act like he hadn't hurt her by pushing her to accept him again tonight.

Lauren stared back at him, her hands loosening against him, and David met the challenge, knowing he deserved the accusation in her face, but it didn't change anything. He was rock hard inside of her, pushing her, and her body was responding to his—he could feel it, pulsing and warm, running with heat and desire and magic. The tears were drama, he told himself, less real than what she actually felt for him. When she thought about this later, once they got to the center and she could feed from this night, she'd understand. She'd have to.

David kept his eyes on hers, seeing the pain there, and swallowed down everything he wanted to say. He'd find a way to make up for being like this later. He would. Right now, though…

He pressed his hips forward, feeling her hot channel contract around him as he twisted against her and she gasped with the new angle, her eyes clenched shut as she moaned out involuntarily, pleasure coursing through her. Bending to her lips, he sucked her lower lip between his and teased her with his teeth as he pumped into her, and then he found her hands with his and pressed them into the bed at their sides.

Lauren whimpered beneath him, her body rocking beneath his, and then she moaned out David's name as a sudden orgasm slammed through her body in response to his rhythm, the magic in her blood spiraling through her veins and sending quivers of pleasure racing through her so that he felt her whole body trembling beneath his as he kept thrusting into her, picking up speed and pressing in deeper. When she gasped again, his tongue pressed between her lips and tangled with hers, arresting his name on her lips.

Feeling her pulsing around him, David slammed into her a last time, gripping her wrists beneath him and grunting into her shoulder as his cock jerked violently within her and she milked every drop of his pleasure into her body, her pussy spasming around him as she whimpered under the weight of him, her body still trembling when he pulled back from her warmth a minute later.

***

When she felt like she could move, she slipped from bed and moved into the bathroom without a word, shutting the door behind her. She washed her face and ran a washcloth over her body to rinse away the slickness and the smell of sex as much as she could. In the mirror, she saw the hickies he'd left on her neck, and she noted how swollen her lips were—the signs of what they'd just done would be visible in the interview, she knew immediately. And because of everything she'd seen from him that night, part of her wondered how much of his passion had been related to wanting her, Lauren, and how much of the passion had been related to making sure their interview went as planned.

And she thought about calling Josh.

What would he say, though? Was it possible that he and David had planned all of this, deciding that it was somehow necessary? She couldn't believe that, but there was the tiniest of voices in her which couldn't help wondering.

Staring at herself in the mirror, at the hickies that looked more and more like new bruises instead of the marks of love that she hadn't really minded getting from him in the past, she thought back to the look on his face when he'd realized she was crying. Because she'd seen it—the moment he'd realized that the moisture he was feeling wasn't just sweat, but actual tears. And, for her part, she'd made the choice not to hide it from him, staring back into those dark eyes she'd grown to love so much that they took her breath away.

So much, she'd worried about hurting his feelings, or making him feel guilty for what was more the fault of spells than his own doing, but this had been him. Tonight had been him knowing he could take advantage of the way her body reacted to him, and doing it.

Even now, she could close her eyes and feel desire at the memory of how his cock had felt, pulsing in her body hard and demanding, and he'd been right that she'd desperately wanted to react—to move against him, asking for more, even as she'd glared back at him for those few moments of defiance. In another second, too, she knew she'd given in. Crying or not, pained or not, she'd given in to him, and given up on resisting. On making him understand.

Maybe she'd forced him to feel hurt for a moment along with her. He'd said earlier that she'd asked to be here in this situation with him, but he'd asked for those tears and any guilt he'd felt for them. He'd known what he was doing, and she hadn't had an ounce of control, or even dignity, pressed there beneath him.

And now? Now she felt disgusted with herself, and ashamed of the desire she felt for him all over again.

Her mind made up, her body wide awake with shame

and desire, she decided she had to get the smell of him off of her. Despite the fact that she'd taken a shower that morning and a bath that night, she turned on the water in the shower and let it run until steam had filled the small room, and then she stepped in and let it do what it could to burn the desire out of her body. At least until she could face herself in the mirror and go back to bed.

Chapter 8

The therapist's office took up most of the in-take center, with only a small lobby and restroom looking to offset the space. Ushered inside, Lauren couldn't help being surprised by the feel of it, as if they'd walked into a luxury studio apartment rather than any sort of clinical setting. Off to one side, there was a large desk set up caddy-corner to a wall of windows, a few comfortable chairs sitting ahead of it, but that was the only sign they were in a business setting.

To the left of the entrance, a huge sectional took up half the space, and Lauren couldn't help thinking that it could probably fit twenty people—all of the people who were said to have disappeared and then some. Against the wall by the door, instead of the bookcases she might have expected, there was a long wet-bar offset by decorative wallpaper boasting a shiny bronze finish. Against the light-colored wood beneath their feet, it was brilliant, especially when seen against the black of the furniture, the green outside the window, and the cloudy blue of the other walls. Everywhere she looked, there was something else to steal her gaze.

"Please, have a seat." The therapist they'd just met gestured them sideways, to a smaller sitting area on the same side of the room as the windows and the desk, and Lauren followed David to the couch. It was stiff and formal, as well as deep.

Lauren had dressed formally that morning, at the men's request, having mostly brought clothing that she would have worn to professional school gatherings and conferences. That morning, she'd put on a dark coal pencil skirt and a sleeveless, filmy white blouse, and covered her arms with a salmon-colored sweater. It was a conservative look, tamer than she'd mostly ever worn, but David's reaction that morning had told her it fit the bill perfectly. Now, though, it left her unsure how to sit when presented with such deep furniture. She finally settled for perching at the edge of the stiff couch with her hands intertwined in her lap, her elbow resting against the armrest. The couch was too deep for her to be able to lean back without her knees being up on the couch, leaving her legs to jut out awkwardly in front of her. Tall as he was, David wasn't having the same problem, and he sat closer to her than she might have liked, right in the center of the couch, his arm draped behind her on its back.

Diagonal to them, in front of the window, the woman who'd welcomed them in took a moment to watch them, and Lauren tried not to shrink beneath her gaze. Her eyes were hard, and reminded her of Nell Everett's in some ways—hazel and unwavering. And her makeup was perfect, as was the designer dress she wore, form-fitting and flattering. This was the kind of woman who'd always made Lauren self-conscious of her curves and her height. Even her smile was too perfect.

Self-consciously, Lauren adjusted her sweater around her neck, pulling her hair forward and hoping the hickies on her neck were hidden. She glanced sideways to David, but he seemed to be waiting for Dr. Samantha Shea to make the first move. Lauren wished he wouldn't. The only thing keeping her heart from beating out of her chest was the thought that he had control here, and that he knew what he was doing.

Everything so far couldn't have been for nothing. He wouldn't have hurt her like he had last night for nothing. He had to know what he was doing.

"Dr. Shea," David finally spoke up, drawing her eyes to his, "we didn't come here casually. I want this marriage to work, and it seems like the retreat mentioned on your website might be a faster fix than weekly therapy sessions."

The woman's lips smiled but the expression didn't reach her eyes, and David had to remind himself to keep his eyes on the therapist as she in turn focused her gaze on Lauren. That hadn't been his goal, and a trace of nerves ran through him. The woman felt wrong, though he couldn't put his finger on why.

"Yes, Mr. Merriweather, I know. And you're busy, which means you want this done and finalized, but there is no 'fast fix', as you say, for a troubled marriage. I imagine your young wife realizes that," the woman said pointedly.

Lauren nodded tightly, and even David could see she was trying to project anything other than the discomfort she clearly felt. You didn't need a therapist's degree to see that Lauren wanted to be anywhere but in this office.

"And the age difference between you is…" the woman hinted.

"I'm 34. She's 25," David answered flatly.

"I see. Lauren, were you the one who was most

adamant about coming here, addressing your problems?"

"She—" David began, but the therapist held up her hand, a glare flattening her lips.

"I asked your wife."

Lauren looked sideways, catching David's gaze. This was a moment where she had to take the bull by the horns and run with it if she could—they'd prepared for it.

"I...not at first," she hedged, "but then, yeah, I guess so. Yes," Lauren added more firmly. "We're...having trouble."

David felt himself relax, and he let himself glance to Lauren. She looked incredibly uncomfortable, however much her outfit flattered her. With her hands twined together, her eyes turned downward, she was the exact picture of what they'd told her this situation called for. What hurt was that he believed it of her, right now in this moment, and knew that she wasn't really having to pretend the role.

"Many couples turn to their family when things go wrong, rather than taking a step like this. What have the two of you tried so far?" Shea asked, her eyes roving between them.

David cleared his throat and answered for the two of them. "My family doesn't live anywhere near here, and we're not close anyway. Lauren doesn't have one, and our friends haven't exactly experienced anything like what we're going through. I'm the type of person who wants to hit a problem right away, hard as I can. That's why I thought something like the weekend retreat you run might make sense for us, rather than week by week meetings."

Shea's eyes met his and held them, as if something about his answer didn't work for her. "You sound like you expect a weekend will fix everything."

"I think it'll be a fair start," he answered evenly.

The therapist leaned back in her chair, but most of her

attention remained on Lauren now, and David had to fight to keep himself from sliding toward her. He didn't trust this woman.

"On the phone, you sounded like a man who is rather…addicted to his business. Will you be able to put aside your business entirely for the duration of the long weekend? And remain focused on your wife and your relationship?"

David nodded, leaning back and attempting some semblance of ease. "That's why we're here." David allowed himself another glance at Lauren, and saw she still hadn't looked up again at either of them. "Dr. Shea, we've read the material on the website, and understand what your retreat is about and how selective you are. We're here because we think it may give us a chance, and we're committed to trying it and taking it seriously if you'll help us."

That seemed to be enough to satisfy Shea, as he'd guessed it would. And there was no wondering why. The retreat's advertisements made clear that these long weekends sometimes bled into longer stays for couples, of a week or more, in order to affect lasting change, and he had no doubt that their ideal couples were those who'd be amenable to such extensions—both in terms of the time they involved as well as the money. As long as they didn't get made as agents coming in to investigate the place, they'd be okay.

Lauren finally looked up, nodding in agreement, and added, "This was the only place David felt would make sense for us. We didn't come here lightly."

David tried to catch Lauren's eye, to read some emotion, but she was entirely focused on Samantha Shea. Yet, when he looked back to the therapist, he found that the woman had been watching him, and he was caught off-guard when she stood.

"David—may I call you David?" Shea asked. When he nodded, she smiled and gestured toward the door. "I think I'll speak with your wife alone first, if you don't mind. You'll wait in the lobby, alright? Just ask the receptionist if you'd like some water or coffee."

David glanced to Lauren helplessly as he stood, seeing that she was wide-eyed, and a heartbeat from standing to come with him. "I'll be right outside," he told her, hoping the edge in his voice would serve a dual purpose of enforcing his persona to Dr. Shea while projecting some real strength for Lauren. He'd known they might be separated for part of the interview, but hadn't guessed it would be this soon. When Lauren didn't protest, he followed the therapist's lead and moved toward the door, but he turned when he got there and stared her hard in the eye. "My wife is used to having me with her in professional settings. I'd rather we do this together."

The woman's eyes remained hard, but her smile softened. "I'm sure you would, Mr. Merriweather, but this is part of the process. Give us twenty minutes or so."

***

With David out of the room, Lauren couldn't help feeling as if the temperature had chilled, and she jumped when Dr. Shea came back to stand in front of her. And then the therapist reached down and picked up her hand in her own rather than sitting back down in her previous spot.

"Lauren, I want you to call me Samantha. Let's go over to the sectional, why don't we? I think you'll be more comfortable there."

Mute, Lauren rose and walked along behind the other woman, noting the way she glided along the floor, her stiletto heels barely making a sound.

"You should put your feet up," the woman told her, guiding Lauren to a corner of the sectional and pressing her shoulders toward the back of the couch so that Lauren found herself all but reclined backward in the overstuffed piece of furniture. Before she'd said anything, Samantha Shea had reached forward and slipped her heels from her feet, placing them on the ground and perching herself on the ottoman a few feet away from where Lauren rested.

"You looked tense even with your husband in the room," she commented. "I take it that he's fairly domineering. Controlling?"

Lauren swallowed, and although she told herself to meet Samantha's gaze, she couldn't quite do it; she stared at her hands instead. "He can be, I guess."

"Dear, did you want him to leave those hickeys on your neck?" she asked next, and Lauren couldn't help jerking her eyes up to meet the other woman's, the change of subject having caught her off-guard. "I take it that's a no," she answered her own question, her eyebrows knitting closer together. "But you want to save the marriage?"

This, Lauren had prepared for, word for word. The men had coached her on the gist of what she needed to say, and she'd all but memorized her response already. "He takes care of me, and I've never been with anyone like him. I don't want to be with anyone else, I care so much about him. I only…want him to respect me," she finished simply. She'd planned to say something else, she realized, but the words had left her at the last minute.

Shea took a moment, and then asked, "You love him?"

Without thinking about it, Lauren answered. "Yes."

Yes.

The word had slipped out without thought, easy and true, and Lauren tried not to consider that. She'd expected the question, even if the men hadn't, and had planned to go around it, but then…she hadn't known whether she could answer yes, or that David would be safely out of earshot when it came up. The fact that she'd been able to say she loved him, without doubt, so simply, was brutal, and not something she'd willingly admit to David. It wasn't fair that she'd fallen in love with him—not by a longshot.

The therapist took another beat and then leaned forward, her eyes suddenly seeming more knowing. "But you want him to be less controlling?" she asked.

Lauren looked at her hands again, letting her fingers twine together. "I don't always mind control," she admitted softly. "But, sometimes, yes."

"He's hurt you? In the past?" Samantha asked bluntly, and Lauren found herself nodding.

In another heartbeat, she was embarrassed to realize that tears were sliding down her cheeks. This hadn't been planned, but to have this woman sitting here, so perfectly together, and with her own life in such shambles, it was as if everything had suddenly fallen in on her. David was supposed to be there beside her answering these questions, and instead she was alone, having to admit secrets that were truths whether she wanted them to be or not. David had the ability to lie, and she knew he would, but it wasn't a luxury for her. For the first time, it occurred to her that not being able to lie wasn't just a danger—it was an embarrassment. Whatever she admitted to the people here, to this woman or anyone else, David would know it to be true.

"I'm sorry," she murmured, and then the therapist was pressing tissues into her hands, rubbing her hand along her calf as if to calm her as she leaned forward.

"No, don't apologize. It's good to be emotional. So emotional," she added.

Lauren glanced up and met her eyes. The woman's

voice had dipped, oddly, as if she was pleased, but her face was all sympathy. "I didn't mean to come in here and begin crying," Lauren said aloud, pressing the tissues to her eyes and willing herself to calm down.

"That's alright. You'd be surprised how often it happens. We go into relationships expecting trust, expecting partnership, and give our hearts to men who then gain an upper hand because of what we've offered. In your case, perhaps you trusted too quickly, or falling in love with an older man put you at an automatic disadvantage when he wished to take more control. And at first it was alright, you thought, until it wasn't. And in the meantime he managed to hurt you…physically and emotionally?" the woman added.

Lauren found herself nodding again, tears still slipping from her eyes. *Maybe I'm not up to this, after all,* she thought to herself. But the woman was already asking her another question.

"Tell me about the first time he hurt you. Can you do that?"

Lauren swallowed. They'd prepared for this. She could do this. It was all about what details she offered. "When we first slept together, he'd been pressuring me…it got to the point where I, I didn't know how to say no. He was frustrated with me, and I hadn't told him I was a virgin," she offered, stumbling on the word. "He was rough, but as soon as he realized I hadn't been with anyone else, he went…he slowed down. He took it easier on me."

"*He took it easier on you,*" the therapist echoed, and Lauren looked up to see her scowling. "That suggests…that phrasing suggests," she corrected herself, "that you don't think he should have had to. Or perhaps…you're looking for excuses to forgive him."

"It wasn't his fault," Lauren said.

Shea stared at her, seconds passing between them.

"Really? Oh, dear, it sounds as if David knew exactly what he was doing and what you were being pressured into."

Lauren shook her head, unable to answer. The picture she was painting of David wasn't fair, and yet it was.

"Lauren, my dear, has he forced himself on you when you weren't ready for him? When you didn't want him to, taking advantage of your attraction and attachment to him? So that perhaps you even gave in by the end, though you hadn't wanted it? Him being your husband doesn't make that right. I want you to be honest with me now. Has that ever happened?" the woman pressed.

That dip of condescension, *assumption*, had come back into the therapist's voice, and Lauren had tears leaking from her eyes again—she felt totally unprepared for this, and wished she could run from the room. Instead, she nodded.

"When was the last time, dear?" the woman asked, and again Lauren found that the therapist was running her hand up and down her calf—as if gentling her, like David had done in the past, calming her. Like she knew Lauren even though they'd just met. It didn't make any sense.

She swallowed, and then answered. "Last night," she murmured, wishing her answer were different.

The therapist muttered knowingly, and told her to go ahead and cry, that it was fine, and Lauren hated her for it. And, just the same, she hated David at the moment, thinking that perhaps he'd known exactly what they were coming into, last night and before, and that that was the reason he'd done what he'd done at all. And what killed her, even now—in the face of this woman who seemed more and more terrifying with her odd sighs and the dips in her tone of voice and her perfect persona and perfect, knowing words—was that Lauren would even now have given anything to have him be the one comforting her, handing her tissues and running a hand along her leg, soothing her.

"We're going to make it better, dear. We'll help him see how valuable, how dear you are. What you mean to him, and how attached the two of you are. I can see you have a special connection to each other, and you adore him, and we'll just make him see that, won't we? We'll make him see how precious you are, and understand that some changes must be in order."

Lauren pressed a tissue to her eyes, soaking up her tears, and found herself nodding once again. The woman's wording—everything about the way she'd just spoken to her about what needed to happen and be understood in their relationship—felt off, double-edged, but still there was nothing to do but nod.

***

David had kept calm and still for the first twenty minutes he'd been in the lobby, but for the last ten minutes, he'd been pacing, and although he could tell that he was making the nearby receptionist jumpy, he'd made no effort to stop.

When the door to Samantha Shea's office finally opened and she stepped into the doorframe, her arm around Lauren's shoulders, it was all he could do to keep from lunging forward and smacking the woman's hand away from her. Forcing a breath into his lungs and a grim smile to his face, he met the so-called therapist's gaze even as he took in the deepened blue of Lauren's eyes that told him she'd been crying.

"It's been thirty minutes," he commented as he stepped forward, lightly moving the woman's hand from Lauren's shoulder and pulling her in closer to his own body. She didn't resist, but he noticed Shea stiffening.

"Yes, sorry about that. Now, Kathy," she said, turning to her receptionist. "Why don't you get Lauren some of that tea that Tony brought over this morning while I talk to Mr. Merriweather?"

David's hand tightened on Lauren's shoulder, but she reached up and gripped his fingers for just a moment. It was enough for her magic to rise some in warmth, reacting to him, and enough for some of the tension to leave him. It was enough.

David met Lauren's eyes briefly as she took a seat on the lobby's couch, and then he followed the therapist, who he couldn't quite bring himself to think of as a doctor, back into her rich office. She moved back to the uncomfortable couch they'd been sitting on before, and both resumed the positions they'd held a half hour earlier, if sitting more stiffly.

"You made my wife cry," he said simply, not trying to hide the edge in his voice.

But the woman across from him just smiled. "No, David, I think you did that."

A retort died on his lips and he glanced back to the lobby door.

"Nothing to say to that? No argument?"

"I told you we've been having trouble. We're here to make it work. Doesn't seem like making her relive every little thing I've done to her is going to manage that, does it?"

"Every little thing," she echoed quietly. "Every little thing? David, your wife may be younger than you, and more sensitive, but she adores you. She loves you. And you've treated her horrendously. She'll say very little because she clearly doesn't want to speak against you, but you've *hurt* her, you've forced yourself on her physically, and you've clearly scared her into accepting the control you have over her."

The room's air grew thick with silence, and David forced himself to be still and absorb the words ringing in the air. As he'd known would happen, stated so largely, so abstractly, there was nothing to argue with. Everything that had been said was, on some level, true, if twisted ever so slightly. And yet, he hadn't expected her words to feel so…personal. Or so true. He looked up and met the therapist's eyes. "I have hurt her. I'm trying to make up for it."

The woman leaned forward. "Really? Are you? Because I'll tell you…when a couple gets comfortable with an uneven dynamic in some respects, when control is part of an attraction, it's difficult to change. It's difficult for someone like you to rein himself in and understand that submissive tendencies aren't meant to translate into anything more than that, assuming those even come naturally to Lauren. You can be the alpha in your family without hurting her or making her cry, in other words—"

"No kidding?" he asked, cutting in, and wondering as soon as he'd made the comment if he was being too glib.

"No kidding," the therapist answered evenly. "So, the question we're left with is whether or not you love her."

The sudden change in topic stunned him into silence for a moment.

"David, I asked you a question."

Taking a deep breath, he felt himself deflating as Lauren's tear-stained eyes popped back into his mind without warning.

"Yeah," he said quietly. "I do. I love her."

Shea smiled. "Alright, then. So, let's talk."

Chapter 9

Out in the lobby, Lauren accepted an over-sized mug from the receptionist and sniffed at the aroma coming from the tea. Sweet, and with a hint of lemon. The taste relaxed her almost immediately, and she found herself curling into the couch with her legs beneath her, despite the pencil skirt and having come in with an intention to look more formal. She tasted sweetness more than lemon, with some suggestion of ginger and chamomile—it was just what she'd needed.

When the receptionist asked if she could offer her another cup, Lauren glanced into it with surprise—she'd been looking out the window absently, trying to calm her heart down after everything that had happened and been said, and she hadn't realized she'd drunk half of it, let alone all of it. "That would be lovely, thanks," she answered gratefully, and gave the woman the mug to refill.

In minutes, another mug rested in her hands, warm and

comforting. Sipping from it, she was reminded of being in the ranch house kitchen, enjoying coffee in the morning or tea in the afternoon, and the many times she'd spent leaning into the island, going over her notes or talking to David or chatting with Josh as he cooked or…she shook her head, bringing herself back to the moment. She'd nearly dozed off, thinking about their kitchen of all things. And yet, she'd been wide awake, strung tight with nerves not long before. She glanced down to the cup of tea in her hands. This second cup had had heavier hints of ginger, and tasted stronger. She only hadn't realized it till now, she'd been so grateful for the distraction.

Feeling like she moved in slow motion, she looked up to find the receptionist's eyes. The woman was in front of her suddenly, reaching for the near empty cup. "Something to relax you," the woman said gently. "Why don't you lay down here and wait for your husband to finish up inside? Just close your eyes and get some rest."

Lauren opened her mouth to argue, but whatever they'd offered her had been strong. She thought of the papers she'd signed in the therapist's office before coming back out. It had all seemed standard, and just been part of the process, authorizing treatment. It only occurred to her now that such treatment probably included drugs.

The woman smiled at her again, and Lauren couldn't remember her name. If she could have, she thought she'd have convinced her to go get David, so that she could tell him they should leave, tell him that they'd made a horrid mistake, but then the woman's hand was on her shoulder again, pressing her back into the couch, sideways, and it was so comfortable…she couldn't help closing her eyes with a sigh, telling herself it was only for a moment.

***

After something like a half hour for his own private session with Shea, David was anxious to get Lauren and go retrieve their things from the hotel. He wanted a few moments alone with her before they came back and then headed off to the retreat. Because they'd done it—they were in. One way or another, they'd convinced this woman they were a good fit for the program, and now it was only a matter of picking up their things and getting back here to catch a shuttle. His truck would be living in a nearby private garage, safe and out of reach, but he'd known that coming in. Beyond that, the woman had given him a brief view of what to expect over the next couple days, and it all sounded standard enough so far, given what he could imagine a place like this might do...but there was no denying that something was off, wrong about the whole thing.

And the fact that the woman had bothered to tell him they'd come for the weekend, "and more if necessary", had been enough of a signal that what they called a long weekend retreat wasn't exactly limited by time in any real manner, so long as he had the money to pay—which he'd assured her he did. Somehow, he got the feeling they'd have been turned away if he hadn't been willing to commit to more than a weekend's funds.

The paperwork took another ten minutes, which he spent sitting on the uncomfortable couch. It was mostly financial, payment for services to be rendered and all that, with acknowledgements of treatment plans "to be discussed" and abiding by the staff's recommendations once they were at the center. That last bit bothered him more than anything, but there was nothing to be done about it—from what he'd been told before coming in, this was a fairly standard contract for a place like this, absolving the staff of responsibility for things that were supposedly out of their control, and if he and Lauren wanted into the center, there was nothing to do but sign. And hand over nearly ten thousand dollars for a single fucking long weekend, of course, but with his agency footing the bill, he couldn't exactly complain.

When he moved into the lobby to collect Lauren, though, he found that she'd fallen asleep on the couch, curled up sideways and into herself, her arms tucked in around her stomach and her head propped on a throw pillow.

"Lauren? Hey, kid, wake up," David said quietly, shaking her shoulder a little bit more firmly. She blinked her eyes open and gazed at him half-lidded for a moment, but when he smiled down at her, she just closed her eyes again, a sigh breathing off of her lips. "What the hell," he muttered.

Looking up from where he crouched beside her, he saw Shea and her receptionist both watching him, as if waiting to see what he'd do. The receptionist had the grace to look embarrassed, but the therapist looked…controlled. "We gave her something to calm her down," she said simply. "After our session, you saw how upset she was. I thought it best."

For a moment, David wished he had his gun. The woman had thought it best? "I could have you…"

"Watch what you say, Mr. Merriweather," Shea cut him off. "Your wife signed off on consent to be treated when we spoke earlier. I judged it in her best interest that a light sedative be given, and so I did so. Now, I hate to be harsh, but we know you're prone to violence, so I won't mince words here. If you threaten me, we'll take your wife into treatment so that she gets the care she needs and you can go down and have this discussion with the police. Otherwise, I suggest you calm down."

David looked down to Lauren and forced himself to take a breath. For whatever reason, it had never occurred to him that they might be facing any sort of drug therapy—it was supposed to be marriage counseling, for Christ's sake. Lauren didn't look near ready to wake up, though, and it was too late to undo whatever they'd given her. She'd just have to sleep it off, and they'd be more careful from here on out. They'd have to be.

He forced himself to nod, turning back to the therapist and her receptionist. "I'll wait for her to wake up and then we'll go get our things," he began, but the woman was already shaking her head, and he saw that her receptionist had made a wheelchair appear from a corner.

"I'm afraid that's not going to work. The shuttle is expected here in a few hours, and the two of you will need to be ready. Lauren may or may not be fully awake by that time, as she seemed fairly exhausted when we spoke. She didn't sleep well last night, I understand?"

Words caught in his throat, David nodded.

"Yes, well, that could mean she'll need a bit longer to wake up, so she can remain here while you go get your things."

"She had two cups of tea," the receptionist added quietly.

Shea nodded, smiling, and looked back to David. "That settles it. She'll need some time to wake up."

Two cups of tea, David thought. *Jesus Christ, what is this?*

David met Shea's eyes. "I'll take her with me. I can carry her."

"Really, Mr. Merriweather, do you think that makes sense? We have a recovery room right here, and she'll be far more comfortable and rested if you allow her to rest," the woman pressed, eyeing him. "In fact, knowing what I do of your relationship, I'm not sure I'd feel safe having you take her out of here at this particular moment."

David had already been bending to pick Lauren up

from the couch, but Shea's unmistakable threat froze him. Maybe this was a test or maybe it wasn't, but David suspected that, if he carried Lauren out of here to the truck, he'd either be dealing with the police in short order, or else this would be the end of any talk of their getting into that center. He'd fucked things up already.

He turned back to the therapist, standing straight. "You can't expect me to leave her here with you, not when you've just threatened to call the cops on me and drugged her without her consent."

"Without *your* consent, Mr. Merriweather. We had hers, remember? Now, again, you can go get your and your wife's things, and trust us as professionals—you have just hired us to help you solve your problems, after all," she reminded him gently, taking a small step forward. "Or, if you're having doubts, we can tear up your side of the contract and you can do as you wish, but I believe Lauren wants our help, and I want to help her. The poor girl's so emotional, I believe she needs our help."

"You run a marriage counseling retreat," he said tightly. "That's what she signed up for."

"Mmm. She signed up for treatment, and there are other centers that can help women in her position if you're not interested in going forward."

David swallowed down whatever he'd been about to say.

He could be to the hotel and back in short order, and nothing would happen to Lauren in the meantime. Adrias had had people watching this center for months—nobody had come in and not come out on their own two feet, and he had no reason to suspect that they'd been found out. After all, the other operatives and agents who'd been sent in here had been called on it and dismissed in short order. No, if they'd suspected he and Lauren were here to investigate them, things never would have taken this turn.

"Alright." He eyed the door behind the receptionist's desk, which he'd earlier assumed led to either a private bathroom or an office supply closet. The receptionist smiled at him as if this were all the most natural thing in the world, and gestured for him to come forward and look inside. Glancing in, he saw that the room held a neatly made twin bed full of throw pillows, and nearby chairs with blankets thrown across them. As they'd said, this was nothing short of a recovery room. But what kind of therapist's office had to plan for a place where patients could recover from being drugged or becoming so upset that they couldn't simply walk or drive away? The question churned against his instincts, but there were no other options.

Silently, he moved back to the couch and picked Lauren up, ignoring the fact that Shea and her receptionist were both watching him. She murmured into his shirt, her hand curling into his button-down as he readjusted his grip on her and faced the women. Then, cradling her against his chest, he moved past them and into the recovery room, where she barely murmured as he laid her down on the bed. He kissed her cheek, letting his lips linger long enough to feel her magic warming her skin against his lips, and then he slipped off his suit coat and laid it overtop of her.

Satisfied she was comfortable and simply sleeping, he dimmed the light in the room and went back out to the lobby, closing the door behind him. "The shuttle's coming in two hours?" he asked.

Shea nodded at him, no sign of her earlier threats on her face as she smiled freely. "That's right. It'll be here at 2:30. You have plenty of time to get your things. Just come back here, and then once your suitcases are in the shuttle, you're welcome to park your truck in the garage yourself or I can have an attendant come over to retrieve it for you."

"And you won't move Lauren?" he asked.

"She'll be on the shuttle with you, Mr. Merriweather. I sincerely doubt she'll move a muscle until you return."

That's gonna have to be good enough, he thought to himself, and then he turned and headed out the door.

✳✳✳

Josh had been sitting in the hotel lobby for an hour by the time his partner walked in. As planned, he'd checked in that day, after the two of them had left so that there'd be nothing connecting them to each other if anyone was watching David and Lauren. Seeing him enter, he waited for a moment, expecting Lauren to come in after him, but when David barely gave him a glance, heading straight for the elevator without any sign that Lauren might be following behind him, Josh rose and hurried to catch up.

In the elevator, he was about to ask where Lauren was when David spoke.

"They drugged her. She talked to the therapist first and then they gave her a sedative while I was talking to Shea. She's at the in-take center and we're scheduled for the afternoon shuttle."

Josh stared at his partner, who was watching the elevator door, his expression flat. When it opened, he pressed between the doors before there was barely room for his body to pass, and Josh followed. "I don't understand—why would they drug her? What happened?"

Pushing the key card into the door, David stepped in and let Josh catch the door behind him. "I don't know. The interview got her upset. I could see she'd been crying, but there was no time to talk before it was me going into the therapist's office. Man, is she a piece of work," he added. Then he looked at their packed suitcases, already ready to go, and seemed to freeze for a moment.

The three of them had talked about doing that, Lauren having suggested it. The only motive for leaving the suitcases there had been so that there'd be one more chance for Lauren and David to touch base with Josh, assuming they got past the interview. If they'd known this might happen, they would have brought them along—as the center had recommended to begin with, Josh remembered now.

David shook his head and finally looked up from their packed suitcases. "This therapist… she had us both sign treatment papers. Lauren signed them while she was talking to her, and it all looked standard, assuming we signed the whole thing. But…shit, Devlin."

Josh stared at his partner as the other man finally took a seat on the edge of the bed, and noticed his fists were clenched. "What?"

David met his eyes. "The way she talked…she was *threatening* me. Not directly, but…she said Lauren needed help. That…that she didn't trust me to take her with me, after what she'd heard," he added tightly. "If I'd tried to walk out of there with her, they would have had the police on me, and papers to show that Lauren had accepted treatment, with their word against mine to say I was an abusive husband trying to walk out with an unconscious woman."

"I don't understand—this place is a marriage counseling center," Josh answered, his mind racing. There'd never been any indication that the center might take one spouse and not another. If there had been, they never would have gone this route. Even Adrias wouldn't have chanced sending a civilian in with an operative and having her stay in alone, no matter what the stakes. He might have been reckless and at the end of his options, but not to the extent that he'd take a chance like that.

"Yeah, that's what I said," David chuckled roughly. "That's exactly what I said. And, I don't know, maybe she was bluffing. Maybe I could have picked Lauren up and headed out and that would have been the end of it, but I guarantee you they wouldn't have been taking us on that shuttle. But Shea said she knew of other centers, places that could help Lauren if I wasn't ready to sign on for treatment for the two of us…." He shrugged. "I don't know if it was a bluff. It might have been some kind of test, to see if I'd relinquish control and follow a plan or…I don't know. I didn't know what to do," he added. "First time in a long fucking time I've been in that position, I'll tell you that."

Fuck. "They won't hurt her while she's there," Josh answered, as much for his own benefit as his partner's. What the fuck had they gotten into? "It was just a sedative?" Josh asked.

"Yeah, it must have been, far as I could tell. She was in a heavy sleep, doped up. They offered us tea and coffee a few times, and she was so shaken up by whatever the therapist talked to her about, I'm sure she would have jumped at a mug of tea. It just never occurred to me they'd drug her. Even separating us so soon for interviews…we rushed this. We weren't prepared," he said, meeting Josh's eyes.

Josh had moved to the window, and he looked out to see a man in a car who was just sitting, and seemed to be eyeing David's truck, which he'd parked haphazardly near the road. One way or another, prepared or not, they were in.

He turned back to David, handing him a small business card for an accountant's firm. "You've got my number on the burner, but if we have to lose that, use this contact.

That office number reaches an extra cell I picked up, and the number listed as the office goes straight to a local operative—guy named Wheatley who I was in the service with. We can trust him if we need to. But if you want to call this off…"

Josh's gut told him they should. That they never should have said yes to Adrias, and past that, that David shouldn't have left the in-take center without Lauren at all, and just called the mission there and been done with it. But there was no longer any doubt that something was wrong with what this place was doing.

And from the look on his partner's face, he'd come to the same conclusions. After a minute passed, though, he shook his head and stood back up, staring once again at those damned, packed suitcases.

"No, Lauren would be pissed if we came this far only to give up when we were ready to go in, and she'd be right," David added. "There's something going on, and we're in a position to figure out what. I don't know what's going on, but Shea kept talking about how emotional Lauren is… something about the way she said it, it was like she admired it. It might be nothing, but it felt strange. There's something to that, if you can think of any way to look into it from your end. And see if there's any indication that the couples who disappeared were actually all-in, too."

"All-in?" Josh echoed.

"Yeah…we assumed, with the divorce lawyers folks were meeting with and the way things looked, that these couples were two side-steps away from divorce. Take another look. See if there's any sign that there was no break-up on the horizon, no matter how bad it got."

"You mean like they were struggling and trying to figure out a way to fix things, but weren't planning on breaking up, regardless?" Josh asked.

David nodded. "Yeah. What they did to us today…the way they separated us." He glanced up to his partner's gaze. "I don't know, maybe I'm jumping to conclusions, but I'm telling you, I felt trapped, Josh. Like they had her, and I could either go along with the plan or give up on…on her. On us. Like I'd have to leave her behind if I wasn't willing to sign on for whatever they suggested, and they knew I'd be in because of it. It felt…planned."

"You think they trap couples by making one dependent on them, or determined to work with them, and if the other's still in love…"

David nodded. "They're trapped. Yeah."

Josh thought about everything he'd read—all of the files, all of the couples. Nothing they'd seen suggested it wouldn't be possible, though they'd never considered it. "It would be a lot easier to suck in one person than two, get them to a point where they felt like they had to be there and didn't have any other options…"

David nodded. "The way she looked on that couch—how…how fucking helpless it made me feel? Yeah. Yeah, that's what I'm thinking, too. Why they'd *want* to trap us when we were about to sign on anyway, fuck if I know…but hell, maybe we've got this wrong. Maybe they're seeing couples and seeing something in one of them they want, and the easiest way to that end is to take both. Because the more I think about it, the more I think they planned on keeping her there no matter what I did."

* * *

Pulling back into the center's parking lot, David saw a shuttle already waiting outside the doors, an array of suitcases being tucked into its back end. He parked and brought over his and Lauren's to add to the mix, nodding to the man who seemed to be in charge of them. "Mine and my wife's for you," he said.

Anxious to get to Lauren, he'd already taken a step away when the man called him back. "Hold on, mister. I need your name so I know which estate to take you and the missus to. Gimme a second," he added, swinging another suitcase up into the shuttle and tucking it to the side.

"Which estate?" David asked. "Isn't this shuttle for the couple's weekend retreat? The counseling weekend?"

The guy nodded and used his sleeve to wipe sweat from his forehead. For early summer in New York, it had become a hot day fast. "There's two separate estates set up for counseling—different issues and all that, no offense. Hell, if I could afford it, I'd probably take my wife," he said with a grin.

David didn't bother to laugh or respond to the joke, and the guy went on. "Everybody's mostly going to the same place—same type of set-up in each place and all that. Knowing which suitcases go to which spot just saves time. So, name?"

"Merriweather, David and Lauren."

The guy pulled a list from his back pocket and gave it a glance, nodding to himself. "You two are going to the South Estate and the others are going to the North one. I'll drop you two off last, at the second stop, just so's you know."

With that, the guy reached for his suitcase and hefted it into the shuttle, nudging it into a space behind some others he'd already slipped inside. By the time he reached for Lauren's, David had turned away, the separation of buildings just one more detail to be considered later.

Inside the center, he found two couples sitting in the lobby. Two women who were holding hands, but about as tense as could be otherwise, and a man and woman who were only connected by the fact that they shared a loveseat, given that both of their heads were tuned only to their smartphones. David looked past them to the receptionist and she immediately got up to meet him at the door behind her desk. "She hasn't woken up," the woman whispered.

Not bothering to answer, David brushed past her and moved into the room, leaving the lights dimmed. True to the therapist's guess, Lauren hadn't moved a muscle. She was still cuddled beneath his coat, sleeping soundly. His watch read 2:02, which meant they still had nearly half an hour to wait, so he decided to let her sleep. He'd just settled into a chair beside the bed when Shea walked in a few minutes later.

"Mr. Merriweather, the last couple just arrived and Matt's in the process of getting the last of the suitcases loaded. Have you tried waking your wife?"

"You said 2:30, so, no, I haven't." With a pointed look from the so-called therapist, David moved to Lauren's side and shook her shoulder lightly. "You want to give us some privacy?" he asked the therapist.

She shook her head, a firm frown on her lips, and David turned back to Lauren, leaning in and pressing her hair away from her ear. "It's me, baby. I need you to wake up, okay?" he murmured, squeezing her hand. "Lauren, babe…"

Finally, a moan slipped from her lips and he felt her breathe in more deeply, stretching beneath his coat and then shifting groggily until her eyes found his. "David…"

"We'll be waiting for the two of you outside," Shea interrupted from behind them, and then her heels clicked away into the lobby, the door remaining ajar behind her.

"There must have been something in the tea they gave me," she whispered, her words slow enough that David could tell she was still working toward waking up.

Pressing down everything he wanted to say, David just helped her sit up on the edge of the bed and then pulled her into his chest. "I know, kid, I'm sorry. How do you feel? Are you okay? They said it was a sedative; I didn't find out what they'd done till you were already out."

Lauren breathed in deeply, and he could feel her skin warming beneath his hands, the energy bubbling up as he pulled her in closer, hoping the contact might ground her. There was no doubt in his mind that she could simply close her eyes right now and go straight back to sleep.

"I like the cologne you've been wearing," she whispered, letting her head rest more heavily against his chest.

"Yeah, well, thanks. But, hey, kid, come on—are you okay?" David asked, pulling far enough away from her that he could try to find her eyes. "Look at me, Lauren," he added when her eyes began to close again, and he could see she was fighting to focus. Her hands were moving on him, as if she were drunk and in that state where she could just enjoy contact, but her eyes were hooded, her lids heavy and being pulled down in slow blinks.

"I'm just tired," she answered after another moment.

"Sleep in the shuttle?" he offered.

"Josh…"

"Shhhh," David cut her off. *Fuck, fuck, fuck. Talk about things going sideways.* "Remember who we are, Lauren," he whispered urgently, his lips tight against her ear. "We're in, if you're okay. But you say the word, I'll get us out of here."

His breath on her ear sent a tremor running through her that even he could feel, and he realized he had desire running through her blood again when she bit back a moan. Being this tired, this weak, and also so close to him…it was too much for her, he realized. She didn't have control of the magic or the sensations, and the way she was pressing into him, he doubted she had any idea where they were. But she nodded against him anyway, even as he realized she had no business saying yes or no to anything right now.

"Yeah, no, I'm okay, David. I can do this. We need to do this. David, we can…"

"Shhhh, alright," he whispered, cutting her off before she rambled further. Worse came to worse, they'd have to change their minds later and find a way out. Standing, he pulled Lauren up with him and steadied her. She let him pull her in tight against his side and hugged his coat to her chest as he half-supported her, and with that they headed out to the lobby and the shuttle beyond it.

Seated on a bench seat beside David, she let herself be pulled in against his chest, and he watched her close her eyes not a moment later.

"Alright, everyone, let me give you a little bit of information as we get started," Shea announced from the front of the bus, having been the last to enter. She braced herself against one of the front bars near the driver as he pulled out of the parking lot and glanced down to a clipboard as if to remind herself of her notes.

David shot his eyes down to Lauren—she'd already gone back to sleep, one of her hands loosely gripping his shirtfront, the other hugging his coat to her stomach. The man belonging to the couple across from them caught his eye as David looked up, mouthing, *She okay?* David nodded, forcing a smile, and that seemed to be enough since the man turned back to look at Shea, and David followed his gaze.

The woman wore her ridiculous heels even here, standing up on this little shuttle of four couples, and her dutiful receptionist sat nearby. This doctor, though…she felt too much the composite package. Too put together,

146

too pretty and relaxed…and too firm and young by half, considering all that she seemed to be in charge of.

"As some of you already know," she continued, "there are two estates. Couples are already staying at each of them. Three couples have stayed over from last week at the North Estate, and there are a number of couples remaining at the South Estate, some of whom have left and come back there directly—yes," she nodded, cutting off a question from the man across from David before he could ask it, "I know you're not thrilled about your vehicles being here, but there's good reason for it. These first few days cannot be interrupted if you're to succeed, so it's best that you don't get tempted to drive off into the sunset or run to the store for your favorite type of beer. If you decide that more time at the retreat makes sense, whether you stay on directly or leave and then come back, your personal vehicles will be welcome."

That explains why most of the missing couples' vehicles aren't in the garage, David realized, thinking back to that being one of the questions Adrias had brought up. He'd hated having to hand his truck keys over to a garage attendant as they'd gotten onto the shuttle, but at least this suggested that his truck would be safe. Safer than them, maybe.

"Now, once we get there, you'll have time to unpack and freshen up. Someone will be on hand to show you to your rooms, and then there'll be a buffet style meal set out for you when you're ready, available from seven to nine tonight. After tonight, there'll be a sit-down meal at 6:30 each night, but this will give you some freedom to take your time settling in. It'll take us about an hour to get there, so we should get there well before 4.

"Are there any questions?"

When nobody responded, the woman gave a warmer than usual smile and nodded her head as if she'd expected that. "Good, then—let's enjoy the drive."

Chapter 10

Lauren woke slowly, her head resting against David's chest for some minutes after awareness began slogging back to her. It felt good, no tension between them but for the slight heat of magic running in her blood and beneath her skin where their bodies were drawn together, even if mostly through fabric. He was talking to a man and a woman about baseball, and some recent game that Lauren doubted she would have understood even if she'd seen it. He sounded like his guard was down, though she doubted that was the case.

When she did open her eyes, she just clasped his hand lightly in hers so as to tell him, and relished the warm squeeze in return that came as their conversation continued. The woman he'd been talking to caught her eye and smiled gently, and Lauren guessed David must have told them she'd simply been exhausted, casual as the look was. What surprised her was the appearance of the couples she saw as her eyes moved around the shuttle. Only she and David were in the semi-casual professional wear that he and Josh had determined made the most sense for this venture. The other couples were dressed as if for a picnic or a shopping trip—leggings, jeans, t-shirts, and shorts. The man across from them even had a ballcap on his head.

"We should be there soon," David commented when a lull came in the conversation, and she nodded against his chest, not bothering to raise her head up. "You okay?" he asked next.

She stifled a yawn. "Yeah, just kind of embarrassed."

"No, don't be." He didn't say more, and Lauren guessed that he'd just as soon not let on to anyone else that she'd been drugged. There were things they needed to talk about, but this wasn't the time, and the man beside her felt like the man she'd come to love and trust, which would have to be enough for the moment.

Soon, she felt the shuttle pulling to a stop and stretched against him as the other couples rose.

"We're the second stop, so just hold tight," he muttered, and she only just stopped herself from asking what was going on—he'd expected the two stops, clearly enough, but this was the first she'd heard of it. Watching as all of the other passengers disembarked, along with that underhanded receptionist who Lauren had only just noticed had been riding along with them, she let herself breathe in David's cologne in trying to prepare for whatever came next. She sat up as he stretched and looked out the window as they began moving again, trundling on from a huge mansion of an estate that made her think of Gatsby and whole flocks of servants. When they moved back onto the winding driveway that had slid by the front of the mansion, they only drove another mile or so before they came to a building that was a near perfect mirror of the earlier estate.

Like the other one, this had a wide veranda out front,

complete with some little two- and three-person café tables and gigantic oaks providing huge puddles of shade. Driving up, Lauren could see a man working on a laptop beneath the shade of one of the trees, and two more coming down from the entrance—to greet them, she imagined.

Shea rose without looking back to them as soon as the shuttle stopped, stepping down the stairs to greet the men with brief hugs.

Lauren leaned into David as the driver exited and he made a show of stretching out kinks in his back. "Two separate centers?" she asked.

He nodded, his eyes on the group outside the shuttle. "For different types of *issues*. There are supposed to already be couples in both of them, but we'll have to see what we find here and then decide if it makes sense to try to scope out the other if opportunity permits."

Lauren looked to the back of the truck as a clank of metal signaled that the driver had opened the door and was pulling forth their suitcases. "We're in it together, right?" she asked, reaching out and gripping David's hand.

He answered with a squeeze and led her down from the shuttle.

Shea and the men had been waiting, and there was a tightness to her eyes that David read as predatory.

"David and Lauren Merriweather, meet Jace and Cary—they'll be taking you to your rooms."

Lauren glanced between the two men, who had smiles firmly planted on their lips but looked ready for argument.

"Rooms, plural? As in, a suite?" David asked.

Shea was already shaking her head, her perfect curls bouncing on her shoulders as if she'd walked out of a goddamned commercial. "No, David, I'm sorry we couldn't tell you earlier, but you'll be staying in separate rooms, as do all of the couples at this estate. Lauren will be welcome to visit your room at any time, but she'll have separate accommodations."

Lauren's hand had tightened on David's, and she found herself stepping closer in to his side, leaving not a breath of space between them. She could feel him breathing deeper, tensing, and she swallowed down the fear she felt in favor of trying to reason their way through this. "Dr. Shea, I didn't want to be drugged earlier, and I'm here to get closer to David. Being apart doesn't make sense for us," she added, looking to the men at Shea's side as if for sympathy, but their expressions hadn't changed, and it suddenly occurred to her that they must go through something like this conversation every time a new couple arrived—this was the way this place operated.

"Lauren, I apologize that Kathy and I didn't ask your permission earlier, but you were so emotional, I judged it best. Now, in your position, given your…admissions, earlier, shall we say? It makes sense for you to have some distance from your husband, and visit him as you wish but have your own home base, so to speak. He won't be able to visit you, and that will offer the freedom you may need to gain clarity on things. It's why the decision was made to bring you over to this estate rather than the other."

David's hand clutched Lauren's, but he already saw there was no way around this. And if not for the reasons he had to be suspicious of this place, if not for the fact that they were there to act out a ruse, he might even have applauded this practice. If the retreat catered to couples where a power dynamic was breaking down the relationship, some separation might make sense. Especially if there was any reason to suspect abuse was involved, as Shea clearly expected was the case with the two of them…but it also all reflected what he and Josh had discussed that morning. Trapping one person as a method of holding onto both.

Shea met his eyes. "David, surely, you'll understand the logic here. And that this is, on some level, a safety precaution…for your wife."

Lauren tensed beside him, but he swallowed down the nausea rising in his throat. "I get it," he said quietly. "But let her come to my room first, so we can both feel assured she knows how to get there. Then you can show her to her room. And we'll see each other at dinner," he added, eyeing the men to see if there'd be any sign of him being leashed along until they were separated. There wasn't, and it even seemed that the three people in front of him suddenly relaxed, their expressions coming more open.

"Sure, you'll see her at dinner," the sandy-haired one commented. "Just decide what time to meet her since it'll be a buffet tonight and you don't want one of you's waiting around for two hours for the other to show."

David nodded, Lauren's hand still tightly gripped in his. He wouldn't let her go till he had to. With nothing else to be settled, Shea excused herself to wrap things up with their driver. The men escorting them each hefted a suitcase and led the way up the stairs to the estate. The one who'd just spoken re-affirmed that his name was Cary—"spelled with a single 'r' and a 'y', not like the girl's name," he emphasized—and told them he'd been working with Shea's retreat for coming up on two years, and that his wife worked in the kitchen while he took care of any number of things, serving especially as a general handyman around the place. He looked to be in his mid-forties, and David had no trouble imagining him breaking up fights between couples at one moment and then going off to fix a toilet in the next; he gave off the well-meaning vibe of a sort of old-style barkeep, and David imagined he'd have trusted him in any other situation. The other man, Jace, was a younger black man who looked to be in his mid-twenties, and who told them he'd been at the estate for nearly as long since getting his own counseling degree. They'd see him as much as anyone, he told them, because he'd be the one on call to answer questions, help them find their way from place to place, or take care of any extra arrangements they needed to make, whether that was calling for extra blankets or needing a mediator in some argument. He'd also be one of their regular counselors, as well as a point person for their treatment plan. David found that he liked both of them, and from the loosening of Lauren's hand in his own, he guessed she felt the same—they'd been well chosen to put new couples at ease, it seemed.

Inside the mansion, they passed by two men traveling through the lobby hand-in-hand, but they weren't either of the gay couples who'd been reported missing as of yet. They were the only sign of living people, but that was just as well since the mansion itself was huge. It was all he could do to keep track of where they were heading.

Rather than walking across the lobby to the giant, circular staircase that wound up to a second level, the men led them to the left and then took a right, pointing further down the hall to a closed door marked "Cafeteria" before cutting off to the left for a bank of elevators.

"The kitchen's closed outside of meal-times," Jace explained, "but we keep all of the rooms stocked with coffee and water, and you can let us know if there's something else you'd prefer to have in your mini-fridge; we'll do our best to satisfy. Lots of the guests like to have juice and granola in their rooms in case they want to skip breakfast or have too much to drink at one of the evening functions. There's also water coolers and whatnot set out all over the place—you'll find your way before you know it—and a few machines that serve hot cocoa or coffee or espresso or whatever floats your boat, no charge."

They got off the elevator on the third floor, and Cary added, "This is the west wing, by the way. There's some private, more solitary rooms over on the east side of the place for when couples want or need more separation, but mostly folks stay over here. Girls—'scuse me, miss, 'women'—stay down on the second floor and men are up here on the third, with gay couples split over the third and fourth floors. Either of you's welcome to visit the fourth floor, should you make a friend up there."   They got halfway down the hall, where Jace began fishing in his pocket for a key, and Cary turned a stern eye to David, eyeing him up and down as if in warning. "There's always a den mother on the second floor, keeping an eye out for men who've wandered out of the elevator on the wrong floor or gone gallivanting—my advice is that you don't do it. You do, you or your pretty wife are likely to end up staying over on the east side of things just so that nobody has to worry about any unwelcome visits."

David nodded simply, thankful at least that, for now anyway, Lauren would only be a floor below him. A floor of separation was something they could overcome easily enough, whether casually or in an emergency.

Jace finally found the right key on his ring and opened up the heavy wooden door ahead of them into what did look like a luxury suite—it lived up to the price tag. The room wasn't huge, but it sported heavy wooden furniture, textured wallpaper, and expensive wood flooring. The bed was expansive, and there was a desk, a dresser, a wall-mounted television, and a small sitting area to boot, this last having a countertop along one wall that ran overtop a small fridge and supported a bowl of snacks, a coffeepot, and a basket of single-serve coffee and tea packets. Off to the side, he saw a door leading into tiled flooring, and guessed that must be the bathroom.

"Your wife's room is a near mirror image," Cary

promised, "a bit softer in color. You need anything?"

David met the other man's gaze and saw something like sympathy there. Now that it seemed they were ready to take Lauren to her own room, her hand had gotten hard in his own, and he thought she might be trembling, if not using his grip to steady herself. "Give us a minute?" he asked.

They each seemed to take their own glance at Lauren, and it was apparently enough that they came to the same conclusion. "Which one of these suitcases is yours?" Jace asked.

David pointed to the one Cary held, and the men set it by a heavy dresser before the two retreated toward the hall.

"Just a minute or two, guys," Jace said gently before they closed the door. "You want to be able to get some rest and unpack before dinner."

As soon as the door closed, David tugged Lauren to the edge of the bed and sat her there, kneeling down in front of her. Her face had gone pale, and she was biting her lip with nerves.

"Lauren, I know we didn't plan for this, but I'm not sure how easily we can back out right now. Are you up for this?"

She coughed out a laugh, her eyes darting around the room. "Don't I have to be?" she asked.

***

Lauren had almost resolved herself to relaxing into a bath and attempting some level of calm before unpacking and meeting David for dinner, but the last person she had any desire to see was waiting for her in her assigned room, perched atop the desk like her own personal Cheshire cat.

"Dr. Shea," she breathed out, feeling herself deflate upon entering. The other woman smiled, and Lauren was barely aware of Jace depositing her suitcase at the door and pointing out a key on the desk before he slipped back out the door.

"Yes, Lauren, I thought we should talk for a few moments while time permitted. Do you mind?"

Lauren shook her head blankly and sat down on the edge of the bed, mirroring the position she'd taken a floor up in David's room, but with far more tension in her limbs. "No, of course not," she responded, reminding herself that attitude meant everything now. As she had in the office, she had to be mindful of playing the submissive wife, timid and young. If she snapped at the doctor or began arguing about her rights, there'd be suspicion thrust upon them immediately.

"I wanted to apologize for surprising you with the sedation, but I truly did feel it best. And, to be honest, I didn't like the idea of David leaving with you after the conversation we had, though I knew you wouldn't feel comfortable standing up to him. Some much needed sleep seemed ideal to suit the situation, as it wasn't as if David would argue about carrying you from our office unconscious. I hope you understand?"

Lauren swallowed down anger. They were painting him as a full-on villain, and there was little she could say in his defense if she wanted to keep their cover. No matter what she felt. "I would have been safe with him this afternoon," she protested weakly.

"Oh, my dear, even you aren't sure you believe that," Shea commented softly, and suddenly she was off the desk and at Lauren's side, her hands on her shoulders. "You love him too much to have a clear mind around him. It's why it's so important that you're here, with some space between the two of you. Even these few hours before dinner. Outside of the house you share, out in public, when was the last time you were separated from him for any length of time?"

Lauren's face must have answered the question for her, and she knew any response she did offer would be damning. Given the situation, of course, it had been nearly a month since she'd been off of the operatives' property and not in the immediate presence of David, if not him and Josh both. There was no explaining any of that, however, and so she remained silent.

"Now that's settled," Shea continued, her point proven, "I want to ask for your cell phone. You don't have anyone to check in with, I understand?"

When she remained at the edge of the bed, still, Shea's grip on her shoulder tightened. "Dear, we discussed this. Everyone needs to be fully focused on the therapy offered through this program, with no outside distractions. And we certainly don't want your over-protective husband to be bothering you every hour on the hour."

Wordless, Lauren got up and moved to her suitcase, where she fished her phone from the side pocket and presented it to Shea. Upon her apparently grateful nod, Lauren watched her move to the door and head back out into the hall.

It was only when the therapist left that Lauren realized there was no phone on the desk or anywhere else in the room, and no way to reach David but to go up to his room and knock. Knowing that was out of the question at the moment, she moved to the door and shot the deadlock before turning to assess her suite.

True to prediction, it was much like David's, but with pastels in the furniture and the bedding, whereas David's room had been more masculine, and here there were flowers in each of the pictures and upon one wall's decorative wallpaper.

Resolved to take advantage of the time alone, Lauren nodded to herself, thinking that this was where she had to be strong. This was where David and Josh were counting on her to keep it together. She pulled her suitcase to the dresser and began unpacking. Then, she decided, she'd get a bath or a nap and be rested for dinner. Taking one obligation at a time, she felt sure she could do this.

Chapter 11

David had thought he'd be the first into the cafeteria, he was so anxious to touch base with Lauren, but when he got there he saw that she'd felt the same—and, apparently, so had others. Lauren was seated at one of the back tables with two men who had their backs to him, but they turned when Lauren's face lit up with relief.

She was up from the table and coming over to greet him even as he recognized them as Phil and Christopher Rollyson—the last gay couple to have been reported as a suspicious entry into this place's walls. Now, they were smiling and waving at him in welcome even as Lauren met him halfway across the room. "They're here!" she hissed as she tiptoed up to meet his lips in a brief kiss of greeting.

"Yeah, but so are we," he reminded her in a whisper, gripping her hand. He'd have thought that the sight of one of the couples alive and apparently well would have calmed the churning in his gut—these guys looked fine, after all—but, instead, the opposite seemed to be happening. These guys didn't look brainwashed, and they also didn't look like they'd willingly walked away from successful lives and forsaken their careers. They looked *normal*. So, what was he missing?

"I'm Phil and this is my husband, Christopher," one of them said, standing as they came back to the table and reaching out to shake David's hand. He took it, and then reached for Christopher's.

Phil had been an architect, he remembered, and Christopher a teacher—his quitting that job had been one of the big eyebrow-raisers. As Lauren began talking, as if to fill him in on who they were, David took a moment to take them in, looking for anything that might suggest they were there against their will, but there was nothing. Phil looked as he had in his pictures, clean-cut with a stylish men's cut to his salt-and-pepper hair. His skin was slightly less tan than it had been in the pictures David had seen, but his eyes looked healthy and aware. Christopher was quiet, seemingly content to let his husband and Lauren do the talking, but looking healthy enough, if tired. He wore a carefully trimmed beard, and his dark hair was just a shade too long to be called professional. David thought he might have lost a few pounds since the picture he'd seen had been taken, but it was nothing drastic.

"So, the guys were saying that this place has really helped them," Lauren finished, looking to them as if to lead them into selling David on the place.

"We're more connected now, communicating better," Phil agreed, glancing between them and reaching up to grip his husband's shoulder. "It took some time—more than planned," he laughed, "but we're good now."

Christopher nodded, murmuring agreement, and David for the first time wondered if he'd been drugged somehow, or maybe smuggled some pot in in his suitcase.

"And how much time…have you guys spent here?" David asked.

At this, the two men finally looked at each other, and Christopher leaned into Phil, though David couldn't have said whether it was for support or out of affection. "It's been weeks," he said quietly. "But we have each other now, and we never managed to be this solid on the outside."

The outside, he says, David thought. *Like we're in a prison.*

Phil looked like he wanted to say more—his face had flashed a seriousness that David wondered about. Was the levity being projected forced? But the moment passed as Christopher spoke up, his voice slow and a bit flat.

Lauren's hand remained in David's as Christopher talked languidly about how they felt more connected, more emotionally stable, more on the same page, and David found himself squeezing Lauren's hand in his own, holding it against his thigh and enjoying the warmth of her skin. Anyone would have said this was a normal conversation, if heavy on therapeutic mumbo-jumbo, but it felt anything but.

As more couples came in, David recognized three more couples from those in their files, but all of the other couples were unfamiliar faces. He tried to take in faces as they got up to wait in line at the buffet line once the food was set out, letting Lauren keep up casual conversation with Phil and Christopher, and realized there had to be fifteen couples there, all in their mid-twenties to mid-forties. Age was the primary constant, though the room's atmosphere also felt…even. Like there were no high emotions in a place where he would have expected them. Fewer tensions than you'd see in an average gathering of couples, definitely. And unlike in the shuttle, most of the people here looked like they were cut from the same cloth in terms of attitude—to a person, the dress was casual business. No jeans or leggings or t-shirts. No tennis shoes, even.

When they sat back down, their trays full of grilled chicken, vegetables, and side salad, David finally asked, "So, what are we supposed to expect? We don't know much, other than that this place is meant to *fix* our marriage," he commented, allowing sarcasm to leak into his voice. He glanced to Lauren with an eyebrow raised, hoping she recognized he was just trying to play a part.

Across from him, Phil shrugged as he cut into his chicken. "It's okay to be skeptical. I was, too, at first—hated taking the time off work, but Christopher here said we needed to work on things, so…so be it," he said, shrugging. Beside him, Christopher was focused on his food and didn't seem to have reacted to the comment. "But then things got figured out. The first weekend, we spent what felt like forever in therapy—at least, it seemed like that to me since I'd never done anything like this before, but I know we had some free time on Saturday afternoon since that's how things go around here—and then we hung out with the other couples at night. That'll be tonight," he added, grinning at Lauren in a way that would have made David nervous if the man were straight. "We'll all just hang out, mingle, drink, play loud music—that's how Friday and Saturday nights are around here, taking off the tension. Saturday afternoons are pretty easy-going, too. You'll enjoy it. Monday came, and we spent half the day in therapy, half the day together, and things were okay. Better."

"Better enough that we decided to stay past the weekend," Christopher added, finally glancing upward. "Most do."

Phil nodded, stuffing food into his mouth.

Across from the two men, David could feel Lauren looking at him, waiting for reaction, but he'd already steeled himself against showing any. He had to remember who he was in this game, and who she was.

As the meal went on, he let Lauren do the talking, getting to know the two men—mostly through Phil, with Christopher keeping to himself again even though his demeanor was friendly enough—and David did little more than nod as a few other couples wandered by to introduce themselves or caught his eye from across the room, apparently in welcome. Couples only came in on Friday, it was clear enough, and so they were the new faces, with everyone else having had at least a week to get friendly already.

But even knowing what was at stake, he kept physical contact with Lauren as the meal permitted, whether by brushing her arm or letting his hand rest on her leg or in the small of her back. Anyone watching, he knew, would see the possessiveness in the gestures, but they were honest. Over and over again, they served their purpose, warming both of them with a reminder of the chemistry between them and the fact that they'd come into this together. Once upon a time, he might have said that feeling stirrings of magic under a woman's skin would drive him away—now, it was reassurance.

By the time the meal was over, another couple had joined them, and they led the way to the so-called ballroom where the night's reception would be held. Walking behind them, David couldn't help noticing the possessive arm of the man around the woman, holding just tightly enough for it to dent the skin of her shoulder and suggest there was a smidgen more pressure there than might be comfortable. Lauren walked by his side, her hand in his, and he was conscious of his tight grip on her upon seeing the couple ahead of them—he'd fallen into his role somewhat too well.

Upon getting to the ballroom, the man turned to them and began gesturing around, pointing out the location's coffee station, bar, hors d'oeuvres stand, and restroom. When his wife Maria reached out her hand and all but demanded Lauren accompany her to the restroom, David moved to the bar with her husband, Garrett, and Phil and Christopher moved off to speak to the barista behind the coffee stand.

"You'll get used to it," Garrett told him. "It's a nice set-up they got here, and the girls are good for each other—like a sorority, you might say. What'll ya have?"

David eyed the wide array of bottles behind the bar, and then motioned toward a bottle of Jamison. "Whiskey on the rocks—a double." Once Garrett had placed his own order for a martini, David focused his eyes back onto the other man's. "What do you mean they've got a sorority?"

The man's caterpillar eyebrows raised and he grinned. "Not literally, my man. I just mean they take all their emotions out on each other, so we don't have to deal with 'em; girls are emotional, right? That's what got us all here, I bet. So, all that emotion back-and-forthing between them, we sit back and get the easy part of the relationship, with all the high-strung bullcrap getting worked out with the therapists and each other and shit. Hell, Maria's more interested in sex than ever, and it's like all the emotional crap gets drained out of her before she ever comes to my room. I could be wrong, but I and some of the other guys have come to the conclusion that the therapists encourage the women to be as accommodating as possible, if you get my drift."

David took his drink from the bartender and looked for the tip jar, but the man behind the bar waved him off.

"It's all taken care of here," Garrett said, taking his elbow and pulling him off toward a table. "Hell, oughta be, much as we pay."

"How long have you been here?" David asked, eyeing the restroom entrance. What was taking the women so long?

"Oh, four weeks now. Seems like it's gone by like nothin'. We quit our jobs, though I could get mine back with a phone call, but after a few weeks, it's almost like you're family here. We're talking about moving into one of their long-term facilities—you heard about those yet?"

"We just got here today," David reminded the man, turning his eyes away from the restroom. "It never occurred to me we'd be here more than a week or two," he added pointedly when Garrett just grinned and shrugged off the comment. "I have no intention of quitting my job." But Garrett's eyes were on two women who were dancing together to a song the DJ had just put on, their arms around each other like they were sisters as they whispered to one another. "Garrett," David hissed, and the man finally turned back to meet his eyes, a lascivious grin on his face.

"Can't hurt to watch, right?"

David didn't bother to answer, instead sipping his drink and glancing toward the restroom again. "You were saying, about long-term facilities? I thought this program was meant to offer long *weekends*, not fucking months."

"Yeah, well, it depends. You get to like the set-up, there are some options. Me 'n Maria, we get along here better than we did outside. It's hard not to think about staying; her fuckin' family drives me nuts, always stopping by—they can't do that here! We hand over our properties and what have you, we're part of the family for life, no more costs involved. 'Course, I'm not stupid. I've got some offshore accounts they'll never know about if we do go that route, and I'll have those when I get out, but for now? No work, all play, living in luxury with a happy wife and no expenses…you'd be surprised how little it costs, once you've been here a while, all things considered. Like I said, I imagine I'll get bored of it eventually, but hell if it's not a nice fuckin' vacation for a while. Give it a year, I figure, and then maybe I'll think about going back to the outside."

That fucking word again—outside. "And what do they get out of it?" David asked. "In return for…all this?"

The man didn't seem to catch the sarcasm, and just adjusted himself at the table, leaning back in his chair and letting his eyes wander back to the women who were still dancing together. "They get the properties people give up, and the family everyone creates by joining in. It's called a therapy circle."

The whiskey stuck in his throat for a moment, David stared at the man and waited for the punchline. When it didn't come, he repeated, "A therapy circle?"

"Yeah, my man. 'We all help each other through marriage' is the company line. But meanwhile, we're shootin' the shit and playing poker with free drinks in hand while our girls pour out their hearts to each other and we get the best of both worlds. Word has it, the long-term facilities have gyms, tennis courts, golf course memberships, the whole bit. Fucking resorts, they sound like. Hey," the man added, suddenly meeting his eye and then looking him up and down. "You ever cheat on her?"

"What? On Lauren?"

"We're not saints, my man, who do you think I'm talkin' about? Less you got another wife wanderin' around."

David glanced yet again to the restroom and then looked back to Garrett, reminding himself of who he was supposed to be and what they'd walked into. His drink had gone empty somehow, and he thought about getting up for a refill right away, but he answered instead.

"Garrett, no offense, man, but we just met. What the hell makes you think I'd trust you with something that might come back to bite me in the ass in a group therapy session tomorrow?"

The man guffawed and punched him in the shoulder, then gulped down the rest of his drink. "So that's a yes, am I right?" He stood up and grabbed David's elbow, pulling him up and back toward the bar. He was about his height, and strung his arm around his shoulder like they were brothers as they walked. "Just take my word for it—you want choice here, they'll make it available. You just wait for Wednesday. I'll have Maria invite your girl to her room for a chick flick and you won't know what hit ya."

***

In the lounge that served as a lobby for the ladies' room, Lauren perched on the makeup counter just outside the restroom and let the four women circling her go on about the estate and what it offered. It all felt a bit manic, actually, maybe even like they were hyped up to have a new face joining their circle and nothing else mattered at the moment. She felt as if she'd been pulled into a nest of giggling sisters who were ready to adopt her, and couldn't help thinking that, odd as it was, *off* as it was, there was a certain charm to it. Her mother had always talked about the sisterhood of the coven, but her mother's group had been so toxic that it had never seemed attractive. Now, with four women around her gushing about how the place had helped their marriages, and how cute David was, and how much the two of them would get out of being there… there was a charm to it. One of them in particular, a quieter and more serious woman named Adrienne, reminded her of Claudia, and it was easy to imagine the two of them sitting back in front of a television and relaxing together while the world moved around them. And what could be wrong about that?

"Did you work?" Maria asked when a lull came in the conversation, and then a woman that Lauren recognized from one of the files, Dora, was there pressing a tall glass into her hand. "Vodka and cranberry," she said, passing out the last of the drinks from a tray she'd brought in for the group.

Ignoring how strange it seemed for a tray of drinks to be brought into a large lady's room—no matter how luxurious it might be—Lauren forced herself to smile in welcome and take a sip from the glass. She'd have to talk to Dora later, but the woman certainly didn't seem to be stressed in any way.

"I was a graduate student before I met David," Lauren answered. "Then…things kind of swept me up and school didn't make sense anymore."

One of the women nodded knowingly. "And before you knew it, you were stuck at home and making sure dinner was on the table at six or he'd knock you down and scream about it."

Lauren stared at her, her jaw dropped in surprise, but the other four women in their small group nodded in apparent understanding, never losing their smiles—one of them even chuckled—with Lauren being the one of them to even have the grace to look uncomfortable.

They find that funny? How was that a joke? Lauren wondered. But they were all acting like it was a common story.

"It's alright, dear," Maria whispered, apparently seeing the surprise. "It's why you ended up here. We understand, so you can tell us whatever it is that's happened when you're ready. Nothing to do but laugh about it after a certain point, especially now that you're here in a better place."

Lauren met the eyes of the older woman who'd joined them at dinner and found herself nodding mechanically. There was nothing else to do.

By the time she was able to find a way to excuse herself, she'd learned more intimate details about the women in the restroom's lounge than she'd known about the lives of most of her friends in school—and they hadn't been shy about gossiping about the other couples, either. Remembering why she and David were there, she'd taken in as many of the details as possible and endeavored to remember them despite the vodka and cranberries that had kept appearing in her hand. Now, for the most part, she knew who'd been to the hospital because of their partner (most of the women there, it seemed), who'd been threatening divorce, who'd cheated, and who'd been attached enough to their careers that giving them up to stay in the retreat had felt, at best, slightly uncomfortable. She also knew too much about which marriages had suffered because of addictions, which couples had tried and failed to have children, and which ones were most committed to staying here for some time further—and that number included all five of the women she'd been surrounded by for most of the night.

What she didn't understand, and what had grown harder and harder to grapple with as the gossip had flown around her, was how these women were coping with the odd circumstances they'd found themselves in, and how they could be so casual about their private crises. Through all of the conversations, nobody had lost their temper or grown emotional—not even when talking about cheating husbands, broken limbs, and gambling addictions that had, at least in Adrienne's case, left her and her husband in bankruptcy. If anything, the women had seemed emotionally flat, dulled somehow behind their apparent good moods, to the extent that Lauren had wondered aloud if anyone was being given anti-depressants, thinking privately that they *all* must be taking them. Instead, the women had admitted to taking occasional sleeping pills, but that was it. And yet, they were casual and easy about the retreat, their own lives, and anything else that came up. But there was no depth to any of the discussions, let alone the women's emotions.

Lauren couldn't help thinking that, had she been in the position of any one of them, she would have found this difficult to talk about. She'd even voiced as much, but been assured that the group therapy the next day would get her past that stepping stone. She couldn't imagine how that would be the case, but she hadn't argued.

Heading back out into the main area of the ballroom, she found that the lights had dimmed, and her own perception was fuzzy at the edges. She'd taken three or four drinks over the course of the conversation, and had probably downed them too fast, given the circumstances, but it had been an excuse to remain mostly quiet. Now, she stood near the wall and looked around. Men and women were scattered everywhere in small groups, with some few dancing and some few others sitting. She spotted David sitting with three men, one of whom she thought was Maria's jerk of a husband who'd joined them at dinner. Another, she realized once she got closer, was one of the men considered a suspicious case, whose file had been laid across the ranch house's island a few nights before. She couldn't remember for sure whether or not he was Dora's husband, but thought he might be. And since he was alone and she was still in the lounge, that seemed like an even bet. He didn't appear concerned with his wife's whereabouts, though.

There were drinks in all of their hands and no women nearby, but Lauren forced a smile onto her face as she approached and slid in next to David's chair as he kept on with the story he'd been telling, even with Lauren standing beside him.

His hand snaked around her waist and he held her there beside him as she took in the men he'd been sitting with—all of them were drunk, all of them close to David's age or a bit older. He still hadn't said anything to her when he finished talking, but his hand was wound possessively around her hip in a way that almost made her wish she'd stayed with the women in the lounge.

"So, this is your girl. Young," one of the men at the table commented, a hint of a leer stretching his lips.

Lauren felt David's fingers tense against her skirt, and she reminded herself that here, in this setting, it was his place to respond—not hers. Not if she wanted to hold their cover.

"Young and innocent enough to fall for a bastard like me," David joked. "Right, honey?"

His face looking up to hers froze her for a moment, but she made herself smile. He was sober enough, but he was also back in that character she'd found herself having dinner with the previous night. "It looks like some of the couples are calling it a night, and it's been a long day," she offered in response, nodding off toward the main door where a few couples could be seen wandering out.

Instead of answering, David's hand pulled her sideways so that she fell against him, off-balance, and landed sideways in his lap, stunned into silence.

"That's how you tell her how you feel, my man!" Maria's husband crowed out, and Lauren felt herself blushing.

"How about you boys go get some refills and grab my girl a drink?" David asked.

"Wantin' a minute of private time to finish putting her in her place, huh? Message received," one of the men commented, and with that he gestured to the other two.

Laughing, the other three men rose and made their way off to the bar, and Lauren felt David's hand nudge her chin, and then press hard until she'd tilted her head up to meet his eyes. The dark grin remained on his face, but his eyes had gone soft and serious.

"It's a boys' club, Lauren. I couldn't just get up and leave when you suggested it. One drink, and then we'll go up to my room and be done with all this till tomorrow, alright? You understand?"

Shoving down the emotion that had been building up in her throat, she forced herself to nod. She should have realized that she couldn't be that blatant about suggesting they leave and then expect him to get right up and walk out the door with her—in another time and place, sure, but not as long as they were here playing these roles.

She let her lips meet his in a kiss, and didn't resist when his hand at the nape of her neck pulled her in tighter so that she knew her lips would be swollen afterward, insistent as he was. When he sucked her bottom lip between his teeth and bit down lightly, she finally found a way to fight against the magic warming her body and pressed her hands into his chest in protest. A small groan of pain escaped her as he finally pulled away, and she pressed two fingers to her lips to relieve the pressure.

Then David was talking, and she turned her head to find that one of the men whose names she couldn't remember was pressing a dark-colored drink into her hand. "Spiced rum and coke, darlin'—David says you're spicy. From the blood on your lip and that smile, I guess it's true."

Lauren felt herself blushing, but accepted the drink as David laughed off the comment, and she tried to relax against him. His hand was warm on her thigh and she could feel the magic heating her blood, but this wasn't how she'd imagined the night would go. As one of the men began talking about how the retreat was saving him money, because his wife wasn't able to shop online 'every goddamned night', Lauren let herself zone out and simply watch the few couples dancing on the dance floor. At least someone was enjoying the night.

Chapter 12

With the other men too far gone to care, and too far gone to give him useful information, David made their excuses and pulled Lauren up along with him.

She'd long since stopped murmuring into his ear that she wanted to leave, that she was uncomfortable, and it was more than clear that she was drunk. He didn't know how many drinks she'd had before she'd come to find him, but her lips had been stained with cranberry juice, and there'd been a fuzziness to her gaze that he'd recognized in a moment. She'd clearly passed well beyond the point of being tipsy, and he'd taken advantage of it, he knew—holding her in his lap, keeping her heat against his and teasing her, with his touch and with the hardness in his pants both, as well as occasional nips to her neck.

She'd have been upset if she'd realized he'd moved her hair aside to reach her there, giving the men they'd been sitting with tell-tale glimpses of the marks on her skin, but the drinks had kept that from coming up. Instead, she'd been a bundle of nerves against him, practically vibrating with the magic.

At first, he'd worried over it, wondering at how he hadn't noticed it before, but then he'd realized it had only been a matter of time. They'd been in such close, constant contact, it had had time to get used to him, and to build up—and now he was ready to really enjoy it.

David's hand remained tight on Lauren's as he led her away from the ballroom and into the elevator, pressing the button for his floor before he faced her and leaned in for a kiss even as the doors to the compartment closed. Reminding himself to be gentle, he pressed his lips into hers, breathing in her upper lip and letting his hands slip to the skin above her skirt, beneath her blouse. Sitting on top of him for the last hour, her skin had been thrumming with warmth, bouncing off the liquor in his blood and begging for attention—all nerves and desire and heat. Now that they'd finally been able to escape the gathering, he didn't want to wait.

He felt her murmuring something into his mouth, but he pressed his lips into hers harder and sucked in the moan she let out as one of his hands found the small of her back and arched her body into his, her belly rubbing up against his hard cock as she tried to stay balanced in her heels. He could taste remnants of cranberry juice and rum on her lips, and feel the wanton magic bubbling up in her, pushing her flesh into his.

"Come on," he muttered as a beep signaled the door's opening.

Pulling her along behind him, he got to his door and fished the key card from his pocket. He could hear her still trying to catch her breath behind him and feel how off-balance she was, but he tugged her into the room behind him and then kicked the door shut.

Lauren landed on the edge of the bed where she'd sat with David earlier, her throat dry and her head swimming. She knew the case should be at the center of her mind, that she should be using this time to fill David in on what she'd learned, but she could see from the look in his eyes that the magic in her blood had been getting to him as well as to her.

And, he was right that this was what she wanted—him, right now, and nothing else. Sitting on his lap for an hour or more, her back or shoulder against his chest, feeling his heartbeat at all times, with his hand slipping under her skirt to her bare thigh and then down her leg, and his lips occasionally nipping at her neck, his hardening dick pushing against her and his lips breathing against her skin… it had been all she could do to stay still and keep from moaning aloud at times, the way the magic had been pushing her blood faster, heating her body and demanding closer contact.   Even now, her body seemed to be pulsing and wet in tune with the magic, secreting away any other thoughts before they could truly surface.

In front of her, he was stripping already. His eyes on hers, he took off his button-down and then his trousers, socks, and shoes till he stood before her in only his boxer briefs, his cock denting the fabric insistently. She didn't protest when he went to his knees in front of her and pressed her backward so that she lay back on the edge of the bed, dizzy with alcohol and power.

"Stay where you are," he told her, pulling down her panties and flipping her skirt up. Then his hands were around her thighs, yanking her body toward his waiting mouth.

The sensation stole any other thought from her. His tongue lapped her juices up, stretching up and down her slit as he moved around her center, collecting the moisture her body had been generating for an hour now. She felt his hands tighten on her thighs, spreading them apart almost painfully so that she was more open before him as she dug her nails into the comforter, giving in to him. His tongue circled her clit and she cried out before he pulled back and then pushed it into her slit, over and over again. Then his hands moved. She felt him slap at her thighs when they instinctively moved to close, and she heard herself mewl in protest as if from a distance, but left them open.

Everything except for the magic was fuzzy and difficult to hold onto, and the control in his voice and his touch was impossible to ignore. Once again, though earlier she'd thought she'd be too sore to accept him, let alone want him, she found herself giving in to desire and quivering with heat, soaked for him.

His hand came down on her belly then, his thumb circling and playing in circles around her clit as his other hand spread her pussy wide open for his tongue to gain better access, and when he lapped at her again with his hand pressing down and his thumb right there, she couldn't help but explode suddenly, screaming out in release as her body bucked beneath his attentions and his hold kept her center pinned to the bed, where he hadn't stopped.… Two of his fingers began pistoning in and out of her pussy, filling her over and over again as his lips came down on her clit and he nipped her there with his teeth so that her eyes clenched shut and she could have sworn her whole body saw stars, suddenly warming up and reacting to him a hundred-fold, her blood pulsing with magic in reaction to the orgasm.

When David lifted up from Lauren, out of breath, his chin and hands were soaked with her juices, and he could practically hear the magic swirling in her blood. If not for the liquor in his system, it might have occurred to him to wonder whether this was dangerous, either now or in the long-term, but for now he just wanted more of her. What were the chances of anyone sensing her magic anyway, or of Nell and Johanna searching for it at this very moment? It all seemed more unlikely than dangerous, and he wanted this—he wanted her, now. His cock was as hard as it had ever been, demanding her, and in moments he'd skimmed off his underwear and moved up to the edge of the bed, gripping her hips. Thank fucking God it was a high bed, he thought, and then, before she'd even opened her eyes and caught her breath from the orgasm she'd gotten from the oral, he pulled her hungry pussy up to meet his cock and buried himself in her heat, groaning out with the pleasure of her tightness as he did.

Lauren's eyes shot open, her lips falling apart in an O of surprise as David's rigid length sank deep into her, filling her channel in one long thrust as a full-body shiver ran through her on the edge of that last orgasm, bucking her body against his instinctively so that he bottomed out against her cervix, pressing into her hard, and she groaned aloud, her hands jumping to his biceps and holding on.

Keeping himself hilt-deep, David leaned in over her and tugged her top up so that her stomach and breasts were bared, her skirt gathered around her waist and her top around her upper chest. In another move, he'd clicked open the front-clasp bra and released her breasts. She closed her eyes when his hands found them, squeezing the soft flesh in his hands as his dick pulsed inside of her. She was hot and wet, with both juices and sweat, and he began thrusting in and out of her, achingly slow, as she got used to him. Somehow, she was always tight for him, always hot and wet and waiting and tight, and it drove him nuts.

When he came, he leaned into it, pressing in deep so that she grunted out in pain and pleasure as he gripped her ass and held her against him, wanting to feel his seed filling her, and her body accepting every drop. She was limp in his hands, exhausted, and he let himself enjoy the sight of it for a minute more, buried inside of her, before he stepped back.

She groaned beneath him at the sudden emptiness, her legs falling limp against the foot of the bed. He could see that she hadn't the strength in her thighs or her arms to push herself more fully onto the bed, and just lay in front of him, letting him look at her as she watched him in return.

He hadn't spoken a word through all of it, but to demand that she keep her legs open for his tongue, and the desire to possess her was practically bleeding from him now—on some level, he knew he was losing control, pushing her harder than he should, but he could feel her magic aching for him, wanting more, and his dick was still hard with the scent of her desire in the air and the way she lay before him, as helpless to the spell in her blood as he felt.

David drank in her glistening skin and her hooded eyes. Even with her bunched clothes and dazed appearance, she looked like a goddess spread out before him—and she was his for the taking, over and over again. He knew the next day would be stressful, and could hold anything. There was no telling what awaited them, but tonight she was here, heated and wet.

Without giving it more thought, he knelt on the bed beside her and tugged at the zipper of her skirt until he'd loosened the garment and could pull it down her legs and drop it on the floor. He untangled her from her blouse and her bra, and she let him, watching him languidly as he moved above her. He loved that she didn't resist, or even say anything. She simply followed his movements with her eyes, and he saw them linger sometimes on the scars he carried before coming back to what his hands were doing.

Her clothes gone, he ran his hands along her torso, occasionally dipping a finger to the moisture of her core and running it along her abdomen or around her nipples. Each time, she caught her breath or moaned in response, offering little sounds of pleasure and surprise. Finally, he kneeled beside her and lay both of his hands on her, resting them there as if to gentle her, one on her belly and his other on her abdomen, simply feeling her skin. This wasn't gentling her, though—this was stirring up her magic, ramping her desire higher and higher with every touch. He could feel the warmth gathering beneath his hands—the magic there trembling, reacting to his touch.

It was intoxicating.

When she'd closed her eyes and clenched her fists against the bedspread, and he could see a flush across her torso and feel building heat beneath his palms, it occurred to him that this was what magic felt like. What raw, natural power felt like. With all he'd experienced, the thought nearly sobered him for a moment—he'd fought against witches and magic ever since leaving the military, and had never given much thought to some supernatural power flowering in his own hands. As unnerving as it was, though, the more powerful thought was that he had power over Lauren, control of both her and her power, whatever was left of it.

Feeling the magic thrum beneath his hands as he traced her ribs and then reached to her neck, stroking his fingertips against her pulse, his dick hardened further as her breath hitched when the magic gathered at her neck, beneath his fingertips, and he stretched down to lay his lips against her there, feeling the heat.

When he rose from playing the magic through her body, she was stretched out and panting, glistening with sweat and flushed with heat.

He'd done some exploring of the room earlier, and

found that the suite was equipped for a variety of tastes and purposes—it seemed this place catered to sexual play as a healing factor between couples, given the stock of toys and condoms and other things he'd found. He knew what he wanted to take advantage of now, though. From the bottom drawer in the oversized nightstand beside the bed, he gathered two silken ropes.

Lauren still had her eyes closed, but she didn't resist when he took one of her hands, and then tied the silk of one rope delicately around her wrist before he stretched it up to the headboard and tied it off, jerking on it lightly to be sure it was secure. When he looked back to her face to see a reaction, her eyes were open wide against his, but she still wasn't protesting. And she looked more aroused than scared, based on her panting lips.

Silently, he took her other wrist and tied it off so that her arms were spread-eagled above her head. The vulnerability hitting her, she'd drawn her legs together, and her knees were up now, triangled above the bed. With both of her wrists tied off, he could see nerves coming out of her, but her nipples were hard buds of desire and there was no doubt of the wanton moisture seeping from her center.

The muscles in her arms flexed, and he saw her tugging at the bonds experimentally, her lips pursed with nerves.

"David?" she breathed out, but he only stood above her watching her. The power of having her here like this, not fighting him, just waiting, with magic running through her and waiting for him…

Wanting everything at once, he moved his lips to her belly, and then down, and he sucked her clit between his lips until she screamed with the sudden onslaught of sensation. His hands landed on her next, his fingers pressing into her mouth and pussy simultaneously, demanding she accept him as he used his tongue to explore her skin, teasing her belly, her abdomen, and then her breasts. His cock was pulsing with want, but he could feel the magic rising in her, running along with his touch beneath her skin, and he couldn't get enough of it, no matter how desperate her gasps or how swollen her lips.

When he pushed three fingers into her soaked channel and she bucked against him reflexively, as if any touch would push her over the edge now, no matter how many times he asked it of her, he couldn't wait any longer.

Lauren's breath was knocked from her when he fell upon her, his lips and teeth finding her neck before she could make a sound. With the weight of him on top of her again, her wrists pulled at the ropes, their knots tightening around her skin as she tried to gain the breath to tell him his weight was stretching her from the bonds, hurting her, but the ache in her pussy had stretched through her blood so that it was desire driving her, and all she could do was gasp as he sucked skin between his teeth and nipped at her, licking at her sweat as he did.

Lauren clenched her eyes shut, knowing he was going to tease her until he was satisfied she couldn't handle more. Already, she couldn't breathe or focus enough to get a word out or tell him it was all too much, the desire running through her in a way that felt as painful as it did pleasurable, soaked as she was with want, but he wasn't slowing down. If anything, he was demanding more, and she'd long passed the point of surrendering. And the thing of it was, she trusted him—even quaking beneath him and furious with him over the night, horrified at herself for wanting him as his dick teased her yet again, his legs holding hers apart and with her hands tied painfully above her, and with that too-knowing look in his eyes, she trusted him completely.

He moved over her and grinned, his eyes on hers as his

fingers played the magic through her blood, making it rise at will. He knew how to use it against her now, she realized, teasing her with the magic's energy as well as pleasure, and it was running in her blood, working to catch up with his touch as his eyes held hers and he tweaked her nipples, brushing her clit at turns and making her gasp when his fingers touched her wetness and then pulled away, tracing it along her body and even dipping between her lips, so that she tasted her juices along with their sweat.

All they'd been through considered, Lauren wasn't sure she'd ever felt this emotionally vulnerable to him, to his charm and his strength and his fucking smile and the way he held her, like she was his—and that was fine, she suddenly realized. Tied down like this beneath him, with him teasing at her nipples so that she could barely breathe, she just wanted to please him, and to be his.

And suddenly he pressed forward all the way, into her, his dick pushing hard into her as she let all of the air in her lungs out and he grunted with the pleasure of it, and she felt the magic building inside of her along with her orgasm so that she thought she'd explode with the heat and the power of it. She wrapped her legs around his thighs instinctively as he began to pull out, and he stopped with only his head inside of her, holding her open before him and trembling.

"You're mine," he grunted when his lips came away for a moment, and then his hand was at the nape of her neck, gripping her hair and tugging her head sideways so that he could better access her neck and bite down as he lunged into her, letting the force of his lust carry his cock all the way into her heated channel so that she knew he could feel the breath hitching and crashing in her lungs, desire fighting natural need.

With his fingers twisted in her hair, he moved back to

her lips and kissed her hard as he thrust into her again and again, finding a rhythm that her hips began to match desperately, and then his fingers found her clit, and she screamed into his mouth. Buried within her, he stayed pressed in deep as she came around him, bucking helplessly beneath him and gasping his name between gulping down breaths, her hands grasping at air emptily above them and tugging at her bonds so that the ropes only tightened further. When she'd begun to catch her breath and come down from the release, he bent above her and sucked one of her nipples into his mouth, his dick still buried within her pussy, as hard and demanding as ever. There were moans coming from her mouth now that she didn't recognize as her own, but one of his hands slid up to her mouth, silencing her as he pushed two fingers deep into her mouth, pressing down on her tongue insistently until she took his hint and sucked at them as if he'd offered her his cock, her tongue exploring and allowing his fingers to play. She could taste her own desire on him, the sweetness of it, and each time he took his hand away to let her breathe more easily, it seemed his fingers were back again only moments later, until there was a rhythm to his fingers and their wetness that matched his cock, pushing into her again and again, and only feeling larger as she grew more helpless, more swollen and wanton around him and for him.

When she opened her eyes, he was grinning down at her, pressing the fingers of one hand against her tongue as his other hand held the hair at the nape of her neck, keeping her still beneath him as his cock and his fingers used her, offering a puzzle of desire and want that she couldn't catch her breath through. His cock suddenly went deeper then, as hard as ever as he bottomed out and kept her pinned to the bed, and then she screamed into his hand as her body shook and the magic ripped through her, centering in on the points of contact between them.

She thought she blacked out for a moment, and then, finally, she had space from him, without any contact. He was lying beside her watching her, as if waiting for her to recover, and she thought he was done. And then he wasn't, his fingers and his cock suddenly back against her wetness, his fingers at her mouth as he landed on top of her again, his cock prodding at her cunt, demanding more from her.

She was trembling around him now, with his fingers in her mouth and his cock pushing her, demanding her pussy keep up with its rhythm as he thrust in and out above her and kept his lips latched onto her nipple. When he bit down and pressed in as deep as he could, she opened her mouth wide in a desperate gasp and tremored beneath him, rocked by a climax she hadn't been ready for.

This time, David wasn't far behind her climax, and he erupted again within her body as her body clenched him, milking him for every drop with a pulsing heat that felt electric. He stayed buried within her, his lips sucking at her nipple as his fingers traced her lips and her neck again, his weight holding her to the bed beneath him as the last shivers of pleasure wracked both of them.

Sensing that some of the pleasure in her blood was giving way to discomfort, he forced himself to pull back and roll to the side, breathing deeply as he let one of his hands fall beside him on her belly. He could feel the warmth of her magic, thrumming in her skin and feeding their chemistry, called into her center by his touch and gathering there beneath the flesh where his hand lay. He got lost in the sensation, closing his eyes and enjoying the power of it reacting to him.

When she shifted upward, a pained grunt slipping from between her lips, he finally actually looked sideways at her, and though her eyes were hooded, her skin still flushed, he could see a sharp edge of pain in the thinness of her smile, overtaking everything else. It was enough to lift the fog of desire he'd allowed to control him, and through the liquor and the magic now, he saw Lauren was as exhausted and pained as she was satisfied. She looked…used, maybe even hurt. Looking up, he saw the way the ropes had begun biting into her skin, cutting into her circulation, and he twisted in the bed to kneel beside her.

"Fuck, I'm sorry," he murmured, the beginnings of sobriety licking at his conscience now that the lust in his blood had been sated. She murmured acknowledgement as he worked his fingers into the knot that had tightened at her left wrist. It was a slow process, the knots had tightened so much with the pressure of their coupling, and when he got her hands loose, he took them in his and looked at the angry red marks left by the silk.

"It was fine at first," she muttered. "It's fine."

He looked up to see that her eyes were already closing, breath still catching in her throat from the climaxes he'd kept forcing upon her.

Swallowing down the worst of the guilt, he nodded, massaging her wrists. "The rest of you must be sore, too, between last night and tonight," he said, suddenly remembering that he hadn't been easy with her the night before, either.

Fuck, what am I doing to her?

She was so flushed, and he'd left more marks on her. Her legs were pulled together in a way that told him she'd be more sore than satisfied in a few hours' time, too. "I got carried away," he admitted, his eyes roving over her arms and breasts to try to meet her gaze, hoping she felt the sincerity, but she was already near on asleep. He hadn't meant to hurt her again. He really hadn't.

"It's okay, David," she murmured, her words barely

audible. "We got carried away. I wanted…everything you did. It's just the magic, the spell…things keep building," she breathed out.

He let her lie there as his own blood and heartbeat calmed, and then he leaned sideways overtop of her and kissed her as gently as he could, letting his lips just barely part hers as his hands rubbed her wrists. He knew they needed sleep, but he also knew that going to sleep like this wouldn't do her much good—she'd wake up sore, and sticky with desire, swollen with what they'd just done. There were healing salts in his suitcase that he'd bought her as a gift, and a bath and a bottle of water might make all the difference.

"Lauren, baby, wake up for a minute," he whispered. She murmured into his neck and he kissed her again, keeping himself from putting any pressure on her as he did.

"I'm sorry, Lauren, but please, wake up for me, kid."

Finally, another kiss pulled Lauren back to the room so that her eyes half-focused. David looked more pained than she felt, and it was almost enough to make up for everything he'd done over the last few days, it tore at her heart so much. And as much as he kept apologizing now, words falling over each other as he told her he'd been overwhelmed by the reactions, by the magic rising to his touch, she could just blink back at him, thinking that none of the apologies were necessary—that, for most of it, she'd been right there with him, at the mercy of the magic in her blood, unable to tell when enough was enough. She'd enjoyed it, nearly all of it, though she regretted it now with the ache she felt in her core, and the rawness she felt around her core and her wrists.

And it was true, Lauren realized. Lying here like this, naked and bruised, with swollen lips and an ache sinking deeper into her body, she was strong enough to admit that she'd enjoyed his dominance, and the balance of pain with the ecstasy. Seeing David lose control with her had even, in itself, been a powerful aphrodisiac.

When she raised up to meet his lips for a gentler kiss, the magic still rumbling in her blood did little to negate the sharp crick in her neck and shoulders from where he'd been biting at her and holding her down, and where her shoulders had been pulled up above her in the binds he'd put on her wrists, and she couldn't quite bite back a sudden groan of dismay, the pain enough to spike adrenaline through her blood.

"How about I run you a bath?" he offered.

Lauren found herself nodding, breathing out and feeling as if she'd caught her breath for the first time in ages. Her magic was starting to settle, the currents stabilizing and cooling down within her body as the heat of their lust and chemistry cooled with their exhaustion and the liquor wore off.

When David had run a warm bath, he came back to the bed and picked her up over her protests, cradling her against his chest so that she couldn't help but lean her head against his skin and feel the pounding of his heart. He bent down and helped her settle into the bath before the magic could truly awaken between them again, and then disappeared from the doorway of the bathroom and left her to soak. He'd managed to find some moldavite bath salts somewhere, and glassy green chemistry of the moldavite began working on her muscles almost immediately, its scent allowing her to lose herself in the water, fully relaxed for the first time since they'd left the ranch house.

By the time the water had turned green around her with the salts, she'd lain a washcloth over her eyes and reclined back. She'd let David wake her up, and rest till then, hoping the next day could be put off just that much longer if she stayed soaking where she was.

In the bedroom, David pulled on some sweatpants before fishing the burner phone he'd brought from within a pocket of spare jeans where he'd put it for safe-keeping. Opening it up, he turned it on and texted Josh that the two of them were turning in for the night, having already seen four of the missing couples—who were fine, it seemed—and having interacted with two of them. Things were strange and suspicious, he added, but they were okay.

That chore done, he tucked the phone away once again and then headed back into the bathroom to sit with Lauren while she bathed. He didn't want to talk about the case or worry about anything more than comforting her and making up to her the lust he'd burned off against her that night. Everything else could wait for the morning, when they'd be learning more anyway, but he didn't want to be apart from her. He'd let himself lose control, and maybe she'd lost control also, but they'd figure it out together. When he got back into the bathroom, though, he saw that Lauren had managed to doze off in the big clawfoot tub, her neck reclined against the towel that he'd lain on the back edge for her.

Sitting on the edge, watching her breathe lightly, he let his eyes rove over her. Her hair lay in a tangled mess, gathered over one shoulder, and her bare neck on the other side showed angry markings as proof of that night and the previous night—he'd truly been rougher with her than intended, and her swollen lips were added proof. He glanced down her body, to her breasts floating in the water, their still pert nipples buds of attraction that had only softened somewhat since she'd come into the bath. Near her belly, both of her hands floated, resting lightly at her side and over her belly. Her wrists boasted angry red markings, and he couldn't help wondering if they'd be visible the next day. He thought they probably would, and his gut tightened when his next thought came—that nobody would care, even when they noticed and understood the bruising was new, and where it had come from. Nobody but him would care he'd hurt her.

At least, not unless they could somehow use it against them.

***

Lauren sat in the center of a circle of women, her legs crossed and her wrists tied together in her lap. Without looking up, she knew she was surrounded by more than a dozen women. All of the women from her mother's coven, and then there were the women she'd gotten to know that night. Rounding out the group surrounding her were her mother and the therapist, Samantha Shea.

The women talked over her head, hypothesizing about how Lauren's magic reacted to David, and what the potential for long-term renewal might be, and how it might be used. Her mother, the once insanely powerful Phillippa Merriweather, preened, pointing out that her spell was proving to be her daughter's renewal and salvation, though everyone had doubted her. Shea agreed, talking about Lauren's value as a source of energy and power, and the depth of her emotion for the man she'd been tied to.

Lauren listened silently, her breath and her voice caught in her throat. Where was David? Why was her mother alive, and how had she ended up at the center of these women who all seemed to find her amusing, a commodity to be used and worked upon rather than a person? She wanted to scream at her mother that her spells had been damning, dangerous things that she was determined to overcome, but found that she couldn't.

Magic was running through her blood again, warming

her painfully, and the ache she'd been feeling in her core and in her limbs was no longer pleasurable, as it had been earlier, but tight and demanding. She gripped her hands together in her lap, fighting to remain calm, and then she began to feel energy bleeding out from her, glistening and warm. Detached, confused, she watched the strands of magic slip from her pores and spread outward along the floor like little veins, running to Shea and to her mother, and beyond them, out from the circle like little rivulets of magic that she no longer had access to.

Where she'd been uncomfortably heated just minutes before, Lauren suddenly found that the magic was stealing not just her energy, but her warmth, and her skin was slick with a chill sweat. She was cold, and cramping and sore, but still the magic kept running away from her as if drawn away on automatic power.

As she began to shiver more violently, she raised her knees against her body and hugged herself into an upright fetal position, gripping her nails into the jeans she wore and telling herself that she had to find a way to call out to David, to find him, if she could only stay awake...

She jerked upright, breathless and freezing. In the dark, she could hear David's slight snore, and make out the shape of the window at the edge of the room. *I'm at the estate,* she remembered. *In David's room.*

Calming her breath, she pulled the comforter up from the base of the bed—she'd grown cold, and thought she must have pulled away from David. Now, she curled her body back against his, and breathed a sigh of relief as he twisted, his arm coming down naturally to pin the comforter to her body and wrap her into him, his body curling behind hers beneath the sheets. Her body was aching and chilled, but she could already feel the warmth David's body brought to hers—bringing her back to herself, reminding her of the pleasure behind the aches.

Satisfied that she could sleep against him like this, she forced the nightmare she'd had out of mind and closed her eyes, shifting her head on the pillow so that she could feel David's breath at the nape of her neck against her hair. With that extra bit of life and contact there, and his body pressed into hers, she knew she'd sleep, and the morning would come soon enough.

Chapter 13

Lauren had gone to her room to shower that morning and then met him at breakfast, but now they'd been separated all over again. Within twenty minutes of breakfast, David found himself in a group of six men that included Phil, the gay man who he'd first met with Lauren, the leering golem of a man named Van who he'd gotten to know the night before, and two other men who'd found their way to the retreat. The man who rounded out their group was the primary male therapist, Dr. Tony Toscano, who'd been introduced to David and Lauren that morning as their primary couple's therapist. He was also David's group therapist, which meant he'd be seeing the man constantly.

So far, he fit the stereotype David might have come up with for a man in his position, though he had an extra bit going for him in that he seemed far more authentic and down-to-earth than Shea. No, this man was casual and easy in his manner—the type David knew would be a lawyer's dream as an expert witness, he was so conversational and clear in his words. He'd have had juries eating out of his hand, no doubt, which was the one thing that put David slightly on guard—other than the fact that he was a therapist at all. Still, he was a good ten years older than all of the men in their group, and wore his authority like a suit, balancing a clipboard on his knee as they sat in the circle that David had dreaded, but expected.

"So, a few weeks in, and I think we're doing better," Phil finished. "Chris says I'm acting more like the guy he fell in love with," he added belatedly, but David couldn't help noticing the fast grin that followed the statement. It gave the impression that the conclusion on his partner's part was the accomplishment he'd been going for, rather than the change that should have driven it.

Tony smiled back—too knowingly, David thought—and then turned to one of the other men, whose name David could no longer place. "When we met Thursday, you said Adrienne was still pushing back against your authority—has that changed at all?"

David's eyes cut back to Tony rather than waiting for the man's response. Wasn't this man supposed to be teaching them how to attain partnerships and peace in their marriages, versus outright authority?

"Yeah, but whatever Shea said helped," the man answered, and David let himself re-focus on the conversation—he'd have to figure out the aims of this place later. "She went off with her girlfriends again Thursday night, but last night worked out. She gave me what I wanted." He nodded to himself, but a frown had creased his lips. "She was still upset."

Tony wrote something on his clipboard. "And did you give her what *she wanted*?"

The man shrugged. "We didn't get to that part."

Van laughed outright and David bit back a sarcastic

comment. From the narrowing of the therapist's eyes, the guy would get it from elsewhere.

"We'll talk about that later, in private session," the man commented simply. And then his eyes moved to David's.

"David, you won't know this yet, but I and the other therapists actually watch video feeds of breakfast— you've noticed the security cameras in the cafeteria."

Noticed them, yes. Understood, not so much. Apparently, that was about to change. He met the other man's gaze and answered evenly. "Worried we'll steal some toasters?"

Chuckling, Tony shook his head. "No, not with what you're paying. Rather, we want to see the dynamics before we move into therapy sessions, or get a head-start on curtailing any crisis that may arise between couples overnight. It's not a perfect system since plenty of our residents skip breakfast on a regular basis"—the man glanced pointedly to Phil—"but it doesn't hurt. This morning, I couldn't help noticing some…evidence, on your wife, that the two of you were together last night."

Jesus Christ. Seriously? Here? "And?" he asked.

"And, that's fine. She's welcome to visit you at night. But given that the two of you are new here and I haven't met with her in private yet, I'd like you to give me some insight into how consensual it was."

David's instinct was to throttle the man, but he swallowed down the emotion and stared back at him. "It might have gotten out of hand, but it was consensual. Completely. But it sure seems like this is something for a private session instead of the group."

The men around them guffawed, Van loudest of all in demanding details, but the therapist only held his gaze for another moment, silent, and then nodded as if he'd come to some conclusion for himself. "Alright, well, now that we've covered introductions and checked in with everyone's progress since Thursday, I'd like to talk about give-and-take. Are you listening, Raul?"

The man whose name David had struggled for sat up straighter.

"You are the dominant factions in your relationships. That is not in question, and we'd be going backwards if we attempted to dissect it or counter-balance that impulse. And, yes," he added, his eyes on David's again, "that means that you'll sometimes lose control, for better or worse. Authority comes with power, and we are not perfect. It happens," he said, shrugging.

Fuck, that's casual.

"But, whether you retain control in all moments or lose control, you have to be able to self-reflect and understand what that means to your partner. If you lose control, do something to make it up to them. David," he said suddenly, "did you do anything to make up for your violence, last night or this morning?"

Caught off-guard, David nearly choked on the coffee he'd been sipping. "I, uh, I ran her a hot bath, told her to soak…but," he added quickly when he saw the other men's faces, "I don't always, I admit. I usually don't, uh, think about stuff like that." He had to remember who he was playing here, he reminded himself. No matter how casual or real this felt, he *was* playing a role. He should have told them he'd rolled over and gone to sleep.

But Tony was nodding even as Raul scowled. "And did she accept it?"

"Accept it?" he echoed.

"Did she say thank you, accept the gesture, et cetera, or did she argue with you or accuse you of losing control?"

Knowing that Lauren could only tell the truth if asked the same, he answered with the truth. "She accepted it. And she enjoyed the sex, too," he added pointedly, unable to help himself. "She knew I didn't mean to hurt her last night."

"But you've meant to hurt her in the past," the therapist responded without missing a beat.

Before David could answer, the man moved on, as if he'd only made the comment for effect. It hadn't been a question, David realized. Just a conclusion that he couldn't refute.

"Men, the point here is that a gesture like that is what's going to keep your partners in a mindset where they trust that these losses of control will be temporary, passing. I guarantee you that David got more pleasure out of hurting his wife and exerting that control than she took in a simple bath, but the gesture, small as it was, allowed for her pride to remain intact and kept her emotions in check. Cooking dinner, running a bath, offering to watch your partner's favorite movie with them or make them a drink—these are all small gestures which express some *give*. Relationships need to have give-and-take. That goes for everything from orgasms to restaurant choices," the man added simply.

"You get frustrated that your partners are emotional, and part of our work here is helping them deal with those emotions so that they don't spill over unnecessarily and cause frustration in your marriage—we have ways to help them focus those emotions elsewhere, and that helps a great deal—but the fact that they show those emotions less does not mean they stop existing. In fact, everything you do drives emotion, and the more passionate you are, the more emotions you drive, even if you don't see them and don't wish to see them. Manipulating the way your partners understand those emotions is what will allow you to continue in peace."

David felt his face going red with discomfort, but he remained silent. He hadn't been trying to manipulate

Lauren into letting him off the hook—not consciously. And he hadn't been ignoring her emotions or trying to pretend they didn't exist. Yet, that was what this man was suggesting made sense: manipulation and trickery in some tug-of-war. It felt disingenuous at best—malicious at worst.

Seeming to see his discomfort, the therapist reached out and gripped David's shoulder, as if for support, but it was all David could do to keep from physically shaking the man off.

"David here instinctively understood he'd gone too far. It wasn't an even give-and-take by any means, but it was enough give to control the situation and keep emotions in rein."

Finally, David shrugged the man's grip off, making a show of sipping his coffee so that, perhaps, it would seem less awkward and pointed. More than anything, he wanted to get out of this room and find Lauren, but it wasn't the time.

"Given the power dynamics in your relationships, you may not ever give up control, and that's fine. Preferable, in fact. But you have to offer proofs that you care when you're with your partner, present for whatever the two of you engage in. Or, what *looks* like proof. They have to feel as if they are getting love in return for putting your desires and needs above their own."

Tony's lips turned up in a smile that David should have found peaceful, but didn't.

"Van," the therapist commented, "you've mentioned your wife spends too much time with her girlfriends, chatting on the phone. Correct?"

The man nodded. "Drives me up the wall. She's cooking and yapping on the phone the whole time. After dinner, she's back on the phone, talking about how she feels and what she wants, over and over again. Then she wants to go out with 'em two nights a week and gets bent out of shape if those are nights when I want her home. You saw last night," he said with a glance to David. "All that time at the reception, she was off with her girlfriends 'stead of with me."

David didn't bother to voice the fact that Van had been dead-drunk and telling misogynist stories and jokes. He hadn't missed his wife for a moment.

"Alright," Tony commented, "so the trick is to present it in terms of give-and-take, making her feel as if she's being given something with those phone calls. Make it clear to her that she can spend two nights out or talking on the phone, but keep control of the situation—don't give it up entirely. Make those two nights of your choosing, or else make it clear, ultra clear, that you get her for the whole of the weekend, no girlfriends in sight or sound."

Van's lips quirked up. "Her girlfriends get two nights, no more, and I get five."

Tony inclined his head as if agreement had been reached and all was right again. "There you have it. Giving up two nights keeps the power in your court, retains balance in your favor, and offers some give for the take. Giving up those nights is far better than the two of you fighting over her attention for five or six nights each week. And once that system is in place, once that arrangement is made, the tension will be removed from the situation and the system will be in place. That will be a rule the two of you can abide by. And she'll retain those nights to focus on her girlfriends *if* and *only if* you have all of her focus at other times, as agreed."

Raul nodded, his eyes narrowed as if he was already determining what his offer of 'give-and-take' would be with his own wife. "It's like business. We keep the upper hand, but make the person on the other side of the deal feel like they're getting the upper hand on us."

"Exactly," the therapist agreed.   Beyond that, if you make your partners believe you have their emotions in mind, and you keep their emotions focused on your own desires as much as possible, and on passion, it will be smooth sailing."

Van grinned as if the solution was simple, but the calm that had settled in felt like ice in David's throat. He didn't know if it was right or wrong, but they were turning relationships into business arrangements, using sex and affection and time as currency—that's why these couples were getting along and how they were learning to get along, leaving aside violence and fighting. And, somewhere, emotion and love were being taken out of the equation, manipulated into another form of currency and pushed down out of sight. The thought stuck in his mind, twisting against the hypothesis that he and Josh had come up with. And then Phil spoke up, answering it.

"I love Chris, Doc. I don't want to blackmail him into doing more around the house, and that's an awful lot what this sounds like. I'm with Raul on this—it sounds like a business arrangement, but I don't know if it's the way I want to run my marriage."

The therapist shrugged. "Emotion belongs in the bedroom, between the two of you—the extreme emotion and connection should show up there only. Most of you are here because it was erupting elsewhere. In struggles for control. In chaos. In violence. That's not sustainable. Extreme emotion belongs between you in the bedroom, and that includes love. Part of your job as an authority in your marriage is to ensure that emotion is kept in check in your partners, and given release as *appropriate.*

"Phil, all of you, understand this: You're setting these deals and agreements because you love your partners, because exerting control and making boundaries is a sign of that love. Phil, you say you love Christopher. You all say you love your wives," he added, looking at each of them in turn until they'd all nodded. "Well, it's that simple. You haven't found a way to sustain relationships without organizing trade-offs like this formally—not without explosions of emotion interrupting your lives and your marriages. In general, remember that give-and-take is necessary. And, remember, it should also be uneven— the type of men you are, a marriage will only be sustainable if you each retain the upper hand, and your partners need to realize that. It's part of the work we're doing here. But whatever satisfaction entails for you and your partners, individually, you have to find a way to make that satisfaction attainable. And if there is some realm where agreement cannot seem to be reached, for whatever reason, that's where you make a deal."

Put so simply, it all almost sounded logical to David's ear, or at least the last part did—until the man added, almost as an apparently obvious afterthought, "And, if they break the deal, you punish them or get Shea and I involved right away."

The comment came near the end of the session, and David couldn't find a way to question it. Not without giving up the role he was playing, or suggesting he'd doubted everything which had been said. The only thing which eased its harshness had been the doubt he'd seen flickering across the other men's faces. The slips of concern, especially on Van's and Phil's faces, had been the only things to make him think they might be redeemable—at least in terms of their relationships. But then, he'd already accepted the fact that some of the folks they'd come in to save were jerks.

Realistically, David knew he ought to be trying to pair off with one of the men at the center of this case, whatever this case was, but everything the therapist had said had only made him feel worse about the way he'd treated Lauren the night before. He left the group session with one focus in mind—finding Lauren and checking in on her. They'd barely spoken that morning, there'd been so little time after they'd woken up, but there was time now, and he was determined to at least spend it with her…even if they couldn't talk honestly about what was happening between them and the way the magic was working in her blood, perhaps even affecting him. He guessed he knew that that was more a signal of his weakness than the magic's strength, but one way or another, they needed to address it at some point. When they could, anyway.

When he got to the break room, he hardened his gaze and hoped his concern would remain hidden, but he moved toward her as soon as he found her in the corner with two other women. He recognized Van's wife from the pictures at the ranch house—Dora, her name was.

And then he was at her, wrapping his arm around Lauren's shoulder before she'd known he was approaching. She'd worn a high-collared shirt to hide the hickeys on her throat and neck, but there was still light bruising to be seen on her wrists, and a swelling to her lips. The other two women greeted him naturally, though, as if his sliding into the room and coming straight to her only made sense.

"David, this is Dora, and Adrienne," Lauren introduced him, glancing up so that he caught the bright blue to her eyes—bluer than that morning, which meant she'd been brought to tears in her own group session. Involuntarily, his grip tightened on her, and he had to force a smile to the two women who stood there. Adrienne was looking at him suspiciously, and he realized from the name that this was Raul's wife. He could understand her being suspicious of any man if she was married to that one. Dora, on the other hand, looked as perfectly naïve and casual as her own husband, Van.

"Pleased to meet you," David answered automatically, but none of them reached out to shake hands, and Lauren shifted in his grip as if to allow herself some space. Holding back a grimace, David only held onto her more solidly, knowing it was what these women would expect. He'd have to make it up to her later. The promise to himself felt flat, though. It seemed that he'd been spending an awful lot of time promising himself that he'd make things up to her. What was the point of making promises if he wasn't in a position to keep them?

Lauren didn't fight his grip, but she didn't hold her elbow back from knocking into his ribs when he pulled her in tighter. She understood this possessiveness was part of the role, but it was getting to her—especially in public. The chemistry between them had started to feel like a physical pressure, and her magic began whirling at his every touch.

And it was beginning to build, uncomfortably.

She'd thought about it that morning, first while showering and then during breakfast as David and Phil had talked politics. Since leaving the ranch house, she'd been actively avoiding any use of her magic. The guys had been adamant about it—no matter how unexpected their location might be, any use of her magic could literally act as a flair for Johanna and Nell. Engaging it for any reason outside of the ranch house was out of the question.

She hadn't expected it to be a problem, honestly, and the promise she'd made to avoid engaging it had been a simple one—she'd given her word without any thought, knowing it was the only smart thing to do. But now…it was building in her blood, making it harder for her to focus on anything beyond her connection to David, which kept feeding it. Being close to him, even through fabric, made things worse—it was begging for use, and the closest it came to finding release was when they were together, skin to skin and feeding off of its connection.

Only today had she realized just how much she'd been engaging it at the ranch house, through the gardening and other small attempts at magic. Giving in to their relationship, their chemistry, had been what the magic in her blood had been waiting for…and now it was building, wanting release. In the cage, she saw now that her exhaustion and fear had dampened it; maybe there'd even been something in that powder on the floor that had affected her, as well. But here and now, with David close by and no life-threatening stressor dampening it, and with her being mostly well-rested and healthy…the magic couldn't stand being contained like this, and it was aching for release.

More and more, it felt nearly like a vibrating cord running through her veins, hot and unstable. She knew she wouldn't have been crying earlier that day if not for the power distracting her, driving emotions out of her, but she hadn't been able to stop herself. She'd made herself look like an emotional wreck all because of it beating at her veins, begging release.

David holding her like this, even in public, sent shivers running through her blood and her skin—want soaking her panties and drying her throat, demanding attention. It was as embarrassing as it was distracting.

Suddenly, she realized that Dora and Adrienne had excused themselves—she stood alone with David in a corner, and had completely zoned out their separation along with their movement into a more private part of the room. He was staring at her, his brow furrowed and his lips parted as if he'd just been speaking. "Lauren?" he asked, quietly, and she got the impression he'd already said it more than once.

Jerkily, she nodded. "I'm okay. I'll…I'll have to tell you later. Just…give me some space when you can, okay?" she asked, gripping his hand and squeezing before she pulled away, hoping he'd understand she was asking for a reason.

Holding her gaze, the man she'd come to love nodded at her, but she could see doubt written over his features. She knew he'd lost control the night before, getting that taste of the magic in her blood, but they couldn't talk about it now. No matter what he was wondering, or how it would affect them while they remained in the center, it would have to wait.

"We've got about ten minutes before our session. You want to take some juice and go sit on the patio?" he asked. "Get some time to ourselves?"

"Yeah, maybe so." Lauren glanced around to the other couples spread around the room, seeing that nearly everyone had separated off into their personal pairings. Unlike the night before, there were no men and women standing together unless they were two who were romantically involved. It was as if an unspoken rule had come into effect, that in this break time, during the day, they'd be focused on each other.

Outside, Lauren took a chair at a small patio table and looked out over the grounds—the estate was gorgeous, truly, and might have offered a perfect vacation if not for the situation they were in.

"So, after lunch, it sounds like we're on our own for a while," David commented, forcing a lightness he didn't feel into his voice.

"Yeah…any thought to what you want to do?" she asked, forcing an ease into her voice that she didn't feel. Truly, she wanted to retreat to her room and sleep, but that wouldn't do anyone any good, and it wasn't as if she could be alone with David without them giving in to what was running in her blood. She knew that well enough.

When he didn't answer immediately, she added, "Christopher said he and Phil might go swimming and we could join them. It could give us a chance to get a better feel for why they're here maybe. Dora and Adrienne seemed interested, too, and I know Adrienne's not one of the people we're here for, but…"

"Works for me," David answered.

Lauren looked back at him, taking her eyes from the view. "Do you know what's going on?" she whispered. "Yet? I mean, there's something, but…"

"We'll figure it out. Soon," he added. There wasn't much more to be said, after all.

Lauren fell silent with the comment, welcoming the space to calm down from the morning. It had been a lot to take in, and there'd been a lot of questions. True to her worries, there'd been no way to hide the marks David had left on her skin, and though she'd been able to say that she'd enjoyed getting them, she'd had to awkwardly admit that they'd hurt her, as well, and that although David had apologized afterward, he'd pushed her, and she hadn't really had time to think about saying no.

It was all true, and yet it also made things sound so much worse than they were. She'd heard what she'd said. And she'd seen the pity in the eyes of the men and women around her with every excuse she'd made, every word that had fallen from her lips. Adrienne had actually reached out and half-hugged her as she'd been trying to explain that there was nothing to worry about, that they should ignore the marks on her wrists. And then she'd begun crying, and it had all gotten so much worse.

There'd been nothing to say then, and there wasn't much to say now.

When David's watch showed that their allotted break time had passed, he reached out his hand for Lauren's.

They were to meet in Tony's office this time. They turned right in the lobby and moved past the group therapy rooms spread along the main corridor before following arrows off to the 'private offices—by appointment only' area. Tony's door was halfway down the hall, a small placard beside it displaying his name and alma mater. Knocking, David waited for word from within before nudging the door open and ushering Lauren inside.

"David, here you are, and this must be Lauren."

The man had taken off his suit jacket, and he stood from his desk to guide them over to a couch and chair that weren't unlike those they'd encountered in Shea's office at the in-take center. Here, though, Lauren didn't bother with preliminaries. Rather than sitting uncomfortably as she had before, she slipped off her ballet flats and curled her legs beneath her on one end of the couch.

"I'm too short to be comfortable unless I sit like this," she explained belatedly when both men stared at her.

"Of course, of course—I realized how wide the seat of that couch was only after I bought it, but wanted room for my clients to lay down. Anything you need to do to make yourself comfortable," the therapist offered as he took a seat in front of them. "Can I get you anything? Tea, perhaps?"

"No," David said overtop of Lauren, a shade too loudly. "Sorry," he added, "but we're fine. A little skeptical of hot tea in therapists' offices right now, no offense."

It took a moment, but then Lauren saw understanding show in the other man's eyes. "Ah, of course. Yes, I heard that Shea and her assistant made the decision to sedate Lauren at her office and should have guessed. My apologies," he added, reaching out and grasping Lauren's hand lightly in his own. "You won't be drugged in this office without your permission."

Lauren's eyes shot to David's as the therapist's hand lingered on hers for what felt like a moment too long. That had seemed like an odd phrasing, but she was so on edge…

"Lauren, dear, you seem warm. Are you running a fever?" the therapist asked, still leaned forward.

Surprised, Lauren pulled her hand back and met his eyes. "Um, no, I don't think so…I'm just…warm," she answered lamely.

"Her temperature runs hot," David broke in.

The therapist's eyes stayed on her as if to examine her from his seat, but finally he leaned back and met David's gaze. "Perhaps a visit to the clinic after lunch, just in case? It's further down the corridor you followed to reach these offices. Rather than turning off after the group rooms, you just keep going straight and you won't miss it."

David forced himself to smile, and nodded without comment. He knew why Lauren was warm—it was the magic thrumming in her. No doctor would be able to do anything about it, whether she was flushed with heat or not.

Even holding her hand as they'd come to the office, he'd felt it, and understood her reluctance to be in contact with him, skin to skin. They'd lost control the night before—the marks on her wrists, visible around the edges of her sweater, were evidence enough. And though he couldn't say why the magic was getting to them now in a way that it hadn't before, that was a conversation for later. For now, they just had to be aware of it, and not let anyone else get a glimpse of what was truly going on between them.

"Alright, then," Tony said, his eyes sweeping back and forth. "I've seen Shea's notes and met David this morning, but this is where we start talking about goals. David, why don't you tell me what your goals are for this relationship?"

And so the session went. It wasn't anything they hadn't prepared for, and the answers came just as easily as the questions; they passed through much of the material they'd created as backstory, and then on through most of what David had told Shea. They'd been in the man's office for near on forty minutes when he finally held up his hand as David began speaking again to answer his last question.

"David, I appreciate your willingness to participate, but I need to hear from Lauren also, even in this session between the three of us."

David looked sideways to her and saw her eyes had gone wide with nerves. Her hands were clutching each other in her lap, her legs pulled tight beneath her in a way that made her look five years younger than she was. Christ, he wasn't even sure she looked twenty right now.

"Lauren," Tony prodded her, "I asked about the last argument you had. When was it?"

"I...I guess it depends how you define an argument," Lauren stumbled, her eyes darting to David's. "We disagreed last night. I was ready to go upstairs before David was...but we didn't argue about it."

"He got his way?" Tony asked gently.

Lauren simply nodded, her eyes going to her hands in a way that flared guilt along David's spine.

"And when did you last argue?" he asked quietly. "Verbally?"

Lauren swallowed, silent. They'd planned for this question, and it had been easy, because their last argument at that point had been at the ranch house, over coming here. Granted, the argument had been related to safety rather than their relationship, but David guessed that half the couples here had at some point argued about whether or not to come to the retreat. But that wasn't the argument Lauren had to talk about now. They'd changed the answer to Toscano's question when they'd been at the hotel, and she couldn't pretend that hadn't happened.

"The night before last, at the hotel. David had…embarrassed me at the restaurant we went to, and I was upset. He said he…" Lauren broke off, apparently trying to figure out what she could say. "He said he'd wanted to demonstrate authority, that I needed to respect that…what he was doing. I told him he'd gone too far. I was upset."

"And what was he doing? To exert authority?" the therapist pressed, holding up a hand in a halting gesture when David went to answer.

Lauren swallowed, hard enough that David could see the struggle running through her.

"He ordered for me, and that was fine. He knows what I like to eat and drink," she explained. "But then…he took his shoe off, and…I was wearing a skirt, and he kept bothering me, reaching under it with his foot—there…" she said more quietly, discomfort radiating from her. "And, I mean, we were in a restaurant booth. I think others noticed and…I was embarrassed. When his voice got loud a few times, it was too much for me."

David let himself focus his gaze out the window, ignoring the truth of what he'd just heard. He couldn't believe she'd said so much, but he also couldn't fault her for it. He'd been playing a role. He knew that. But he also knew that he hadn't been playing any role the night before, and he'd still hurt her. How many excuses was he going to give himself?

"And how did the argument end? Did he apologize?"

"I… I think so? We fought at the hotel. I got a bath and he went down to the bar. I wanted to be asleep when he came back, but I wasn't. We argued then."

"Were you still angry?" Tony pressed.

Lauren nodded, visibly nervous.

Once again, David forced himself to look away. As she'd predicted, this all sounded worse than it was. But, at the same time, in view of what he and Josh had discussed…he could see how the therapist in front of them might read this. Toscano would view all of this as evidence of her being afraid of him, afraid of some sort of punishment for telling the truth. And that was what scared him. They couldn't explain that Lauren was afraid to lie, afraid of them, without giving away their cover, but what would happen then? And if the therapists kept reading this as being abusive, and him and Josh were right…well, if that was the case, then the only thing keeping them from being just as trapped as anyone else was that cell phone upstairs, and the assumption that they wouldn't be forcibly separated.

"But did you have sex anyway?" Toscano asked next, and David watched Lauren's eyes jerk up to his, surprised.

"I see by the look on your face that you did," the man said gently, and Lauren nodded helplessly, her lips pressed tight together. "I don't know, of course, but I would hazard to guess that the argument fizzed out without resolution or sincere apology, and David wished to reinforce his dominance, so that, to him, sex was the only thing that made sense."

David's gut clenched, guilt rising up and threatening to explode as he tried to remember whether or not he'd apologized, and what exactly had been going through his mind. How much of it had been desire, and the case, and how much of it had been him wanting to possess her and satisfy his own wants above hers, or even the needs of the case?

Lauren glanced to him, and he knew she was looking for reaction, but he avoided her gaze and looked out the window again. He was sick to his stomach over it, but he couldn't disagree with anything that was being said. And, if he was being honest, he wanted to know what she'd say.

"David?" the man asked.

"I'm not sure what I was thinking," he answered.

Lauren looked back to the therapist, and David followed her gaze when the silence hung a moment too long. Lauren had gone deathly still beside him, but Toscano's face suggested the reason. His eyes looked almost…amused? It didn't seem like that could be right, but he could swear there was a lightness there that hadn't been present a moment before.

"Doctor," she interrupted, drawing Toscano to look back at her. He did, and David heard her emit an unintended gasp. He reached sideways and gripped her hand, hoping it would remind her to stay calm, to stay present and aware, and then Toscano's eyes came back to his, as if sensing the intention. There was amusement there—and cruelty.

His breath stopped in his throat. *We shouldn't have come here.*

Then Toscano looked back to Lauren, seemingly unaware of what he'd shown them. "Lauren?" he asked simply.

"I…I want you to know that we want this to work," she stuttered.

"Yes, and we wouldn't have brought you here otherwise," the man said. The line of cruelty in his eyes had vanished now, replaced by the veneer of caring he'd been giving off earlier.

If he hadn't known better, David might have thought he'd imagined it. But he hadn't, and he felt sure Lauren had seen it, too. Her hand was trembling in his, and he knew she was struggling to keep it together now.

"I haven't been an ideal husband to her," David offered, leaning forward suddenly, "and I'm not gonna say I have been. But we're here to fix stuff moving forward, so it'd be good if we could get off the fucking past."

Tony's gaze moved back to David's, narrowing on him, but then he stood up as if in dismissal. "Yes, well, that's the goal. I'll see you both separately tomorrow, and I think we'll make headway then now that everything is laid on the table. The three of us will meet again together the day after tomorrow, Monday, same place and same time, and re-evaluate your progress at that point to see whether or not the weekend was enough. For now, you two should go get some lunch, and then either rest or visit the clinic," he added, his eyes coming back to Lauren's. "Carve out some time to talk about this morning's sessions together also, and we'll reconvene to talk about outcomes."

David didn't bother to comment. It was all he could do to remain outwardly calm as Lauren pushed her feet back into her discarded shoes. They moved toward the door with David ushering her out with his hand on her back— wanting the contact, if for no other reason than to remind her that he was there behind her, pushing her out of the office of whatever they'd stumbled into.

Chapter 14

Back in her room, Lauren slid into the swimsuit she'd brought along. Swimming at the house, she'd worn tankinis that showed her midriff, but had decided to bring something more conservative when David had told her that this place advertised a pool. Or, at least, she'd thought of it as being more conservative. Now, she wasn't so sure.

The suit, which she'd let Claudia order for her when they'd been shopping more for the other woman, had a sort of old-style, pin-up vibe to it. It was a one-piece with fabric that came just low enough to look like tiny shorts, and sported extra fabric in the front to give the impression of it ending in a mini-skirt. The V-neck with a sweetheart neckline elevated her breasts and bared her back completely. As a red suit with black trim, it had looked cute and playful in the pictures…worn on her, though, in this context, the way it accented her hourglass figure seemed more risqué than she'd intended.

And, to make matters worse, there were the marks that

showed up far too clearly on her pale skin. What had she been thinking when she'd agreed to go swimming? Her only comfort was the fact that Dora had similar marks, as did some other women. The fact that the marks had already been seen earlier in the day, around the edges of her sweater, didn't offer much solace. With the bathing suit on, they stood out in stark relief to the rest of her skin, and she couldn't help wanting to kick herself for not thinking about the fact that going to the pool would put her in this position. She hadn't been thinking about anything other than connecting with Adrienne and Christopher, spending more time with them, and now here she was having set herself up to be humiliated.

Still, it was all she had, and the bruises wouldn't even make her stand out all that much from the others. Seeing herself in the mirror, she could only blame herself for not trying the suit on ahead of time or thinking about what these bruises would look like with nothing to cover them.

With little choice, she pulled out a short black sundress she'd brought as a cover-up and slipped into it before heading out the door.

Pool-side, she found David already sitting in a lounge chair beside Phil, both of them in boat shorts. Beyond them, she could see Christopher in the large pool with Adrienne and her idiot of a husband, as well as a few other couples.

Perching on the chair beside David, Lauren leaned in and pecked him on the cheek before she sat down. If she could help it, she dared not do any more than that. She'd wanted to explain, between the therapist's office and lunch, that the chemistry between them was building up magic that didn't have any outlet from her body, practically driving her crazy, but had finally decided it would just have to wait for that night. If she couldn't use magic, which she couldn't, it wasn't as if there was anything to be done about it anyway. They just had to get out of here as soon as they could.

David's hand caught her forearm and held her lightly as he kept talking to Phil, their eyes on the pool. Figuring the water was her best chance of cutting contact, she pried loose his fingers and stood up to lose the sundress. Before it was even fully over her head, though, whistles rang out, and she knew she'd made the wrong choice in wearing the suit.

The dress fell to the floor and David's hands landed on each side of her waist, holding her still in front of him. Even Phil's gaze looked appreciative, but David's was…hungry.

"I want to go swimming," she told him.

"You look gorgeous, baby," he told her, and in another moment he'd pulled her in closer, so that she stood between his thighs looking down at him, her hands having come to rest on his shoulders. He still wore a t-shirt, and Lauren imagined it wouldn't come off since that would reveal his scars and prompt all sorts of questions, but standing this close to him…

"David, I want to go swimming," she whispered as he tightened his arms around her waist, looking up at her and holding her with both his legs and his arms now.

"And I want to look at you."

She closed her eyes as his lips met her chin, and then her lips, and then moved to her ear. Even the air was electric between them, and she could feel her body warming to him all over again, her breath catching in her throat.

Christopher called out from the pool, and she barely recognized his voice or understood him, she was so far gone into David's touch.

"David, dude! You want to go up to your room or let the lady swim?" he called out.

Suddenly, David leaned back away from her, releasing her so abruptly that she nearly stumbled from the sudden loss of pressure against her skin. His eyes were on hers as she caught her breath, knowing and hot. He could feel the energy, she realized.

"You look gorgeous," he repeated.

Blushing, Lauren whirled and hurried to the pool. The water was blessedly cool, and Adrienne and Christopher met her at the base of the stairs.

"You do look really good—I don't particularly blame him," Adrienne offered, grinning.

Lauren swallowed down her nerves and returned the compliment. The other woman was in a light blue bikini that showed more skin than Lauren would have been comfortable showing, and she looked amazing.

"Phil's already got David drinking, so you can blame his antics on him if you want," Christopher told her with an easy grin when David let loose another piercing cat-call of a whistle, hitting home the fact that he'd fallen back into character.

Lauren forced herself to ignore it, and she gave Christopher a smile as she leaned back against the side of the pool beside him. Still, she'd seen his eyes glance off of her bruises, and Adrienne's had also. She wished it were Dora here in this little circle, who had some bruises of her own. Christopher had a dark hickey on his throat, but it didn't come close to measuring up to the bruises Lauren's skin exhibited.

She could hear David from where she was, talking too loudly about her body and the way she'd run away from his attentions, so much so that she could feel herself blushing. Phil began joking back with him, his voice just as loud, and Christopher shrugged it off helplessly in a way that Lauren realized meant he was used to it. Adrienne dunked her hair in the water and then laid back in the water to half float and half tread water in front of them.

"Be glad Raul's not with them—he's worse than the two of them put together, the way he gets with a drink in his hand," she commented, her eyes going unfocused as if to think about it.

Lauren dunked her head beneath the water, letting the coolness of it chill her skin and her blood as much as it could, and reminded herself of what they were doing there. "I saw the bar when I came out here," she told Christopher, who'd turned to give his own partner a disgusted look. "David would have found it if Phil hadn't guided him there."

Adrienne rolled her eyes toward her own husband and the couples at the other end of the pool, all of whom were standing around with drinks in their hands. There was a deep section between their small group and the other, but both main ends of the pool were only four feet, built for conversation more than exercise. "Nature of the place," she commented. "We'll be drinking, too, soon enough. They'll be easier to put up with then," she commented wryly.

"Naturally," Christopher offered, glancing over to his own husband, sitting high and dry with David. "It's why we're here, right? Trying to get things worked out with a drink in each hand and a smile on our faces." But he frowned at the thought, lines creasing his face in a way that made him look closer to the age Lauren knew him to be.

Adrienne flipped to her feet, meeting Lauren's eyes. "You love him, right? No matter what he does?"

Christopher caught Lauren's eyes, breaking in before she could answer. "It's okay, Lauren, you don't have to be ashamed of what you guys do in the bedroom or what the relationship looks like. None of us have anything near perfect relationships, but we're still in love. Mostly," he added, side-eying Adrienne, who only shrugged and looked away. Christopher turned his gaze back to Lauren's. "You love your guy just the same as most of us love our jerks. It is what it is. You don't have to be embarrassed. Not here," he added, his eyes jumping to Lauren's wrists as if to reinforce what he'd just said.

Lauren nodded, swallowing down the embarrassment and the condemnations she would have liked to offer over Raul and Phil. The two people in front of her were good people who she genuinely liked. David was playing a role, and it embarrassed the hell out of her, as did the marks on her wrists right now, but she was all the more upset that this behavior was considered normal by the two people in front of her.

Christopher swished water at the two of them. "Cheer the fuck up, girls. We're all in the same boat, sink or swim, and there's worse places to be. Lauren, seeing you in your suit reminds me—I've been meaning to ask about that tattoo. It's something else," he commented.

Lauren turned her own eyes down along the line of her arm, and the metallic tattoo that had already saved her and David once. It was a welcome distraction. Gleaming with water, it shone in the light, and she thought you could almost see the metallic shadings. The lacing of the vine highlighted her toned upper arm, and then curled around her lower arm to wrap around her wrist. It didn't exactly match the shy graduate student persona that she'd been selling at the retreat.

"I got it on a, sort of…uh, whim. I never wanted one before, but the idea of this one made sense."

"It really is gorgeous," Adrienne offered, actually reaching out and tracing her nail down along the vine.

"I thought about it, but Phil's not a fan. I gotta sell him on it. I've seen him eyeing yours—it might be a step in the right direction if I can come up with an idea he likes. Could I get the name of the artist from you?"

Turning her arm in the light, Lauren looked as far back to her shoulder as she could, and saw David and Phil watching her from their chairs. Blushing suddenly, she turned back to Christopher, putting her back to the men outside the water. "I don't know it off-hand, but I could email it to you after we leave. Or David might remember—somebody he works with…connected us to the place. I do love the way it came out," she added, hoping they wouldn't have noticed her stumbling, or ask for more detail about how it had come about.

"I'll take you up on that, too," Adrienne commented. "You know, Chris—and you also, Lauren—I'd love for us to stay in touch once we leave…Lauren, we just met, but relaxing around you guys has meant a lot to me. I don't have many friends outside of Raul's circle."

Christopher's eyes darted up above Lauren to Phil as he agreed. "Staying in touch would be good. Once we leave. Lauren?"

Her heart felt like it was up in her throat, but she nodded. Her circle of friends and acquaintances had shrunk drastically over the past few months, but even so, she'd rarely had close friends. Despite the fact that these two in front of her didn't know who she truly was, or the truth of her and David's relationship, they already felt like friends.

Breaking the awkwardness of the moment, Christopher splashed water up over his shoulders and onto his face. "So, Lauren," he said a moment later, "this was your and David's first morning—the first real day, I guess. How'd it go?"

The question brought her back to the moment, and to the emotion of the morning. "It was… stressful. I thought this would be a good idea, but I'm no longer so sure, to tell you the truth. David and I are okay when we're by ourselves, but when Tony and Shea get involved…" Stuck for words, Lauren shrugged. There was only so much she could say, in any case.

"You'll feel better in a few days," Adrienne promised, stretching out to float on the water's surface again. "It sort of ebbs and flows around here."

"Emotions, sex, everything," Christopher agreed. "Something about the vibes. See how you feel Monday and judge by that, after you've had a few days of therapy. Things change overnight around here."

"Seems like it," Lauren admitted, thinking about how different Christopher himself seemed from the man she'd met the day before. Adrienne didn't seem different, but he seemed more open—more alive, almost.

"But if you can leave then, don't hesitate, babe. We'll stay in touch," Adrienne said.

Something in her voice was rough, like there was meaning there Lauren couldn't reach, but she saw Christopher reacting to it—dunking his head underwater as if in denial of something. "It sounds like most people stay more than the weekend," she said quietly, feeling like there was subtext to all this that she was missing.

"That they do," Christopher said, as if trying to close the subject. "Adrienne, don't you think it's a little early to be chatting about going or leaving?"

The other woman shook her head, frowning, and Lauren wished David were there to try to understand whatever it was she was missing. Unable to let it go, she pressed, "And you don't miss…life outside?"

The man shrugged, seeming to think about it, and then splashed water up over his shoulders and onto his face again. Lauren followed suit, calming the heat from the sun and giving him time to answer. He did seem different from the day before—he'd said more in the last few minutes than the whole afternoon yesterday, and he was certainly acting less dependent on his partner. She couldn't make sense of it, but to think that he must have been having a bad day the day before.

"I mean, the food situation is less than ideal, I admit—it sucks not just picking what we want to cook or order every night, relying on the kitchen—but beyond that? I sure as hell don't miss getting yelled at every day and not knowing what to do without just calling it quits on Phil. And it's not like I'm close to my family. Some friends, I miss, yeah, but I'll see 'em when I see 'em. And, in here, you two gals aren't bad company," he joked, suddenly reaching out and yanking Adrienne's ankle so that she fell out of her float, spluttering and splashing water back at him.

Lauren found herself laughing at the spectacle, and then Adrienne was splashing her and the three of them were pushing water at each other like kids, shrieking with the fun of it.

A giant splash to her side announced the presence of David and Phil, and suddenly she felt David's arms swooping around her, plucking her from the pool and tossing her into the deeper water nearby. She came up spluttering, treading water, but grinned back at David from where she rose up for air. Catching her breath as she watched Adrienne and Christopher begin ganging up on Phil, she sank back beneath the water a few seconds later and made a darting swim for David's knees—the coolness of the water was balancing out the heat in her blood, and two could play at the game he'd started.

She landed just above his knees and knocked him sideways before shooting to the surface for some air. In moments, he'd come up beside her and wrapped her up against his chest, pressing her back to the side of the pool and coming in for a hard kiss. Before her shrieking laughter got cut off, she had a moment to recognize that his face was practically glowing with the fun of the moment, and it was easy to relax into his grip and forget, at least for a little while, what they were really playing at.

* * *

"David, Lauren, I was thinking the three of us could have dinner together," Shea called from behind them.

The two of them had been heading toward the elevator after a few hours in the sun, and David had been feeling relaxed for the first time since Lauren had left his room that morning, but the sound of the therapist's voice brought him back to the wrongness of the moment. The naked fun of the afternoon disappeared as he turned back to face the woman, automatically reaching out to Lauren and putting himself slightly in front of her. Tony, he wasn't sure about yet, but this woman…whatever was going on, she was at the forefront of it.

"I thought we were meeting after dinner for another couple's session with Tony," he commented. Beside him, he felt Lauren tugging her sundress down, fidgeting in the cold of the hallway.

"Well, we all have to eat, and you've been connecting so well with the other couples…" Shea offered, stepping in closer. Her eyes moved over the two of them, and David wondered if any of his scars were visible through his wet t-shirt. Nobody had commented on anything at the pool, but it occurred to him now that he should have worn a darker shirt. "I thought," the woman continued, "you'd prefer meeting over a long dinner so that you could spend more time with the other couples afterward, since tomorrow will be busier. I'm glad you took advantage of the pool today," she added.

For the life of him, he couldn't have given a single

reason why she seemed threatening—her voice was all warmth and welcome. But she nearly reminded him of Nell Everett.

"That would be fine," Lauren interjected, taking a step up to stand beside him. Her hand tightened on his. "Should we meet you in the cafeteria?"

"Oh, just come to my office and I'll have food brought around. It's just down from Tony's, on the right. Say, six o'clock? That should give you time for showers and some time to yourselves."

David forced a smile and nodded, knowing he ought to be glad for the extra time to examine the woman. He'd just have preferred it be without Lauren by his side.

With the night's date confirmed, David pulled Lauren on into the elevator and hesitated over the buttons. "You want to shower grab clothes from your room, then come upstairs?" he asked quietly.

Lauren nodded and leaned into him, her head pressing against his bicep. She was trembling.

The elevator dinged to signal the second floor and David reached out to hold the 'Door Open' button down. Lauren hadn't moved from beside him. "Why don't you just grab clothes and come back—we'll shower upstairs and I'll hold the elevator for you. I'll wait right here."

Lauren nodded against him, but it took her a few more seconds to move. "You'll wait? You don't mind?" she asked from the door.

He shook his head. "No, just go."

When she walked away, he glanced out into the hallway, his hand still on the button to keep the doors ajar. Down the hall, in the direction Lauren had walked, he could see a desk set into a little alcove, and glimpse sharply manicured nails above it shuffling through papers. Whoever sat there exchanged some words with Lauren as she passed. That had to be the woman stationed on the floor to keep men away. Tempted as David was to follow Lauren, he'd been told clearly enough that catching her eye or being seen on this floor, outside the elevator, would only bring trouble. It wasn't worth it.

Lauren was back in less than a minute, a bag clutched to her side.

When David shut the door to his suite and locked it, Lauren landed in his arms a moment later, radiating with warmth and energy as her arms wrapped around his middle and her face pressed into his wet t-shirt.

"You okay, kid?"

Still silent, she nodded. A few seconds passed, and he just held her, waiting. Finally, she near-whispered, "It was just such a good afternoon…it was fun, right? And then, Shea…" she trailed off, and David thought she might actually be close to tears. Emotions had been running through the top of her blood all day, he knew, as if she'd been on the razor's edge of one extreme emotion or another, whether joy or despair. Phil had told him that Christopher was the same around here, but he hadn't had enough time to think about what it meant. He needed to find a way to guarantee they weren't still being drugged, but couldn't imagine how that could be the case since they were all eating and drinking together. Was something about their therapy group actually working up emotion on purpose? His own group session had been flat enough, but…maybe?

"Listen, why don't you go get a shower running. I'm gonna check in with Josh on the burner."

It took a moment for her to disengage, but then she nodded and glanced up to meet his eyes. "Don't go anywhere, okay? I want us to talk before we go to dinner."

"Promise."

With that, she headed off toward the bathroom, but he

didn't miss the fact that she left the door slightly ajar behind her. He'd join her soon.

Josh picked up on the second ring. "How goes it?" his partner asked.

"Yeah, I don't know. We're okay." David stopped there, trying to figure out what more he could say. What did he know, really? Besides what he was feeling about this place? "Lauren's off," he said after another moment. "She's okay, but something's off. If she's no different by Monday, or gets worse, I'm pulling the plug and we're getting out."

"What's going on?"

The shower was on now, and David guessed she wouldn't hear anything over the water, but he moved to the far side of the room anyway and turned to the wall, his voice projecting away from the bathroom as he answered. "I don't know. I wish I did. It's almost like she's slightly drunk—her emotions are all over the place, is the only way I know to describe it. Like everything's elevated somehow. From what Phil Rollyson told me, his husband Chris is the same."

"And they're okay, too, but for that? You guys have talked to them?"

"Hung out with them and some others most of the afternoon, yeah," David answered, turning back to lean on the wall so that he could keep an eye on the bathroom door.

"Any way they're being drugged?" Josh asked after another moment.

"Not that I can figure out," he answered, releasing a sigh. "We ate from a buffet last night, and everything we've drunk today has been out of community water coolers or coffee pots. Breakfast and lunch served cafeteria-style right in front of us—they'd have to drug all of us or none of us, going that route. And we had some drinks at the bar this afternoon, but Lauren just had one, and I ordered it for her along with one for me—no way the bartender could have known whose drink was whose."

"And Lauren hasn't had anything you haven't?" Josh pressed.

"I mean, yeah, but nothing that wasn't available to everyone. They have water coolers and coffee and snacks set up all over the place for anyone to grab. The therapists take stuff from the same supplies. And I'm fine, far as I can tell."

"Yeah…you sound fine, for what it's worth. She's feeling okay, though? And you still think something's off about the place as a whole?"

"On both counts, yeah. Any news on your end? New leads or whatever else?"

David could almost hear his partner grimacing over the phone, just from the sigh that came across the line. "Nah, not really. Another couple got reported, but that's it. A Raul and Adrienne Rivers."

David smiled tightly. "Well, the good news is that they're fine. Lauren's actually made friends with Adrienne Rivers and Christopher Rollyson more than anyone else—we were with them all afternoon."

"That's something, I guess. Listen, you guys just be safe. I'll keep Adrias in the loop and let him know you're thinking about calling it on Monday, if not before. Check in tonight?"

"Yeah," David agreed. "I'll just send a text that we're good if there's no news, and call tomorrow."

"Good enough. Stay safe, brother," Josh commented, and then he disconnected.

David turned off the phone and then tucked it back into the pocket of his luggage where he'd been keeping it.

In the bathroom, he could see Lauren's form through the shower's glass door. She had her hands up, running soap or conditioner through her hair. He dropped his own soaked clothes on the tiling beside hers and parted the door so that he could slip into the spacious shower behind her. Her eyes were closed, soap running down her forehead, but she must've heard him—she didn't jump when he put his hands on hers and took their place, massaging the shampoo or conditioner she'd been using into her dark hair as she turned and leaned into his grip, her hands finding his chest and resting there.

After another minute, he prodded her into the stream of the rainwater showerhead and worked the water through her hair until it ran clear.

"Was that the soap or conditioner?" he asked.

"Conditioner," she answered, finally opening her eyes and looking up at him. With both of them partially under the spray, but its focus on Lauren, David worked soap into his hands and began rubbing it along Lauren's skin— over her shoulders, down her arms, and then into her breasts and stomach. She closed her eyes and rested her hands on his shoulders, practically purring beneath his touch as he went lower, going down to his knees so that he could reach the rest of her. When he prodded her to turn around, she did, and he rubbed his hands up along her back, into her muscles. He reached around her and let his fingers explore around her center, slipping along her wet folds that were already slick with her juices, but he didn't go beyond the point where she murmured with only the beginnings of pleasure—far as he was concerned, shower sex was more of a slippery pain than it was worth, good as her skin felt beneath his.

"You, it's your turn," Lauren murmured, and he didn't argue. He stayed on his knees as Lauren slipped around him, moving easily in the oversized shower so that he could get the full benefit of the spray as she massaged shampoo into his hair and then ran soap over his shoulders, his back, and his chest. He stood when she moved lower, letting his hands wander through her hair and over her slick shoulders as she ran soap along his belly and then lower, going to his legs and then coming back upward to the part of him that was now standing straight, pointing at her.

He was about to suggest they turn off the water and head to the bedroom when Lauren's tongue darted from her lips and she leaned forward, one of her hands finding his member as her other wrapped around his thigh and she leaned in. The touch of her tongue was warm, and her lips followed. He shot one of his hands up to the hold attached to the soap dish at chest height and held on, his other hand finding its way to Lauren's shoulder, resting there as he told himself not to push her. But, fuck, this felt good.

Lauren's tongue ran up along the vein at the underside of his dick and one of her hands found his balls, cupping them as her lips and tongue kept exploring. He let his hips press forward against her grip as her lips circled his head, and the thought that she had to be tasting his pre-cum now made him harder. She sucked him into the hot warmth of her mouth, until he was near halfway in and he could feel her struggling to fight a gag reflex. The struggle he sensed in her was enough to remind him that she hadn't ever done this before, little experience as she'd had, and the thought made his dick jerk in her mouth, wanting more as desire spiked in his blood.

"You've never done this," he grunted, trying to hold himself back from pushing her. "Go slow."

She nodded slightly, the head of his cock still in her mouth, and he groaned aloud at the sensation of her mumbling an answer around him. Every instinct in him wanted to grab the back of her head and press forward, but he knew he couldn't. Instead, he held himself back and let her explore him, making him harder as her tongue

230

licked along his shaft and her lips pressed up and down.

When her hand became firmer on his shaft and he realized they were moving in rhythm, he gulped and pressed his hand into her shoulder. The water was running cold over his back now, and while he wanted to cum into her mouth some time, this wasn't the time or the place. She fought him for a moment, her lips still wrapped around him, and then leaned back with a gasp, her eyes coming up to his as she licked her lips. "Okay?" she asked.

"Jesus, Lauren." His dick was throbbing, it was so hard, and she was still licking her lips, naked and on her knees before him.

With one hand, he reached back and found the lever to cut off the water, and then he was pulling her up against him, pressing his lips against hers. Her whole body was slick against his, her lips salty with the taste of him and slick from the shower. Breaking the kiss, he stepped from the shower and pulled her behind him, grinning at the giggle he heard slipping from her throat as he yanked her out of the bathroom.

He'd seen extra blankets in the closet and he went for those now, knowing they'd regret it later if they soaked the bed. With her watching him, he grabbed down the velvety blankets set aside for cooler nights and formed a make-shift pallet. When he was done and looked up at her, he didn't have to say anything. She was in front of him in another moment, down on her knees. He didn't argue when she took him back into her mouth, and his hands found the nape of her neck as his hips pressed into her. He felt her gag and pulled back, looking down at her. Her lips were in an O, spread around the head of his cock, her eyes wide and looking up at him, watering, but he could see pleasure there, too.

Swallowing down his desire to press for more, faster,

he let her set her own rhythm and relaxed into it, her hands exploring his balls and the base of his rod as her lips and tongue focused on what they could reach. The soft warmth of her mouth and the press of her tongue were constant, making him want more with each moment so that it was all he could do to let her set a pace she could handle. Each time he glanced down at her, her eyes were wide, raised and focused on the expression on his face, and finally he couldn't take it anymore.

He pulled back from her, treasuring the slight moan that slipped from her lips when his dick left her, and then he pressed her back into the floor from where she'd been kneeling. Her legs were still bent at the knees, and he pressed her thighs further apart as his lips landed at her core. She was drenched with desire, and he let his lips begin exploring her, pulling in her juices as she mewed above him, her hands kneading his shoulders as her core pulsed beneath him. When his thumb found her clit, her body bucked beneath him and she called out hoarsely. He could feel how swollen she was, her body still recovering from the night before, but she'd started this, and he wanted to finish it.

He pulled back while he could still feel the orgasm thrumming through the heat of her blood, reacting to his every touch, and moved up above her without a word spoken between them. Her eyes opened wide again when he pressed into her in one slow lunge, filling her.

She gasped beneath him, her pussy as hot and tight as it had ever been, and he froze above her while she got used to him, her body pulsing and stretching, allowing him to fill her once again as the orgasm that had been subsiding began building again and her nails clenched into his forearms beside her, where his hands were at her side, holding him up above her.

"You ready?" he breathed out, feeling his dick

throbbing within her. It was hard and demanding, and didn't want to wait any longer.

She was panting beneath him, but nodded, and he leaned down to run his lips along her throat as he pressed into her balls-deep, bottoming out as she gasped.

In another moment, she'd lifted one leg to wrap around his thigh, and her center pressed up into him, her eyes turning to find his. "Ready. More," she gasped out, and with that he let himself begin moving, his dick building toward the rhythm it had been wanting, with all of the hot pressure of her channel there to take everything he'd been aching to give her all afternoon, since seeing her in that suit and feeling her body beneath his fingers. The desire had been constant, anxious, and her lips sucking at his dick had only heightened the demand.

He let his lips find her neck and his teeth nipped her skin as he pulled nearly all the way out of her, until only his dick was encased in her tight cunt, and then he pressed hard, all the way in so that she shuddered beneath him, another orgasm ripping its way through her as she screamed out his name and he pressed in deep, spasming inside of her with his own release. He held himself against her, his dick throbbing as she milked him for the last of his cum.

"I needed that," Lauren murmured, feeling the magic running calmer in her blood than it had since mid-morning.

David choked on a laugh beside her, still laying naked on the makeshift pallet at her side. "Shit, *you* needed that? After seeing you wearing that suit, I'd say the need was all mine."

Lauren shifted against him, letting her body curl deeper into his. She could feel his dick, semi-hard against the back of her thigh, his chest warm and muscled against her back. She let her hand wrap around his bicep and squeeze, feeling the heat and strength of his body beneath her grip.

"I didn't have time to tell you earlier, once I realized it. I didn't know how to tell you, I guess," she murmured, more to herself than him. His hand wrapped around her shoulder, and his lips touched the back of her head and lingered there.

"Tell me what?"

Lauren relaxed into him and tried to think of what to say. She didn't want to either exaggerate or downplay what her body was experiencing, but she also didn't want him to call this mission off. Every instinct she had told her that the people in this retreat were in trouble, somehow, even if they didn't know it. It had been bad enough knowing they might be in danger when they'd been strangers. Knowing what she did now, she couldn't help feeling responsible to Christopher and Adrienne, and even to their partners and the other people she'd met.

"The magic in my blood. I need to talk to you about it."

David tensed against her, but he didn't pull away. One of his legs instead wrapped over her ankles, entwining his body around hers. "I'm listening."

"Yeah, I know," Lauren breathed out. A shiver of heat ran through her along the line of her body touching his, and she felt his dick twitch against her in response. She swallowed down a moan, blocking out the sensation— they had to have this conversation before she got lost in him again.

"The magic's been building in my blood, from being so close to you so constantly; I know you've felt it, too— it's why my skin feels fevered, because the only outlet is sex, when we're together like this…that seems to calm it. But then, I think it's also making it worse. Like, soon after we stop, it wants more. Like…like it's got its own mind and needs the distraction of you, or else it's running in my blood, looking for an outlet, waiting for me to use it. Which, of course, I can't. I know that doesn't make sense, David—I've been trying to figure out how to describe it, but this is totally new. I'm not sure I know what I'm dealing with, and it's not like I have anyone to call to ask," she added more quietly.

David remained silent for a minute behind her. Then, she felt him pull back a little, giving her more space, though his arm and leg stayed wrapped loosely around her. He leaned away so that she fell onto her back and could meet his eyes as he lay sideways, propped up on one elbow. "I know it got to me last night, feeling it in you. I could tell it was stronger, but there wasn't time to talk about it today, and you weren't up to it last night, which is my fault. I lost control, Lauren," he added, his eyes on hers. "I knew I hurt you, but I didn't know the magic felt so different for you…that it was so present. Is it hurting you?"

"No… no, not really," she said, maybe too quickly, but she could see the concern in his eyes, and feel that he was only a step away from calling everything off, and she couldn't let him do that. "It's hot… it makes it hard to concentrate sometimes," she explained, "and sometimes I do feel almost like I have a fever. It's uncomfortable— yeah, like a fever, that's the best I can describe it. But it doesn't hurt. It's *not* hurting me," she said, her voice steadier. "But it's like…it's heightening every emotion, destroying my focus completely. I'm afraid I'm going to fall into accidentally taking advantage of it, too, it's so present. I think I did earlier, maybe, reading Tony's expression," she admitted. "And at the pool, it was all I could do not to go over to the flowers and pet them."

"*Pet* them?"

Lauren shrugged, glancing away from his gaze for the

first time and knowing she was probably blushing now. "It's been my nature for so long, you know? Working with plants and herbs. Feeling their natures, feeding their health…it's almost automatic. I know how strange it sounds."

David sighed above her, and when she looked back at him, she could see the new tightness in his face. "You're saying that our being together at the house was okay because you had an outlet for the magic—you were using it—and now that you're trying to keep from using it at all, it's building up in your blood."

"And because we're spending so much time together," Lauren acknowledged, relieved he'd understood without her having to say more. "I think it must have been okay in the warehouse because I was so tired, or the wards in that room could have affected it, for all I know. And maybe I was using it without realizing it, in trying to fight against…" she trailed off, wishing she hadn't brought it up, but it wasn't as if David had forgotten those days.

"The energy," David finished for her, his eyes distant.

Lauren breathed out, a catch in her throat as she nodded and then leaned her head into his arm. "And then at the house, I wasn't using much…but I was using it. Stocking up the poultices for you guys and Barry, and getting together those you passed out to other teams. And then there were the gardens, and we weren't together that much until near when we left, so I barely felt any magic in my blood at all—honestly, I was starting to think it was gone again, but for when I was with you. But now…I don't know what to do. I think being with you builds the magic, but the only time it really settles, or has any outlet, is when we're in bed together."

"Having sex?"

"Yeah." Even now, she could feel her magic rumbling in her blood, drawing attention to the pleasant ache at her core from where David had been filling her not a half hour ago. His dick was semi-hard still and again against her thigh, and the thought of it filled her throat with emotion.

"I think," she went on, "maybe I feel like you did in the warehouse. Like I've had enough, but I haven't, and there's no answer."

David's hand reached to her chin and he pulled her face toward his until their eyes met—his were harder now, though. More agent than lover. "But we're not in the cage now, Lauren. We can leave. You say the word, we're out."

Pulling away, Lauren sat up beside him and hugged her knees, pressing her forehead into her knees and trying to think. This was what she'd been afraid of.

His hand found the base of her spine and began rubbing up and down along her back, drawing a shiver up from her blood so that she had to fight down a moan of pleasure. Instead, she answered, "We can't leave. Not now. We're in and we have to find out what's going on. What's the worst that can happen?" she tried joking. "I'm sore when we leave from wanting so much sex? I feel like I have a fever for a few days? That's nothing compared to people being kidnapped."

David's hand kept moving on her back, but she could feel tension in his fingers. "The worst is that you get forced into using real magic, doing more than just reading an expression for lies or emotion," he answered quietly. "And whether that means Adrias finds out or you catch the notice of Johanna and Nell, either way, it's not good. Worst case I'm worried about isn't sex or a fever, Lauren—it's the witches coming after us while we're here and unprepared."

A few seconds of silence passed before he added, "You feel like you're close to losing control of it?"

Lauren shrugged, but she didn't meet his eyes, and she couldn't answer.

Chapter 15

Samantha Shea guided them over to a card table that had been set up for an intimate meal near the couches in her office. The space wasn't unlike the one they'd seen in the in-take center, outside of having fewer and smaller windows, and David felt Lauren's hand tighten on his as the door closed behind them. He couldn't blame her.

"One of the kitchen staff will bring us a meal shortly, but I thought we'd start with a glass of wine?" she offered, already reaching for a full bottle she'd set near the table. Noting that the wrapping was still over the cork, he nodded, but looked sideways and caught Lauren's eyes as the woman reached for a corkscrew. Knowing Lauren, he felt confident she'd gotten the message—neither of them would be taking a sip until Shea did.

Lauren sat across from Shea and David sat between them at one side of the table, placing himself so that he'd see the door and anyone entering.

"How was your first full day?" Shea asked, filling the

three wine glasses with a deep red blend. Lauren reached up and put her fingers on her glass' stem, and David pressed into her hand beneath the table. She nodded, barely, and he knew she'd wait to drink until Shea sipped hers.

David shrugged at the question and put his own hand around his glass, though he didn't bring it to his lips. "This morning was a lot, meeting everyone in group. Emotions and all that. It went alright. I'm not sure I'm feeling the effects of the money we're spending yet, though. We could have spent an afternoon at a pool with friends if we'd stayed home," he pointed out.

When the therapist took a large swallow of her wine, he felt Lauren relax a breath beside him and he took a fast sip of his own—no odd taste.

"Yes, we do start out rather slowly," Shea admitted. "Part of it is so that the therapists have a bit of time to observe the dynamics—not just in new couples, but in those who've been here and are progressing through therapy. But the two sessions you had this morning weren't a cakewalk; I imagine you already recognize how exhausting those were. A full day, right off the bat after just getting here, would be too much for many couples. Tomorrow will be a fuller day, as will Monday."

Nodding, David glanced to Lauren. They'd agreed not to let her know that Monday might be their personal cut-off day, despite the fact that they weren't expected to leave until Tuesday, at least. "And you always have a private dinner with the new clients?" he asked.

Shea met his eyes, smiling. "Suspicious much?"

He forced a grin, hoping he was playing the sleazy businessman more than a government operative. "Always."

"Well, it depends on the couple," she allowed, leaning back and roving her gaze between the two of them. "In cases where a couple seems to be fitting in with the other couples, making friends and connections and so forth, yes. It allows you time to socialize afterward and doesn't break up the tempo. On the other hand, if a couple comes in and is more stand-offish…if they'd spent all afternoon in their room for instance, and left last night's party early, not really connecting to anyone outside of therapy, then I'd want them to have dinner in the cafeteria with the rest of the couples and hope they took the time to make some connections. In a case like that, I wouldn't expect them to gather with the others for long after dinner, so meeting with them afterward wouldn't be interrupting anything anyway, but would hopefully offer more time for getting to know the other couples during a meal."

"When they couldn't run away, since everyone needs to eat," David finished.

Shea smiled. "Exactly. Some people need more time to open up to others because they're set in their ways, staying to themselves. They need that time in the cafeteria for more structured socializing."

"Makes sense," Lauren murmured from beside him. "But if you always meet with couples…" her eyes came up, meeting his and then moving to Shea's. "That must mean you have a purpose for meeting tonight?" she asked.

"Perceptive, aren't you?" Shea asked, her eyes narrowing slightly.

David felt Lauren's hand tense in his beneath the table, but forced himself not to react. The woman's tone had been condescending, but the woman Lauren was playing wouldn't react to it. She kept quiet, and he realized she must have come to the same conclusion. *Good girl*, he thought to himself, his eyes still on Shea and waiting for her to continue.

"Yes," the therapist said after taking another sip of her wine. "I do have reason to meet with you privately. I want to talk with you some about this morning, what to expect tomorrow, and also what you might think about going forward. I'll spend most of tomorrow at the other estate and Monday will be very busy, but this will give you some time to think about what you're doing and consider options. You'll also," she added, smiling particularly at David, "have a chance to ask other couples questions about their experiences tonight, while you're together, whereas tomorrow night there'll be separate gatherings.

"You'll see the other couples at meals and in group sessions, of course, but tonight will be the final major social gathering, with everyone in the same place, until Tuesday night, when you may or may not be here."

Lauren finally sipped at her wine, and David thought he felt her relaxing a smidgen more beside him. "We're all ears," David answered, glancing to the door as someone came in wheeling a cart.

"Family-style," their waiter explained, setting a large casserole dish on a placemat in the center of the table and then putting out plates, silverware, and a pitcher of water and glasses.

Shea's eyes came up to David's as the woman doled out salad onto each of their plates, portioning it out from a single large bowl. The relief he felt at the style of the meal was short-lived only because of the gaze. He couldn't help thinking that Shea was looking at him as if to say, *"See? I'll be eating the same food as you. You've got nothing to be suspicious of."* The steady gaze was so canny, in fact, that it set a pit of nerves into his stomach. Maybe she was simply a very good therapist who understood that he'd be suspicious. Or maybe she'd somehow figured out that there was more to them than their adopted roles.

Nevertheless, he set the tempo by settling into his meal, helping himself to the salad and then the casserole, which turned out to be sausage and cauliflower—something he'd have said sounded disgusting, but turned out not to be half bad. Beside him, Lauren ate less, but she did eat, and they let Shea do most of the talking.

True to her word, the woman laid out the schedule for the next few days, which was straight-forward enough, and then began telling them why or why not they might decide to stay for a longer period of time. The only surprise came when she covered pricing. David had expected a heavy sales pitch, given the topic, and that she'd ask for at least half as much as they'd already spent if they decided to stay past Tuesday. Instead, she told them the majority of expenses came from observation and turn-over, and that they could remain at the center for another week free of charge, if they were invited to stay come Monday.

"Invited?" Lauren echoed at that point, her fork stilling in front of her mouth.

Shea smiled again, too warmly, as her eyes stayed on Lauren's. "Of course. If we don't feel we can help you, it doesn't make sense for you to stay. Obviously, I feel we can or you wouldn't be here now, but if a couple is clearly a bad fit or a marriage seems not to be destined for recovery, then, in that case, we'll be up-front with you."

"You've told couples that before? To leave?" David interrupted, not hiding the skepticism in his voice. "Seems like a funny way to run a business, chasing off paying clients."

Shea's eyes met his, that smile still plastered on her lips. "That's true, but we're not a business. We're a family, remember?"

David felt Lauren's leg jerk beside his, and knew the tone of Shea's voice had sent a chill through her body, as it had through his. The woman before them had a way of making the most innocuous of phrases sound anything but. Forcing himself to take another bite of his food, he nodded his head in allowance of the center's motto.

The three of them were on their second glass of wine, having finished taking slices from a small cheesecake that had replaced the casserole, when Shea's voice became harder and she broke the silence that had accompanied the serving out of dessert.

"I do have to mention one more serious topic—I'd be remiss not to. *Safety* is a concern."

David looked up from the cheesecake on his plate and saw that the therapist's eyes had become focused on his expression. Beside him, Lauren sat stiff in her seat. She'd said very little over the course of the meal, but he could feel her hand hot on his knee now, gripping him as if to steady herself. Both of his hands were above the tabletop, one on his fork and one on his glass of wine, and he forced himself to remain still. "Safety? As in fire alarms? What are we talking about here?"

Shea smiled, tightly and sipped her wine, but her gaze never left his. "You think I didn't notice the marks on Lauren's wrists—from rope, if I'm not mistaken—or the bruise on her shoulder? I saw that while the two of you were at the pool today."

David's breath froze in his chest, but Shea kept going.

"Lauren, you'll forgive me for bringing it up, I hope, we were having such a lovely dinner… but since I won't be seeing the two of you tomorrow, I want to make sure this is something the two of you are considering. Your safety is a part of this marriage working—that's all there is to it."

"The bruises were an accident," David said quietly. "We saw the rope in the room; thought we'd try it. It's your center that left it for us to use," he pointed out. The words were stale in his mouth, though. Lauren's face had become stricken, going three shades paler than it had been before, and he knew there was nothing he could actually say in his defense.

"And you're a grown man, Mr. Merriweather," Shea said flatly, carving out a small piece of cheesecake with her fork. She took the bite, chewed, and then continued, "If you can't forego temptation, that doesn't speak much for Lauren's safety in the future. You could buy rope or anything else, yourself, should you want to. And," she added, smiling tightly and meeting his eyes, "such toys can be used without causing bruises. It's those that concern me more than how she got them, beyond that they came at your hands."

"It was an accident," Lauren said, but her eyes were on her untouched plate of dessert. Her grip on his knee had gotten tighter, so that he felt her nails against his skin.

"Yes, dear," Shea answered, the condescension heavy in her voice once again, "but that's beside the point, isn't it?"

David pushed his plate away and took another swallow from his glass of wine. His chest was heavy now, and he knew what was coming before he asked, "And your point, in bringing this up? In saying safety has to be considered?"

"It's the same point I was forced to bring up in my office at the in-take center, Mr. Merriweather. If we cannot help you and suggest the same, or if you choose to leave as planned, and I and Tony don't feel that Lauren is safe with you, we'll have to make sure that you leave without her, and get her somewhere where she'll be safe."

The woman's tone had been friendly, even casual, but there was no mistaking the new threat in her words. It was all David could do to keep from pulling Lauren to her feet and dragging her from the room. And yet, he knew that this had been planned. Shea would have prepared for that. Given the casualness with which she'd brought up the topic, and even the marks he'd left on Lauren, and their conversation at the in-take center, he had no doubt that guards somewhere between them and the front door knew exactly what was being discussed right now. If he pulled Lauren to her feet and out of the room, Shea wouldn't stop him.

But someone would.

He had no doubt that he'd never get Lauren out of this place tonight if he left right this moment—he'd end up being forced to separate from her for the night, or else leave her behind entirely and come back with Josh. She'd come to the same conclusion. Her grip was almost painfully tight on his knee now, and she'd wrapped her ankle around his as if to ground him in his seat. Words were sticking in his throat, and he forced himself to pour another glass of water and take a sip.

Beside him, Lauren spoke up. "David knows he has to be more careful of me. He's trying." She sounded as if she wanted to say more, but cut herself off, and David could only nod.

"Yes, dear, I'm sure he is," Shea answered. "But, now that's settled and we're all on the same page, let's enjoy our dessert."

When they finally managed to excuse themselves, David's heart was in his throat. Lauren had gone silent beside him, walking back toward the salon where the night's gathering would already be in full swing.

At the front door, he saw outside to where three guards were gathered on the front patio, standing casually in a circle and smoking. One glanced in at him and nodded, his mouth set in a threatening line.

Two men, David could have handled. But three? Without allowing either of them to get hurt or stuck in the process, and not even knowing whether the men were armed or whether there were others nearby? There was no way to do it safely. And even if he could have, what then? How far off was the closest vehicle? His best bet was to call Josh and demand an extract, but even aside from opening up a legal nightmare, that'd be a dead giveaway for why they'd been here and kill any chance of finding out what was going on.

Rather than continuing forward into the hall leading to the salon, David tugged Lauren's hand sideways toward the grand stairwell and lowered himself to sit on the third step, pulling her in close ahead of him so that she stood between his knees, facing him, gripping his hands.

Her face was ashen, and he found that he couldn't look at her. "I fucked up," he breathed out. "We shouldn't have come here, Lauren. I'm sorry."

Lauren's hands tightened on his until he looked up and met her eyes. They were dark, blue and watery and full of emotion, and he could feel the warmth of her magic beneath her skin, in her legs standing close to his and her hands on his. She was holding it together, but he could see the struggle. "I know," she finally said, "I know. But we're here now, David, and I'm glad we are. We need to help the people who've gotten sucked into this place—because something is wrong here. You and Josh can do it if anyone can. We'll figure out what's going on and we'll get out."

When he didn't answer, her fingers entangled his. "Right?" she pressed.

David pulled her in closer so that she leaned into him, her head still just above his because of his seated position and her incline. She rested her head down, her forehead on the top of his head, and he felt her warm breath on his forehead and the hot magic running just beneath her skin as he released her hands to run his fingers up along the skin of her forearm, tracing the front of her tattoo and letting her closeness calm down the panic in his own body. He could keep it together for her. "Right," he answered.

"And you're not leaving me here," Lauren added. "I won't fucking let you."

The curse surprising him, he choked back a laugh and held onto her forearms, anchoring her against him. "That makes two of us."

Another few seconds passed, and then David forced himself to release her. She stood straight and he met her eyes. "We should go to the party," he said quietly, wishing like hell that he could say anything else.

"Yeah," Lauren answered, her eyes darting sideways to the hall.

She made to move and he caught her hand, pulling her back a step. Her eyes met his, and he watched her freeze in front of him.

"Lauren, I don't think I have it in me to play things like I did last night, but if we're going to be here…"

"We have to stay believable," she whispered.

"How about we just stay away from each other tonight, and you come up to my room later?   We'll be together then. I'll come get you to leave in a few hours, but if you can, you stick with the women tonight. You learn what you can and I'll do the same. That way, I won't have to be the jerk I was last night. That okay with you?"

He saw Lauren swallow down whatever she'd been about to say, and then she nodded. With that, he got up and moved ahead of her, leading her down the hall to the salon.

Chapter 16

Adrienne met her nearly as soon as she came in the door, wrapping her arm around her waist like a sister and pulling her away from David with barely a word said to him, and Lauren didn't argue. David's plan for them to stay separate made sense, much as her blood was all but demanding she stay locked to his side, and Adrienne's was a face she thought she could deal with as she got past the visit in Shea's office, to the extent that it could be called that.

Adrienne tapped Dora's arm as they passed her by, but they kept walking. They walked on by the restroom and lounge where they'd spent most of the previous night, and soon Lauren found herself in a corner of the small cafeteria, sitting on a bench beside Adrienne.

She'd been ready to force a smile and ask how the party was going and what she'd missed at dinner, but a single look at her friend's face told her that Adrienne knew exactly the conversation they'd just had with Shea, and the sympathy there was too much for her. Clenching her eyes shut, Lauren pressed her hands together in front of her on the table and willed herself not to cry. It was like a ball of grief and emotion and pain that could be held in just until one got hugged—but Adrienne's expression had been the proverbial hug, and suddenly Shea's threat to separate them and the condescension in her tone came barreling into Lauren's throat. In moments, she couldn't help the tears streaming down her cheeks, and she couldn't catch her breath for how violently she was sobbing.

Adrienne's arm was still around her, and Lauren leaned sideways into the other woman, shaking her head as if to deny the whole night. Tissues were pressed into her hands, but Adrienne otherwise let her cry against her without a word. Soon, she sensed more than saw Dora sitting down on her other side, smelling the other woman's perfume as another ball of tissues was pressed into her fist. For the first time since she'd met her, the woman wasn't speaking or bubbling out excitement and gossip.

"She got upset about the bruises and threatened to separate you guys? Send him away and keep you here?" Adrienne asked gently once Lauren's tears had slowed.

Pressing the tissues Dora had handed her into her cheeks and eyes, Lauren nodded. "It never occurred to me...I never thought..." Lauren shook her head again, thinking she sounded like a broken record of a stereotype, but it was also all true. "He didn't mean to hurt me," she finished helplessly.

"I could make some tea?" Dora asked. "Or do you want something stronger?"

"Something stronger," Lauren muttered.

The woman headed back toward the salon and the party they could hear going on in the distance, and Lauren pulled her head up from where it had rested on Adrienne's arm. "I feel like I'm going crazy—like everything keeps getting worse, out of control," she let herself say. And it was true. Her blood and her magic were pulling her emotions in every direction, and it felt like all she could do to keep herself in check, to keep control of herself. And then, every time David turned into the man this role called on him to be as an agent, and every time he or Shea spoke harshly to her, it seemed that things got that much worse. Like, every time she thought she had some control, it was yanked from her, the world and the situation made that much worse.

Beside her, Adrienne was nodding, thinking she knew what Lauren was saying. "It's okay. It's part of the process. Me and Dora both went through it—Dora calmed *me* down after Raul and I had that conversation with Shea, if you can believe that. You're handling it better than I did, you want to know the truth," the other woman added more quietly. "Christopher and Phil had it, too, I found out a few days ago, and Chris said he thought Phil was going to deck Shea. But we're all still here, doing okay."

Lauren swallowed down the tears that were threatening again and asked the question that had been burning in her throat. "Is it the reason all of you are still here?"

Adrienne's hand had been rubbing a soothing pattern on Lauren's upper back, and it froze with the question. "It's not why I'm still here," she finally said.

Lauren nodded, and then glanced sideways at her. "But Dora and Christopher..."

Adrienne shook her head. "It's their business."

The non-answer was answer enough. "You and Raul got past it then, and just decided to stay."

Adrienne shrugged beside her, and her hand began running in circles again on Lauren's back. "I think I'm done, you want the truth. I don't know if I was scared to admit it before or what, or maybe I just didn't want to be divorced. Raul loves me, but I'm just…trying to figure out what to do. How to break it to him that our marriage is over, maybe, even if he and everyone else seem to think otherwise. I guess I have to figure out where to go, too. It's gotten kind of easy to sit around here with Dora and Christopher, drinking and eating away Raul's money."

Lauren smiled stiffly. Of Phil and Van and Raul, she'd take Phil or Van in a heartbeat—it was something of a relief to know that Adrienne didn't plan on staying with the man.

In another minute, Dora returned, Christopher trailing behind her. "You mind that I'm here?" he asked. Lauren shook her head as Dora pressed a clear drink into her hand and Christopher sat down across from them.

"Gin and tonics seemed like a right choice for the conversation," Dora commented, taking a gulp of her own. "More cranberry seemed too…happy."

Christopher held up his glass in a sardonic gesture of cheers and the women did likewise, all of them taking sips before he commented, "You had 'the talk' with Shea—I thought about warning you it was coming when I saw those bruises this morning, but wasn't sure how to bring it up. Us just meeting and all."

"Oh, shut it, Chris," Dora told him simply. "We all heard the way David was talking last night and saw who he was hanging out with. That talk would have been happening regardless. And that's not the point." Her shoulder nudged Lauren's. "The point, my dears, is whether or not you enjoyed getting the bruises?"

Lauren stifled a giggle and felt like the tears might finally have run their course. It was true—the marks around her wrists were raw and her joints were stiff from where David had tied her to his bed the night before, but she'd enjoyed getting them. She only hadn't guessed they might lead to Shea threatening to separate them, or speaking to them as she had—judging them like she had, and making use of it.

Adrienne spoke up after another minute. "Guys, Lauren wanted to know if it's why you're still here. If you want to tell her…"

Lauren might have expected Dora to speak up, but it was Chris, across from her, who answered, and Lauren looked up to see that his eyes had gotten that serious look she'd seen flicker across his face earlier in the day, the frown lines coming back to his forehead and gesturing to his age.

"Phil and I were ready to go after our first weekend, Lauren," he admitted. "We never planned on being here for more than one long weekend, though it's got its perks."

"They wouldn't let you?" she asked.

"They said they were worried about my safety. We'd gotten into it, our first day here—a real yelling match. Phil's a lot louder than me when we fight, but he's all bark. Me having to hold him back from throwing Shea out a window after that talk didn't help. We were totally blindsided, though. Shea and Tony said he was welcome to leave, but that they thought I needed to stay here or in another center for rehabilitation or some shit. Guess they would have moved me to somewhere else if he'd left," Christopher added, his eyes off in the distance. "He wasn't gonna leave without me, though. They put us off for another week, and then another week…. That's when I told Phil he should leave by himself," Christopher added. "He wouldn't."

Adrienne's hand moved from Lauren's back to pick up the drink in front of her. "I offered to leave and get a lawyer, but Van took another look at the contract we all signed before we came in. It spells everything out. We gave ourselves up to their care, to their *expert* opinions. For as long as it takes if they judge us to be a danger to ourselves or others."

"You can leave, Adrienne," Dora pointed out quietly. "Shea told you guys as much on Wednesday."

"Yeah," Adrienne allowed. She turned sideways, her eyes meeting Lauren's. "They've given up on me and Raul, I think. I have, too, as I said." A sigh left her lips, and her gaze moved around the table. "I just hate to leave you guys stuck."

"So, it's like a prison," Lauren murmured, her eyes finally lifting to glance around to the faces of her friends.

Christopher shrugged, his eyes coming back to hers. "Yes and no. You look at it from the outside, you gotta face that it looks like we're all—excepting Adrienne—in abusive relationships. Just depends on how you define abuse, but we signed onto this for their so-called expert opinions and help. They're not keeping everyone here. They're just saying that you and me and Dora, here, at least, can't leave with our husbands."

"And they won't leave without you," Lauren finished.

"Right. And from the way David looks at you, I'd bet he'll be in the same boat as Phil and Van when push comes to shove."

"Someone's going to have to leave," Adrienne pointed out. "Sometime soon, too; this can't go on indefinitely. And who knows if it's affecting other couples we don't know, as well? I mean, everyone is off in their little groups, in cliques—I don't know anyone as well as I know you guys."

"Yeah, but who's going to leave, honey?" Dora asked. "The only way to fix this is to get a lawyer and another expert involved, and because of the power-of-attorney clauses, that's only going to happen if one of our husbands leaves to make that happen. And Van's a good lawyer, but I can't convince him to go without me. I've tried," she added, taking a heavy gulp of her drink.

Lauren saw something change in Christopher's face then, and held his eyes. They'd gotten darker, suddenly, and it nearly made her heart stop to see it. "You know something else," she whispered.

He looked startled, and she realized it had been her magic more than her intuition coming to the right conclusion, but that didn't change anything. "What is it?" she pressed.

Beside her, Dora had stiffened. "Chris? What's she talking about?"

The man across from them stared back at her, unblinking. "You're awful good at reading people, Lauren Merriweather."

When she didn't answer, he shifted his gaze to Dora's. "Get us another round, babe, and I'll tell you. But don't say I didn't warn you," he added.

Dora was out of the room in a moment, and Lauren found herself and Adrienne leaning into each other. Adrienne's arm had wrapped around her waist and Lauren felt thankful for the comfort of the contact.

Dora was back faster than seemed possible, a small tray of drinks in hand. She pressed a tall glass into Christopher's grip and then passed the others to Adrienne and Lauren. "Talk, Chris," she demanded.

He looked to Adrienne first. "You might not want to know," he said simply. "You're about to be out of here. I don't want to jam you up."

Adrienne's grip tightened around Lauren's waist, protective in a way that reminded her not for the first time of how she felt around Josh. "You guys are my friends."

Christopher nodded, and then his gaze went to Dora. "Phil's been trying to figure out how to tell Van, but they don't exactly get along, and I hadn't been able to figure out how to tell you."

Dora scowled, but nodded, and spoke up in explanation as she looked over to Lauren. "Van's from a small town, in case you couldn't tell. One of our regular arguments is over the fact that he thinks being gay is a sin of all sins. I keep waiting for Phil and Chris to convince him otherwise, but he's a stubborn son of a bitch. He and Phil aren't exactly friendly."

Shrugging, Christopher took another sip from his drink. "Well, he might have to change his mind so we can all figure something out together. Phil, uh...hell, this is the other reason I didn't want to talk to you guys about this. One of our fights is about cheating, and he went and slept with one of the prostitutes they brought in last Wednesday."

Lauren spluttered up gin, one of her hands flying to her mouth. "He *what?* They bring in...fuck, are you serious?" she asked.

Chris' eyes had opened wide. "Shit, you didn't know? Fuck. Sorry," he added.

Adrienne sighed beside her. "It happens Wednesdays—they bring professionals in for anyone who's got the urge to stray. We're not supposed to know, but..."

"We do," Dora finished for her. "Didn't seem like there was a point to telling you that bit of bad news yet," she added.

Lauren looked between her friends, trying to find the joke. "You can't be serious. This place is supposed to be fixing marriages, for fuck's sake."

"Two 'fuck's in near as many sentences. You must be surprised," Christopher quipped. "Sorry," he said next, shrugging off the glares of the women.

"Raul told me, and I told them," Adrienne said wryly, her eyes meeting Lauren's. "I guess the logic they spout is that they don't want hopeless cheaters to try to break into other marriages and turn this place into a soap opera of folks sneaking in and out of each other's rooms."

"But," Christopher cut in, "you ask me, it's just one more amenity to keep folks satisfied and happy here."

"It works for Raul," Adrienne acknowledged.

Lauren sat silent, trying to wrap her head around the fact that a retreat dedicated to marriage therapy would actually be facilitating cheating. And how would that affect her and David? Would his role mean he'd feel compelled to cheat, just to uphold his cover? She felt sick at the thought of it, but couldn't discard the idea out of hand.

"Christopher, you were saying…" Dora prodded.

The other woman's pointed reminder brought Lauren back to the conversation. The fact that this place brought in prostitutes or escorts or whatever else was news to her, but not to them. Whatever Christopher had been holding back was bigger.

The man across from her had near finished his drink, and now he took a final gulp, swallowing the rest of it down. When he raised an eyebrow in request and gestured for Lauren's, which sat mostly untouched, she nodded and pushed it toward him. He took a sip, then slid it back to her.

"The guy he slept with is a regular here—comes in most weeks when gay couples are here, I guess."

"I can't believe Phil told you," Lauren commented suddenly, despite having told herself that she wouldn't interrupt.

Christopher met her eyes and smiled. "Seems our relationship has improved—we're getting better about honesty, anyway," he said. "Anyhow…so, this guy, he's a regular. Some guy, a while back, told him he was in the position Phil and I are in, but decided to cut out anyway.

Planned to leave his husband here because Shea and Tony said it wasn't safe for him to leave together with his spouse. Same stuff they've told us—that it'd be against professional judgement, they'd be liable for the results, the spouse didn't know what he was thinking because of being abused and couldn't say no…all that shit. Well, this guy was gonna leave a few days after talking to the escort, supposedly.   Planned to come back to this place with a lawyer and his own expert; take his husband somewhere else for evaluation if he had to, figuring that if that was what had to happen, that was what had to happen. Anything to get the two of them out of here and on a road forward, right? Back to normal life?

"So, anyhow, this escort who Phil slept with, he ran into that guy a month or so back, and I guess he liked Phil enough that he wanted to warn him."

Christopher went silent and reached across for Lauren's drink again. His hand was shaking now, she realized, and rather than let him grab her gin and tonic, she darted her hand out and gripped his, hard, willing some of the strength and magic in her blood into his. It worked, and he steadied. He looked up to meet their eyes in turn, and then faced Dora head-on, his hand still holding Lauren's across the table.

"Guy was drunk, but the escort believed him. His story goes… he said he came back here not two days after he left, with a lawyer and a high-priced therapist. Shea and Tony claimed his husband had left on his own. Said he felt like himself again once his husband was off the estate, and they gave him enough money to get started again. Had a whole song and dance about that being where some of the money we pay goes—into a savings account in case someone needs it to get away, get a new start. They said the guy took the money for a new start and headed out, and it wasn't their fault if he hadn't called his abusive husband to formalize a divorce."

Christopher went silent, but his grip stayed tight in Lauren's hand. She didn't know what to say, or even what to think.

Before anyone answered, he added, "This guy, when he told the escort this… he was drunk. Seemed like he'd been on a bender for weeks. He'd hired a private investigator to look for his husband, called all their friends, the whole nine yards. No sign or word from him. And he swears up and down that his husband loves him more than life itself. That he never would have left and not called him. Says Shea and Tony must have kidnapped him—who the fuck knows why?—but it's his word against everyone. Shea and Tony even let an investigator and a cop in to search the place for the guy, supposedly, and they came up with nothing. So, everyone but this guy is of the opinion that his husband left cuz of the state of their marriage, but he swears his husband never would have left like that. Never would have left the place without calling him. And, of course, Shea and Tony deny that they forced his husband to stay to begin with; say the guy just stormed out one day after a big fight. Lawyer and the outside therapist ended up siding with them, telling this guy to get lost."

Adrienne's grip had tightened on her waist, and suddenly Lauren realized that Dora had begun crying beside her. She reached out and took a heavy swallow of the drink in front of her.

"Maybe the guy's husband really just left—maybe he just wanted to spread rumors and get this guy to feel sorry for him, or his marriage was a lot worse than ours," Dora suggested.

Lauren felt Dora shuddering with tears beside her, and reached sideways to put her hand on the other woman's shoulder.

Across from her, Christopher nodded. "Yeah, maybe."

Silence fell across the table. Christopher's acknowledgement had rung false to all of them, and there seemed to be no question that Phil only would have told him if he himself believed the story was worth reading as a warning.

"Phil's not going to leave," Lauren said quietly.

"No," Christopher answered. "And neither will Van or David."

Adrienne gulped down the last of her drink and then coughed pointedly. "So, maybe Raul and I leave this week, and I bring back a lawyer and expert. I mean, that would work…right? If they're glad to let us go, there's no suspicion. If something's hinky with all this, with the couples they won't let leave, you guys would be here regardless."

For a moment, Lauren found herself agreeing, and then Dora commented, "Haley and Jana said they were going to do that. They said they were leaving because they didn't trust things around here, and that they were going to come back with their own cars to pick us up. I mean, we weren't talking lawyers and therapists…but I don't think they came back. It's not like the place is hard to find. Did I tell you guys they both said they were coming back? I guess I probably didn't," Dora answered herself, her voice soft, "but I kept expecting they'd come back. That was a week ago Wednesday, when they left. I figure Tony or Shea must have said something to stop them."

Christopher shrugged again. "Either way. They had marriages and lives to go back to. Maybe they figured we were over-reacting once they were out and had more space to think. They could also show up any time."

Lauren had only half been listening, processing the grip of Dora's hand on hers and the nerves she could feel radiating from Adrienne. And then the names struck her.

Haley. Jana. She turned sideways to face Dora, and gripped her hand tighter. "Dora, what are their full names? Or do you remember their husbands' names?" Lauren asked.

Dora stared back at her for a minute, her eyes watery and liquored up. "Uh, Lauren, babe, I don't know *your* last name, or Adrienne's or Chris'. I think Haley's husband's name is JD, but I don't know what the initials stand for. Why?"

Lauren's breath had already stopped up in her chest and frozen her still when Christopher spoke up, "For what it's worth, Haley and JD's last name is Vincent. Jana's last name is Spanbauer—don't ask me to spell that—and her husband goes by Pen. What does it matter, Lauren?"

There weren't any words to press back the questions. Haley and Jason Vincent. Jana and Pence Spanbauer. The names matched the two most recent couples who'd told their families they were retreating from life to join a sheltered community, leaving behind their other lives. The two recent couples whose names hadn't come across her and David's radar since they'd arrived, until now.

Lauren reached sideways and grasped Adrienne's hand, and then she turned to look the other woman in the eye. "I can't tell you why, Adrienne, but you can't leave this week, okay? You and Raul need to stay here until…until we figure out how all of us get out of here. At the same time. Promise me?"

The other woman's eyes were dazed, and Lauren realized she was bleeding some of her magic into her, willing her to go along with her, but at the moment she didn't care. Maybe this was on the border of right magic or wrong magic, but either way, it was necessary. Lauren couldn't let her and her husband leave and try to get help until they'd figured out where those other couples had gone and what was happening here.

She could feel the confusion radiating from Dora and Christopher, but blocked it out and held Adrienne's gaze until the other woman nodded belatedly.

"Okay, Lauren, yeah, sure. I promise."

Lauren loosened her grip. Catching her breath, she forced herself to look up and meet Christopher's gaze. He looked suspicious, but wasn't arguing. She swallowed down the nerves in her throat and willed her voice to be steady. "I just think we need to all be on the same page and get a feel for what's happening…for what they're really thinking…before we separate. Power in numbers and all that, ya know?" she offered.

It took a moment, but Christopher nodded, and then Dora leaned her head against her shoulder, mimicking the pose Lauren had held with Adrienne earlier. "Lauren," she offered, slurring slightly, "I'm glad you and David came here. I'm sorry you're not happy, but I feel…like, like…"

"Like you're gonna help us figure this out," Christopher finished for her.

Lauren nodded as he reached across the table and gripped Lauren's forearm, and Dora's hand, as if in solidarity. Trapped as she felt, there was nothing she could say.

When the drinks were finished and Dora had stopped crying, Adrienne got up to get another round. Christopher left a moment later, telling them he'd be back, but that he was going to tell Phil he needed to tell David and Van what he'd heard, rather than laying the responsibility of the news on Dora and Lauren. The girls nodded, and Lauren took Dora's hand in her own again once Christopher had left, willing some of her magic to leave her blood and offer whatever strength and healing it could to the woman beside her. She didn't know, at this point, whether it was responsible or not, using even the slight magic she was parceling out, but that was a question for tomorrow. For the moment, Christopher and Dora needed anything she could offer them. And it was too late anyway—she'd used it to steady Chris, and then to convince Adrienne to her way of thinking. A little bit more flooding out of her now wouldn't matter.

Chapter 17

*Y*ou *want out tonight, we'll do it.*

David stared down at the text message, his brain cycling through what made sense. The simple truth was that they had no proof of anything they'd been told that night, or even of Shea's threats to separate the two of them or hold Lauren there. They didn't even have anything more than the word of men who, best case scenario, could be painted as abusive control freaks in a courtroom. And, they had nothing to go on in terms of tracking down the couples or the individuals who'd supposedly disappeared—they were still just missing, and nothing but hearsay could suggest anything suspicious about a couple disappearing together into a commune or a single individual fleeing an abusive marriage.

And what held him from calling it quits even more was Lauren's determination to stick it out until they had proof, or at least leads. Right now, yeah, they could get Josh to pull them out, but that would be the end of the case— beyond continuing to keep an eye out on things and potentially helping the couples who already wanted out, who they could take with them. But what about the ones who'd already disappeared? Or the ones who'd show up next week and get trapped in the same way?

Staying a few more days would give them a chance to at least look for some proof, or even just a suggestion of where they'd gone. And, come Wednesday, David could maybe track down the sex worker who Phil had talked to, assuming he'd be back at the center again.

Fighting down his conscience, David texted back. *Not yet. We don't have anything real and we're not in any danger from the looks of things. I'll text tomorrow. Keep looking out.*

A minute went by before Josh answered: *Lauren on board with that decision?*

For the first time since she'd filled him in on what she'd heard from the girls and Chris, even beyond what Phil had communicated, David grinned. It appeared his girl couldn't be scared off from anything. He typed back, *More on board with it than me, brother. She's all in.*

K. You guys stay safe. Night.

David nodded at the message before telling Josh to do the same, and then he tucked the phone back into its hiding place. Lauren was in the shower, but tonight he didn't want to join her. The drinks he'd had were still running through his system, along with the adrenalin that had come along with all they'd learned that night. Now they knew people were essentially being blackmailed into remaining here out of fear that they'd be kept from leaving together, or direct threats of the same. In a courtroom, it would be a he-said-she-said mess of pointing fingers, but that was a courtroom. In his gut, David knew the only thing guaranteeing him and Lauren safe passage out of this place was the burner phone in his luggage. That was the one thing, along with Lauren's tattoo, that had enabled him to make the call to stay.

The water stopped running and David rose up and wandered over to the bathroom doorway. Lauren had left the door ajar, and he watched as her naked arm reached out from behind the glass partition and plucked a towel from the rack. Her blurred figure dried itself behind the glass and he met her eyes when she stepped out. Flushed from the hot water, her skin glowed tan with the sun they'd gotten that afternoon, and her eyes were blue with liquor and fresh tears.

"You talk to him?" she asked.

"Yeah. Filled him in," David answered as he moved over to her. He stepped in close, backing her up against the glass of the shower, and lowered his lips to hers. She hadn't dried her face or her lips, and he licked at the moisture before he sucked her lower lip between his and bit down lightly so that she whimpered. Catching her wrists in his hands, he held her arms to her side and the towel fell down to the floor, leaving her wet body to press into his clothing. Her breath hitched, and he felt the tremble of magic that ran through her throat, her lips, her blood, calling to him—he'd never get tired of it.

"Come to bed," he whispered into her lips, and he felt her nod against him.

He'd thought they just needed to rest tonight—that the day had been too full already—but he could feel Lauren's magic bubbling under her skin, pressing her into him, and he didn't want to go to sleep without working through the fear and frustration they were feeling. The next day would be long enough without them depriving each other tonight.

Pushing her to lay back on the bed, David climbed up over her and leaned in so that he could breathe into her throat, feeling her pulse shudder in reaction. She was still damp beneath him, but her skin had begun warming to him. At their side, he traced his finger along the vinework running up her arm. He couldn't feel it, but knowing it was there offered the connection he wanted right now.

"Our insurance policy," she whispered.

"Yeah, but we won't need it," David promised, lifting up from her so that he could look into her eyes. They were still that deep blue they got to be after she'd been crying. He stayed on his knees watching her and then ran two fingers along her cheek, then over her lips. "You were crying in the shower."

Her lips pursed, but she didn't answer.

"You sure you want to stay? Nobody would fault you for wanting out. Tonight. Now. We could get the others out, too."

Light showed up in her eyes for a moment, but disappeared just as quickly. She shook her head, holding his gaze as she did and catching at his wrist with one of her hands so that he had to stop tracing the vinework and focus on what she said. "But the others who've already disappeared—we wouldn't have a way to help them. We wouldn't have anything new to go on. That's what you said earlier. And we couldn't shut this place down."

"It doesn't matter. We can figure that out later. If you want to go, we're out."

He didn't need to see her expression to know what she was thinking—he didn't want to, either. She wouldn't beg out of this mission anymore than she'd give up the friends she'd made over the last 36 hours.

Instead of answering, Lauren shifted beneath him and sucked one of his nipples into her mouth. He froze above her with the heat of her tongue pressing into him and let her explore, her teeth nipping into his skin and hardening the bud of flesh in her mouth. Propped up above her on one elbow, he braided his fingers through her hair and closed his eyes, enjoying the sensations of her mouth on his body. When she moved sideways and took his other nipple between her lips, he reached one hand down between them and, without any warning, sank two fingers into her wet folds. A mewl of pleasure vibrated against his skin and she pressed her hips up into him, meeting his hand as he thrust his fingers into her, stretching her.

"David, please…"

"Un-uh, baby, just wait. Quiet," he cut her off, and he pressed two fingers into her lips to emphasize the direction, so that her eyes widened against his gaze. His other fingers felt the reaction from below, though—her juices were warming to him, her body reacting to his touch and begging for more.

She swallowed down whatever she'd been about to say next, and he grinned down at her.   Then he added a third finger, enjoying the whimpers that came from her throat as his other hand found the nape of her neck and wound through her hair, knotting itself there and holding her head back, arched before him.

With three fingers buried inside of her and his other hand tight in her hair, holding her prone, he lowered his lips to her neck and ran his teeth along her skin from earlobe to shoulder, up and down, feeling the rush of blood beneath his breath as her body soaked his hand and her pussy pulsed around his fingers, tight and wanting. When he bit down on her earlobe, a shriek left her lips and she bucked beneath him, her hands going to the forearm that stretched down between them and gripping him as her body spasmed, held to the bed with his weight and his hands. When he could feel the violence of the orgasm begin seeping out of her, and she was swallowing her own words to keep from calling out, he let himself lick the sweat from the hollow of her throat and simultaneously pressed his fingers in one last time, as deep as they'd reach, just as his thumb reached for her clit and made her buck and scream beneath him again.

When he pulled himself to a sitting position above her, her lips were parted with desire and he could see the flush in her skin had spread down along her torso. The moisture left from the shower was gone but for in her hair, and he rested some of his weight on her thighs, anchoring her down into the bed. His cock was already hard and ready, but he wanted to enjoy her some, and exhaust some of the magic that had been playing her emotions so much that day.

Her hands landed on his thighs, but he focused on her torso, tracing his fingers along her mound, her abdomen, her breasts, playing his nails into her skin lightly and drawing little gasps from her as he sent chills and tickles running through her. He could almost see the magic racing along beneath his fingers, trying to keep up with his touch as it warmed her blood in reaction to the chemistry between them at every point of contact. When she began squirming beneath him, trying to press up into him again, ready for his cock, he moved two fingers to her slit to steal some moisture and then ran it in circles along her clit so that she moaned. He saw her mouth open to form his name again, and he pressed one hand over her mouth as a reminder to stay quiet before rolling off of her so that he could remove what was left of his own clothing.

His cock had been hard and ready for her practically since they'd reached the bed, but he'd wanted her primed first, soaked and wanton.

When he moved back overtop of her, she spread her legs for him instinctively, and he caught one of her legs beneath the knee and pressed it up into her chest. Watching the way she caught her breath at the fashion in which he'd spread her open, he met her wide eyes and let himself breathe in the scent of her desire. He wasn't sure how many orgasms he'd pushed through her, the way they'd been bleeding into each other as he'd touched her and teased her magic up and down through her veins, but she was trembling before him now, her lips panting for him.

Catching her hands in his, one by one, he pressed them to her sides palm-down. "Hold onto the bed, not me," he told her quietly. "I won't lose control this time, but I want to see you helpless with want, Lauren. Giving yourself up to it," he told her, desire tightening his voice. "And keep quiet, baby," he commanded her again, wanting to know if she could meet the demand, and then he leaned down over her and took one of her breasts into his mouth, sucking at her skin and running his tongue along the hard bud of her nipple. When he felt her skin warming with magic beneath his mouth, he anchored himself with an elbow by her head and pressed two fingers, soaked with her juices, between her lips even as his cock found her pussy. Her gasp pulled his fingers in and over her tongue as he lunged into her, pushing into her channel as her magic reacted across her body, from the leg he still held tight against her chest to her core to the breast where his teeth teased at her nipple up to her mouth where she sucked against his fingers desperately, the magic running through her confusing her blood and warming the whole of her so that she was shuddering with want beneath him.

He opened his eyes as he pulled upward for a breath and pistoned his cock in and out of her again, and he saw her hands white-knuckled against the bedspread, clutching the fabric for purchase as her body ran hot with desire and magic and she panted for breath.

Letting his hand leave her mouth and hold to her shoulder, he shifted above her so that his hips dug deeper against hers and began thrusting faster. He could feel her pulsing body struggling to keep up with the rhythm, soaked with desire and already exhausted with pleasure.

Slowing down, he pressed into her more slowly. Her body was clenching around him on autopilot as he glided in and out, but he could see her panting for breath. Her eyes opened again, desperate, and he grinned down at her, knowing she could see the control in his features even as the magic kept running warm in her blood.

"You look like you've got a fever, baby—what's the matter?" he teased her, but she didn't have the breath to answer, and he captured the moan that escaped her lips in a hard, bruising kiss. Speeding up again, he pressed his cock into her faster and faster, and then he told her to hold onto the bed, knowing she'd hear how close he was in his voice.

At the moment he jerked with release, coming hard, his fingers found her clit and squeezed, and she spasmed around him, a scream erupting from her to be muffled against his shoulder as his own curses signaled his climax.

Her pussy milked him for all he was worth, and he ran kisses along her skin and her lips as he rested his weight atop her and their pulses began slowing, his cock still sunken into her warmth.

She was asleep nearly as soon as he pulled away, and he knew she likely wouldn't awaken when he moved her beneath the covers and curled her body into his. For now, he left her to sleep under the weight of her own magic as it calmed into her skin, and with one last glance over her sweat-soaked body, he caught his own breath and headed into the bathroom to shower, wondering again whether sleeping under this roof for another night was more reasoned or more foolish.

***

David settled into Tony's office couch with a coffee in

hand, anxious to get their one-on-one going. He'd left Lauren with Adrienne and Chris in the cafeteria, working on some sort of self-actualization bullshit project that they'd been assigned in their group the day before. For his part, he didn't have any intention of writing the letter to his past self that had been assigned—Tony had told everyone to have the five-page letter ready for the following Friday, and he had no intention of being there that long. How he or any of the other men would have written five pages in answer to Tony's prompt was, in any case, beyond him. What had been telling about the whole thing had been that nobody, to a person, had mentioned leaving before that due date.

"The two of you have remained very close since coming into the center," the therapist started out now, setting his own coffee down on the table between them. "I believe Lauren's been in your room every night."

David let his eyes rest on his, trying to measure what he was fishing for. "Yeah. And?"

"Have you given her the option of not coming to your room?"

A laugh left his throat before he could stop it—if Tony would be asking questions like this, it wouldn't be hard for him to remain in character. "You guys did that yourselves, remember? By giving her a separate room? I'm not dragging her up to mine—I'm sure you would have stopped me if I were."

A wry smile tilted the other man's lips and he re-settled his legal pad in his lap, its top page still blank. "Touché, yes, I'm sure someone would have. Be that as it may, have you told her she doesn't have to come to your room at night?"

"Honestly? I don't remember, but I can tell you that she's made it blatantly clear she wants us together at night, and since that has to happen in my room…"

"Alright, well, let me put it this way. Would you be offended if *I* made it clear to her she's welcome to sleep alone on any night when she wants to—tonight, for instance—and that there'll be no repercussions for doing so?"

The words hung between them for a few seconds, until David realized the implication of what the other man meant by 'repercussions' and leaned forward. "You don't know what you're talking about. I'm telling you, she wants to be in my room. She wants us to be sharing a room, but we're abiding by the policies you guys set up and trusting they'll do us some good. I came here for her, and I'm here, but I'm getting fucking sick and tired of you and the doc suggesting that Lauren's looking for excuses to stay away from me. You tell her she can stay away from me till you're blue in the face, and do it with my blessing, but it won't make a difference."

Forcing himself to sit back in the couch, David took a gulp of his coffee and attempted some curbing of the vitriol he'd just spit at the doctor. They ought to be able to tell by now that the two of them were close if they were paying any attention at all.

"And there'll be no repercussions if she decides she *does* want space?" the older man pressed.

David glared at him silently for a moment before he replied. "No, no *repercussions*. No fucking problems, no issues. She wants a night alone, she can have it. But I'm telling you that she doesn't."

"You're feeling protective of her," the therapist offered. "That's good, as long as it's not taken so far that it becomes unfounded jealousy."

"Fuck you," David spit out before he could stop himself.

Eyes narrowing, Tony nodded and sipped at his own coffee in silence for a few seconds. "Shea had the talk with you, and you're angry. I can understand that. But you do understand where she's coming from. That we have Lauren's best interests in mind."

David's eyes stayed on the therapist's, but he didn't bother answering. Theoretically, the reason and logic of the situation was on their side and they knew it. If you separated out instinct and passion and actual history, they made all the sense in the world. As long as you assumed that David couldn't control himself and that Lauren was weak—which was exactly what he and Lauren had built into their characters in making sure they'd get pulled into this place, and exactly what had trapped them.

"So, how do we get out of here together, Doc? How do we get our relationship fixed to where we're happy and you think we're good to go? You tell me. I want my marriage back, and I want Lauren safe, but I'm starting to feel like I'm the only one with those priorities in mind."

"You're assuming we won't let you leave together come Tuesday."

David stared at him, waiting. Shea's intentions had been perfectly clear, whether she'd voiced them or not.

"Very well. You're right, David, we don't think it's safe for the two of you to leave together right now. None of us do. If you want to leave without Lauren come Tuesday, you're welcome to, but she needs this program. So, if you're true to your word and you want things to work out, then you go through the program. You work on the marriage and you give Lauren enough space that we feel confident she can *take* space if and when she wants it."

"And you're going to tell me how to do that?" he asked more quietly.

The doctor stuck out his hand across the table, offering it to David. "You have my word."

David accepted the handshake and then picked his

coffee back up before he leaned back into the cushions of the couch. "Okay, Doc. So, what now?"

"We talk. You answer some questions."

With that said, the man launched into a litany of questions. They passed the hour mark on the appointment and kept going. The questions were, for the most part, exactly what David might have expected—a history of their relationship, a history of his past, a wholly fictional overview of what his life looked like now. Broad as the questions were, and undirected as they remained, the only difficulty came in making sure that he stuck to a story that would match up with what Lauren would have to say when she came in, though the thought of that made him cringe. Any truth she could tell Toscano—and it would all have to be truth, of course—would paint him as a villain, without question. However he played things now, there was every chance that their only way of getting out of here together would be through calling in the cavalry, given what would have to come from her lips when these same questions were put to her.

"And you've remained faithful to her?" Tony interrupted him. "Since you became serious?   Say, since you were engaged, and since you moved in together?"

The nod was instinctive, and easy, but the re-setting of the therapist's jaw was what told David that he'd had this man's abilities wrong from the beginning. "Perhaps you didn't quite cheat… and didn't quite not?" he pressed.

A knot had developed in David's stomach. He'd underestimated this man and let his guard down, in a private therapy session of all things, and Toscano had seen through him, albeit for only a moment. He'd been so focused on giving reality to the larger picture of their relationship that his eyes must have betrayed him when it came to the details.

For a moment, he thought to deny it, but what was the

point? He was playing a jerk, after all, and jerks cheated on their wives. "I kissed a woman recently," he admitted, "and it could've gone further but it didn't. I was drunk, pissed off, and she came on to me. I stopped it before anything else happened."

He didn't add that, had they not been in a bar, something might very well have happened, given the fact that he'd very nearly fucked a stranger in a restroom.

The man across from him nodded and jotted another line down on his legal pad, but didn't seem surprised. "And Lauren, as far as you know? Has she remained faithful? What do you know of her relationships before you?"

"She's never cheated on me," he answered simply, "and she won't," he added, letting the sleazy confidence of his persona slip back into his voice. "And I'm the only guy she's been in love with—you can bet on that, too."

All of it was truth, though he knew the tone in his voice put a darker spin on it than was necessary. *Let the guy think what he wants. We're gonna have to get Josh involved anyway.*

Tony's eyes had come back up to meet his. "And that makes it easier to keep her in hand for you, doesn't it?"

Sudden doubt edged through him and David steeled himself against flinching. Every time he fell fully into the character they'd created for him, it seemed he fell more completely into not just what he needed them to believe, but into being what they wanted. And, just as telling, there was the fact that they were getting to him, somehow homing in on details that did strike a chord with him whether he wanted to admit it or not.

It had never occurred to him, coming into this, that they could trap them based on character versus circumstance, but now…he couldn't deny that the balance in the scales felt like it was shifted in their favor.

***

Rather than heading to the cafeteria for dinner, Lauren wandered outside of the center. The large oaks scattered around the property offered enough shade that their bases were covered in shadows, and she headed for one of the larger ones. Reaching its trunk, she sat down against it on the side opposite the center and brought her legs up to her chest so that she could hug her knees with her arms, curling into herself. She'd worn a long skirt despite the warmth of the day, and she tugged it down around her and tucked it beneath her feet and bottom, wanting to hold off any ants as well as to make sure that nobody from the center would glance out a window and see her.

She could feel her breath shuddering through her, threatening to erupt in sobs, and they couldn't afford for her to fall apart. Her friends couldn't afford for her to fall apart.

Everything had been fine earlier, and easy enough, but once again the day had gotten later and it felt like things were disintegrating around her, going from bad to worse. The morning had been laidback, relaxed, filled with the assignments from group that were now all but completed, and she found herself liking Adrienne and Christopher more with each moment she spent with them. Afterward, lunch with David had been just as easy; the condescending remarks he'd traded with Raul had even been easy to ignore with Adrienne across from her, so that they could share the frustration of the conversation that the men had dominated.

And then it had all gone to shit, and gotten worse.

In Tony's office after lunch, she'd had to balance along the line of what she could say about David that was both truth and in line with his story, and that didn't amount to much.

They'd met in a bar, he'd coerced her into sleeping with him—and yes, she'd had to admit, there'd been tears and bruises involved on her side—and they'd been together on and off since then. She'd begun to guard even the truths that she could have shared, knowing what picture they painted of David, but her non-answers had been the same as answers when Tony had pushed her to talk about any time when David might have forced her to do things she wasn't interested in, or frightened her or left bruises.

In the end, it had been as if she'd painted a monster out of a movie, and as much as it was all true, the context and the full story made it something else entirely. But she couldn't talk about magic or witches or kidnappings or cages made of energy, or let on that her mother had been a murderous serial killer who'd left David and his partner at their wits' end, or that Lauren had gone back to him because of a spell and an attack and a possessive coven that had left her in need of a safehouse.

She couldn't, essentially, say anything about him which wasn't based in emotion and her own feelings, none of which the therapist was willing to believe, however truthful she was. And while she'd thought that telling him about the man who'd raped her, when he asked about her other sexual encounters, would allow her to show him some good about David, in talking about how he'd helped her recover, the look in Tony's eyes had dried her mouth with its pity. Clearly, he'd understood everything she'd told him about that period in their relationship to be covered by David seeking control, and her falling under his charisma—her seeing David as a hero when, in Tony's eyes, she should have seen him as a monster.

And there'd been nothing she could say to change his

mind.

The whole conversation had left her feeling dirtier than she'd ever felt, as well as powerless. And then, with her emotions already shot, he'd told her David had kissed another woman just days before they'd come to the center. Not even a week before. And very nearly done more.

And she'd laughed.

When would he have kissed another woman? How?

The thought of it had been so ridiculous that she'd passed it off without trying—it had even made her feel better about all she'd shared, because if Tony had believed that of David or felt the need to make it up and lie to her about something like that, either one, any supposedly professional opinion he could have of their relationship had to be off-base. He'd let her leave his office soon after that, and there'd been a smile on her face even as she'd promised to ask David about the kiss. She'd looked forward to laughing with David about it.

And then she'd found him in the break room having a beer with Van. She'd thought about putting off the joke since Van was there, too, but had decided she had to talk to him anyway to let him know she was done in Tony's office and was going to spend some time with Dora and Adrienne before dinner.

"Hey, baby," he said. "Ready to go upstairs?"

Ignoring the suggestion that she knew was meant more for Van's benefit than her own, she went up to him and grabbed his hand, reached up to give him a quick kiss at the side of his lips as the magic curled along her skin beneath his fingers, and joked, "You'll never believe what I heard—Tony told me you kissed some woman last week and almost slept with her. I guess they're really trying to get us to hate each other, huh?"

The look on his face had drained the laughter out of

her voice even before she'd finished speaking, and though she wasn't sure whether he'd been about to deny it or not, the look on her own face must have communicated clearly enough that his expression said everything.

She didn't know what David had been saying as she'd backed up and then fled the room, or how Van had reacted to the exchange. She'd simply gotten out of the room as fast as she could, fleeing to her own room and only emerging when it was Adrienne and Dora who were begging to know she was okay from the other side, the hall mother having called security on David when he'd gotten to the floor and tried demanding her room number. His yells had gotten her friends' attention, and Lauren had heard David, as well, but she hadn't emerged from her room.

Thankfully, they'd gotten the gist of the story from David's ranting, and she hadn't had to fill them in. Instead, they'd played a mostly silent game of cards in Adrienne's room. When it had come time for dinner, Lauren had begged off, asking that they pass David a hurriedly scrawled note that Adrienne had all but insisted she write. All things considered, she'd acquiesced, promising David she'd come by that night so that they could talk, if only to satisfy her friends.

For now, however, she only wanted to be alone. She'd passed Tony inside, and he'd told her to come to his office after dinner rather than focus on journaling about the weekend's therapy, as the weekend plan had dictated. He'd seemed apologetic, and she could guess well enough that he could imagine, easily, where the tears had come from, assuming he hadn't actually seen their confrontation or David's outburst on video. She didn't even mind the prospect of it, as it would be one more thing to allow for postponing talking to David about whatever had happened.

Chapter 18

Lauren woke up in her own bed with only the haziest of memories of being in Tony's office and feeling everything catch up to her. Her emotions had been all over the place, and she'd had another crying fit over everything, she'd felt so overwhelmed. And once she'd calmed down, she'd gotten so tired…and Tony had told her he'd have Jace carry her back to her bedroom because she was nodding off…. Had she argued? It seemed so strange that she wouldn't have, but it was all so fuzzy. And she didn't even remember seeing the younger therapist, let alone getting to where she was.

She lay still for a few minutes more, knowing she was in her clothes from the day before and should shower and change, and knowing she should be upset about everything from David to her lack of memory over the night, and even the possibility that she'd been drugged again, but she couldn't quite bring herself to feel more than slightly embarrassed over any of it. Only barely upset, to the extent that she could almost put it all out of mind…as if it had all happened months upon months ago instead of last night. As if all of her emotions were dampened.

Maybe she'd finally cried them all out.

Somewhat grateful for the odd blankness that had overcome her, she stretched and pulled herself from bed. The clock told her she was already missing breakfast, but a shower felt so much more important right now.

Standing, she saw that Jace had left her a note on the bedside table: *After breakfast, you and David come to my office and we'll talk.*

Nodding to herself, thinking that that made sense enough, Lauren stripped out of her clothes and drifted under the warmth of a hot shower, where she leaned back against the tile and closed her eyes, content to let the water run over her. Content…that's how she felt, she realized. Just easy and content. Even her magic wasn't bothering her or distracting her this morning, so maybe the night away from David had done her good, after all. Maybe she'd only needed space.

Distantly, she knew she should be panicking right now—barely able to remember the night before, and unable to care, and barely able to sense the magic in her blood that had been so overpowering the night before. But she couldn't quite bring herself to be concerned.

***

David stood at the window in Jace's office, looking out over the grounds and waiting for Lauren. He'd already been told she'd fallen asleep crying in Tony's office the night before, and that Jace and the hall mother had gotten her into her room. Nobody had let him know what was going on with her until breakfast, but he hadn't been incredibly surprised when she hadn't shown up at his doorway the night before, despite what her note had promised. What made it worse was that he still didn't have any explanation that meant anything. And now she'd not just missed breakfast, but was twenty minutes late to the session.

When the door sounded behind him, he expected to turn and see Lauren boiling over with emotion already, or maybe ready to throw something at him.

Instead, she looked refreshed, if dazed. There were no circles under her eyes, no evidence that she'd been crying, and when she looked at him after meeting Jace Gathing's welcoming hug—and returning it—he saw nothing more than recognition. No condemnation or anger...no emotion at all.

"Lauren?" he tried. The nerves had sounded in his voice, and he said her name again. "Lauren, are you okay? I'm so sorry."

Waiting for her to respond, David tried to get a read on what she was feeling, or thinking, but there was nothing. And the blankness in Lauren's face—the total lack of emotion—was impossible to read, though it sent a tingle down his spine, knowing it could only signal how badly he'd fucked up.

Jace had been standing back by the closed door, as if to let them have the space to talk, but David almost wished he'd break in and offer some sort of push forward. Instead, he finally moved over to his desk to look at some papers, as if he could wait through a forever-long silence without blinking.

"We just need to talk, right?" she finally asked, her eyes meeting his.

His throat had closed up with emotion. *She sounds confused. Confused as I am, maybe.*

David nodded tightly and then gestured over to the couch. A table in front of it held a plate of fruit and pastry that he'd brought for her from breakfast when he'd realized she was skipping the meal, and Jace had provided three glasses and a pitcher of water already. Not sure what to say in response, he sat down on the couch and then looked back to the woman who'd perched herself beside him and immediately reached for a glass of water. In fact, the water seemed to have all of her focus, and she drank one glass down and poured herself another.

Jace sat down across from them after a moment. "Lauren, David said he was expecting you last night, but we both understand why you needed some space. How are you feeling this morning?"

She finished her second glass of water, and David nudged the plate of fruit and pastry closer to her so that she could reach it. Only when she was filling her glass yet again did she begin speaking. "I think I should be more upset than I am," she offered, "but I'm not…I guess I feel like it happened, and I don't want it to happen again, but it is what it is."

It is what it is? What the fuck?

It took him a moment to process that he hadn't imagined her response. "You should be pissed at me, Lauren," David said, too loudly.

He'd made Lauren jump in surprise, he'd spoken so forcefully, and he caught the look that Jace shot him, but he couldn't help it—how could Lauren be this casual right now? She'd been upset the day before, but now… it was as if she didn't care. "You're *allowed* to be pissed," he emphasized, waiting for Lauren to look at him.

Instead, Jace pulled his attention with a wave of his hand. "David, it sounds like you want her to be pissed. Does that mean you kissed another woman to get some reaction from her? Some passion?"

"What? No! Jesus, Jace—*Lauren*," he said, turning back to her and ignoring the therapist, "I wasn't thinking, alright? I'd just had that meeting and I was pissed, and I ran off and got drunk. Thinking about you made me stop, alright? And I came home. But, yeah, I want you to be pissed, I guess," he added, glancing quickly to Jace and then back. "I want you to give a shit and be angry and be jealous. Hell, hit me if you want to, but don't act like this doesn't bother you."

Lauren finally looked up, and she met his eyes, but the flatness in hers chilled him. The fullness he was used to seeing in them—the bloody emotion and magic—was absent. She could have been looking at a fucking cup of coffee instead of him, for all he saw in her gaze. "Like I was yesterday," she said, and then she took a bite of the pastry he'd brought her.

There was a knot in his throat, but he forced himself to nod. "Yeah, Lauren. Like you were yesterday."

She took another bite of the fucking pastry and then her eyes turned to Jace's. "But I'm not angry, so what does that mean?"

Nonplussed, the other man finally picked up the journal where David had seen him take down notes before. He glanced back over other passages, and when he looked up, his eyes moved between them before finally settling on Lauren. "Maybe it means you've finally had all you can take of David taking advantage of your emotions."

Beside her on the couch, David stilled, waiting for her to protest, but the one thing he could feel radiating from her was confusion. And, perhaps, apathy. As if everything between them had been boxed up and put to the side.

"I don't know," she answered, and her voice had gone back to that quiet, flat shell of her voice that he'd first heard her speak with upon entering, even any curiosity gone from it.

"I don't take advantage of her emotions," David bit

out. "I didn't kiss another woman to make Lauren angry. I did it because I was drunk and stressed and I'm a fucking idiot. I just want to know she's angry because she should be—I fucked up—and if she cares about me and our relationship, she'd be pissed that I kissed another woman, no matter whether I meant to or not." He'd spoken for Jace's benefit and Lauren's both, but he was looking at Lauren. When she didn't respond, he reached out and picked up her hand, gripping it between them.

The chemistry he'd come to expect wasn't there, though. It just wasn't there.

Her hand was solid and warm, but it felt no different from any other hand, and his breath caught in his throat. They couldn't know she had magic, so how would they have known to affect it? Had she done something to drain herself of reserves? What? And how?

In the background, Jace was talking and Lauren was answering him, but David put all of his focus into her hand in his. Slowly, full minutes later, he felt some new warmth—some sluggish sign of the magic that usually responded to him with just a brush of skin, within milliseconds of contact—but it was nothing compared to what he'd felt from her in recent days. Nothing even compared to what he'd felt in the cage when she'd been exhausted and scared. If he pushed himself to remember what he'd felt in the beginning, when he'd touched her casually after she'd first come to the ranch house to recover, all the way back when he'd mostly been avoiding her and she'd shied away from his touch…then, maybe, he could compare this response to the chemistry he'd thought he'd imagined then, before he knew of the vestiges of magic in her blood. But that was it. Her magic right now was as apathetic as she was—shelled, and vacant. Indolent, even.

He forced himself to look back up at Jace and offer

some sign of recognition, if only a grunt. He couldn't tell the man in front of him that Lauren was a witch and that they were bound together and that now her magic wasn't responding to him, connecting them. All he could do was hold her hand and wait, hoping it came back. Hoping she came back.

***

As the day wore on, he let her out of his sight—and out of contact—only when she used the restroom. Despite the raised eyebrows, despite what it might do to their cover story, he couldn't do anything else. Outside of Jace Gathing's office, he sat with his leg against hers as they followed directions and journaled about the weekend, and then he held her hand when they traded journals and he got to read what she'd written. Her entries might have been written by a computer, for all the emotion they held, while his brimmed with frustration and worry that he hadn't been able to hide, even knowing he should.

At lunch, his leg was against hers beneath the table, and that was when it finally came to him that he'd already seen other couples go through this Friday, and was seeing it play out between them now.

On Friday, when they'd first met Christopher, he'd been a shell of the man they'd hung out with and gotten to know over the weekend. And, today, just the same, Dora and Adrienne were both shells of the women who'd befriended Lauren, leaning on their husbands and looking around as if they were two steps behind in each conversation, each interaction. Where Lauren seemed more robotic, they seemed drugged, but it all came out to the same thing—a lack of emotion, a lack of energy, a lack of presence. And now that he knew what to look for, he could recognize it among other couples and remember it from the day before in still others who he'd interacted with. Of Lauren's group of friends, Christopher seemed normal today, but he clearly wasn't surprised about the way the girls were acting, either. Like they were all used to it. Like this was evidence of those cycles they'd talked about, which David had chalked up to therapeutic, self-help mumbo-jumbo.

He stopped eating, the food going stale in his mouth and catching in his throat. This wasn't natural, but it was all around him, and it had been around them since the beginning. And now it was affecting Lauren. When he thought about any given gathering, meal or otherwise, he could focus in on men and women who ran through a day with this dazed presence, both within the small group of friends they'd been focused on and among the couples he'd not gotten to know so well. The flatness, the fucking detachment, was worst in the morning, and eased as a day went on. And it only showed up in the men and women who were on the underside of the power dynamic in their relationship. But what the fuck did all that mean, given that he still couldn't figure out how any of them might be ingesting drugs? Not to mention the fact that, if Shea and this center weren't charging couples an arm and a leg once they were kept around, what the hell were they getting out of the set-up at all?

And, no matter what was happening, what did that have to do with Lauren's magic? And what did that mean for her?

The questions were piling up as quickly as the threats.

After lunch, he convinced Lauren to take a nap with him, and led her to his room. For once, the magic beneath her skin didn't even tempt him to undress her—he feared that that would only scare her off. Instead, he lay beside her in the bed and let her sleep, hoping it would make a difference. He'd taken his shirt off so that there'd be more contact between them, and her cheek and hand and forearm rested in the crook of his shoulder and on his chest while he lay awake and let her rest. He had his hands on her, one on her arm over his chest and one snuck beneath the rim of her shift, resting on her side above the waistline of her skirt, and like this he could truly feel how sluggish the magic was.

He knew it had been driving her crazy the last few days, building up within her blood and finding no outlet, but neither of them had wanted a complete absence of it. Maybe, it was true, that would make things easier in the long run, if her magic didn't run her emotions so ragged or drive him to distraction whenever he touched her, but the listlessness of her was killing him.

They were near the end of the time they had when he really felt the warmth beneath his hands that he'd grown accustomed to rising in her skin, but it was enough of a reaction that he could feel her shifting in her sleep.

Shifting sideways so that he could kiss her forehead and prod her toward waking, he ran his hand along her back and murmured her name until her eyes blinked open, slow and confused.

"Hey, kid."

"David…fuck, I guess I needed that," she whispered. Her eyes landed against his, and he wondered again if it was possible she'd been drugged the night before. But what with? And how would the others who'd gone through the usual routine have been drugged?

"How do you feel? You've been…off today," he commented, trying to keep his voice light.

She nodded as if she knew it, and lay her head back against his shoulder. "I don't know… I don't know how I feel. I want to be angry at you, but I'm not. And I feel like I should be scared, but I'm not."

Fuck, but her voice was slow, preoccupied. It didn't sound as flat as it had earlier, which was something, but David couldn't curb the feeling of dread nestled in his gut. "Jace is expecting us in the cafeteria for a group session in about fifteen minutes. You up for it?" he asked.

Still lying against him, she nodded belatedly.

When she didn't move, he added, "Lauren, I know we need to talk more, when you're more yourself, but we need to get through this. I can't apologize enough for what happened, but we have to be on the same page. I need you with me on this so we can get everyone out of here and get safe. So I can get you safe."

That flat, slow nod came from her again, her cheek against his chest, and he could guess that her eyes were half-closed. Whatever they'd done to her, she wasn't going to slip out of it easily. And whatever they decided to do now, or uncovered about this place, it looked like the next steps would be on him alone.

***

With Lauren in a private session with Dora and Adrienne in Jace's office, David could only trust that there'd be safety in numbers when he retreated to his room after dinner. He had about twenty minutes before he was supposed to join them, along with Van and Raul, so that all of the couples could be in the same spot for one last session today. He hoped he'd be able to retreat to his room again with Lauren at his side at that point, though he wasn't confident—he'd gotten the impression that he and the other husbands would only be joining the group briefly, and then getting pushed back out. There was nothing he could do about that now, however.

When Josh picked up the phone, David didn't bother with any of the pleasantries, or even real explanation.

"You guys need to get us out on Thursday. They're not gonna let us leave together, and we're not staying longer than that. Can you make that happen?"

"You guys okay?" Josh replied immediately.

"I don't know. I mean, yeah, but something's going on with Lauren. It's like all of her emotions are being held in check—evened out. And her magic's flatlining. It was—hell," David cursed, realizing he'd never really gotten around to explaining how Lauren's magic reacted to him, even to his partner. Things had moved too quickly. "It was reacting to me, when I touched her. Like, I could feel it under her skin, in her blood. And I was reacting to it, too, getting carried away by it. Now, it's barely there—like it got used up, but I don't know. It's been constant in her, between us, until today."

Silence greeted him for seconds, and then Josh answered, "And you were gonna tell me this when?"

"I'm telling you now," David said simply, a sigh pushing out of his lungs as he sat down. "It was between us, and we were trying to figure it out. It got worse once we got here. Lauren thinks it's because she wasn't using her magic at all once we left the house, not with gardening or anything else, even slightly, so it didn't have an outlet. If we'd known it'd react like it did, we wouldn't have come, but it is what it is."

"Yeah, alright, well…the flatlining emotions could be an antidepressant. But it's not like we have any idea how drugs affect magic—Lauren would know that, if anyone."

"I don't know if she's been drugged or not; beyond the magic, this is happening with others, the whole emotions being held down thing. I just know something's going on and I don't want us in here past Thursday. I've seen this effect, this flatness, in other couples, but I didn't realize how unnatural it was till today. And also, there are some other couples here who want to leave together but haven't been able to. If you guys come in hard, we'll get everyone out and figure out what the hell's happening together."

"I can come tomorrow," Josh answered quietly. "But I'm not gonna sugarcoat it—Adrias wants proof. He told me this morning he's ready to pay for you guys to stay in there for a month if it'll make a difference."

David gulped down the anger he'd been about to spew at his partner, knowing it wasn't his fault. "Yeah, well, we're not. And I'm not confident they're not gonna try to really keep us separated at some point, which is why it's Thursday. That'll give me time to try to track down this guy Phil talked about and get his story firsthand since the escorts come in on Wednesdays, but I'm not waiting longer than that. Hell, I want us out now, but I don't have a good enough reason to forego the chance of talking to this guy. Plus, with more people on the property, that might be a good opportunity to find some proof, which I hope to have before we get out. Just text me a time tomorrow, alright? I gotta go."

"Yeah, and you guys stay safe. You change your mind, let me know, and tell Lauren I say hi."

"If she hears me," David muttered, but his partner had already hung up.

Downstairs, he found Van and Raul waiting in the hallway already, passing the time with beers in their hands. Van nodded to the 2/3rds-full six-pack on the floor and David picked up one of the lagers for himself, forcing a grin in thanks. "So, this routine? Girls in session, we slide in, and then…"

"We'll probably head off without them and Jace'll keep 'em for another hour before they shoot off and find us or go to bed," Van answered. "You up for a few rounds of poker tonight? Way they are now, the girls'll be sleeping the day off and we might as well."

Jace pulled open the door and gestured them inside

before David could answer, and he followed the other men into the office. The girls were sitting on cushions in a circle that had been laid out on the floor, all of them sitting cross-legged and looking a bit dazed.

"*Meditation*," Raul whispered with a roll of his eyes.

David took the cushion beside Lauren and reached out for her hand. She squeezed back, and he felt a hint of the warmth he'd come to expect, but at no level he would have noticed if he hadn't been looking for it.

"We've been talking about centering ourselves, redirecting heavy passion and emotion into focus," Jace offered, looking around at each of them and meeting the men's eyes, in particular. "I'd asked the girls to practice this morning, and you may have noticed that they were a bit more withdrawn today—it's all part of the process. David, you look like you have a question?"

Given how he felt, he guessed he probably looked like he had a rant more than anything, but he bit his tongue and shook his head rather than say what was on his mind. "Lauren didn't seem like herself."

She squeezed his hand lightly, and he squeezed back, but Jace only shrugged. "Maybe you don't know what it's like for her to be so herself that she's comfortable?" he suggested. "But that's something for tomorrow, perhaps. For now, I want you to close your eyes and clear your minds."

David did as requested and went along with the thirty minutes of crap that Jace spouted, but Lauren's hand remained in his even when the therapist pushed them to keep their hands in their own laps. He'd liked this guy upon meeting him, and felt like he was more trustworthy than the others at one point, but he'd begun to feel like he was more full of theory and proverbs than anything, and nothing he said during their 'calming circle' dissuaded him.

When it was time to head out, he leaned into Lauren's ear before rising. "Come to my room tonight, okay? I'll see you then?"

Absently, her eyes on the floor, she nodded and met his lips with hers for a brief kiss.

Chapter 19

Her first sensation was of the cold air, a hard floor beneath her, and a wish for a blanket. And then she opened her eyes.

She'd woken up to cinderblock walls that were gray and faded, as if in warning that she wouldn't see the sun any sooner than they'd allow. Oddly, the floors were a warm hardwood, oaky and dark in color, smooth beneath her skin. It was like she'd been plopped into a bomb shelter with luxury-level flooring.

Her eyes searching the room for any further hint of where she was, Lauren tugged her sweater tighter around herself, glad for its warmth, and sat up in a cross-legged position, leaving herself in the center of the room. Her feet were bare, sticking out from her jeans, but she couldn't remember if she'd been wearing shoes. Last she remembered, she'd been at her desk in her little room on the second floor, in these clothes, writing that letter and wondering if David was already asleep, or whether he was simply waiting for her to knock at his door.

Had she been wearing shoes or socks? Probably not, she thought now.

Mentally, she went over the space, feeling oddly detached from everything but the chill in the air and the inviting warmth of the wood beneath her feet. The room was square and stifling—maybe ten feet to each side and across, and up to the ceilings, too. The door was little more than a line in the cement wall, itself built of more gray cement and barely visible in the dim light. If she didn't focus on it, she lost track of where it was, it blended in so well. What light there was came from naked bulbs attached to the ceiling, but they were more yellow than white. She struggled to hear anything beyond her own breathing, but there was nothing to be heard, just as there was little enough to be seen.

With minutes passing, she began to wish she could fall asleep, if only to pass time. Finally, she lay back down, curled onto her side, and did her best to at least pretend the floor was warm enough to heat her whole body, and softer, and that David was just behind her, near on to joining her. Soon enough, it became easier to imagine herself all but melting into the wood of the floor, gaining comfort from it as she would have from David, and then she slept.

***

When Lauren didn't come by as promised, David had to assume she'd been too tired, or that her anger had come back to her in full force. It had been a rough day, he knew, and with little to show for it. And as relaxed as she'd been in Jace's office, she'd looked exhausted and wary of him. But hours later, in bed and awake, the worrying was beginning to get to him.

Maybe everyone around them thought they were

quarrelling, and God knew they had been, but he'd needed to see Lauren tonight. He'd needed to see her coming back to herself, whether that meant anger or love or anything in between. Over a poker game, both Van and Raul had assured him that this was how things went around here—the emotion built up and exploded, and both their wives had days where they were 'out of it' and withdrawn, but it passed after a day. The girls went back to normal. They'd assured him Lauren would be back to herself tomorrow.

But Lauren had said she'd be joining him in his room. Had she really been that tired, that she might have just gone to her room to change clothes or shower, and changed her mind and gone to bed instead? Or forgotten her promise? The more he thought about it, the more he worried. Whether she'd been too tired or forgetful, either way, that wasn't her. When he looked at the clock a last time before drifting off, it was nearly 4 AM.

Even before the room's alarm sounded, though, he'd showered and shaved and been headed for breakfast—no matter that he'd be the first one in the cafeteria. He'd wanted to be there when she arrived.

Filling time, he helped the two kitchen workers who were present, setting out silverware and cups, dropping off carafes of juice and water. By the time they'd finished and he'd gotten some coffee, adding too much sugar, the kitchen staff had begun uncovering trays and other guests were beginning to trickle in, but Lauren wasn't among them.

As he had the day before, he joined Christopher and Phil. Today, Christopher was having another off-day, as he had when they'd first met him. He was quiet and withdrawn as Lauren and others had been the day before, but Phil ignored David when he asked about it, as if it was a bitter subject. Awkwardly, the three of them settled into a mostly silent breakfast and waited for Lauren.

When she finally did walk in, David had to fight the urge to jump to his feet and greet her; instead, he stayed at the table as he watched her move into line to get breakfast, and listened to the inane chatter of other couples who'd joined their table. He thought he'd done a decent job of acting out his role the last few days, but he was running low on patience. Especially now that Lauren once again didn't look herself, walking around as if she was in a daze, not even having glanced his way. Seeing her like this, pretending to listen to the conversation around him, he was glad that he hadn't jumped up to greet her. He needed this time to try to figure out what was happening, and exactly what had gone wrong.

David leaned over his empty plate and caught Phil's eye. "Lauren yesterday, Christopher today—you guys said this goes on and off. A day at a time. Fine, okay, but Lauren…"

Phil took the prompt and looked across the room. David watched as the other man's eyes narrowed. He'd come to respect this man's intelligence, and knew he was one of the ones who felt trapped, anxious to get out of this place and angry that he'd become stuck along with Christopher. Now, his lips tightened. "Two days in a row?" he asked, but it was more a statement than anything.

David nodded, but it wasn't needed; they both knew she'd been dazed the day before also, and everything anyone had said suggested that these phases went in single days—maybe two per week, maybe three—and the men David had actually talked to about it seemed to ignore it willfully, knowing they couldn't do anything about it or offer any explanation.

"Let's hear what she says," Phil said quietly. "Maybe she's just tired, or taking it harder than the others."

"*It?*" David hissed.

Across from him, Phil shrugged. He nudged Christopher, looking for a response, but the other man's gaze was focused on his coffee, and moved upward only languidly. "Did you see Lauren last night?" Phil asked.

Christopher's gaze wandered across the room slowly, finding her and then coming back to David, and then to Phil. It was slow, unemotional—robotic—and David fought the urge to reach across the table and splash water into the other man's face, if not actually strike him. These two were the closest thing he and Lauren had to allies in this place—he didn't need to start a brawl in the cafeteria when they clearly didn't have any more of an answer than he did.

Christopher shrugged, his head already turning back to the conversation running beside them.

Giving up on any further reaction, David looked over to see Lauren headed to the coffee bar. She was moving more slowly than usual, even more slowly than yesterday or after she'd gotten that concussion, and there was no expression on her face. Her eyes didn't wander at all and her movements were measured, if steady—lifeless, if movement could be described that way. He looked back to Phil. The other man's face was tight with nerves, and David realized he actually looked pained right now.

"We get through the bad days because of the good days," he said quietly, "and because I don't know what choice we have. But, David, be careful if you ask about it. I didn't see Chris for four days after I brought it up, but for mealtimes and forced therapy sessions—I couldn't get him alone, much as I tried. And we did try. I don't know if it's drugs or what, but we shouldn't talk about it here. Just… think about it before you ask," he finished.

David forced himself to nod, despite the chill he felt at the idea of a separation like that, and of what these people had already gone through, to get to the point where this was accepted. *Four days.* "We need to talk. Later." He'd decided that morning that he'd tell Phil, and maybe even Van, what he was doing there, and that they'd be getting out Thursday. He needed help to try to find the proof Adrias wanted, and with the clock ticking, there was no reason not to get the other men involved. Worried as they were about their spouses, he was done worrying if they'd tell Shea or Tony their secrets—the look on Phil's face during this conversation had been confirmation enough of that by itself, if anything. And while he couldn't get a read on Raul, he felt fairly sure that Van felt the same.

When Lauren finally reached the table, there was none of the warmth he was accustomed to—she sat down with a small, mechanical smile offered in his direction and then began to eat her toast and eggs, her eyes on her plate. Like Christopher across from her, her gaze wandered to whatever conversation was loudest around them, but didn't seem to take anything in. Beneath the table, David reached sideways and placed his hand on her knee, beneath the hem of her skirt, but there was no reaction— not in her body language, not in her skin or her magic. She simply kept eating.

The night before, her chair had been nearly against his, as usual. Her leg had been crossed so that her foot rested against his lower leg—she'd wanted the contact, clearly, and he'd thought she'd been getting back to normal in behavior if not in expression. He'd been glad for it, and taken her after-dinner behavior in Jace's office as a symptom of the meditation, foggy as it had been. But before that, through dinner, they'd talked lightly and traded glances—they'd been on the same page even if she had seemed withdrawn, slightly removed from her normal self, and even if her magic had been dulled, less heated. Even yesterday morning, in Jace's office, he'd felt more connected than this on some level—there'd been confusion in her glances then, and questions he could work with.

Now, there was just distance. They could have been strangers, to the extent that he even caught some of the other men and women at the table glancing their way. The meaning was clear, mirroring his own thoughts. *This is Day Two. What happened?* Adrienne and Dora especially looked worried, making it clear that they were back to being themselves. It was only Lauren who'd remained in the fog.

Rather than sitting and watching her nibble at her food, David finally left her to Phil's watchful eye and rose for another trip to the coffee bar, fixing himself a second cup that he'd be able to walk away with. For the first time, he was glad that the two of them were scheduled for a private therapy session sooner than later—it wouldn't be alone time, but maybe it would be private enough that he'd be able to figure out what the hell was going on here without another therapist pulling her away from his sight. Hell, maybe the goddamned therapist could even help him figure this out since it seemed as if this wasn't normal even by their standards.

When the bell rang to signal all of the couples that they should head to their first commitment, David met Lauren at the exit and moved with her down the hall, biting his lip to keep from saying anything, and waiting. There were too many people around to talk about her magic, and he didn't know what more to say beyond that she was acting odd, which hadn't done any good the day before. And, after what Phil had said about his experience in asking questions, they couldn't afford to take chances. Not after he'd already gotten these therapists' attention for all of the wrong reasons.

He stepped up to open Tony's office door for her, and

she said, 'thank you', and it was the first time he'd heard her voice all morning.

Inside, David ushered her to the couch and tried to quell the unease running through him—something was wrong, even more so than yesterday, and he couldn't fix it if he didn't know what the problem was, but he doubted a meeting with Toscano was going to help matters.

The man was already seated in his chair across from the couch, eyeing them keenly as they entered. Was he watching Lauren more closely? David couldn't be sure, but it seemed like he might be.

"And how's everything this morning, Lauren? David?" he asked as they sat.

Lauren just offered that mechanical smile again, but David answered, "Alright, I guess. Quiet," he added with a glance sideways. Lauren had sat down next to him, but there was space between them that wouldn't normally have been there.

"Lauren, you were quiet yesterday, but today you seem more placid than usual, am I right?" Toscano asked next. "More than over the weekend, certainly?"

"I feel fine. Good," she answered immediately, but her voice was flat. As if the answer had been programmed into her—she'd known it was right, so she'd said it, simple as that.

"I'm sorry," David said after another moment of what was beginning to feel like maddening quiet. "Doc, could we have a minute of privacy?"

"Something you don't feel you can share with me?" he asked, an eyebrow raising the only sign of movement from him.

"Just...I'd like to speak to Lauren in private, if it's alright." David only just caught himself from clenching his fists—every instinct he had was telling him to grab Lauren by the hand, pull her out, and call the whole damn investigation off. Suddenly, he felt sure he should never have agreed to bring her into this. *Thursday's too far out,* he realized. *We can't wait that long.*

"Well, David, if you and Lauren both feel adamant that you need a few minutes of privacy, I suppose I won't stand in the way of that, but are you both on the same page?"

Toscano looked at Lauren, seeming to gauge her. "Lauren, do you feel the same?"

She glanced toward David, not bothering to meet his eyes, and then she shook her head. "We're fine," she answered. "We shouldn't waste this time with you, Dr. Toscano. Right, David? Isn't this what we're here for?" she asked.

David let his nails dig into his palms until the pain convinced him he was awake, that this was happening. "Fine," he grunted after a moment, his eyes refocused on their supposed therapist. *Don't ask about her blankness. Don't give them a reason to separate you—Phil warned you for a reason.* The other man's warning echoing in his mind, he focused instead on their broken plan from the evening before. "Last night, I expected her to come by my room. She'd been off all day and she's off now, but I thought we were on the same page. I thought we were starting to get past what...what happened over the weekend; that we could talk it out. But she kissed me goodbye in Jace's office with a promise she'd be by after and then she was a no-show, an hour after promising she'd come by. Then she comes into breakfast this morning and doesn't say a goddamned word to me. Treats me like I'm a fucking stranger. You tell me if you wouldn't want alone time for a fucking second after a turn-around like that."

"You sound angry, David."

'You sound angry.' Are you fucking kidding me?

Another few seconds went by as David processed the scene unfolding around him. Toscano looked confused by *him*, and Lauren looked…well, she still looked fucking flat, or maybe slightly embarrassed, if anything. What the hell was going on?

"You wanna psychoanalyze what I'm feeling right this second? Fine. Try confused, maybe a little hurt. You wanna lay blame now or what?" he asked, leaning back into the couch.

"Do you think that's what this is about, David? Laying blame?" Toscano asked next.

This is like every bad therapy session in every movie, he thought, pushing him again to wonder how many of these therapists were charlatans. Shaking off the thought, he refocused. Lauren was looking at him along with Toscano now, both apparently waiting for a response.

"No, I don't," he finally answered. "But I thought we left off yesterday on a good point, and I want to get back to our life together sooner than later."

"Fair enough," Toscano answered, leaning back across from them.

As the man began offering a mini-lecture on communication between couples, David forced his body to relax, but when his leg shifted a few minutes later and his knee came to rest against Lauren's, she shifted away, and he saw Toscano noting the move even as he himself processed what it could mean.

"David, I think Lauren and I may need to discuss a few things in private—I'm seeing signs that perhaps she is on a different page, and you may have been right earlier, that last night needs to be addressed. Would you excuse us?"

He glanced to Lauren, waiting for her to insist that he stay—that they remain together, as they'd agreed to do yesterday, keeping either of them out of private therapy sessions as much as possible—but she was looking at her hands again, her face flat. Instinctively, he knew she wasn't about to disagree, and short of causing a scene, there was nothing for him to do but leave.

***

With David out of the room, Lauren shook her head to try to wake herself up again. She knew Toscano was staring at her, and she knew something was wrong, but she was just so drained. The day before, she'd felt unemotional and flat…but she hadn't felt like this. Now, she felt almost detached from herself, as if the role she'd been playing had eclipsed the person she'd been all her life, and now she was…nobody. Nothing.

"Lauren, are you alright, dear?" Toscano asked.

"I don't know," she answered quietly. He gave her time, and she looked up to return his gaze. "I only vaguely remember yesterday, and I don't remember telling David I'd go by his room, but maybe…"

"Maybe you forgot?" the therapist finished for her. "Perhaps you're dissociating because of the problems in your relationship. You've spent the last two nights apart, I believe—maybe that space has given you time to…come to yourself?"

No, that couldn't be it, she told herself. She loved David, for better or worse—the way they connected, space away from him was the last thing she wanted. Could she have told him she'd come by, and then forgotten?

"I…if I told him I'd come by, I must have forgiven him," Lauren murmured, fighting to remember either anger or forgiveness at this point.

"Ah, for kissing that woman. Did he tell you the extent of it? Did you talk about it?" the therapist pressed. "Perhaps he talked you out of being angry with him—

that's my fear, if you agreed to go by his room last night," the man pointed out, and Lauren thought she heard an edge of something more than regret in his voice. Sarcasm? But that didn't make sense.

Everything was just such a fog, and even with knowing that she shouldn't trust the man in front of her—that David was the only one anywhere nearby who she should let her guard down around—her instinct now was to fall into the role they'd built for her and see if Toscano could help her get back to feeling like herself. To feeling…something. She remembered Christopher telling her yesterday that she'd feel like herself again today. Not worse. And David had been so frustrated…at least Toscano seemed to mean well. And while she thought David had been angry at the therapist more than at her not showing up, maybe she could use this time to get back to herself, and then help David figure things out so they could all leave this place. At the thought of that, a dagger of desperation slid through her—she wanted to leave this place and go home, to the ranch house with David. Anything that got her there, she'd do, even if it meant getting help from this man in front of her.

"I don't remember last night, but David means everything to me. I don't want to disappoint him," she said. "If you can help me remember…I know we can work things out. I could go get him now, and we could all talk."

Toscano handed her a tissue, and Lauren realized there were tears leaking from her eyes. She hadn't even realized she was crying. Did she feel sad, even? What was wrong with her?

"Let's bring David in later, Lauren. And don't be embarrassed that you're crying—yes, I can see it in your face, dear. It's only natural, with what you're going through. David must give you the space and time to not worry about disappointing him. So that you can focus on yourself, not on his reactions to what you're doing or thinking. I wonder if he is?" the man added.

Lauren glanced up and then down, overtaken by nerves and confusion. For a moment, she almost thought Toscano had smiled with pointing that out, little sense as that would make, but she was too tired to think about it. She was so tired.

"If you don't remember last night," the man before her went on, "perhaps it's due to stress. Or perhaps your body just needed the rest away from David again so badly that it took the opportunity to shut down for the night, given the privacy? I'm sure you'll remember yesterday later."

The words rang hollow to her, but what else could it be? Without speaking, she nodded jerkily and stuffed the soiled tissue she'd held into a pocket.

"So, let's talk about privacy, Lauren. How jealous is David, exactly? How much space does he give you?"

Remembering the whole of their story and what David might have shared, Lauren forced herself to come back to it, and to think—however briefly—of David as the mean character they'd created, rather than as the David she knew. When she looked back to meet Toscano's eyes, about to tell more half-truths, he cut her off.

"I know you sanitized things before, Lauren, bad as they sounded. I could see on your face that you were holding back. I want you to tell me about your relationship in more detail, alright? And about your feelings, as well, and not just the good ones. You skated past the bad things before, and I let you, but that's what I want you to focus on today."

Lauren had said so much already—admitted so much—she'd felt as if she had focused only on the bad, and now she was so tired, parceling out the truth and thinking about how it would look seemed nearly impossible. Closing her eyes, Lauren took a deep breath and realized that she'd simply have to follow his directions, and tell him all she could, come what may, and maybe later they'd get past everything to what her brain was doing, in blocking out the day before. Nothing made sense at this point, but if a professional was telling her what to do… maybe that made sense. And what did it matter anyway, if she and David would be leaving together, and nothing they said here mattered? Josh would be coming for them if they didn't leave on their own, and it would all be fine somehow, and none of this would matter.

Thankful that she was too tired to feel the weight of what she shared, she told Toscano the whole of the story, to the extent that that was possible, slipping into the role David and Josh had drawn for her and blocking out the meaning of her own words. Josh and David had been careful to talk to her about how she could pick and choose what she said, leaving out context so that she wouldn't have to lie, and she'd done it before more carefully, attempting to make it sound to Jace and Shea like their relationship had been more than sex and violence, but now that Toscano was rushing her past the good side of things, and her positive feelings…saying it all aloud, she realized how horrible it all made David sound, to say that he'd tied her up and teased her after they'd met, until she'd given in to him, and then she hadn't known where else to go for help when she'd needed it. And then he'd been protective of her to the extent that he'd ordered her not to leave their house, and, yes, she'd quit school after she'd met him, and he'd forced himself on her more than once when she'd told him she wasn't ready or felt too tired. That he'd left bruises on her skin over and over again, and that she never, ever left the house without him. All of it was true… but without the whole of the context, it turned him into a villain when, more often than not, he'd been her protector.

"And he was like this with you from the beginning?" Toscano asked when she'd stopped speaking.

Fuck, how do I answer that?

Lauren met Toscano's eyes and forced herself to think of when she and David had first met. She thought of the bar at first. "He was—he *is* mostly nice," she corrected herself. "You have to understand that. When I met him, I couldn't resist him, from the beginning. He listened to me. He cared about what I was saying. I liked the way he put his hand on my back and ordered for me, and looked at me. And the chemistry between us…that was so strong, from the moment we met. Like nobody else I've ever been around. But after we left the bar…after that first night…it's all been, I don't know, a roller coaster," she added helplessly.

Toscano's silence said all it needed to, and she thought of just after that night at the bar, when she'd woken up at the ranch house in the men's interrogation room. "He got cruel, I guess, soon, but he was focused on work instead of a relationship," she said carefully. "And he could tell I was attracted to him."

"How?"

Lauren looked out the window, away from the therapist, but he clicked his fingers and brought her eyes back to him.

"You've glossed over things, Lauren. Hidden them. If I'm going to help you, you have to tell me what you're thinking. How did he know you were attracted to him? You said he tied you up; wouldn't let you leave his home—did you try? And, when was he first cruel? Was it at the same time, loosely?"

Lauren swallowed down the drive to lie back on the couch and close her eyes. She felt like she'd said too much now, but didn't know how to back up. Why had she told him all that? Why? Toscano's eyes were following her every breath, and she finally answered. "He…I couldn't help reacting when he touched me. He told me he could see me reacting. He said he could tell I desired him, from the way my eyes changed, and I…shivered. When he touched me. When he said my name," she added quietly, remembering those days in the ranch house when his presence had been both a comfort and something to be feared. She'd spent so many hours alone, sometimes she'd desperately wanted him to walk into that room and talk to her, but she'd so often regretted it as soon as he had.

She looked back at Toscano. "I don't know what he saw—why my reaction to him was so easy to read. But it was."

"And when he was first cruel to you. Tell me about the first time he hit you," Toscano prompted her.

Lauren's eyes jarred up to his, and she felt a flush rising to her cheeks. "I don't want to talk about that. I think I need a break," she found herself whispering.

Toscano shook his head. "No, if you leave this room, you'll go find David and convince yourself that these details are only details of the past, not worth talking about. We've started now. I want to finish. Tell me about the first time he hit you."

Lauren closed her eyes. "Can I have something to drink?" she asked.

Toscano set down his legal pad and got up to cross the room to a small mini-fridge. He returned with a bottle of water that he set in her hand, and Lauren couldn't help shivering at the cold of the bottle—it was one more reminder of the cold bottled waters that David had brought to her during that first week at the ranch house.

"Go ahead," he prodded her after she'd drunk some of the water down and rested the bottle on her leg.

Her mouth was dry again already, but maybe this was the hard part that David and Josh had warned her about. Going over these things she'd rather forget. For the sake of the other people who were stuck here, and had gotten wrapped up into this, at least, maybe she just had to keep going and get through this session.

"He was asking me questions I didn't want to answer. About my past. I guess he wanted specific answers…that I wasn't giving…and he wanted to get my attention, to push me to answer. He slapped me. It wasn't hard, but it surprised me."

"With the palm of his hand or the back of his hand?"

"The back," Lauren whispered.

"And how did you feel?"

Lauren blinked, a wave of tiredness running through her. She only wanted to sleep. "I was more upset than hurt. I mean, it hurt…but I liked him, still, even though I didn't want to. I don't know if he could tell or not."

Toscano was quiet for a moment, and then he pressed, "You don't sound like you think him hitting you that time was cruel. But *you* used that word. When did cruelty come into things, Lauren?"

She gulped down the rest of the water, feeling suddenly breathless. *I shouldn't be talking about any of this*, she told herself. But somehow, it was as if her brain and what she knew were disconnected from her mouth, and what she was able to control. "Before we slept together. That day. He pointed out that he was hurting me, and that I still desired him. That I was afraid of him and in pain because of him… and still wanted him to touch me. He teased me, about wanting him, and I was ashamed…but it was true."

"Ah," Toscano breathed out. "And that, my dear, is what he's been running with, I'm afraid. That memory is in his mind also, you see. It feeds into him excusing his own behavior, the way he treats you."

Lauren took another tissue from the offered box and shook her head helplessly. It was all one-sided, but nothing he'd said was false, either, she guessed. David had told her as much the night before they'd gone to the in-take center, hadn't he? He'd said she was submissive, and liked his control, and that that had made it alright, alongside their goals. She'd had no defense against any of his reason, and had felt nearly as helpless then as she did now.

"Well, I'm glad the two of you came to us. That shows he wants to do better," Toscano replied after a few seconds more of silence passed. "Needless to say, the way things stand, I don't think the two of you can think of leaving this week as planned, and I've told David as much, but if he cares as much about this marriage as he claims to, he'll be willing to stay for as long as this takes. I think, though, it's my expert opinion that it would make sense for the two of you to spend some time apart, rather than for you to be trying to visit him at night. Whatever drove you to stay in your own room last night, I believe your instincts were correct. You'll make him understand what he stands to lose if this doesn't work."

The man's eyes were glued to hers, and Lauren had to force herself to nod. That was the last thing she wanted, and yet she felt strangely blank, as she had all morning, ever since the moment she'd woken up.

"Good. I'll tell him so. First, I want to get you settled in the east wing."

Chapter 20

Y ou've got her in solitary confinement? You can't be serious," David fumed. "We're here to work our shit out *together*."

"Not confinement, David—retreat. It will give her some time to recover herself."

"And us?" he asked, taking a step in toward the therapist. "How about recovering us?"

"I suppose that remains to be seen, doesn't it? In any case, I wanted to let you know of the situation's turn, but I have another appointment now. You'll be speaking with Dr. Gathing tonight after the evening meal," he added.

The air seemed to close in on David after the door shut behind Toscano. He found himself sitting heavily at the desk. Staring at the bag that held his burner, he couldn't think of what to do next. What was all this? Was it just because of the story he and Lauren had presented, or was the morning's strangeness, and this new separation, what the couples who they hadn't met had experienced before disappearing? And, more to the point, did it mean Lauren was actually in danger, or that they were getting closer to what had brought them here to begin with?

And does it matter?

Either way, his fingers were itching to shut this down even if it meant calling it quits on the case and those who'd already gone missing. He just couldn't do that safely when he had no clue exactly where Lauren was—there were too many variables now for him to call it off before he found her.

Closing his mind to the possibility that she was out of reach for anything beyond a few hours, he ran his hand through his hair and pulled on a button-down over his t-shirt so that he could head straight to dinner—or out into the woods—without returning to his room first.

Outside the door, he saw one of the security men standing nonchalantly on the other side of the grand staircase, barring anyone passing into the other wing, but he relaxed visibly when David didn't engage. From the look on the man's face, David was certain he'd been led to expect a fight, or at least a confrontation. Instead, David nodded to him and headed downstairs, where he planned to double back toward the corner stairs and explore the floors above them, which the grand staircase didn't reach to. He didn't need this man seeing the buttons on the elevator go up instead of down, however, or seeing David head for the other staircase just to avoid him. Let the man guard the other, private wing where his other half could be found. Just for now, he had other plans, and figured he might have more maneuvering room than he'd had before—if only because they'd mostly be cautious of him seeking her out and not sneaking around in general.

At the corner staircase, David glanced around only long enough to make sure he wouldn't be seen, and then he slipped into the rarely used door—these had been presented to them as fire stairs more than anything, and stairs to reach the upper floors when extra guest rooms were needed, but it was hard to imagine they'd leave three floors barely used. He passed by the first few floors and came to the top, the sixth floor. He'd yet to speak to anyone who'd been up to these floors, and if they were so proud of only taking in fifteen couples at a time, ever, and thus needing only thirty rooms in this wing…why these upper floors? He could think of a lot of easy explanations. He could just as easily see many of them being lies, too.

It almost surprised him when the access card he'd lifted from a guard that morning allowed him into the hall—maybe the man had been too embarrassed to report it stolen, or maybe they weren't so monitored as he'd thought. One way or another, it worked in his favor.

The hall looked just like the ones below except in that the doors leading off of his hall and Lauren's had small windows in them. There were curtains to cover them from the inside, sure, but there *were* windows. These had none—not even spy holes. And, light switches were found in the hallway, just beside each door.

David tried the first door he came to. It moved heavily, as if it wasn't used to moving or weighed three times what a door ought to, and he soon saw why. Inside, the space was empty—and odd. The floor was a gorgeous hardwood, like he'd expect in a new luxury home. The walls, in absolute contrast, were gray cinderblock—and this was why the door hadn't wanted to move. There was cinderblock held to the back of it, with no handle visible. With the door closed, he saw that someone shut into the room wouldn't just have no exit—they might not even realize where the door was, the seams were so tight and rough, and the room so dim. There was no light switch on the inside of the room, and hitting the light switch in the hall showed that the light inside had been left on—it went from dim to dark and back again.

Examining the door from the outside, he saw that it could be locked with a key—an actual key, not a key card like he had.

He moved to the next door, which was also unlocked, but this one opened smoothly.

Inside, he found a sort of lounge. Both the walls and the floor were covered over with the deep, expensive hardwood he'd seen previously, and there was a variety of pillows and cushions spread throughout the room. There were also a few small writing desks, as if meant for people who were sitting on the floor and wanting a surface. Beyond these, there wasn't much to see—it was clean, blank and waiting, and maybe twice as large as the stifling cinderblock room next door.

Moving down the hall, he found a repetition of this same pattern. An odd cinderblock-walled room followed by a hardwood lounge in a constant back-and-forth pattern. The more he explored the rooms, the more he was uncomfortable with what he saw. But at the same time, there was nothing here that he could even begin to paint as being incriminating or suspicious in relation to the missing couples. And there were no cabinets or spaces even to be searched for clues—there were hard surfaces, little lap tables without drawers, and pillows, and that was it. It was all just strange.

When he got to the last room, it was an odd one out, so he wasn't sure what to expect behind the door—whatever he'd have thought of, though, it wouldn't have been what he got. This space looked like a state-of-the-art security space, built just to keep an eye on all of the rooms he'd just passed by.

But then there was the wall opposite the computers and monitors showing those rooms. This wall had bottles hanging from the wall, each of them with three levers above them. Each set of three levers was labeled with a room number, and a quick glance back down the hall assured him that the numbers listed belonged to the cinderblock rooms.

What the fuck? He pushed against the security door again, slipping inside and letting it shut behind him. Closer up, he could see the bottles were attached to tubes leading into the wall. Still no labels, though. He turned to a cabinet against the wall and opened it up to find the answers. Rows and rows of bottles, all neatly labeled.

Two of the formulas he recognized, and his gut clenched. Rohypnol and chloroform. Whatever the others were, he didn't imagine they were any less suspicious. On the lowest shelf, there was a covered tray, and a quick glance showed it to be full of hypodermic needles already readied with heavy doses of adrenaline.

Back out in the hall, he went into the first cinderblock room he came to—as he'd expected, there were air vents, but there were other vents also, parceled into the floor. Waiting, he felt sure, for the aerosol versions of the chemicals he'd just seen.

Whatever these people were doing, they wanted their victims alert, but they didn't want them remembering a goddamned thing. And they wanted control over their senses—awake, unconscious, aware…it was all semantics. Whoever was making decisions here was treating their subjects like push-button dummies.

There'd still been no sign of anyone else when he hit the staircase again, wavering between playing it calm, searching for Lauren, or getting Josh on the line and calling this whole thing off. Now he had evidence of something…he just didn't know what, exactly.

The decision was made for him as he reached the second floor and nearly ran into Samantha Shea, who he hadn't seen practically at all since their last meeting.

Predictably, her demeanor was cool, but he reminded himself he was nothing more than a jerk of a white suit to her, who could reasonably enough be expected to search for his wife. Having been upstairs didn't mean he would have noticed anything suspicious—he could have just been coming from his room on the next floor up, after all.

He spoke before she could, hefting anger into place to cover the concern he felt ringing through his brain.

"Where is she? I didn't agree to this, and you keeping her from me isn't—"

"Mr. Merriweather," she stopped him, that implacable smile covering her lips. "Let's talk about this like adults, please."

"Adults don't get put in time-out, lady, or go into a therapy unit with the plan of feeling like they're in prison, which is about what we're getting to," he gritted out, his fists already clenched. "Where is she?"

Her smile was forced now, but too late he noticed that her own hand had slipped into her pocket. Even as he caught the meaning and went to slip past her, two of the security guards who he'd passed dozens of times came pushing through the door into the next level. Before he could decide whether he'd be better off running or continuing his charade, she'd stepped out of the way and he'd been shoved up hard against the wall.

He was expecting cuffs or threats when he felt a sharp sting at his neck, and then things went dark, with nothing left for him to consider or fight through.

***

The fog Lauren had felt that morning had been slow in fading, but now that it had, she was having a harder time reconciling herself to the way she'd treated David that morning, and more recently, how she could have let that therapist convince her that they needed time apart. What had she been thinking? And why in God's name had she said so much or gone along with him?

For the fifth time in thirty minutes, she paced to the window and then back to the door, and then tried the handle again. With the door to her admittedly swanky room locked, she'd been cut off from him entirely.

No other course of action before her, she finally began using her fists on the heavy wooden door, slapping into it and rapping at it alternately as she called out for attention. "Hey! Someone! I want to talk to someone! Hey!" She paused and took a breath, and then went for it, screaming for all she was worth. "HELP! SOMEONE, HELP ME! HELP!"

The sounds of her yells were beginning to hurt her own ears by the time the door was yanked forward from beneath her palms.

"Lauren, dear, you need to calm down," Dr. Toscano spoke without taking a beat.

Swallowing down the nerves she felt suddenly, inexplicably, Lauren took a step backward. The therapist she'd gotten to know stood calmly in front of her, but he looked far from harmless, flanked as he was by two large guards she hadn't seen before. "I've changed my mind," she said quietly. "I'd like to go back to my regular room…please."

"I gathered that." Gesturing for the guards to wait in the hall, the man stepped further into Lauren's room and walked in to circle the space, dipping his fingers along the dresser and bed as he moved. "And why would that be? Perhaps because you fear your husband will be angry with you for agreeing to the separation?" he suggested.

"What? No! No, I just…I've changed my mind. I don't know what I was thinking."

"That's right," Toscano commented, turning suddenly

to face her. "You don't know because he doesn't give you time to think, or space, and so it was overwhelming and confusing when you took a moment to think for yourself, wasn't it?"

"No, that's not…"

"But it is, Lauren," the man interrupted her, and with that he placed one hand on her shoulder and guided her toward the armchair by the window. "You need to relax. Given space, you leapt at it, but now you're afraid— partly because it's so new. You have to trust me on this, dear. You're not the first to come here seeking relief from an overbearing husband."

Lauren took a glance at the door and the security guards beyond it, shaking her head. "I want to talk to him then, at least," she offered.

"Tomorrow. For now, how does coffee sound?" he asked, smiling too brightly.

Tomorrow? "I thought I'd be having dinner with David?"

"Not tonight, dear. You need some space."

Lauren shook her head again, but allowed herself to be pressured backward into the chair. The doctor, she could maybe get past, but those guards in the hall? There wasn't a chance. She was trapped.

***

David woke up stiff, with a pounding behind his eyes that suggested he really ought to try to pass out again, but instead he twisted his neck to look around from where he'd been lying on a hard floor. Stretching, he rolled onto his back, blinking up at the ceiling a moment later. He was in one of the cinderblock rooms.

"Hi, David. Feeling calmer?"

He rolled upward into a seated position on the hardwood floor, one hand reaching naturally to his forehead. He stared at the doctor and propped himself forward, elbow on knee. "What is this?" he grunted, glancing around again and then meeting Jace Gathing's eyes. The young therapist sat on a fluffed up pillow a few feet away, the security guards who'd stopped him earlier just behind him.

"This is me wanting to know more about your wife. What you know about her."

"What I know about my wife? Are you listening to yourself?"

The man smiled and went on as if he hadn't heard the sarcasm. "She feels things solidly—at first, we didn't realize the depth of the emotion, to tell you the truth. And then we didn't realize how tightly the emotion was tied to you. We're still getting a feel for that, I admit. I'm curious, though—it seems she has both natural magic and magic affecting her emotions, binding her to you more closely. It's stronger near you. Why is that, I wonder? You don't seem like the warlock type. So, did she cast the spell on herself, and was it on accident or on purpose? Before or after you hurt her?"

David shook his head, closing his eyes against the doctor's prattling and trying to think beyond the pounding in his skull. "I don't know what you're talking about," he muttered. What the fuck was going on here?

"Let's not, alright? You and I both know there's magic involved here. Since we've been watching more closely, we've seen you feeling it, reacting to it. Pretending won't do any good, beyond wasting time."

David looked up and met the man's eyes. They were harder than he'd seen them in the past—more like Shea's threatening gaze.

"Or maybe you paid someone else to cast the spell on

her, knowing she'd have difficulty walking away from you after that? Hmm? You took a liking to her pretty, young figure, her submissive tendencies, and didn't want to let her get away?" he prodded, leaning forward from where he sat, set some six feet or so away from David. "Maybe you don't even believe in spells—I've seen that before, too. Or, you didn't before you saw the way it affected her. It wouldn't be the first time that's happened. On a whim, someone pays for a spell they don't believe in… and then they aren't prepared for the magic to be realized."

"Neither of us had anything to do with the fucking spell," he answered after a moment, "so, fuck off and tell me what it is you want from us."

"Ah, there we go. At least you're admitting it now. And that look you're giving me… You don't act much like a bank manager, Mr. Merriweather. I'm beginning to wonder whether the profession suits you."

David didn't flinch, staring forward, though he was surprised that their cover wasn't broken. Maybe he should have pretended ignorance of the spell, after all, but there hadn't seemed to be much point. "You don't always act much like any therapist I've ever heard of, either," he finally said. "You guys make surprise injections and forced separation part of your repertoire with all couples? Or did we just get lucky?"

"Surprise injections? You were over-excited, endangering yourself and our personnel. As licensed professionals, we only naturally gave you a sedative."

"Where's Lauren?"

He smirked, leaning forward. "Tell me about the spell."

David stared at the man for another moment, and then sat up straighter. The man across from him didn't appear ready to give up, or remotely skeptical—and David could too easily imagine him walking out of this room and disappearing for hours, leaving him trapped here without another word if he didn't offer up something. Maybe if he gave him something, he'd get something. And Lauren couldn't contradict the story, after all—for once, her inability to lie would work in their favor.

"Her mother," he said. "The woman was crazy. She had trouble with her husband—cheated on him and then got pissed off when he returned the favor, or maybe he started it. I don't know. It was a fucked-up marriage, and she thought putting a spell on her daughter would be a good idea to keep her from going through the same thing. It wasn't. End of story."

Jace Gathing squinted, his lip quirking up. "If that were the end of the story, Mr. Merriweather, we wouldn't be having this discussion. We've established the spell exists, and now where it came from. What does it do, exactly, is what I'm asking."

For a moment, David saw Lauren's fear in his mind— the hesitation he'd become used to after she'd come back to the house. The tremble in her skin when he'd touched her when she wasn't ready. Even now, if he concentrated, he could practically feel the electricity and warmth between them, if he tried. Instead, he pulled himself back into the moment at hand and willed emotion from his voice before he spoke.

"Her mother thought tying her to the first man she had sex with would be a good idea. When I took Lauren's virginity—when she gave it to me," he corrected himself, "her body became tied to mine. She reacts to me… in a way she can't, and won't, to anyone else," he finished. "Us being together, touching, amps up what natural magic she has, and her emotion."

The air stilled between them, and David saw the young therapist processing the spell's implications. Spoken out loud so simply, he'd thought it sounded almost innocuous, but in the relationship they'd presented…

"So even if she wanted a divorce…"

"She could get it, but she'd never enjoy being with someone else. Not physically, anyway," David acknowledged.

The other man nodded, eyeing him, and David thought he saw pity showing itself in his gaze.

"It's only a cruel spell if she doesn't love me," David said flatly, before Gathing could say anything else. "So, don't pretend you understand it, alright?"

"Your wife, Lauren…she feels *magic* when she's with you, specifically. Physically?"

"I…maybe so, yeah," he finished lamely. "We both feel it some, but nothing happens if that's what you're asking. It's just there," he finished lamely. What the hell was happening here? "It's not useful, just there, but I didn't do it to her, so you can leave off thinking I did. Now, where is she?"

"Mmm. A spell like that…I imagine the emotion, the connection between the two of you, is almost tangible. Addictive for both of you, am I right? And that she misses you desperately when you are apart?"

David looked up to the guard, who looked as interested as Gathing, but neither man looked surprised by anything which had so far been said. "What the fuck do you want from us?" David asked.

Before any answer came, Shea appeared at the door. "We don't normally answer that question," she replied. "But then again, we don't normally have a couple like you and Lauren at our disposal. Jace," she said, her eyes still on David, "why don't you arrange an early dinner for the three of us in one of the lounges? I believe a discussion of things might actually be in order for once— and perhaps, Mr. Merriweather, we can all benefit mutually. You'll get your wife back, and we'll have something special, as well."

The other therapist looked to her as if for confirmation and then rose and got to his feet. As he left the room, Shea gestured for David to join her. In moments, he was being escorted down the hall he'd skulked down earlier, back to the security room.

"Take a seat," she offered. "Would you like some aspirin? I imagine you have a headache."

Figuring they'd be less obvious about drugging him if that was their plan, David nodded and was rewarded with a few pills and a bottle of water. Shea sat down beside him in front of the monitors showing the various rooms, the guards stationing themselves near the door once again.

"We don't normally have guests who believe in magic or anything supernatural," the doctor said casually. "But you do."

David shrugged. "Even before I met Lauren, I'd seen things. It's not a part of my life, but yeah, I know shit happens that can't be explained without it."

A huff of a laugh escaped the woman, and her voice got softer. "And do you know what succubi are, Mr. Merriweather? Or incubi?"

David looked sideways to her. Her eyes were wide, suggestive. "Energy through sex, right?" he asked, but there was a catch in his voice.

"You could say that my colleagues and I are related," she said, leaning back in her chair with her eyes on his.

David's breath stopped in his lungs for a moment, and then he answered, "You touch Lauren, and I…"

"You misunderstand. I'm not saying that we feed off of sex, but that's likely the closest thing you'll have heard of. We feed off of emotions, energy. Sexual energy also sometimes, though not often in this particular facility."

This facility. David glanced from Shea to the guards.

They hadn't moved, though one of them looked surprised—not disturbed, however. Just surprised that David was being told all this, it seemed.

"Them, too," Shea answered before he could ask. All of us who work here are a particular type of succubus, or incubus, as the case may be," she added with a nod to the men. "But we feed off of emotion, not sex. This center is something of an ideal place for us, and couples like you and your wife—like the friends you've made also—are such generators of strong emotions…love, anger, guilt, fear, pain, ecstasy…you're just the type that we find particularly useful," she finished.

One of the guards nodded from where he stood and David's eyes went back to the monitors. The one sitting in front of him showed a guard carrying a limp form into one of the cinderblock rooms. He placed the form on the floor and then backed off, and David saw it was Dora. Her eyes were shuddering as if she was dreaming, and he saw her lips moving, but she lay still as the guard backed off and closed the door on her.

"She's fine—falling into a deeper sleep," Shea commented. "Normally, we'd only drug her once she got into the room," she added, nodding to the bottles on the wall, "but I suppose Tony thought this might make more sense, rather than have you get upset or cause a scene. It's often easier to draw emotions and sensations from sleeping bodies, and why we have the hard wood, which is conducive to what we need to do to pull them out. Natural elements of the earth and all that. Shall we?" she asked.

Before David could think to say anything, one of the guards had stepped forward and yanked him up from his chair with a grip on his bicep. He let himself be guided down the hall, into one of the rooms filled with pillows and hardwood. In front of him, Jace was already settling down onto the floor, his head on a pillow. He lay on his back, with his palms pressed into the hardwood. His knees were bent so that the soles of his bare feet could do the same.

Shea pushed David toward a pillow and then turned to the guards. "You'll keep an eye on him and feed later," she announced. "Set the chemicals for a minimum drawing from her—I want to enjoy myself later, and we only had her up here two nights ago," she added, her eyes jotting sideways to David. "I misspoke earlier. Dora will be something of an appetizer more so than dinner tonight."

David watched as she reclined on the floor nearby, removing her shoes and then lying down in a position similar to the other therapist.

"She won't feel anything," Shea commented, closing her eyes. "But she and Van have had a good day—the endorphins, the sex, the love between them…not such a powerful meal as what we've been getting from Lauren, but nothing to neglect."

Nausea rose up in David's chest and he pushed it down. He pulled his eyes away from the two monsters laying down nearby when one of the guards stepped up beside him, smirking. In his hand, he held out a tray with a sandwich, chips, and another bottle of water. "Dinner for you?" he offered.

***

The fact that Lauren would have to be drugged—because they insisted on it—didn't make things any easier. Most of what they'd said had, in fact, been a blur.

He'd watched Jace and Shea feed, ignoring the food that had been offered to him for his own dinner. Where their flesh had been in contact with the floor, there'd been the slightest glowing, and he'd felt something like a low reverberation from the floorboards beneath the cushion he'd been sitting on. As he'd watched, the two therapists had twitched and shuddered at turns, expressions running over their faces, and the impression had, undeniably, been that they were getting pleasure from the sensations they fed on. Watching them, he'd been glad he couldn't see Dora at the same time—whether she'd been experiencing something at the same time or sleeping through all of it, he wasn't sure. He also wasn't sure which would be worse.

Eventually, the hum had left, and the almost jealous expressions of the guards watching him had lifted. Waiting for the therapists to wake up, David had eventually eaten the food he'd been provided, figuring he needed the energy. He hadn't tasted a bit of it, though he'd appreciated the large tumbler of whiskey that a guard had brought him to chase it down.

Apparently, these guys could read emotions and needs just as well as they could feed off of them.

When Shea had finally stretched and sat up, looking for all the world like a satisfied lioness, David had been glad for the steadying liquor in his system. "You done now?" he'd asked quietly, even as Gathing's eyes blinked open languidly and the man's gaze wandered over the room, finally settling on David.

What had followed had been blurred by the pleasure in their voices, and the disgust in David's own veins. They'd talked about the way it all worked, the way the variations they'd developed out of rohypnol, adrenaline, and chloroform, along with other chemicals whose names went over David's head, served to relax the human system and amp up dream states, enabling a sort of purified emotion to run from dreams and memories, the wooden floorboards serving as a conductor to pick up the emotion and sensation and spread it out to whatever other bodies were there, flesh to floorboard, to collect it.

He couldn't help thinking it all sounded like a sort of reversal of *The Nightmare on Elm Street* plots, though these monsters talking to him appeared civilized enough and didn't seem to be drawing blood.

They were actually proud of their set-up—that was clear enough in the way they talked about it. Bringing in couples whose emotions were tied up in knots, and feeding tensions and attachments so that emotions ran higher than ever. Then, taking the more emotional, submissive partners to feed on at night, to use, and most of the time leaving them none the wiser in the morning. They'd told him that Lauren's dreams were all terror and pleasure, variations of fear, love, and pain coloring different moments and dreams, but that feeding on her had been like a meal made from five different people, and stronger. They'd compared it to a filet mignon being enjoyed after a week of hamburgers, and he'd felt sick to his stomach as they'd gone on about the variations in 'emotional flavoring' as they'd termed it.

And now, there wasn't much choice but to keep feeding them in just the same fashion—they'd been painfully up-front about the choices.

They wanted Lauren's emotions and magic to be pulled back up to the levels they'd been at when they'd first tasted her, and had two therapists from another center coming in that night to experience her emotions firsthand. There was no question of whether or not that was happening. Shea had been able to read between the lines of what Gathing had related about the spell Lauren had connecting her to David. Intuitively, she'd already understood that Lauren's connection to him fed into her pleasure and magic, and some of the nightmares they'd been reading and getting glimpses of had been based on her being raped in the past, after the spell had been activated. Now, David could either feed into her magic and their connection by making love to her, and these monsters would feast on the pleasure and endorphins that came from that connection, along with her magic, or they'd find someone else to hurt her, and they'd feast on the pain and the roiling magic that came from that. Either way, it meant Lauren being used for an emotional feast on their end. It all came down to whether or not he could involve himself and be a willing accomplice.

Whether or not he'd come exploring, they'd planned on retrieving him tomorrow at the latest, Shea had said, rare as it was that they told couples of their set-up at this place. They'd wanted his participation up in these rooms, so that they could feed more easily from Lauren's connection to him and see how his direct presence would affect things. And now that he knew, they wanted him to drive the present night's plans. It didn't make him feel better to know that other couples, once they left here to move to long-term facilities, were also made aware of the arrangement, though at least that meant they were alive. It also didn't change things for him and Lauren. Not now.

One way or another, these monsters needed her emotions and her magic to be pulled up to the overflowing levels they'd reached before, and in the short-term, that meant ensuring her either pain or pleasure, awakening that spell that had been feeding into her emotions and bleeding into the woodwork. They weren't willing to wait, and David didn't have any leverage with which to put them off. Even before he'd said a goddamned word, they'd had some idea of what they were dealing with, and Shea hadn't needed them to tell him—although she had—that if he'd said nothing, they'd have been experimenting on Lauren tonight anyway, teasing out whatever they could from her magic and blood. Whatever that meant for her.

When Lauren was guided in by two guards, supported between them, it was all David could do to keep from rushing at them and pushing out into the hall. There'd be no point. They'd take her from him, and there'd be no chance of them remaining together until Josh could get in and get them out. Not to mention what they'd do to her in order to amp up her emotions if he refused to be involved. They'd admitted that simply putting her to sleep tonight likely wouldn't have achieved the desired effect, and implied that hurting her wouldn't have been off the table—if David didn't participate, that was.

Holding back curses, David got up from where he'd been sitting against the cinderblock wall and moved across the room to take her from the guards. She was on her feet, but moving as if in a dream, her eyes fluttering closed and then open and then closed as she leaned into his chest. He was half-supporting her when the guards stepped back.

"She's going to be unconscious?" he asked quietly.

The second guard shrugged. "She'll wake up—the doc just gave her a low dose of the drug to get her up here so she wouldn't remember. Wait fifteen or twenty minutes, she'll be awake enough. Figured this made more sense than doing the initial dosing in the room, you being in here and all," he added, smirking. "This way, you'll be aware enough and make sure we get what we need—don't want to knock you out, too, by accident. Not tonight, anyway."

David swallowed down the curses he wanted to offer in return and guided Lauren into the center of the room as the door shut behind the guards. On the floor, he pulled her in so that she was leaning against his chest, curled up against him, and held onto her. Waiting.

Even now, he didn't know if he was doing the right

thing. Maybe he should have tried to put them off longer, until Josh could get there, but he couldn't have forgiven himself if they'd gone ahead tonight with hurting her and just left him out of the picture. And was this really any worse than what he'd done to her at the hands of the coven? Honestly, he wasn't sure anymore, he'd hurt her so much.

The thought of all he'd put her through sent another run of disgust running through his heart, and he held her tighter. He could feel her arms warming beneath his hands, slightly, and her cheek warming through his shirt; the sensations made him wish he could go back in time and kill her mother himself, for putting this spell on her. It seemed like the chain of side effects was never-ending, like each time they had it figured out, there was another complication to be dealt with, either between the two of them or getting used against them. No matter how much pleasure it gave them in private, he wouldn't have wished it on anyone.

When she finally stirred against him, he let one of his hands wander beneath the waistline of her blouse, running above her jeans along her hip. Her eyes hadn't opened yet, but her body was stirring against his—he could feel the magic warming her blood and his own body responding. He wanted to distract her before she really realized where they were or what was happening. She murmured something unintelligible against his chest, and he craned his neck down and shifted so that he could meet her lips. The kiss was soft, gentler than anything he felt, and she returned it.

Not giving himself time to think about what he was doing, David twisted the two of them sideways so that her back was down on the hardwood floor and he was on top of her—as fucking instructed—having barely broken their kiss. Her tongue slipped into his mouth and he sucked, biting down lightly as one of his hands found its way fully into her shirt and pulled at the lace of her bra, finding a nipple and playing with the hard bud as she released a slight moan beneath him and arched into his hand. Straddling her, he could feel her body warming up, her breath coming faster, and he used the desire radiating from her blood to feed his own, blocking out everything around them. It didn't matter where they were or why they were doing this—for now, it was just them, and it was what they needed to do to get through this night together without Lauren getting hurt. Shea had made some comment about Jace having his eye on her, and that the young therapist would have been disappointed to hear that Lauren couldn't enjoy being with anyone but David—the last thing David was going to do was give him a chance to test the spell and get her hurt in the bargain.

David raised her shirt some so that he could kiss his way up her abdomen, and then he found one of her breasts and sucked a nipple between his teeth. Lauren's hands had found his shoulders now, but she still wasn't fully awake. She murmured his name and he pressed his hands into her sides, holding her still and acknowledging the heat coming from her blood, radiating from her in waves of magic and desire.

"David…David, we should talk," Lauren whispered, and he felt her shift as if to move from beneath him, but he bit down on her breast instead of releasing her, and pressed his hard dick against her leg—through his jeans and hers, he knew she could feel him.

"Later," he muttered back as he rose up to find her lips again. Her eyes were open now, dazed, and he brushed one hand over them. "Close your eyes. Try to relax."

"This room," she murmured.

He sucked the lobe of her ear between his teeth and let

his hands toy with her breasts, straddling her body and letting his dick press into her core through the fabric that was still holding them apart. Her bare back was mostly to the ground, as well as her upper arms and her feet. He wanted to leave her her dignity as long as he could while still giving these monsters what they'd demanded.

"Don't worry about it, baby," he whispered, and then he began kissing along her neck and her throat, relishing the fact that her hands were grasping his own shoulders and back, returning the affection even through her confusion. "Just go with me."

His hands on her breasts, his lips at the small of her throat, he let himself press into her harder, proving how much he wanted her, and she sighed beneath him, arching into his body as a mew of pleasure whimpered from her lips.

When one of her legs lifted and wrapped around his thigh, he knew she was more than ready for him. That's what he'd been going for—he didn't want to disrobe her and taste her in this room, like he would have in private, or play with her the way he had been each time they'd come together lately. Already, he could feel magic coming from her in waves, reacting to their coupling, and her skin was hot to the touch.

He pushed his own jeans down to his knees first, trying to ignore the fact that they were most assuredly being watched, and that others still were probably feeding on the emotions coming from this girl beneath him even as he moved overtop of her, and then he pressed her jeans down around her hips, down to her knees.

She was whispering something, and he glanced at her face and realized there was panic there—she was finally awake, looking around and trying to figure out why they were here, doing this—but he dropped down into her and sucked her lips into a kiss before she could scream out or question what was happening, or doubt this, which they had to do.

When her hands came to his chest and she started pressing against him, trying to get him to move off of her, he caught her hands in one of his and let go of her lips only long enough to pull her hands above her head and allow her a gasp of air. Before she could protest, he had her fully prone beneath him, both her slim wrists encased in one of his hands above her head and his other hand on her hip, holding her still beneath him.

"It's gonna be okay, kid, trust me," he whispered, leaning up and finding her ear to speak to her just as he let himself lunge into her, pressing his cock deep into her channel. She was drenched, soaked with want and ready for him, but tighter than ever since she hadn't yet found any release or even been touched there, and he groaned with the pleasure of her warm heat swallowing him up, stretching around him, his lips at her ear and murmuring nonsense as her body yielded, wet and tight around his shaft as he moved back and forth, working his way into her again and again.

She was protesting beneath him, squirming in protest, but her body was reacting, her pussy hot and warm and pulsing around him as he pressed in still deeper, and he heard a gasp when he bottomed out at the entrance to her womb, so that she let out one of those whimpers that was half pleasure and half pain, which he'd come to rely on telling him how she was feeling, and where she was. He pulled back a few inches and let her gasp for breath beneath him, but her body was pulsing with pleasure and magic, and she was soaked for him.

Pressing her wrists into the hardwood floor, he found her lips again and sucked her murmured protests into his own mouth, swallowing them down with the self-hatred he felt in the moment so that he could get lost in the physicality of what they were doing and forget everything else.

With his free hand, he reached between them and pressed into her belly, pressing down each time his cock pushed into her again, building the rhythm between them so that her words turned to moans and he closed his own eyes. He still wore his t-shirt, and he could feel sweat soaking through now as he kept pushing into her, making himself last. He didn't want to do this more than once, or have to hold her down and force her to accept him again after he'd already come once, so he was determined to make this last and make this one round count for everything.

When her breath and the pulsing of her cunt around him signaled she was close, he moved his fingers to her clit and sucked her lower lip between his teeth. The orgasm ripped through her, drawing a scream from her throat as she bucked into him, and he held himself still and hard inside of her, anchoring her against the hard wood floor.

When the scream was gone and she was gasping for breath, he began licking at her lip, tasting blood where he'd bit down and murmuring apologies as he began pushing into her again, letting his hips find a natural, slow rhythm of pistoning in and out as she remained beneath him, held down. She couldn't catch her breath now, and the difference in her body chilled him. Some of the heat from her body had leaked out, as if the orgasm had released more than an explosion of pleasure, letting go of sensation and magic at the same time. Beneath him, her body was getting cooler, her panic and her magic both bleeding out into the floor, distilled with her pleasure as if they'd suddenly crossed some boundary, to where the process had started.

His own sweat went cold, and he swallowed back the

rage and horror at what was happening as he kept pushing into her. Her eyes met his, but they'd gone flatter and more confused.

"We're dreaming?" she whispered.

Instead of answering, he caught up her lips in another kiss and let go of her wrists. She'd stopped fighting now, as the confusion had built with the loss of her emotions and her magic in that release, and her hands found his back, gripping at his shirt and his skin with the pressure of the magic leaking through her body, tremors of her last release still pulsing through her and working to heat her blood.

David's hands had the freedom to explore now, and with her shirt pressed up above her breasts, he found one breast and let his other hand snake around to the small of her back, levering her against him as he pressed into her again and again. Much as he wanted to cum, he could remind himself of what they were doing and the cooling of her body, and it pulled him back from the edge so that he could keep pushing into her.

And yet, the urgent self-hatred and pain he felt at taking advantage of her had leveled off, leaving a dull pain in his mind that allowed him to focus more on their pleasure than the surroundings. Intellectually, he could concentrate and feel the heat of the wood against his knees and his forearms, and the yielding flesh of Lauren's body as she gave in to him, and he knew that he was being affected by the room and the drugs in the air just like she was, the hardest edges of his energy and emotion seeping into the floor and into the girl beneath him, but his mind was still caught on how tight and wanting she was.

When she moaned again, in what sounded like torture as much as pleasure, he felt her pussy clench around him suddenly and he finally let himself go, pounding into her with all of the anger and force he'd been holding back that night so that she gasped for breath beneath him, bucking against him as he screamed out his release above her, his cock hard and pumping into her, filling her as she pulsed and shivered around him.

He rested his head against her chest then, feeling the coolness of her skin and his own climax ebbing as he worked to catch his breath. Tangled up against him, she'd gone limp, but her breath was heavy, and her body was still pulsing around him. He pulled out of her and looked up to her face, ready to apologize, but her eyes had already closed, the room having sucked away her energy along with her emotion and magic.

A hiss pulled his attention sideways before he could decide whether or not to try to wake her. He didn't see anything, but the sound was coming from one of the vents at the edge of the room. The sight of it froze him momentarily, but then he caught his breath and held it. Hurrying, he righted Lauren's bra and blouse as well as her jeans, all before he finally retrieved his own kicked away jeans and yanked them back into place after tucking his still hard dick into his underwear.

His lungs burning, he left his belt hanging loose and settled for jerking up his zipper before he lay down behind Lauren and pulled her body into his, letting his own back take the hardness of the floor as he turned her against him and rested her head against his chest, cradling their bodies together before he released the breath he'd been holding.

Within a minute of breathing out and gasping in new air, he felt the drugs covering over his consciousness and he reflexively grasped Lauren tighter against his body, only hoping that the bastards controlling their fate right now would keep their word.

Chapter 21

When Lauren woke up, her first awareness was of an ache that seemed to run deep through her veins, all across her body and then into her core. She'd felt stiffness like this before, but it had never been so complete. Lately, waking up at the center, there'd been a dull ache in her body that wasn't unlike what she'd felt after her magic had first seeped away at the ranch house—a sort of empty thickness. She'd felt it in the mornings over the last few days, but never like this. Now, she felt wholly drained of energy, magic…anything beyond breath. And on top of it, heavier on her body, was the ache of used muscles and joints, dull and stiff and complaining like they'd been for those days in the cage.

With that connection, her eyes jarred open.

But she wasn't in the cage, she saw—she was in yet another room, luxurious and impersonal but for the glaring style of the center. It wasn't either her room or David's, or even the room she'd been sent to in the east wing, though it also wasn't unlike any of them. Somewhat smaller maybe, if anything.

She forced herself to sit up, rising from the mattress in a fashion that would have suggested to any observer that she was closer to sixty than twenty, and let herself look around. The bathroom door was ajar, and she could hear the water of the shower running within. A window looked out onto the woods at the side of the center, and she guessed they were higher up than they'd been before from the look of the trees—on the fifth floor, maybe. The light was soft, just showing beyond the trees. It was dawn, then, or close to it.

Jerkily, she moved off the bed and toward the bathroom. From the doorway, she could see David's outline in the steamed glass of the shower. His belt, jeans, and shirt were crumpled on the floor. Wanting to be close by, even if uncomfortable, she perched on the countertop and leaned back against the mirror, waiting for him to finish. Her mind drifted over her body and she let herself close her eyes, trying to remember the night before.

She remembered being separated from him, and realizing what a mistake she'd made in going to the other wing, and wishing that they'd had Josh give her a burner phone also, despite it doubling the chances of them getting caught...and then, nothing. She didn't even remember lying down in bed. Her body ached, though, and now that she thought about it, she could feel a tackiness along her upper thighs, making her shift in her spot and note that her jeans were stiff with... it had to be cum, she realized. The tackiness plus the way she ached meant she'd had sex, and didn't remember a moment. But it must have been with David, right? Surely, the spell's effects would have made for violence she'd be feeling a lot more strongly now if anyone else had taken advantage of her while she'd been...what? Asleep? Drugged?

When the water stopped, Lauren's eyes met David's at

the moment he pulled open the shower, and the flash of discomfort she saw there was all she needed.

"What do you remember?" he asked.

She stared at him for a moment, but he looked away as he began drying off, and then he shook his underwear out of his jeans to pull it back on. "I don't," she answered. "I remember being separated from you. Was I awake with you during the night? It feels like we—"

"Yeah," he said gruffly, pulling on his jeans. "We had sex, and you were in and out. I wasn't sure if you'd remember any of it. We need to talk."

Lauren didn't bother responding—she was too tired. There were so many emotions roiling in her blood right now, none of them pleasant, and yet she felt dull and detached, as well. It all amounted to her wanting nothing more than to go to sleep. The relief she'd felt at finding out David was with her again had disappeared in the wake of his casual admission that he'd had sex with her even when he'd known she'd barely been aware, and with her memory of finding out that he'd nearly fucked another woman, just days before they'd come here together.... Maybe her mother had been right about men being sex-driven bastards, after all.

When David made to take her hand and pull her from the bathroom, Lauren gently shook off his grip, wondering why she couldn't garner up outright anger. "I need a shower. Will you be here when I get out?"

David's eyes met hers for a moment and she could see he wanted to object, but she wasn't budging on this. She felt disgusting, and disgusted with herself. If he could take time for a shower, she could.

"We'll talk when you get out," he finally acknowledged. He leaned in and gave her a quick kiss on her forehead, squeezing her hand as he did, but his touch didn't warm her at all, and then he left her to it.

She shed her clothing and found what she'd expected. Dried cum that had leaked out of her, and the sticky musk of sweat and saliva. Hickeys on her neck and light bruising around her wrists and the backs of her shoulders suggested they'd been on a floor and that the sex hadn't been gentle, and she thought she could even see light marks on her hips—left by David's grip, she imagined.

Trying to shut out the turmoil, she retreated to a long shower, keeping it hot enough that, by the time she turned off the water and emerged into the cooler air of the bathroom, she had to sit for a moment on the toilet and catch her breath, her body reacting to the change in temperature.

As in the rest of the rooms she'd been in, this one had robes folded neatly under the sink. Much as she disliked the idea of leaving herself undressed with all that had gone on, she couldn't bring herself to put on the soiled clothing she'd woken up in. After drying off as best she could and leaving her hair mostly wet, she pulled a robe tight around her body and tied it, and then headed out to confront David and find out what had happened.

"We don't have any fresh clothes here?" she asked upon seeing him.

He'd been standing by the window, staring out over the land and into the tops of the trees beyond it. Hearing her voice, he turned and shook his head, and Lauren finally saw what she'd missed before. His eyes were red, more than if he'd just been losing sleep. She'd never seen the man in front of her cry, but from the set to his jaw and the look of his eyes…she guessed he had been. If not while she'd been in the shower, then before she'd woken up.

"I'd probably be more comfortable if I'd put on a robe, too," he acknowledged. "You okay?"

Rather than moving closer to him, Lauren forced

herself to perch on the bed and meet his eyes from a distance. "I need to know what happened last night—I guess you remember?"

David nodded, and then he turned back to the window and began talking. And kept talking. He told Lauren about finding out she'd been taken to the other wing, and going exploring on the sixth floor, as well as what he'd found. He told her about the conversations he'd had with the so-called therapists, and what they were doing, and that her magic being tied to her emotion and their relationship somehow made her emotions all the more attractive for them. And then he finally told her about the choice he'd been given—to fuck her in one of those rooms, and draw out her emotion and her magic even when her body had already been exhausted from the night before's drawing, or else leave her to be prey for someone else.

"They joked about separating us when we weren't in those rooms, but I'm not so sure it was a joke anymore," he said finally, turning around from the window to face her. "They also know they can't trust me to not go looking for you if they don't put real distance between us. And they have long-term facilities set up to hold couples once they leave here, if they want them. I get the impression they want to know what'll happen to your emotions if they do separate us for any length of time. Tomorrow's Thursday, but…"

But you don't know when Josh is coming, or how much time we have, Lauren thought, finishing the sentence on his behalf, silently. He hadn't needed to say the rest, and she could tell from the way he'd been parceling his words out that he was worried they were being listened in on.

He hadn't moved any closer to her, and Lauren thought that was probably for her benefit—he had to have seen the unease spiraling through her mind when she'd left the bathroom. She'd never expected any of this, though. After what he'd told her, snatches of last night were coming back, and maybe the nights before. She could picture the room David had described, and remember the feel of the wood beneath her body, and how cold she'd felt when lying there alone, which she supposed must have been from one of the earlier nights.

"I thought that room was a dream," she admitted quietly. "I woke up thinking of it yesterday, but just…I just thought it was a dream."

Rising from where she'd been sitting on the bed, Lauren moved over to stand next to David and then let herself lean against him, shifting his way slowly. She was close enough to hear him release a heavy breath, and then his arms wrapped around her, hugging her against him. The warmth she usually felt from his touch was still recuperating—she could only barely feel it stirring at his presence—but his arms felt good around her, and she raised her hands to embrace him in return, holding onto him and relishing the tightness of his own hold, nearly squeezing the breath from her.

"I'm so sorry, kid," he whispered into her hair. "About everything. What happened before we came here—it was a mistake, and I was drunk, and me stopping it is no excuse for it starting. I know we need to talk about it, but we have to get out of this first. I just need you to know I'm sorry."

Lauren nodded her head against his chest, not bothering to look up and meet his eyes. He was right that they had to keep their focus right now. Feeling his breath on her and the pounding of his heart, Lauren clenched her eyes shut and tried to focus only on being with him, right now where they were. She had to find a way to hold onto this, and everything else could get figured out later. She wanted to cry, too, but the heaviness in her body hadn't left, and though she was warming to his presence, she could feel the truth of everything he'd said. Her magic was practically absent, and her emotions were sluggish, stilted and detached.

"Can we just go to sleep for a while?" she finally asked. His hold on her had loosened, though he still held her against him. What could they do besides wait for Josh at this point anyway? She should have felt elated that they'd figured out what was going on, and that now this place could be shut down, but didn't have it in her. What David had found out and seen would be more than enough once tests were run and remnants of the drugs were found in patients' systems. But, for now, she was just so tired.

"Not yet, Lauren." David leaned down to her, and his lips came practically to her ear so that he could whisper. "I saw the looks on their faces when they talked about you, and when they talked about separating us. I'm worried that's the plan, and that it won't just be to separate wings of this place now that I know what I know. We need to get out of here." He paused, and then added, "Lauren, how strong has your magic gotten? Can you get us out of here?"

Lauren's breath caught, and something hitched in her throat—either a sob or a laugh, though she wasn't sure which. "David," she whispered back, "the magic is gone—you said yourself that you felt it leaving me last night. I can barely feel it now."

"But if you could?" he pressed. "Josh will be able to get everyone else out. It's us I'm worried about. He'll probably come in at night, first thing tomorrow or tomorrow night, either way—that leaves a lot of time for them to move us, which they've already talked about."

She processed that, leaning into him and the silence, but she was having trouble focusing. And then she realized what he was expecting to come next. And if they separated them, to other locations…

"And you don't have a tattoo or any way for them to track you, do you?" she asked.

The silence was enough of an answer. Now that they knew her tattoo worked, there were plans for the program to be expanded to other operatives, but at this moment, she was the only one who had one. If they separated her and David, and took them to separate locations, Josh would be able to track her within a week or two, but not David.

"And I'm worried…" he added.

"What? What aren't you telling me?" she asked.

"I'm worried they're going to want to see how you react to someone else besides me, what emotion and reaction that draws out with your magic. The way they rushed last night… there's no reason to think they'd wait long enough to where Josh could find you first. I don't know how far they'd let things go if they realized you were going to be hurt by it, but I don't want to find out. And I think they're already suspicious of me being something more than what they know. If they find out who I am, or even suspect it, things are going to change fast.

"So, that's why I'm asking. We're on the fifth floor in a locked room that's probably guarded, on an estate that belongs to them and covers a lot of ground, and right now we're stuck. If your magic built up more, is there anything you could do?"

Holding onto him, Lauren tried to consider the question and think about where they were. Even before she'd gone to graduate school, when her life had still been up in the air, the type of magic David was talking about had never been something she'd worked on. Sure, her mom and the stronger witches in her coven had been able to disappear at will, and move to other locations with little more than an expense of energy and memory. But besides the fact that they'd needed years of practice to build those abilities, Lauren had never even tried it.

Her focus had always been on the natural world…on determining the healing qualities of chemicals in plants, on fostering growth and healing, and sometimes on finding particular herbs or everyday items that had been lost. But escaping from locked rooms and armed guards? That had been her mother's world, if anyone's.

Gently, Lauren pulled away from David and moved closer to the window, where she stood shaking her head. She felt helpless, but there was nothing she could do.

He moved up behind her and his hands found her waist, and then his lips were at her ear again. "What about a weapon of some kind. Something to give me an upper hand? I can get us past the locks, but I can't take on more than two guys at once and not just get us in a worse position unless I'm armed."

"I've never even thought about building weapons," Lauren whispered back.

Images of the energy burns David had sustained while fighting the coven came to her mind and she shut her eyes against them. Even if she could, were injuries like that something she could bring herself to dole out?

David stood straight behind her, and one of his arms wrapped around her shoulders and pulled her to lean into him so that they stood together at the window. "That's okay," he said quietly. "I figured it was a longshot. Worse comes to worse, we'll count on this vinework," he added, tracing one finger along her arm from her wrist, back and forth along her forearm.

Vinework. Lauren jarred from David's arms and pushed her forehead into the glass of the window, staring downward. Five floors below, off to the side, the center's pool sat still and calm. And while she couldn't see the wall beside it, she remembered it. There'd been thick vines climbing a trellis against the estate's brickwork, running at least fifteen feet up around the doors leading back into the center and stretching above the trellis, running along the brick walls.

Could I do that?

David's hand came back down on her shoulder and she turned to face him. "How long do you think we have, for my magic to build up?"

"You have an idea?" he whispered back by way of answer.

"Maybe?" she offered. She went on tiptoes to reach toward his ear, and he met her halfway. "The vines growing by the pool. You remember them?" she asked. He shook his head. "Bricks are made of clay and shale—those are natural substances that can carry magic, just like the wood they use upstairs. If I had enough energy, magic…I think I could reach out to those vines, and bring them up to us. If I could get them this far, I could get them to the roof, and they could anchor in there. They'd probably be strong enough for our weight."

David leaned back from her, meeting her eyes. He glanced outside next, and she could see the doubt playing in his eyes. "Are you serious?"

She shrugged.

His lips came back to her ear. "They'd *probably* be strong enough for our weight? Baby, we're five stories up, and there's a hard patio below us."

Lauren grimaced, but the point was the same. "You put a lot of vines together, weaving together, with anchors at both points, they're strong," she whispered. "We'd have to test them, but… yeah, I think they'd hold us."

David's eyes went back to the window, and then he turned to glance back at the door and look around the room. There was no question of the fact that there were only two ways out of the room, though. The vents weren't large enough for either of their frames, and short of busting their way through a solid wall or ceiling, that left the door or the windows.

"So, how long do you think we'd have?   If we at least wait till lunchtime, and stayed together, touching, maybe that would be enough…"

"After you've been drained three nights in a row?" he answered quietly.

Swallowing, Lauren saw the hopelessness of that and shook her head. But why had he been so intent on finding out if she could help if they didn't have enough time for her to recover from the night?

And then his lips moved down to her neck, and Lauren caught her breath with the feel of his heated breath on her pulse. Before she could think to say anything, his hands had found the tie to her robe and begun tugging at it.

Lauren pulled away and backed into the window, staring at him. "You can't be serious."

"We can wake up your magic again," he told her. "I did it last night. We can do it again. You have to trust me."

Lauren's mind spun, struggling to catch up. She was already so stiff and sore, sex didn't sound even remotely appealing. David had had his hands on her for ten minutes now and her body had barely woken up—that was how tired the magic and the desire in her blood were, and how spent she was in terms of energy and emotion.

"You really don't think Josh will get here till late tonight? Or even tomorrow night?" she asked.

David's eyes darkened, and he opened his mouth as if to say something and then didn't. Instead, he moved over to the desk and sat down in the chair, where he propped his hands on his knees and stared at the carpeting for a few moments before answering, and she had to approach and lean on the desk when he did, just in order to hear him speak.

"I'm not going to force this or demand we try, Lauren. I know you're tired and sore—it's written all over you, and I know better than you why. I wouldn't be suggesting it if I didn't think it was worth thinking about but... you want to know the truth? I feel like we're back in that fucking cage. I feel helpless, and like I'm being forced to hurt you, and I'm fucking sick of it. I shouldn't have brought you into this—it's been torture for you since the moment we left the ranch house, practically—but I did, and it's too late to go back.

"If I had any other ideas, we'd run with them, and if it were just me here, then I'd sit back and wait for a chance to show itself, but my gut's telling me we don't have that luxury if we want to avoid shit going from bad to worse."

Lauren reached sideways and let her hand rest against David's shoulder, searching for the heat in her nerves she usually felt when they were in contact like this. Usually, it was like static electricity arose between them if she was within inches of him. Now, she was touching him and barely felt anything—she could have been touching Dora or Adrienne and felt the same.

"If I knew it would work," she began, "I wouldn't be hesitating, so I guess... I guess that means we should try?"

David's hand reached up to his shoulder and landed on hers, pressing her skin into the fabric of his shirt for a moment as if saying thank you—or giving her a chance to change her mind.

Steeling herself, Lauren appreciated the chance to back down that she sensed him offering, but she couldn't take it. In the seconds his hand had rested on hers, it had occurred to her that she'd never forgive herself if David's fears came true to the extent that not only were they separated, but in a way that would leave him missing in action and with no immediate means of their tracking him. If she had a way to avoid the chance of that happening, she had to give it a try.

Maybe she ought to be furious with him right now, and hurt, but they were tied together. And she loved him, whether she'd told him that or not; she loved him.

Without giving herself more time for doubt, she shifted away from the desk and landed on her knees in front of him, tucking the soft robe she wore beneath her own knees to provide more cushioning. A glance upward showed that his eyes looked doubtful, but he didn't move to stop her as she reached for his belt and began tugging it loose. Instead, he slouched toward her and lifted his hips so that she could pull away his jeans and his briefs and tug them down his legs.

His cock was barely semi-hard when she reached for it, moving closer as David spread his knees further apart and gave her room. One of his hands found the nape of her neck as her hands landed on him—one on his shaft, the other reaching beneath and finding his balls. She swallowed the nerves she felt and moved her lips to his head, playing her tongue around him before she took him into her mouth.

She could feel him hardening as she traced her fingers along his length and set to exploring him. The sensation of him thickening in reaction to her lips and her tongue was new, and powerful enough that she felt her heartrate speeding in response with the adrenaline of it.

Pulling back, she took a deep breath and then shifted his cock so that her lips could reach its base, and she licked her way up each side as her hand kept moving along his shaft in a slow rhythm. He'd gotten to the size she was used to now, harder and longer in a way that was just short of threatening, and she tasted pre-cum when her lips went back to his head and licked up the salty liquid before encasing him again and sucking him deep into her mouth, to where she could only just keep herself from gagging as his hands clenched in her hair and he began moving her with a rhythm he set. One of her hands found his thigh for purchase and her other stayed on him, grasping and exploring as his breath caught above her and his dick jumped against her tongue, hard and demanding.

When he pulled her backward from his cock, she was out of breath, and his face glowed with the lust she'd become so addicted to seeing in him, but the tight hold of his fist in her hair was enough to suggest he was on the edge of control, reacting to her every breath.

"Good start?" she breathed out, and he loosened his grip on her so that she could lean in and begin nuzzling her lips against his hard shaft again, teasing out a rhythm with her own fist.

"Jesus, Lauren."

David pulled her up then, and had her robe undone in moments. It hung loosely on her as he pressed her sideways to sit on his thigh, and then his lips found one of her nipples and began to return the teasing she'd been doing. One of her hands found its way between them and moved along his dick in a gentle fisting movement as he suckled at her, his hands exploring her ass and her breasts. Her breath hitched each time his teeth nibbled at her flesh or teased one of her nipples and she closed her eyes and leaned into him, willing her body to warm to him. The reaction was slower than it had ever been, but she'd felt her blood reacting even when she'd had him in her mouth—it wanted him, as it always did, but was sluggish and drained enough that each iota of warmth and energy seemed to require whole minutes of build-up rather than the moments they'd become accustomed to.

His teeth came down on her nipple and she arched into him, her hand freezing on his dick with the tight sensation his mouth delivered. She could feel her pussy leaking with desire now, but felt glad he was taking his time about moving his attentions—as it was, desire was fighting against the ache she'd felt in her body since waking, and as much as want was beginning to soak into her blood, there was a large part of her that didn't feel ready for another round with him.

When he bit down again, he did so harder, and she whimpered and nearly lost her balance from the surprise of it. In another moment, he'd stood with her and brushed the robe from her body so that it landed on the floor. She made to go to her knees before him again, but he caught her elbows instead and backed her toward the bed, his lips locking onto hers in a demanding kiss.

Her breath was knocked out of her as she fell backward on the bed, David having gone to his own knees and landed between her legs a moment later, his tongue pressing into her slit and then licking upward as his hands held her thighs wide apart and pulled her closer. Her fists found the bedspread and clutched it. She heard herself moaning, her blood heated and reacting to him now as she couldn't help arching against the bed so that his lips were suddenly on her, exploring and driving a shriek out of her body just as he pulled away and then pressed into her deep with two fingers, his thumb reaching up to find the button of her clit as he held her against the bed.

The orgasm hit her violently, and she couldn't help screaming out as the stabbing heat of it raced through her core and across her system, sending shocks of sensation through her blood. He was saying something as he pressed into her with his fingers, finding that rhythm he knew too well and wracking the full of the orgasm from her, but she could only focus on the feeling of his hands on her and the white-hot pleasure he'd just brought on.

She'd barely caught her breath when his lips came

back to her slit and she shuddered in an aftershock of relief as his tongue began lapping at her juices, his hands holding her legs wide open so that he could explore her more easily. When she couldn't slow the sensations enough to catch her breath, she finally reached to his shoulder and gripped him, hoping he'd understand—she could feel herself swollen with both use and want, both raw and still desiring him, and knew they were already on a line where his entering her would bring as much pain as pleasure. She wanted to reach that point soon and be done, hoping it would be enough for what they needed. Dizzying as her thoughts were, she could feel the heat in her blood now, reacting to him, and even if it wasn't as powerful as usual, it was at least awakened and wanton, building energy from the chemistry between them.

David moved overtop of her as he felt the energy beginning to rise under her skin, but knew they needed more of it. With that in mind, he sucked her lower lip between his teeth and bit down lightly, pressing her into the bed as he let his fingers open her up, and then he was into her, his cock pushing into her tight channel and feeling the heat of her surrounding him.

She felt tighter around him than she had the night before, swollen from use, and a slow press forward drove a whimper out of her chest—the kind that drove him crazy, so that he had to hold himself back from speeding up right away.

He let go of her lip and moved to her ear, licking along her earlobe and up the edge as he pressed into her harder, beginning another rhythm to push both of them into a release. "Stay with me, baby," he whispered. She was already shivering underneath him, sweat running along both their bodies now. Something unintelligible passed her lips and he pushed as deep into her as could go, feeling the breath rush from her lungs in response as she called out again and he sped up. She was hot and wet, the pulsing of her body around him was signal enough that she was on the edge again.

He reached beneath her and gripped her ass with both hands, bringing her body up to meet his hard thrusts as he found her lips and swallowed down the scream that ripped out of her lungs when he rammed into her again, filling her swollen hot pussy and feeling rivulets of magic rushing to her skin, meeting his body's touch with its own rush of quiet release.

"Fuck," he breathed out, lifting his lips from hers and meeting her dazed eyes. They were unfocused, and her lips were swollen now from his kisses—panting with both pain and pleasure, he guessed. He could feel her channel pulsing around him, holding his cock inside of her and milking him for any cum that could be left, and he let himself hold still inside her, enjoying the sensation. She groaned when she moved her arms, pressing her hands lightly into his chest.

"David, I'm sore. I need a break," she breathed out, her eyes closing on a sigh as if she might fall asleep right there beneath him.

"You trust me?" he asked before he could stop himself.

Her eyes opened, and she met his gaze, but he could see the nerves in the way she was looking at him. The confusion he'd seen when she'd first woken was gone, and some of the blankness had even been replaced by awareness, but he could see she was struggling to focus, her nerves and exhaustion still fighting against desire.

"I'm sore," she repeated, instead of answering.

He nodded, and pulled out, but he didn't move from overtop of her and instead repeated, "Do you trust me?"

Finally, she offered a hesitant nod, and he leaned in to give her a gentler kiss on her lips than what he'd offered before. He didn't think she'd like what he was about to try—not at first—but maybe giving her body some unfamiliar sensations would give her magic the boost they needed.

Pulling up from her, he nudged her sideways and she lay on her front with a sigh. She started to roll away from him, but he pressed her back down into the comforter. "Just relax," he told her, moving over her and landing on her thighs, his semi-hard cock poking at her ass so that she spooked for a moment and began to pull away before his hands landed on her lower back, and there he began a slow massage.

Forcing himself to take his time, he pressed his fingers into her muscles, moving from her lower back up to her shoulders and neck, then working her arms from shoulder to wrist before moving to her ass and then back to her back, going slowly and building up a new layer of sweat as she groaned beneath him, relaxing into the pleasure of the massage. He could feel her magic following his fingers, warming the skin beneath him. It was still sluggish, still playing catch-up, but there was a new heat in her body that hadn't been there when they'd first gotten to the bed—it was waking up.

The massage gave him real time to consider what he was doing to her, and the way the magic worked, which he'd mostly tried not to consider—at least when he'd been sober and in control of himself. The truth of it was, he'd been on board with taking away her magic. There'd been guilt involved, at the time and ever since, but magic made him nervous. It was one of the reasons he'd joined this force of operatives—to be one of the people working against it, making sure witches were kept in check and held back from hurting people. Now, he was actively using it, building it up in this girl beneath him, engaging it on purpose. It wasn't anything he'd ever envisioned being willing to do, and the feeling of it thrumming beneath his fingers was unsettling even as Lauren moaned in pleasure at each move he made, his kneading fingers being echoed on by her magic gathering in her veins.

He could see desire leaking from her with his cum, as well, and knew that as sore as she was, he could ask her for more if he focused on the rest of her body now. When he felt like the sensations were putting her to sleep, he moved his hands lower, and edged back along her body as he massaged her thighs, and then her lower legs and her feet, and then he made his way upward again, but stopped at her ass this time and let his fingers explore further below her body, pressing into her hips and then coming back to her round backside.

She jerked in surprise when he let one of his fingers play at her back entrance, teasing the rosebud of a point there to see how she'd react.

As expected, she bit out his name and flinched beneath him as if to move away, and he forced himself to ignore the nervous edge in her voice when she said his name. Trying to gentle her with his voice, he reminded her she trusted him, and then he ducked a finger into her pussy, pressing in so that she sighed and relaxed into him despite herself. When he moved the finger back to her ass, covered in her own juices, he felt her jerk beneath him, but he pushed forward anyway.

She was tight, and whimpering in discomfort beneath him, but his palm pressing into her lower back was enough to keep her mostly still, and then his finger was inside of her, stretching her open, the tight ring of her virgin entrance clasped around his finger as he murmured to her to relax and remain still, willing her to get used to him. She squirmed, whimpering and trying to pull away, but he held her where she was, remaining inside of her with his dick thickening against her thigh again, demanding its own satisfaction.

When he felt her beginning to give up and relax, he pulled back and felt her sigh in relief, but then his finger was gathering her natural juices again, and pressing in again. God, she was tight.

Lauren tried pulling away from him more sincerely this time, scrabbling to move off the bed, but he was faster, holding her down and pressing into her further, letting his finger thrust back and forth a few times, as far in as he could go. Her breathing was coming faster now, little whimpers of pain sounding out each time he pressed into her or his knuckle ran against that tight ring of muscle, but he kept going, feeling her channel stretch around him anew each time he pressed inward. His cock was rock hard now, wanting her, but he knew she wasn't ready for that.

When he pulled away from her, he could actually see the tension escape her body as she collapsed back into the comforter. He hadn't processed any of what she'd said, any of the words that had left her lips, he'd been so intent on playing with her ass and her reactions, but he knew he was pushing her harder than he'd intended once again.

Still, his cock was hard, they needed magic, and there was something he'd been leading up to.

While she remained collapsed into the bed, he moved back to the dresser at the bedside table, hoping its contents would be identical to what he'd found in his own room and left untouched. Sure enough, the bottom drawer offered the same options.

Clearly, this place was built for couples, and it was built to keep them happy and entertained—entertaining each other. It expected night-time visits, and encouraged them in its own way. He was about to take advantage of that again.

Nestled in the drawer were a number of options. Besides assorted condoms, there were sealed packages of lubricants, cuffs, silk ropes like he'd used in his room, and a variety of toys. He reached for one of the smaller toys, which was identical to what he'd seen in his own nightstand. The plug was maybe the width of his finger, but slightly longer and tapered at each end, and with a flat base attached to a ring so that it could be controlled. There was a weight to it that surprised him, and he realized it was larger than he'd thought—bigger than what he would have chosen for this point between them, had he been given the choice.

Glancing to Lauren to make sure she wasn't watching him, he examined the packaging more carefully, making sure it was original to the supplier. Seeing that it was, he did the same with a small bottle of lubricant, and then he closed the drawer.

Lauren was still lying on her stomach. One of her arms was beneath her forehead, a small pillow offering space between her panting lips and the comforter. The other was splayed backward loosely—she'd been pressing at his hand, trying to get him to let her go and back off before he'd stopped, and it had landed there when he'd finally released his hold on her. He could see her body still breathing deeply, and the moisture surrounding her cunt and ass, and the desire leaking from her still. Her body was all but glowing with desire, in fact, and although he wasn't sure she'd admit it now, he'd felt the heat gathering around his finger, pulsing in her veins as he'd pressed her for more give.

Without warning her, he came back to perch overtop her thighs, pressing her body into the bed again with one hand landing in the small of her back.

She jerked beneath him, her head turning to find his gaze, and the distraction offered him time to force a pillow beneath her hips, raising her ass. She tried to squirm sideways, but he pressed her down harder—he'd already decided what came next. "Don't fight me on this, baby," he said simply.

"David, that's enough," she breathed out, her eyes on his. "I don't…that was…that was enough," she said.

Swallowing down his own doubts, David leaned forward and let his chest press into her back.   His hard cock landed along her ass and he felt her jump at the sensation, and then she was shaking beneath him, squirming, but he didn't let her roll away. Instead, he held her down and he kissed the nape of her neck, pushing her hair aside, and let his hands run along her arms, down to her wrists, tracing back and forth until he could feel her shiver.

"You can't take me there," she whispered. "You're too big—I can't take that."

"I'm not going to, not now," he answered. He licked along her neck and then bit down lightly on her earlobe, eliciting a hitched breath and then a whimper. She hadn't said anything to his 'not now', but he'd felt her body quiver beneath him in reaction, so he knew she now understood he wanted that—eventually. She was right that it would only hurt her right now, though, and so he was thinking of something else. "Just trust me a little bit longer, baby," he whispered into her ear, and then he sat up on top of her thighs, looking down at her. She'd stopped squirming, and lay helpless beneath him, but she was also tense, and he knew she'd become restless with wanting him to move off of her and let her up.

For a moment, he thought she was going to argue or really start fighting to get away from him, and he wasn't sure what he'd do if she did. Now that they were this far? Building up her magic seemed like their only chance to get free before Josh could get to them, and having come this far, he didn't want to give up on it, but instinctively, he knew they needed more energy in her blood if they were going to have any chance.

He ripped open the packet of the butt plug he'd taken from the dresser, and before she could say anything, he'd pressed it into her pussy, pushing it in and out and pressuring sighs from her body as she tried to catch her breath and ask what he was holding, what he was doing.

Instead of answering, he opened the lube he'd taken from the dresser and squirted some along the already slick plug. She was splayed out before him, and his cock was as hard as it had ever been, aching for her, but he moved his leg from overtop of one thigh so that he could spread her further apart, and felt his own desire spike when she whimpered in response, squirming to get away.

Before she could look back to see what he was doing, he'd landed the small plug at her ass and his other hand had found her clit, his fingers beginning to brush along the small bundle of nerves. Her body flinched in response and he used the motion to his advantage, pressing the plug into her with a pop so that her anal ring caught it and held it, a yelp of surprise that bled into a whimper sounding out as he moved his hand to her hip and held her still, letting her know that the squirming wouldn't change anything as he pushed it into her, all the way to its base. Moaning in protest, she reached back for it, maybe thinking to remove it or stop him from playing it in and out of her ass, but he batted her hands away, and then, when she wouldn't stop grabbing for his hand, without thinking about it, he delivered a hard spank to her ass that brought a loud cry to her lips and froze her beneath him.

Everything had happened so quickly, Lauren found herself breathless and reeling.   The massage had felt amazing, nearly putting her to sleep, and though she'd felt David's cock full along her thigh, she'd all but moved beyond thoughts of another round, she felt so swollen and tired. Once that massage had begun, his hands had felt like perfection, and she'd thought that had been the reason he'd wanted her on her stomach.

And then…she'd never thought about him, or anyone, touching her there, at her back entrance. Maybe she'd come across it in a book or two, but more than that? It hadn't been something she'd thought about, not with him or anyone, and it had felt tight and burning and shameful to have his finger invade her like that, though she'd felt the magic reacting, trembling against him…and then he'd pistoned in and out of her, forcing her to get used to him. It had hurt, and then just been uncomfortable. But now, he'd put something foreign into her, filling her *there*, and she couldn't catch her breath. His fingers had been on her clit, shivering pleasure into her all over again, and with her focus there, he'd suddenly pressed something else into her; she'd felt it pop into her, filling her uncomfortably, both firm and giving, and ever so wet, all while his finger strummed against her clit so that she couldn't catch her breath enough to protest. She'd begun trying to pull away from him, to get away at the same time as she swatted her hand back, wanting to remove whatever he'd pushed into her. It felt so strange, unnatural—she'd just wanted it out, she felt so uncomfortably full and warm, and then there was the way his hand had hit her ass, freezing her. Her mind couldn't catch up with what was happening and the sensations, but the feeling of having the plug inside of her…

And then his hand came down on her ass again, shaking her body with the force of his palm and making the plug shift weirdly, uncomfortably, practically vibrating inside of her with the quivering running through her blood in reaction to the new sensations and David's hands.

Her body went suddenly white hot again, David's fingers pressing that circular rhythm hard into the flesh above her clit as his palm pressed into her pelvis and his body pressed into hers from above, his cock hard and pulsing against her thigh with that thing inside her ass and her magic roiling between them, practically quaking with desire. She found herself screaming into the comforter, the warring feelings of pleasure and pain erupting against each other as David's hand came down hard on her ass, spanking her again, and then again, so that his fingers kept jarring along her clit and the plug vibrated inside of her.

Each time she thought she was gaining the breath to speak, another shockwave of sensation hit her, her body confused and hot beneath David's attentions.

Unable to think, she started to pull forward and bring some space between them, instinctively wanting a moment to regain control, but then he was directly over her, one of his hands seeking out her wrists and holding them together ahead of her as his other found a breast and squeezed. Then his lips were at her neck, sucking, and his cock was at her pussy…

She groaned, and then felt herself filling as he pressed into her, his cock forcing itself into her channel.

"Too full," she grunted, but he wasn't listening. "It's too much."

His hips kept thrusting into her, vibrating the plug in her ass with each thrust forward, shifting it inside of her as he used her, and she could feel the foreign object and his cock inside of her together as he moved, pressing further and further into her again and again as she gasped for breath, the sensations too much to keep track of.

His hand left her breast and moved back to her hip, and she felt him controlling her movements as she gasped for breath, and then thrusting the plug in and out of her ass as his cock used her pussy, with all of her consciousness gathered at her center, the magic thrumming in her body and reacting to the feeling of being more full than she'd ever been, with his hand at her hip again, urging her to meet his rhythm as he kept pressing her forward, insisting on more, but whether it was pleasure or pain, she didn't even know anymore. It was just all heat, desire, and the feeling of him filling her again and again as his fingers played with the plug and then pinched and teased at her along with his lips, not allowing her the breath or the focus to beg him for a break, let alone make an attempt to get away.

And then something of her magic shifted inside of her as he pounded in deeper, her body clenching around his and the strange plug as she screamed again, a climax streaming through her in a blinding run of magic like none she'd felt before. Her breath lost, she felt herself go limp beneath him, giving in to him completely.

When he sped up, she found she was pressing backward into him, but still she couldn't speak. The fullness had gone from being painful to feeling exquisite, and his cock pounding into her pussy was heightening and evening off the pain and the pleasure in turns.

He let go of her wrists, and she could feel him crouching behind her, pressing deep into her as his hands spread her thighs open further and she felt herself clenching both him and the plug in reaction, vibrating with pleasure and pain as he began to thrust more violently, pulling her body in to meet his as he did.

When his fingers found her clit and his open palm slapped hard against her ass as he bottomed out, she couldn't stop herself from screaming out, her arching body erupting with another orgasm as he jerked his own release into her and she felt herself overflowing with his seed again, unable to speak with the power of the pleasure rushing through her flesh.

Panting, she felt his fingers press into the flesh of her

ass then, massaging her so that she whimpered with the sensations on top of the fullness, both his cock and the plug still buried within her. It felt like ages before he pulled back, leaving her pussy empty first, and then his fingers whispered along her ass and she breathed out with discomfort again as he pulled the plug from her.

She lay still, open and breathless, and tried to calm her heartbeat as he moved around the room. After some seconds had passed, he covered her with her robe and she curled beneath it, not a word spoken between them. When she closed her eyes, she just hoped he'd let her sleep, but she hadn't barely dozed off before his voice interrupted her.

"Lauren, are you listening to me?" he asked as his weight shifted the mattress beneath her.

She let herself mumble in response. He'd been talking before, and she'd blocked him out. Her body was aching and warm, and she'd let her focus drift to trying to dampen down the desire she felt running in her blood, as if it had a mind of its own. Her core felt unnaturally heated, and her blood was still shivering from the orgasms he'd wracked from her.

His hand touched her shoulder and she shifted away, pulling the robe with her. "Leave me alone, David, please."

It took seconds for him to respond, and she tried to ignore the pain in his voice when it did.

"I can't, Lauren. I'm sorry, but I can't. We need you to get dressed. I've got your clothes here."

The dryness of her mouth sent an acute ache down her throat when she swallowed down the things she'd like to say to him, but she couldn't help groaning aloud as she shifted to her side and looked at him.

He'd pulled on his jeans, and sat beside her grimacing. He was half faced away from her, and she could see nail marks on the backs of his shoulders where she'd alternately gripped him and tried to shake him away from her with pain if not with begging. He'd said earlier that he felt like he was back in the cage, being forced to hurt her, but now he'd left her in the same spot. She was aching, sore and hot, and it had seemed again like he hadn't heard a thing she'd said. Hadn't heard her whimpering or begging him to stop, or felt her trying to push him away. And to make it worse, she didn't even know how she felt about what he'd put her body through—it had hurt, especially at first, but there'd been pleasure also, shaking its way through her violently. But the plug, and the spanking…and she knew without looking that he'd left bite marks on her shoulders, and that her lips and her pussy both would be swollen and raw from his attentions. She hadn't been ready for any of that.

Between them, he'd placed her jeans and shirt from the day before, as well as her undergarments. She could see from where she lay that her panties had cum caked into the fabric, and shivered in response to the sight of it. Her body was still running hot with desire, unable to admit when it had had enough.

She shifted, unspeaking, and reached out for the clothing without letting the robe fall away from her. Tossing the panties to the side, she slithered into the jeans by themselves, wincing as they came up around her hips and she felt the rough fabric against her sex. Putting the sensation out of mind as much as she could, she reached out for her bra and hooked that hurriedly at her back, the robe having fallen away with her maneuvering, before she took up her shirt and slipped that on, as well.

David still hadn't looked back at her, and her voice cracked when she spoke. "You and Josh didn't want me to use magic here, off the ranch's property. You made me promise not to," she reminded him. "Now you really want me to try?"

From where she sat on the other side of the bed, she saw David's Adam's apple move as he swallowed down the first comment he might have spoken, and then she watched the muscles in his arms and chest clench, as if a shiver had run through him. Instead of answering her immediately, he got up from the bed and headed over to the floor where his shirt lay. He picked it up and pulled it on, and then he finally turned to look at her.

His eyes were red, hooded and swollen, and she could see marks from his nails in his palms, where he must have clenched his fists at some point—there were enough markers of grief on him, and the sun looked bright enough outside, that she realized she must have dozed off after all, and been lying in bed for some time.

"We don't have any choice," he said. He moved over to the desk and picked up a sheet of paper before he came back to the bed. She shifted away from him as he sat, unready for the further heat she knew would come with contact, but he reached out to her elbow and pulled her in beside him, letting her go only when her ear was close to his lips so that he could whisper, and then show her the note he held as he read it aloud. "It got pushed under the door while you were sleeping."

He looked down at the sheet, held in one hand, and read, "*The two of you together are quite something, but it's been decided that you need some time apart. Try to enjoy your morning together. We'll bring by lunch, and then discuss your future accommodations at separate locations. Your things are being packed now, and we'll have separate transportation available this afternoon. Please be prepared to cooperate accordingly so that this can all go as smoothly as possible, and accept our guarantee that the upcoming therapy sessions will not have you separated for more than a week at a time, should you cooperate fully with the treatment plan being laid out.*" David's eyes came back to hers, dark and pressing. "They told me not to tell you about anything I learned, anything of last night," he whispered. "I guess that's why they're sticking with the therapy line."

Lauren finally looked up from the note when his hand touched her chin, shifting her face toward his. He didn't have to say what he was thinking now—the fact that they were packing their things on their behalf this morning was enough of a warning. If they touched David's suitcase, there was a good chance they'd find the burner phone. "It's ten-thirty," he said quietly. "If we're going to make a move, we need to do it."

Chapter 22

The windows were painted shut, so David had broken the glass with his fist wrapped in a towel and then used an extra fixture he'd found in the bathroom to knock out the extra glass before wedging a pen into the edges of the window, over and over again, until the seal could be broken and they could get it open. While he'd worked on it, Lauren had washed her face and tried to bring herself back to life with some coffee from the in-room Keurig. She'd also listened at the door for a while—true to David's guess, there were guards out there who she'd heard bantering back and forth. She'd heard at least four voices coming from different points in the hall, two of whom had spoken quietly from right near the door and joked about the noises she'd made that morning. She'd felt heat rise to her cheeks upon hearing it, and soon gone back to the window to watch David's progress.

Once he got the window open, he gave her a nod and retreated to leaning on the desk. What she hadn't expected were the ripples of nerves that went through her at the thought of trying to actually work magic in front of him.

Before, it had been different. He'd sensed it when they'd touched, and maybe even seen her using it when she'd been in the gardens outside the house, but it had never been visible—not like it would be now if this worked. At most, he'd witnessed its effects when plants or herbs had grown more quickly than usual. He'd probably seen results in the cage without realizing it also, given that they'd come to the conclusion her magic had likely been feeding healing into her own blood, cannibalizing itself on her behalf so that she wouldn't be really hurt by how rough he'd been with her. But all of that had been unspoken, unrealized in some fashion.

Now, as Lauren leaned slightly out the window and pressed her palms lightly to the brick outside of it, she was painfully aware of David's eyes on her, and of the fact that he'd been the one to originally try to take her magic away entirely. And, he and his partner had recently insisted she not use it or access it at all unless she were on their property, and told her Adrias couldn't know it still existed in her blood because of her mother's spell. All of that had, no pun intended, necessarily gone out the proverbial window, but she couldn't erase any of it from her memory.

Closing her eyes, she pressed her palms into the brick and tried to block out David's presence. Instead of thinking of him, she reached for the vines growing up the brickwork below, sending out her own tendrils through the clay and the shale, picturing her magic as little slips of energy elongating from her body and then being embraced by the natural materials of the earth. At the moment when the bricks accepted her energy, she felt herself pulled into the elements and leaned herself further into the embrace of the window. She hadn't been sure it would work, and now she wasn't sure she'd be able to offer enough magic to get the results they needed, but she had her answer—if she could just keep it up.

With her palms warming against the brickwork outside, she rested her chest against the window frame and reached out further along the brick, holding her eyes closed and willing her magic outward. There was warmth all through her body now as it roiled inside her, finally getting a real request for use, and then it began rushing out of her.

She barely felt David's hands land on her hips as if to anchor her when she leaned outward, instinctively pushing herself in the direction she wanted her magic to go as it bled from her.

Now she could feel the upper tendrils of the vines themselves, the pieces that had been actively growing, reaching higher across the structure, and she tugged gently at them with her magic, fostering shivers of growth to bring them upward, faster and then faster again.

Fighting the urge to lean out even further as her magic pushed for more connection, to allow her to reach for the vines herself, she pressed her magic harder, letting it ride off of the remnants of desire and the heat in her blood as it reached downward in heavier doses, and then she began feeling the vinework really creeping upward as a wide expanse, and not just as single vines and tendrils—first by millimeters, then by centimeters, and then by inches and feet. Tiring, she leaned her brow against the window frame. There was a new sheen of sweat on her skin now, all over her with the pressure of pulling magic from her blood that wasn't quite ready for use, and unfamiliar with what she was asking. She could feel it on her skin, on the slickness of the window frame all around her.

"Don't let me fall," she whispered, and the tightening of David's hands on her hips told her he'd heard her. She leaned further outward, no longer worried about keeping herself grounded in the room as she stretched her arms out against the brickwork as far as she could reach, her hands straining toward the vines while lying on the bricks and bleeding magic. Clenching her teeth against the heat of the magic in her hands and the cool feeling in her body that told her she'd already given too much, she continued willing the magic from her body, sending it into the vines below.

The brick had already been warm with sunlight, but it had grown warmer still with the heat of her magic, and she could feel it flooding out of her now, sapping her strength in favor of the strength of the burgeoning vines and the shale and the clay that were thirsting for it, pulling it in and spreading it across the widening expanse of greenery on the building's sides.

When the first tendril of greenery touched her finger, she let her hand be overtaken by it before she realized what was happening and urged it sideways, upward toward the roof. Behind her, she heard David gasp as some of the greenery crept into the window ledge, but she kept her focus outward.

She could feel the vines twining together now, anchoring into the brick and then reaching higher, climbing upon each other and twisting as they rose unnaturally, pulled upward at a rate that should have taken decades and was instead taking minutes.

Her hands burned painfully with the energy running from her into the vines and brickwork, so much so that it seemed like she was touching hot coal, but she kept them pressed hard into the building, forcing her magic and energy outward. Feeling herself slip into a daze, groggy with the power running from her into the clay and the vines that she could now touch, she finally made herself blink her eyes open and look around. The sun had moved in the sky, so much time had passed, and she felt weighted, heavy. But she also knew that the vinework was heavy along the side of the building, anchored in the roof above. She looked upward and saw a curtain of green.

Still willing the little bit of energy she had outward, she let herself lean further back so that her feet once again found the floor, and David's hands relaxed some against her hips—she hadn't realized how off-balance she'd been, how far out, but her knees had been at the window frame, her arms reaching outward, and he'd been the only thing keeping her from falling. She reached the floor, holding her hands curled against her chest, and spoke quietly. "Try it. Tug on it. See if it's strong enough."

Having a hard time believing the sight in front of him and what Lauren had managed, David reached out the window and wrapped his fist in some of the vines running up toward the roof. He pulled gingerly at first, and then he tugged, yanking on them with as much of his weight as he could without actually climbing out the window. When the vines barely seemed to give, he reached his hands upward, took hold of more of the vines, and hung there, his feet off the floor and his body slanted into the window. Again, he barely felt any give in the vines. They were sturdy and tangled, knotted together and digging into the walls as if they'd been there growing and digging in for centuries, not minutes.

Looking up and down, he could see the vines running from the base of the building all the way up to the roof, up and over the edge of the flat-roofed building. "Okay, then," he breathed out. "You're going first. I'm going to sling a sheet under your arms in case the vines give as you start climbing down and it'll catch you if…what?" he asked, breaking off from what he'd been planning.

Lauren was shaking her head, sitting on the floor

beside the wall. "I'm not going, David. I can't climb. You go, and call Josh—get him here."

Still at the window, it took seconds for David to process what she'd said. And then he noticed how her hands were curled against her chest, as if she'd been injured and felt the need to protect them. They weren't closed, but limp and curled, as if she were holding invisible softballs or mimicking claws.

When he kneeled in front of her, he smelled the vines, but there was also another scent hanging in the air. Burned flesh, and energy. With his gut clenched in knots, he reached out and gently took hold of Lauren's forearms, and he pulled her hands further from her body so that he could see them. The smell of energy had made him picture the energy burns he'd gotten from Nell, but this was something else. Lauren's flesh wasn't opened, from what he could see, but her palms and fingers were a brilliant, painful red, with the burns continuing over her wrists and fading as they rose up her forearms, as if she'd laid her hands onto a hot stove and left them there for long seconds, allowing herself to be burned, her wrists and forearms given near the same treatment, but less so.

"I don't even think I can close my hands right now, let alone grip anything well enough to climb," she said quietly. "I'll be okay, but not in the next few hours. This is my magic, so it's not toxic, but I need time to heal."

"Fuck, Lauren," he breathed out, staring at the burns. "You should have let go sooner."

"Then we'd both be stuck," she replied, her voice flat, as if she'd begun going into shock. "Seriously, David— go. Maybe they won't even move me, they'll be so busy looking for you," she added belatedly, pain radiating from her as her voice cracked on the words. "Even if I could climb, it wouldn't be any use. I'm exhausted. There's no way I could run like we'd need to once we got to the base of the wall, so you'd just have me stuck there instead of here. Same difference. You're going to have to leave without me."

He didn't bother answering. There wasn't a chance in hell he was leaving the room without her. He walked back to the window, but instead of looking downward, he looked up.

They were on the fifth floor, maybe ten feet down from the lip of the roof. Twelve feet, at most. Before he could change his mind, he wiped his hands on his jeans and then sat down in the window, facing into the room. "I'm going to take a look at the roof. If that door opens, you scream, okay?"

Lauren looked up at him blankly—she was dazed.

"You hear me?" he asked. "If that door opens, I need you to scream. But I'll be right back."

Her head slipped forward in a half-hearted nod, and he knew he'd have to let that be good enough. He didn't want to waste anymore time. Swallowing down his nerves, he swung his legs outward so that he was sitting in the window, and then he reached sideways and wrapped his right hand into the vines. Standing up in the window, he used the vines for balance and turned around so that he was facing the building now.

With both hands in the vines, he forced himself to leave behind the window, using the vines as ropes and bracing his feet against the vinework. They were tangled and thick enough that he thought he could use them for footholds, and tried experimenting to see if it would work, not allowing himself to look downward. Barefoot, he could feel the tangled vines beneath his skin, but they didn't feel steady beneath his feet or knotted enough to rely on, so he went back to bracing his feet against the wall as if he were mountain climbing on a sheer cliff with a rope. What he wouldn't have given for a rope right now, though.

Hand over hand, he began pulling himself upward, and once he got the hang of gripping into the vines and relying on them, he made fast progress. When he pulled himself over the edge of the roof, he found just what he'd been hoping for. True to the impression he'd gotten from the ground, the roof was flat, designed to work as a sundeck that had long been out of use or ignored. There was one door in what looked like nothing more than a single-room space that he guessed held nothing but the top landing of the corner staircase, and the roof was otherwise bare—but for the vines. True to Lauren's hope, the vines had wound their way upward over the ledge of the roof, curling into and around rain gutters, and then creeping all the way across the roof to the shed, anchoring into and around it for purchase. The vines that covered a good forty-foot-wide stretch of brickwork on the building's face became narrower here, winding together into what looked more like a fallen tree than vinework, pulled together and stretching across the roof with little tendrils tucking into the roof's surface. Seeing it, and the way it had come together, there was no doubt in his mind that the vines could carry both his weight and Lauren's, and then some.

It was just a matter of getting her up here to safety and keeping her hidden until Josh and the cavalry arrived.

It took seconds for him to sling himself back onto the building's side and return to Lauren. She'd fallen asleep, and he moved immediately to the bathroom and retrieved a wet cloth. She came awake as he wiped at her brow, and looked more aware than she had a few moments before, if barely.

"You listening, kid?" he asked gently, his eyes on hers.

It took a moment, but she nodded.

"Here's what we're gonna do. The vines are steady—

it's amazing. I don't know how you did it, but you did fantastic, kid. They'll hold us. Now, you're gonna get on my back, your arms over my shoulders, piggy-back style. I can get us to the roof like that, and I'll leave you there. When they see this window and the vines, they'll think we both went down—it'll never occur to them to check the roof. I'll get you up there, and then I'll climb down and get word to Josh to move in. Think you can hold onto me for five minutes, baby?" he pressed, gripping her forearms to hold her attention.

Seeing her, he wasn't sure she could, but he didn't see any other options. He knew he could handle climbing with her on his back for the short time it would take to get them to the roof, but he needed his hands to climb. They didn't have enough sheets for him to pull her up from the room to the roof if she couldn't hold on and would need a sling, so this was the best option. The only option, from what he could see.

"I don't know," Lauren said. She seemed more aware, and looked at her hands. "I can't hold onto you."

"No, but you can wrap your arms around me and cross your wrists, and your legs can wrap around my waist. I know you can do it," he added simply, projecting a confidence into his voice that he didn't quite feel. They'd been through so much, they wouldn't fail at this juncture. He wouldn't let them.

Finally, she nodded and met his gaze. There was fear there, but she looked willing—he'd take that.

Helping her to her feet, he positioned her next to the window and then swung his legs outward for the second time. He didn't allow himself to look down, but instead took hold of the vines directly beside the window and gently eased out onto them, remaining as close to the window as he could. Then, he tentatively let himself down further, so that his shoulders were just above the window ledge.

"Come on out," he told her. When she'd hung her legs out the window, just as he had before, he nodded at her hands. "Wrap one of your arms around my shoulder, Lauren, tight as you can, and then ease yourself out. Start with your legs on mine and then wrap around my chest. You can do it.   Just don't look down or think about it."

Tentatively, she reached out for his shoulder and let one of her injured hands come to rest between his shoulder and the wall. "Are you sure?" she asked, eyeing his position. "I don't want us both to fall."

"I'm sure," he told her, re-wrapping one of his hands into the vines and re-bracing his feet. He let go of the vines with one hand and held her arm, steadying her as she eased out the window and awkwardly wrapped herself around him. He only released her when he felt her legs locked around his waist, and her arms crossed over his collarbone so that her breath fell hot on his neck. "Slow and steady. Just don't let go, alright?"

Against his shoulder, she nodded, and he took a deep breath. Maybe because of the adrenaline, she didn't feel any heavier than the packs he'd carried when hiking in the mountains, but there was no denying the danger if he lost his grip or slipped, or if she grew too tired too fast, and he had to remind himself that this was their one option.

Hand over hand, he ignored the heat of her soaking into his body and pulled them upward, small steps and hand changes making for slow progress that seemed to take forever but carried them closer and closer to the roof, until he was finally able to reach for the ledge and get a handhold on something other than greenery. With a grunt, he pulled them up and over. As soon as Lauren had untangled herself from him, he collapsed beside her, laying on his back and panting for breath, rubbing feeling back into his shoulders where they'd grown numb from the pressure of her weight, most of which had been focused on his upper back and shoulders.

"I can't believe that worked," Lauren breathed out, lying on her back beside him.

Unable to catch his breath, he just grinned back at her. "What did I tell you? Piece of cake."

Lauren shook her head, a small smile creasing her lips, but her eyes were hooded—he guessed he had maybe five minutes until she was out cold.

Pulling himself to his feet, he pressured Lauren to hers and led her over to the outcropping that housed the roof entrance point, where he guided her into a seated position in its shade, putting her on the side adjoining that holding the door. He looked at her hands again, but the red hadn't calmed and there wasn't anything he could do at the moment—they'd have to wait.

"You give me five minutes to get down, max, and then you try to pull some of these vines overtop of you. I don't think they'll look for you up here, but it can't hurt to be camouflaged if they do. You cover yourself up as much as you can, and then you can go to sleep and I'll be back before you know it. Lauren, you hear me?" he asked when her eyes wandered sideways rather than offering answers.

Finally, she nodded, but he doubted she'd be awake long enough to do as he'd suggested. For a moment, he thought about covering her now, but knew there was no telling what that might do to the stability of the vines, and he couldn't chance using the stairwell. Rather than press her further, he leaned in and kissed her forehead. "I love you, baby," he whispered, but her eyes were already closed.

From the edge of the roof, he looked back to see her slouched sideways on the other side of the roof, her hands curled loosely in front of her as if cupping air. She looked worn and helpless, but there was nothing else he could do for her up here. The best thing he could do would be to get down as quickly as possible, so that nobody would have a hint that she hadn't escaped into the woods already.

Swinging over the edge of the roof, he moved more quickly once he got the hang of going down. After a few awkward moves downward, he resorted to letting his feet dangle in the air as he lowered himself hand over hand. By the time he got to the patio, he was soaked in an all new layer of sweat, but he was safe and on firm ground again. With a glance upward, he noted that nobody was looking out the window at him, and with that he hurried to the patio door. Inside, he saw some couples strolling by and waited for them to pass before he entered.

A glance at the schedule posted on the board told him that all of the therapists were engaged in sessions in their offices, so he'd have to interrupt one of them to get to a phone—there was no way around it. Adrienne and Raul were in a private session with Tony Toscano, and that seemed like the best bet. He might not be a fan of Raul, but he trusted Adrienne and knew that Lauren did, as well.

Moving as quickly as he could without being spotted, he made his way to Toscano's office. A touch to the door told him it was unlocked, and he didn't bother knocking. Without preamble, he moved inside, interrupting Raul mid-sentence. Tony moved immediately for the desk and David launched himself at the other man, knocking him to the floor with a grunt and landing a punch before the therapist got his bearings and rolled him sideways, grappling with him and landing a hard punch to his kidney that loosened David's grip so that the man could scramble to his feet. Toscano had to be older than him by ten years, but he'd gotten his feet back quickly.

Rolling sideways to avoid the man's boot slamming

into his head, David for a moment wondered whether Tony had been one of the ones to feed on Lauren and himself during the night, and it was enough to send a growl through his lips as he kicked up to his feet and faced off against the therapist.

The man had gotten a knife from somewhere, but it was a small one, nothing more than an average pocket knife, and David feinted left with his arm to draw the blade. Toscano fell for it, swinging the blade down faster than David could pull back and managing to slice a long cut into his forearm, but it had been enough of a distraction that David had kicked into the man's other side, knocking him off balance so that he fell to the floor and the blade skittered away.

He heard Raul yelling something in the background, but Toscano had fallen toward his desk and lost no time in crawling for it. Before he got there, David tackled him sideways, sending the two of them rolling sideways until David was able to plant the other man against the glass of the window. The man got a hold on his neck with one hand, his other grappling for better purchase, but David had the advantage now that they were hand-to-hand and managed to loose himself long enough that he was able to deliver a hard punch to the side of Toscano's head, knocking him out instantly.

When he stood up to catch his breath, he saw that Raul stood frozen and staring down at the unconscious doctor, surprised into silence. Adrienne had risen to her feet but not moved from the couch, her eyes having gone wide and unblinking.

"Get the door," he demanded, and Adrienne moved for it without further instruction.

David took a step toward the phone and then thought better of it. Toscano was fit, and not someone he wanted to underestimate. A quick glance around told him there wasn't much of anything he could use to restrain him, but scissors beckoned from the desk. In one move, he'd grabbed the scissors and the suit jacket that had been hanging on the therapist's chair, and begun cutting it into strips. When he had a long strip, he willingly handed both the scissors and the ruined garment to Adrienne's waiting hands as he moved to tie Toscano's hands before the other man could wake up.

"Who are you?" Raul asked, moving to stand over his wife as she kept cutting into the jacket as David had just demonstrated.

"I work for the government," David said flatly. "Get his legs," he added, throwing a strip Adrienne had just handed him to Raul as he tied another around his wrists for added measure.

"We were worried about you guys," Adrienne said as David gestured for another strip and moved to gag Tony. His eyes had just fluttered, and David knew he'd be awake soon. "I told Christopher I thought something had happened, but we didn't know what to do…"

David finished the gag and gave an experimental tug to the tie around the man's ankles, but Raul had tied him tight, despite his clear doubt.

"Where's Lauren?" Adrienne asked next, even as her husband moved to Toscano's sideboard and began pouring out a glass of whiskey.

David held up a finger, gesturing for her to wait as he dialed Josh's number. When his partner's voice came across the line, he almost laughed, he was so relieved. Instead, he just told him to get there, and to hurry, and to bring an ambulance or two along with the cavalry, and as soon as Josh confirmed they were safe and that he was on his way, David hung up.

Toscano was blinking himself awake and just beginning to struggle in his bonds when Raul came back to the desk and silently handed David a glass of whiskey. Adrienne was scowling, but he sipped it anyway, grateful for anything to wet his throat.

"She's on the roof," he finally answered. "We got out the window and climbed up. She's got some bad burns on her hands, and couldn't make it down here with me. I climbed down the vines to get to the patio and make this call, but she's exhausted and I didn't want to leave her stuck—"

David was cut off by the door banging open, four guards pouring in within seconds and dropping both David and Raul to the floor.

Chapter 23

David didn't bother looking up when Shea entered the room. One of his eyes was near swollen shut, and he wouldn't do her the courtesy of wasting his other's sight on her. Instead, he let his gaze remain on his own feet, stretched out before him and tied—with rope, not strips of jacket—at the ankles. For now, his best bet was silence and he knew it. The guards had given up on beating information out of him, but time was on his side now. It didn't matter that he had a black eye and some broken ribs—those would heal. What mattered was that they'd used up time, and they also hadn't moved him from the center; and the fact that they'd been demanding to know not just who he was, but where Lauren was, told him well enough that she remained hidden on the roof, none of them the wiser.

And their beating had taken real time, too; it had, he guessed, been thirty minutes since he'd called Josh, and he doubted his partner had been more than an hour away, considering they'd been planning on raiding the center sooner than later.

"David, I respect your commitment to silence," Shea began, "but I need to know who you are, and we need to know which direction you sent Lauren in if we're to have any hope of finding her, so you'll have to excuse me. She's weak right now, after all, and neither of us want her dying of exposure out in the woods."

He should have seen it coming, but between the exhaustion catching up to him and the beating, he was a second too late to move in time. Shea's hand came forward with a needle sticking out of it and caught him in the bicep, going through his shirt and direct into his skin before he could wholly process what had happened.

When he yanked his arm sideways, the syringe clattered to the floor between his body and Shea's, but it was empty by then.

"Now, we'll just wait a few minutes and see if you want to tell me what I need to know, shall we?" she asked, retreating to the other side of the room and taking a seat in a chair positioned across from him.

For the second time in as many days, he felt nausea rising up in his stomach at the sight of the grin on Samantha Shea's face, but there was nothing to do but wait and hope Josh got to the center before the drug took effect.

***

Lauren blinked her eyes open against the sun and found herself staring into Adrienne's tear-streaked face.

"Jesus, thank God you're okay," the woman muttered.

Before Lauren could reply, Adrienne had wrapped her arms around her and hugged her close, and it was all Lauren could do to keep her hands cupped protectively against her chest. "David?" she breathed out.

"He called someone. A partner, I guess?" Adrienne suggested as she sat down heavily beside Lauren, still holding onto her.

Lauren leaned into Adrienne, allowing the embrace to offer the comfort she'd been wishing for after David had disappeared over the edge of the building.

"The guards took down him and Raul, and I ran, right after," Adrienne added. "David said he climbed down the vines and that you were on the roof—it's funny, I never realized how thick they were or that they went all the way up to the roof. I figured they'd hold me if they held him, though."

"You climbed up?" Lauren asked after a moment.

Adrienne nodded her head against Lauren's, tightening her embrace. "I figured, if he felt it was safe enough for you to hide up here, it was the best place for me to hide. And I wanted to check on you," she added. "I didn't know what else to do."

Lauren's throat had gone so dry, she couldn't speak. She simply nodded and then closed her eyes again.

***

The first indication that the drug had taken effect was an urge to talk. About anything.

Despite the dryness of his throat and the aching behind his eyes, he felt the urge to talk. And, instinctively, he knew that he wouldn't be able to hold anything back once Shea began speaking to him, asking for the answers he'd so far kept silent.

Out of options, he lay back on the floor, ignoring the pinch in his wrists that resulted from the new pressure on them, tied at his back as they were. He didn't bother closing his eyes—it wasn't as if he could avoid answering Shea if she asked if he was awake. He did, however, hold his breath, and hope that she hadn't ever trained in martial arts or self-defense.

Within a minute, his ruse worked better than he could have hoped. Not only did she approach, but she actually leaned in over him, offering an easier target.

Without warning, David snapped his legs up, connecting to her skull with the balls of his feet and demolishing the stupid canary grin that she'd worn upon leaning down over him. As soon as she was down, dazed, he kicked out again, hitting her in the right temple this time and knocking her violently into the wall.

Even at the point when an operative broke in the door an hour later, she was still out cold, blood oozing from her scalp.

***

When Lauren woke up again, she was surrounded. Josh was reaching out a hand to help Adrienne to her feet and David had leaned in over her, one eye swollen shut and a deep cut lancing down his cheek. She gasped at the sight of him and his lips landed on hers. The kiss was what convinced her he was really there, that this wasn't some teasing dream leading up to a let-down she'd feel only upon awakening.

When he pulled back, she moved with him, holding the kiss. Instinctively, she moved to wrap one of her hands into his shirt, and the pain of the fabric against her burned skin was what yanked her away from him with a yelp of pain, her eyes and his both shooting down to her palm even as he grunted in pain himself and grabbed his ribs.

She swallowed against the sudden sting in her palm, tears beginning to slide down her cheeks. When she looked up again, Josh was kneeling beside her, his eyes on the burns. "There's an ambulance downstairs."

Shakily, she nodded, and each of the men grabbed one of her elbows to help pull her to her feet, David nearly stumbling himself as they helped her up. In another moment, Adrienne was at her side, Raul standing as an awkward shadow behind her. "David, you're barely on your feet yourself. Let me," she added, nudging him to the side.

Lauren caught Josh grinning at the authority in her voice, and while David scowled in return, he didn't argue. Lauren met his gaze and nodded, the weight of the last few days suddenly heavy between them and thudding in her chest. "He needs one, too," she said, her voice sounding rough in her own ears, but it had been loud enough.

Josh was already nodding, gesturing to his partner to head down the stairs ahead of them. "And don't fall—I don't want to have to carry you out of here," Josh commented as David stopped at the top of the stairs to glance backward and make sure they were following.

"Fuck off," David grunted as he leaned on the bannister and started downward. "Let's see you scale that wall a few times and take a few nutjob succubi down, and then we'll fucking talk."

"Remind me who just got beat up by a bunch of therapists again."

"Do they always act like this?" Adrienne asked.

Lauren felt tears leaking from her eyes again, but she found herself grinning despite them. "Always."

The relief of knowing they'd be out of the center in minutes—not hours or days—gave her enough adrenaline to last for a few flights of stairs, and to keep the pain in her hands at bay, but then she stumbled, and stumbled again. The second time, she nearly took Adrienne down with her as the other woman helped to keep her from falling, and Lauren felt the exhaustion overtaking her faster than she could explain herself. Mumbling some apology, she sat down heavily on a stair between the fourth and fifth floors, and leaned against Adrienne when the other woman sat down beside her. David had stopped on the landing below, looking upward at them as he caught his own breath, one hand resting on the wall. When one minute of rest turned into five, Josh crouched down in front of her, taking another look at her burns and then finding her eyes with his.

"Are those toxic?"

She felt Adrienne's confusion coming from beside her, but didn't have the energy to explain any of what was happening. That would come later. She shook her head. "They just hurt."

Josh moved down to David, and she closed her eyes and leaned into Adrienne as the two men spoke in hurried whispers. Next, she heard David begin moving down the stairs, and she opened her eyes to see Josh crouching in front of her. "I'm going to carry you the rest of the way," he told her flatly.

"Yeah," she answered, and then acquiesced as Adrienne and Josh helped her to her feet so that Josh could pick her up. Relaxing into his arms and body, she kept her hands cradled against her chest, curled in so as to avoid coming into contact with even the fabric of her shirt. Adrienne was coming down the stairs just behind him, and Lauren vaguely heard her saying something, asking questions, but the energy of following the conversation was too much for her.

She'd wake up at the bottom of the stairs, she told herself, and then she'd convince Josh to just take her back to the ranch house and let her sleep while David took the ambulance to get checked out, and everything would be fine, because they'd be out of the center, with everybody safe and this place shut down—she could already hear operatives below them, questioning so-called guests and moving along the floors. Despite the barked orders and the heavy sounds of boots, the chaos was welcome. It meant this was all over. In just a few flights of stairs more, they'd be out of the center, and she and David could be together. Everything else could wait.

About Your Author

Michaela discovered Stephen King and Piers Anthony when she was in fourth grade, and there was really no going back from there. She penned her first full-length novel in 7th grade when she fell in love with *seaQuest*, and passed the time between seasons by coming up with her own adventures for the characters; now, she knows to call it fanfiction, but back then it was for her the beginning of a life-long writing passion, and the stories were as real as anything else in the world. From the beginning, her stories ranged from horror to science fiction and fantasy, and involved danger, passion, and character-driven nightmares.

A constant reader and writer, she grew up in Virginia, spending most of her time in the backstage area of her high school theater or wandering the woods near her home, wondering what it would be like to cast spells or meet a vampire. Eventually, she moved to South Carolina and her escapades expanded to sipping whiskey and skinny-dipping in dark lakes where she'd still like to believe monsters lurk.

Now, she lives and writes in southwest Florida, where she works as a full-time book editor specializing in horror, dark romance, suspense, fantasy, and anything at all involving the paranormal. Her own writing always takes dark turns, but tends toward character-driven stories, which blur genre lines and ask the questions that she believes we sometimes even hide from ourselves. *Spells in Therapy* is her second novel, and she's already working on the sequel since the characters in the book aren't people she's quite found a way to walk away from just yet. Her work has also appeared in various anthologies you can find by taking a quick look at her <u>Amazon page,</u> and you can keep up with her latest news and releases by following her on Twitter <u>@MichaelaLCane</u> or on Facebook <u>@Michaela L Cane</u>.

Other HellBound Books Titles
Available at: www.hellboundbookspublishing.com

Spells in Waiting

For as long as she can remember, Lauren Merriweather has fought to separate herself from her mother - by focusing on school and developing her healing powers. Like her mother, she's a natural-born witch, but unlike her mother, Lauren is not a killer driven by hatred.

But, when a fight with her rampaging mother drives Lauren to seek relief in alcohol and mindless flirting, her world is twisted violently out of her control.

Lauren's attraction to David is as immediate as it is undeniable - to the extent that she forgets about the spells that have, until now, kept her from getting close to a man. But, David Fredricks is the government operative investigating her mother for murder, and he and his partner have determined that Lauren is their best lead.

As far as David is concerned, Lauren and her mother are both witches, and that makes them little better than monsters. Lauren's allure doesn't change the fact that her mother is a vicious serial killer, and he's prepared to do whatever it takes to stop her.

An interrogation goes too far, and Lauren finds herself bound to David in a way that neither of them could ever have imagined - and her very survival depends on her trusting the same people who stole her identity.

Follow Him

True love doesn't die - it devours. Just outside the sleepy town of Dreury, a mysterious cult known as The Shared Heart has planted its stakes. Its followers are numerous. More join every day. Those who are lost and suffering seem to be drawn to it; a home for the broken. When Jacob finds himself in need of such a home, he abandons his dead name and gives himself over to the will of The Great Collector. However, love refuses to let Jacob go so easily; his ex-fiancé, Nina, kidnaps him in the hopes that he can be deprogrammed. As she attempts to return Jacob to the life they once had, a terrible fear creeps in: what if there isn't enough of her Jacob left? When The Great Collector learns of his missing follower, the true nature of The Shared Heart is unleashed. Nina discovers what Jacob already knows: that hidden behind the warm songs and soaring bonfires is a terrifying and ancient secret; one that lives and breathes and hungers. And it's coming for them.

The Devil's Hour

A new and altogether awesome anthology of all things horror!

Seventeen spine-chilling tales of the darkest terror, most unpleasant people, and slithering monsters that lurk beneath the bed and in the blackest of shadows…

Satanic Panic

An incredible homage to 1980's horror!

Satanic Panic, a mass hysteria created in the nineteen eighties, has returned to a small college town in the Midwest.

Ritualistic murders and the presence of the occult have bled below the surface of the town in the form of icy accidents and other coincidences.

And when three lifelong friends find themselves on the radar of a killer—and leader of a satanic cult—they must fight for what's good without being seduced by the evil that possesses their campus.

The Toilet Zone
RESTROOM READING AT ITS MOST FRIGHTENING!

Compiled and edited by the grand master of 80's schlock horror, Bret McCormick, each one of this collection of 32 terrifying tales is just the perfect length for a visit to the smallest room....

At the very boundaries of human imagination dwells one single, solitary place of solitude, of peace and quiet, a place in which your regular human being spends, on average, 10 to 15 minutes - at least once every single day of their lives.

Now, consider a typical, everyday reading speed of 200 to 250 words per minute - that means your average visitor has the time to read between 2,500 to 4,000 words, which makes each and every one of these 32 tales of terror - from some of the best contemporary independent authors - within this anthology of horror the perfect, meticulously calculated length. Dare you take a walk to the small room from where inky shadows creep out to smother the light and solitude's siren call beckons you?

Dare you take a quiet, lonely walk into… The Toilet Zone

Invasive Species

A monster has come to Maldus, Arkansas, and the residents of the small mountain town are too busy to notice. With the monster comes something even more terrifying and threatening than gnashing teeth or razor-sharp claws.

The monster has brought change.

The residents of the small mountain town are too busy to notice at first. Busy with things such as addiction, racism, work, or land deals. Unnoticed, the change the monster brings in its insidious wake spreads like wildfire.

Unnoticed, the town of Maldus falls prey to an Invasive Species.

Micheala L. Cane

**A HellBound Books LLC
Publication**

http://www.hellboundbookspublishing.com

Printed in the United States of America